enjoy it.

Fred

Home Visit

by
Fred Scaglione

A Stevie Corra Casework Mystery

NYNP
Books

Copyright © 2012 by Fred Scaglione

Cover design by Marcia Rodman Kammerer

NYNP Books
New York Nonprofit Press LLC
P.O. Box 603
Rhinebeck, NY 12572

www.NYNPbooks.com

ISBN 978-0-9857427-1-3

For Birgit

*Who filled my life
with love, laughter
and two wonderful kids.*

1

The setup was obvious. Two young black men in their early twenties lounged with an air of bored hostility on the steps of a corner building just off the avenue. Stevie Corra took in the scene at a distance as he approached from their right along the opposite sidewalk. Straight ahead, on Stevie's side of the street, was a third player, even younger, tucked in next to the tall stoop of a dilapidated brownstone townhouse. He knew there would be another just around the corner, watching for surprises coming up or down the avenue. For now, however, in the baking heat of this July afternoon sun, business was slow. No one else – neither cops nor customers – was in sight.

Stevie continued at a steady pace, even as his pulse began to quicken. He recognized the familiar emotion – a cocktail of anticipation and fear fueled by a surge of adrenaline that never lost its kick. Instinctively, his right hand slid behind him, hovering over the place where a gun once would have been. Now, there was nothing; just absence with a weight all its own. No gun; no shield; no radio to call for backup. Stevie was alone.

The taller one in the Knicks jersey picked him up as Stevie crossed the street, heading diagonally for the building where they stood. He heard the muffled murmurs of warning and watched as languid eyes flashed to attention, searching the street for anyone else that might be coming. At his far right, Stevie could see the youngest corner boy prepare to break from the townhouse steps with their package.

The shorter of the two, with a black tee-shirt and jailhouse build, now clearly in charge, stood and started down the steps towards him. "Looking for something?" he said, his eyes both wary and threatening. "You're not going to find it here!" His partner continued to scan the street in both directions.

"Relax," said Stevie. "I'm here on business, but not your business."

The boss' eyes narrowed for a few moments as he silently processed the response. "You a cop?" It was half question, half statement of fact.

"No"

"Social worker?" the young man asked again. "Child welfare?"

"Excuse me," said Stevie, stepping slightly to one side in an effort to go up the steps. "I need to go in." The two drug dealers exchanged silent glances; then separated just enough for him to slip by.

Stevie turned to the Plexiglas covered listing of tenants on the entranceway wall. There were eight apartments in the narrow, four-story building. "Saunders" was crudely printed with a blue ballpoint pen next to "2-B". Feeling two sets of eyes from behind following his every move, he pressed the button and heard a muffled buzzer from deep inside the building. Stevie waited; then waited a little longer before buzzing again. Nothing. No answer.

"Looks like nobody's home," said the Knicks jersey.

"Don't worry; somebody's home," Stevie replied, pressing the buzzer buttons for all of the other apartments at once. Within seconds, he got an answer as the wood framed front door rattled free of its lock.

Stevie stepped inside and closed the door carefully behind him. He turned to see a long dark hallway on his right and a narrow staircase, rising to the upper floors, on his left.

"Who's that?" shouted a voice from the end of the darkened hallway.

"Sorry, I pushed the wrong button," he answered before hearing an apartment door being shut and bolted.

Stevie climbed unsteady and creaking stairs to the second floor and headed for the rear apartment. The dull glow from a filthy skylight above the stairwell barely cut through the gloom of the hallway.

He rapped his knuckles on the door of "2-B", hearing the sounds echo through the building. "Mrs. Saunders!" he called, knocking again, "Melody!"

Nothing! There was no answer, no sounds at all of life from inside. He rapped the door and called once more.

Suddenly, Stevie heard a lock open, but from the apartment door at the other end of the hall. A head peeked out from behind the doorway and stared at him without saying a word.

"I'm looking for Melody Saunders," he said.

"There's nobody home," answered the woman who looked like she could be in her 80s with a weathered, chocolate face topped by unruly wisps of gray frizz.

"Do you know if she will be back soon?" Stevie asked. "I'm looking for Mrs. Saunders and her son Shaquan."

"Nobody's home," the woman repeated. "Nobody's been home." The door closed firmly, followed by the metallic clang of one deadbolt turning into place, then a second.

Stevie stared at the shuttered doorway and felt a wave of concern. This wasn't good, he thought to himself. He turned and walked down the staircase and out the front door.

The arrangement of street players remained unchanged, with one important exception. Now, the crew boss was focusing his attention on the building entrance from which Stevie emerged.

"You take care of your business?" he asked.

Stevie shrugged. "Do you now the people who live here?" he asked. "Do you know Melody Saunders?"

He could feel the young man's muscled body stiffen as his gaze hardened.

"Don't know her," he said flatly. "I never knew her."

"How about her son Shaquan?"

"Don't know him."

Stevie stared into the crew boss' cold, black eyes and felt a second wave of despair, this time stronger and deeper.

2

"Damn!" Jackie spat in a combination of anger, worry, frustration and remorse. "Goddamn it!"

As Director of Foster Care at Brooklyn Family Services, Jacqueline Johnson was Stevie Corra's boss. During his five years with the agency, she had also become a close friend. He knew that Jackie felt a personal responsibility for each of the children placed in their care. Try as she might to keep an emotional distance, Johnson couldn't help feeling – and reacting – like she was their own mother when things went wrong.

"I thought we had gotten past this with Shaquan," said Jackie, as much to herself as to Stevie.

They both had known the boy since he first came to BFS four years earlier at the age of 12, fresh from a long series of failed placements with foster families at another agency. Shaquan had already been in the system for four years at that point. He didn't like it… and didn't want to stay. Shaquan was a runner right from the start, unusual for a child that young. It didn't matter if the foster home was good or bad; the foster parents caring or cold. Shaquan wasn't interested in having a new family. As bad as life had been at home, that was where Shaquan wanted to be.

Melody Saunders had been just a child herself – 16 years old – when she gave birth to Shaquan, a going away gift from a brief relationship with an older man in the neighborhood. Surprisingly, Shaquan was Melody's only child. A lack of pre-natal care, followed by a difficult delivery, left her unable to have other children.

Melody, who had known little love in her own life, loved her son. But, she also needed a man. Abused as a child, she believed that violence was an everyday part of all relationships. Shaquan's father – long gone by the time of his birth – was followed by a chaotic succession of other men – each one seemingly harder and meaner, both to Melody and her son. Some stayed for a night; some for months; only one longer.

The drugs which Melody took to dull the pain hadn't helped. Her life – and Shaquan's – began to unravel. Sometimes she would be there; sometimes not. Sometimes there was food; sometimes not. Shaquan's appearances in school became less and less frequent, noticeable even in a system where tens of thousands of children miss months of class every year. Eventually, his teachers referred the case to Children's Services for "educational neglect". It didn't take the City caseworker long – once she finally tracked down the family – to find what she was looking for – scars and bruises, old and deep, like stains on a worn carpet that never come out. Melody and Shaquan each had their own physical histories of abuse. Yet, they shared them like a family resemblance – the same discolorations up and down their arms, bruises on their backs, partially-healed cuts around the eyes and mouth.

Eight-year-old Shaquan spent that night at the City's Children's Center at Bellevue Hospital, where he was examined by a doctor and interviewed by a social worker. The next day, he transferred to a foster boarding home in another Brooklyn neighborhood. It would be the first of many. Melody stayed in the run-down, Brownsville apartment alone – no son, no man – and in tears. A little before midnight, she set out to find relief, paying for it the only way she could. For her, as well, it would be the first of many nights to come.

"You really think she's gone?" asked Jackie.

"It's just a feeling," said Stevie. "There was no answer and I couldn't get into the apartment. I've called her cell phone about ten times. I'll try the apartment again tonight."

Jackie turned to face him with a look of concern. "You be careful," she said.

11

"Don't worry," he answered. His tone acknowledged the basis of her concern while assuring that he wouldn't take any unnecessary risks.

"What does Joseph think?" she asked. Joseph Otinga was House Manager at the BFS group home where Shaquan had lived with seven other youth from similar circumstances.

"He's surprised. Everything had been going pretty well. Shaquan seemed happy enough. There hadn't been any problems in the house. Then, out of the blue, he was gone. He must have slipped out during the night. Joseph called me right after breakfast once they realized he was gone."

"And, he thinks Shaquan would have gone home?" asked Jackie.

"Sure," said Stevie. "So do I. There is no place else that seems likely." They both knew that when Shaquan had run in the past, he had always run to Melody – even if it generally ended badly. Shaquan had always been one kid who was easy to find when he'd gone AWOL.

"OK," said Jackie with a deep sigh of resignation. "Let's call it in to ACS and file the Missing Persons Report with the police."

The regulations were clear. Foster care agencies had to notify the City within 24 hours any time a child in their care went missing. They also were required to file a police report, even if many cops saw the disappearance of another 16-year-old foster kid as just one more meaningless exercise in paperwork. Some local precincts even refused to file a report, claiming that they were under no legal obligation to do so.

"I'll do it," said Stevie, gathering his files and turning to leave.

"You know someone?" asked Jackie.

3

"Yes," he answered. "I know someone."

"Stevie! Come on in," said Lieutenant Jack Schwinn as he strode into the precinct lobby, radiating the authority that comes with rank. "He's with me," he added to a patrolman seated behind a raised desk against the wall, who nodded his own approval in response.

"It's been a long time," Schwinn continued as he led Stevie down a hallway and through a large, brightly lit squad room filled with rows of desks. "You look good. How you been?"

"I'm fine." It had been years since he'd seen Schwinn – or anyone else from the old unit for that matter. Jack had put on a few pounds, but not a lot. At six-three – a few inches taller than Stevie – with broad shoulders, a barrel chest, and thick bushy blond hair, Schwinn could still make quite an impression.

"You're looking prosperous," said Stevie as they settled in on either side of Schwinn's desk.

"It's not much, but its home," Jack answered with a cavalier wave of his hand. As a squad commander in the Brooklyn North Narcotics Division, Schwinn had finally escaped the bullpen and gained the first important privilege of rank – an office with a door that he could close behind him.

"Congratulations on the bump up. Those bars look real good on you. God knows you earned them." Stevie meant it. He had worked with Jack for three years, two of them as Schwinn's own commander after Stevie had been promoted to Lieutenant. Jack was a good cop... and would make a good boss.

"Thanks," said Schwinn, his voice uncharacteristically soft. "I learned from the best. You know that." There was a moment of awkward hesitation before he continued.

"So.... What's this all about? Something tells me you didn't just drop by to have a beer and catch up."

"No," Stevie chuckled in response, "although that sounds pretty good. One of our kids went AWOL and I need to file a Missing Persons Report.

"What?" blurted Schwinn, half question; half instinctive indignation. "That's not really my department any more. That's why God invented desk sergeants."

"Sorry," said Stevie, holding up his hands in surrender. "But, you know the deal. I thought you could at least get them to take the report. It's not like I expect anybody to do anything about it." He waited a second for effect before continuing.

"And, I wanted to pick your brain about something else – something that is your department."

Schwinn raised an eyebrow as he gazed at Stevie with a questioning look. "Go ahead," he said slowly.

"Our kid, Shaquan Saunders. His mother Melody Saunders lives in a building at the corner of Utica and Livonia. I went over there this afternoon looking for him. There was no sign of him... or his mother. But, there was a pretty lively little street scene going on outside. Do you know the place? Know any of the players?"

"Oh, yeah. I know the place," said Schwinn, leaning forward in his chair. "Who did you see?"

"The shift boss was a short, bald guy; built like a brick wall. He looked like Mike Tyson before the tattoo, but darker. There was another guy – taller – and a couple of kids."

Stevie could feel Schwinn's interest growing.

"Yeah," he said. "That's 'Back' Thompson. He played linebacker for DeWitt Clinton, or something like that, before dropping out," Schwinn added in response to Stevie's unasked question about the nickname. "I guess he liked to hit people. He still likes to hit people. They work for 'Rue' James. Do you remember him? Back in the day, he ran a corner down on Livingston and Ashford. Now he runs all the corners in Brownsville... or, I should say, he did."

Stevie looked at Schwinn questioningly. "What happened?"

Jack brushed the query aside. "So," he said, "you're looking for mom...Melody Saunders?"

"That's right. She lives in that building. I figured that's where Shaquan went, but there was no sign of either of them."

"Well," said Jack with a sigh. "You're not the only one looking for her."

"What do you mean?" Stevie asked, puzzled.

"So am I."

"What?"

"Rupert 'Rue the Day' James got popped right outside her window last night. We'd like to know if she saw anything... and wants to talk about it. But, as you say, there is no sign of her."

"Christ! What happened? Do you know who shot him? Do you know if Melody was even there?"

"We have some ideas, but nothing solid," said Schwinn. "As you might expect, no one saw or heard anything. All I know is that the shooting took place about ten feet from the Saunders woman's window. If she was there, she would have had to have seen something."

Stevie sat in silence. A host of possible scenarios, none of them particularly good, scrolled through his mind.

"Any idea where she might have gone?" asked Schwinn. Their roles had reversed. Stevie had come seeking information, now he was the one taking questions. "Do you know if she has any family or friends she might go to?"

Stevie tried to work his way through the case file in his head. "She has a mother and sister who both live in Bed Stuy... I can't remember where... but they weren't exactly close. Anybody in the building give you an idea about whether she was home or not?"

"No," said Schwinn. "This is the kind of building where nobody wants to know too much... or say too much... about their neighbors."

The two sat, staring at each other, in silence.

"Anyone else likely to be looking for Melody?" Stevie asked, voicing a concern that was already obvious.

Schwinn shrugged. "Could be," he said slowly. "I don't know for sure, but there certainly could be."

Stevie nodded and rose from the chair.

"If you have names and addresses for the mother and sister, I'd like to get them," said Schwinn.

"Sure, I'll email them."

"Thanks," said Jack, taking a more upbeat tone. "And, don't be a stranger. Let's get together for that beer. I'd like to hear more about what you've been up to."

"Sounds like a plan," said Stevie as the two men shook hands.

After a moment's hesitation Schwinn continued. "I'm really sorry about what happened."

"Me, too," Stevie answered slowly, turning to leave the office.

"It wasn't your fault!" said Schwinn quickly.

Stevie stopped and waited a moment before turning back to look at Jack. "Yes, it was."

4

Shaquan's group home was an oversized, white brick, single-family house surrounded by large, covered porches on three sides. Unlike some of the mansions just a little further west, the structure had always been on the less fashionable side of Flatbush Avenue. Even in Brooklyn's heyday before the Dodgers left for Los Angeles, the house had never quite measured up to its own aspirations. It was more tacky than majestic. Today, the house was tired; clean and well maintained, but weary from a century of use, most recently by an ever-changing "family" of eight troubled teenagers plus a revolving cadre of child care staff and clinicians.

Joseph Otinga had worked at the Flatbush Group Home, or others like it, for almost twenty years. Born in Ghana, Joseph had migrated to the United States in his early twenties, joining a vibrant and rapidly growing West African community in Brooklyn. Through relatives, he soon found work as an entry-level child care worker watching over the endlessly exploding number of children being removed from their families due to parental abuse or neglect.

It seemed as if Otinga was born to be a child care worker. Short and stocky, with a smile that lit up his round, ebony face like a sunrise, Joseph was simultaneously gentle and strong, soft-spoken but firm. He could defuse almost any confrontation without raising his voice. His inner calm and self assurance was infectious. Most, if not all, of the youngsters with whom he worked quickly came to understand that he cared for and respected them. Despite four years of college and decades of experience, Joseph never thought of these kids as foster children, juvenile delinquents, or any of the countless other mental health diagnoses that come to define children living in institutions. For Otinga, these were simply young people struggling to find their place in the world – often against unfair and apparently overwhelming odds. And, most important of all, Joseph believed – and could sometimes make them believe – that they were capable of doing just that. He was simply there to help.

"Hello, Steve," said Joseph, as he opened the heavy front door. His lilting African accent was still strong despite two decades of living in New York.

It was just after dinner and Stevie nodded to several of the kids watching reality TV in the living room.

"Carlos is in his room," said Joseph, leading Stevie up the long, steep staircase to the second floor. Each of the eight youth living in the house shared a bedroom with another boy. It wasn't always ideal, but it worked. In many cases, as with Shaquan and Carlos, the boys became close – breaking down the sense of isolation that came with any type of out-of-home placement. These two had roomed together for over two years, ever since Carlos moved into the group home.

"Hi, Carlos," said Stevie, knocking on the half-opened door. "Can we come in?"

The youngster, listening to an I-pod while doing his homework, nodded.

"You find Shaquan?" he asked, pulling out the earphones.

"No. That's what we wanted to talk to you about."

"Sure," he answered with a shrug to show it was no big deal.

"Could you tell me what happened?" Stevie asked. "Did you see Shaquan leave?"

"I already told Mr. Otinga," said Carlos with a huff of irritation.

"I know, but tell me. I need to find Shaquan. It's really for his own good, so he'll be safe. Maybe you saw or heard something that can help me."

"I didn't see anything. I was sleeping. When I woke up this morning, he was gone."

"Do you have any idea where he went, or why?" Stevie coaxed, as gently as he could. "Were there any problems here at the house? Was Shaquan having trouble with any of the other kids?"

"No," answered Carlos. "There were no problems here. Shaquan was down with everyone."

"Did he say anything about wanting to leave? Where do you think he went?"

"No, he didn't say nothing!"

"So…. Where do you think he went? Friends in the neighborhood, maybe?"

"No! Shaquan didn't have any friends back there."

Stevie waited a moment before pressing again. "So, do you think he might have gone home to his mom?"

Carlos looked at Stevie for a second before turning away. "Maybe."

"That's what I think. Joseph thinks so, too." Otinga nodded in quiet agreement. "Had Shaquan talked to his mom recently?"

"Shaquan was always talking to his moms," said Carlos, avoiding Stevie's searching gaze.

"I know. But did he talk to her in the last day or so before he left?"

The boy seemed torn between not wanting to snitch and knowing that it would be best for Shaquan to come back home – to the group home.

"Come on, Carlos," Stevie said softly. "You know we just want to make sure he is OK."

Carlos hesitated again, fighting against an almost instinctive code not to say anything. "She called him yesterday morning. He got all quiet afterwards."

"Thanks," Stevie nodded. Another wave of worry washed over him. Melody's call had come the morning before Shaquan went AWOL.

Joseph put his arm around the boy's shoulder. "It's OK, Carlos," he said with quiet warmth. "You made a good decision. You are helping Shaquan. Why don't you go downstairs; Mrs. Ramirez is making a surprise snack."

As Carlos left, Stevie stood and walked to Shaquan's side of the room. The wall was decorated with a few hip-hop posters, some little league medals and a large, brightly-colored, diamond shaped kite. Joseph had been flying kites since his youth in Ghana and taught all of the group home kids how to make and decorate their own. He believed that the sport was almost spiritual – allowing youngsters to see their dreams rise high to the heavens, riding on the silent but powerful forces of nature. It taught patience... and sensitivity to the subtlest shifting of the winds. Try too much, too soon, and you came crashing down. Catch the right current and you could soar up among the clouds.

Above the desk, on a framed corkboard, Shaquan had some notes and pictures, including one of himself and Melody taken during a family picnic earlier that spring. "I'm going to borrow this," said Stevie, pulling out the push pin and slipping the photo into his jacket pocket.

"Don't worry, Steve. You'll find him," Joseph said reassuringly. "He'll be home soon."

"I hope so." Corra wished he felt as certain.

Stevie tried calling Melody's cell phone one more time as he walked to the car. Again, he got only her relentlessly up-beat recorded message. "This is Melody Saunders. I'm sorry I can't answer the phone now. Leave your name and number and I'll call you back as soon as I can. Have a blessed day!"

He thought about driving out to Brownsville for another look at the apartment, but then thought again. Darkness would soon be falling over Brooklyn. If Melody – and Shaquan – were back home, they'd still be there first thing in the morning. And, his visit would be less likely to create a stir in the neighborhood.

Instead, Stevie steered his seven-year-old Subaru into the slow-moving line of traffic going west along Church Avenue and headed for home.

5

Stevie parked in the driveway and picked up a small pile of bills and junk mail as he walked in the front door of his one-bedroom, ground floor apartment. Windsor Terrace was less than two miles – barely a 15-minute drive – from the Flatbush Group Home; separated primarily by the rolling green fields and tree-lined paths of Prospect Park. Nevertheless, it felt like a different world.

The neighborhood, once a solid part of working class Brooklyn, had ridden a roller coaster of ethnic and economic change over the past thirty years. Earlier waves of Irish and German immigrant families had largely evaporated – the children fleeing for suburbs on Long Island as their aging parents passed away or moved into nursing homes. Black and Puerto Rican newcomers inherited the neighborhood during the 70s and 80s.

Before long, however, Windsor Terrace had become the destination for a new round of immigration. The neighborhood had always been a poor cousin to Park Slope, with its long rows of fashionable, finely-detailed, turn-of-the-century townhouses, around the corner on the west side of Prospect Park. Now, Windsor Terrace accommodated the gentrification overflow; young urban professional families of all colors and national origins who could not afford the insanely skyrocketing real estate prices of "brownstone Brooklyn".

Stevie had bought the two-family row house as an investment – together with his former partner, Jimmy Sullivan – seven years earlier, when times were good and there had been plenty of overtime on top of his lieutenant's salary. He had never expected to live here.

After things went bad, he had given Sandy the house in Sheepshead Bay as part of the divorce settlement. Stevie worked out a deal with Jimmy. He moved into the small downstairs apartment and Sullivan took the rental income from the two-story, three-bedroom unit upstairs. It had been a good deal for both of them. Certainly there was no other way Stevie could afford to rent a similar apartment – while also paying child support and graduate school tuition – on his current caseworker's salary.

Stevie walked past his bedroom and into the combination, living room/dining room/kitchen at the back of the apartment. The space was light and airy, looking out through large windows and a sliding glass door that opened onto a small deck and garden.

He rummaged through the refrigerator and came away with a foil-topped glass bowl half full with the leftovers of yesterday's pasta salad. Stevie suddenly realized that he was starving. He grabbed a bottle of beer to go with it and headed out onto the deck.

It was almost eight and the sky was turning a deeper, richer blue in the dwindling twilight. The evening air was cooler and there was a slight breeze that swept along the row of back gardens.

As Stevie ate, he picked up the photo of Shaquan and Melody that he had taken from the group home. The boy was big for his age, at 16 already taller than his small, thin, almost fragile looking mother. In the photo, they stood together, Shaquan with his arm draped around Melody's shoulder as if to protect her from all the pain and danger he knew was out there. They both smiled; he with a flash of boyish pride; she with less assurance, and perhaps a hint of shame.

Suddenly, Stevie's cell phone rang. He looked at the incoming number. It was Sandy.

"Hi," he said.

"Hi! How are you?" After six years, their conversations were still awkward.

"I'm OK. It hasn't been the best of days. How about you?"

"The same," said Sandy, showing no inclination to go into details. "I wanted to let you know that Joey's game is going to be at

10:00 on Saturday… at the Parade Grounds… I have to go into the city so I can drop him off, either at your place or the field."

"If you could drop him here at 9:00, that would be great. How is he?"

"He's good," she said, hesitating before going on. "He's looking forward to seeing you. Look, I have to run. I'll see you on Saturday."

"Sure, thanks," said Stevie. "See you then."

He hung up and was left with the same heavy feeling of sadness that followed each of their conversations. It wasn't that he missed Sandy or their life together. That had proven to be a mistake early on, long before he left the force and they split up. Rather, Stevie regretted what that mistake had meant for her… and their son. He and Sandy had met early and fallen in love young. Unfortunately, they had grown up in a world where kids in their 20s weren't afraid to rush into marriage – despite all the available evidence that it wasn't a particularly good idea. They hadn't given themselves time to fall out of love – or to find out that they were very different people who wanted very different things. Sandy longed for a home and family, with lots of kids and a husband who was always there for little league games and family barbecues. Stevie wanted to be a cop… and live a cop's life… just like his own father. And, that meant that the job came first, always. Home was a place where you came to crash after double shifts and 18-hour stakeouts; where you kicked back with another scotch after stopping by the bar with your partner; where you made love to your wife with less and less joy, less and less often.

Joey! Joey was different, thought Stevie. "The day Joey was born was the happiest day of my life." He had said it a thousand times, and he meant it. Yet, Stevie realized now, the very next day he had left for 36 straight hours to oversee the final takedown of a major operation that provided crack cocaine in wholesale quantities to half of the corners in Brooklyn. There were 22 separate arrests. It was the case that made Stevie's reputation as the department's rising star – and a fitting son and successor to Chief of Detectives Joseph Corra. Stevie came home a hero. Sandy and Joey had come home from the hospital a day earlier – driven by her mom and dad. When he picked up his baby and kissed his wife, Sandy had tears in her eyes. Stevie had thought they were tears of joy. They weren't.

He made a note about Joey's game time on the calendar and got himself another beer. He tried to shake off the sadness that had come with the memories, but couldn't.

After a few moments, he picked up the photo and studied Shaquan. Despite his painful past, you could still see the child in the boy. His almond shaped eyes were soft, despite the defensive façade. There was a gentleness in his smile. Big and solid, Shaquan still had a light covering of baby fat over his increasingly muscular frame.

Shaquan was wearing a black, hooded sweatshirt – hood down – for what had been a brisk spring day. Stevie looked at the sweatshirt and then at the boy's face again. He looked into the boy's eyes and felt a chill run up the back of his neck. Suddenly, Stevie was seeing a different youth, the same age as Shaquan, from a different time and a different situation; a boy whose face he could never forget. He felt a wave of nausea and dizziness wash over him.

Stevie closed his eyes as tightly as he could, but the image of the boy remained. He could not shut it out.

6

Stevie rose early and jogged the two blocks before beginning his three-and-a-half mile run along the drive that circled Prospect Park. Even in the relatively cool morning air, it was clear this was going to be another hot and humid day. He was back at his apartment by 7:00, ate a light breakfast and showered. At 8:00, he climbed into the car and set out across Brooklyn towards Melody's apartment.

This time, Stevie drove the street first before approaching on foot. It was a totally different picture than the day before. There was no sign of Back Thompson or the other street dealers on Melody's steps or anywhere else near the corner. There was some light foot traffic along the avenue as neatly dressed women hurried towards the subway stop two blocks away. He found a parking place and headed for the building.

Once again, there was no answer when Stevie pressed the 2-B buzzer. He tried a second time with no success, before hitting two or three other apartments and finally getting a response. Stevie closed the door behind him, quickly climbed the stairs and turned towards the rear of the building. What he saw stopped him cold.

The door to Melody's apartment was open. No one was there, but the door was ajar. It clearly had been forced open. The door had shattered around the lock and handle. The door jamb itself had split vertically along the grain from where the lock had been kicked free. This wasn't a quiet break in. Someone had been in a hurry and simply planted a very heavy boot squarely on the door and burst it open. They weren't worried about noise. Whoever had done this wasn't worried about anything.

Stevie used his own foot to gently nudge the door open further. He didn't bother to call. No one was home.

Inside, the apartment was a wreck. Clothes, papers and even furniture were scattered everywhere. Stevie knew that Melody wasn't much of a housekeeper, but this was different. Someone had been here looking for something or someone. Pretty much anything Melody had – which wasn't much – had been searched and discarded. The kitchen drawers had been emptied out on the counter tops. The couch had been ransacked and a small bookcase swept clean of CDs and tacky knickknacks. Her bed had been stripped and searched; her clothes ripped from the closet and tossed into a heap on the floor. On the dresser lay a small pile of personal papers – telephone bills, correspondence from the Human Resources Administration and Children's Services, photos, mostly of Shaquan when he was a baby.

At the foot of the bed, a crude curtain had been torn aside from a window overlooking the back alley behind the building. Stevie stepped over a pile of debris and peered down at the stretch of ragged concrete. To his right, where the alley opened up to Utica Avenue, a single strand of yellow "Police Line" tape had been strung in a futile effort to seal off the crime scene. On the cement, immediately below Melody's window, was the fading outline, sketched in chalk, of a sprawled human body. In his mind's eye, Stevie could see "Rue" James, blown backward by the force of the shots, his right arm thrown out and over his head, his left laying limp by his side. Looking closer, he saw the broad patch of stained concrete – surrounding the chalk silhouette – where the drug lord's life had drained out onto the streets from which he came.

Stevie stared at the scene in quiet thought. If Melody had been there – awake and not numbed by drugs or alcohol – she would certainly have seen everything. She would have seen James die… and who had killed him.

He turned and scanned the wreckage around the apartment. There was nothing to indicate that Shaquan had been here – no backpack, no school books, no clothes or dirty laundry left behind. Where was he? And, where was Melody?

Stevie slipped past the overturned furniture in the living room and walked out into the hallway. Staring at him, just like the last time he had been here, was the little old lady from the apartment next door. The only thing that had changed was her faded, flowered housecoat. With a firm grip on both her door handle and the inside of her apartment, the woman barely moved as she studied him with penetrating eyes.

"What happened?" Stevie asked, knowing instantly that this was the wrong question.

The woman just shrugged, not even bothering to answer.

"I'm looking for Mrs. Saunders' son, Shaquan," he tried again, gently. "I'm worried about where he might be." He slowly pulled out the photo of Shaquan and Melody and held it out towards her.

The woman remained motionless, tucked in behind the half-opened door, but her gaze softened. After a lifetime in buildings like these, she seemed to sense instinctively that Stevie posed no threat.

He took a cautious step forward, then another – holding the photo in his outstretched hand like a peace offering. "This is Melody and her son," he asked. "Have you seen the boy? Has he been here?"

The woman's eyes flashed from Stevie to the picture and then back again. After a moment's hesitation, she reached out and took the photo, her hand trembling ever so slightly, the skin almost transparent with age. She stared at it for a moment and a tiny smile flickered on her lips. "Yes, he comes here," she said, giving the photo back. "He's a nice boy."

"When?" Stevie asked. "When did you see him?"

The woman gave him a confused look, as if wondering why he would ask such a question. "All the time," she said. "He comes here all the time."

Stevie stood speechless, trying to understand what the woman was telling him.

Suddenly, the entire building seemed to rattle as the front door opened on the floor below them. Stevie stepped to the hallway railing and looked down the staircase. Just as quickly he heard the apartment door next to him close firmly, followed by the metallic echo of one deadbolt, then another.

Whoever had come into the building walked straight to the first floor rear apartment and went inside. Stevie listened to that door close as he stared at the shuttered apartment door in front of him. Then he turned, walked down the stairs and headed for his car.

7

Stevie drove as if on automatic pilot back through the heavy morning traffic towards downtown Brooklyn. His mind was elsewhere, replaying first the scene of devastation in Melody's apartment, then the halting, unfinished conversation with her neighbor. Where was she? And, where was Shaquan? The questions pierced through his mind like screams; pleas for answers that simply were not there; almost physically painful to contemplate. It had been more than 24 hours since the boy had gone missing – a day, one full night and at least part of another. He was worried. It was a frightening world out there and Shaquan seemed headed for greater danger, rather than less.

Stevie grabbed his cell phone and called Schwinn, telling him about the break-in at Melody's apartment. The police lieutenant responded with a moment of silence followed by a grunt. "O.K. I'll send someone over to take a look. I've got to go. I'll let you know if we hear anything."

Twenty minutes later, Stevie pulled into one of the parking spots that Brooklyn Family Services kept at a small lot near the main office. He was due in Family Court.

Shaquan was only one of 18 children for whom Stevie was responsible. Most were adolescents who, like Shaquan, had been in foster care for many years. For some reason, he never got the babies. No cute little, grubby-faced toddlers, smiling and giggling amidst the wreckage of their families, with new adoptive moms and dads lined up and waiting for a judge to issue that Termination of Parental Rights.

No, Stevie got the older kids, those who had never been adopted.

Maybe it was because they hadn't been particularly cute to begin with…bad skin or a slightly damaged expression from all that crack they'd shared with mom during nine months in the womb.

Maybe it was because they had come into care when they were old enough to know, if not fully understand, what was happening. They had felt the pain of being abandoned; the panic of being taken away, physically removed from the only home and family they'd ever known, no matter how flawed, dysfunctional or destructive. They and their moms had shared the same searing screams of separation, filling their run-down apartments with a discordant harmony of terror, not knowing if or when they would ever see each other again.   They had prayed to God…sworn to God… that if he let them stay they would be good… their moms would be good. Please, don't take me! Please, don't take her! Please! I'll be good! We'll be good!

But, no! They had to go! It was for their own safety!

Stevie knew that it was true, at least some of the time, maybe even most. Regardless, it was a horrible, painful, life altering decision to make. When do you take a kid away from his mother? Are you doing it too soon? Are you going to wait until it is too late? There was always plenty of room to second guess yourself; or be second-guessed by parents, the kids, your boss, attorneys, family court judges, cops and reporters.

Sure, there were those rare cases – thankfully very rare – where a child was obviously in the process of being gradually beaten to death… or tied to the radiator or kept in a locked closet.

But, most of the time… maybe 99% of the time… it was a judgment call.

Is it better to leave this little girl with a mother who slaps her when she does something wrong or doesn't send her to school for days or weeks at a time; who leaves her alone with a little brother at night when she goes out?

30

Or, will she be better off coming with me so she can spend the rest of the day in what will feel like a police station and then go to live with a series of strangers...some of whom will give her the best of care, others not... maybe for weeks, months or years... maybe for the rest of her childhood?

There were always a thousand questions. Is mom on drugs? Or, is she just tired, overworked and stressed? Was she going out to play...or to score? Or, to work the late shift at Wendy's? Was there a baby sitter who was late; or a sister/girlfriend who forgot to show up? Who is that boy friend? How often is he here? Does he ever hit mom? Does he hit the girl? Does he ever *touch* the girl?

It goes on and on! How clean is the apartment? Are we talking just messy or are we talking real filth? Is there food in the refrigerator? If not, what day of the month is it? If it's early, where did this month's food stamps go? If it's late, maybe mom just couldn't make the meager ration stretch.

Most important of all, who is this mother? Does she want to be a good parent? Does she know how? Can we help her? Will she let us? Do I want to tear this family apart? Do I have to tear this family apart to protect that little girl...and her brother... and even the mom? And, if I do, will we ever be able to put them back together again?

It was a tough job and, thankfully, not one that Stevie had to do. The City's Child Protective Services made the initial decision whether or not to remove children after reports of abuse or neglect. Stevie was convinced that CPS workers had the worst job in the world. It took its toll, emotionally. He knew one experienced and highly-regarded CPS worker who, after years of responding to calls, had simply walked up to an apartment and stopped dead in his tracks. He stood there staring at the door but couldn't bring himself to knock. He just couldn't do it one more time. He was done. After a few minutes, he turned around, went back to the Brooklyn Field Office and quit.

Luckily, Stevie worked with kids and families where the decision had already been made. The children were already out of the home, living with foster parents or in a group home. His job was to help them find a way to get back together. To make sure mom was in substance abuse treatment or rehab; attending parenting classes; getting her own life together. He tried to help kids get past their own anger and hurt, or maybe give up on unrealistic expectations of who their parents were and what they were capable of. He shepherded them to therapy sessions, dealt with problems at school and mediated conflicts with foster parents or group home staff. He would bring kids and parents together for visits, supervised at first and then on their own, hopefully leading to longer and longer stays, including overnights and weekends.

It was true that Stevie had to make decisions about whether it was safe to send a child back to his mom… or whether they should remain separated. But that was different. The pressure wasn't the same. For one thing, these weren't spur of the moment choices, made without any real understanding of the situation or the people involved. And, they weren't made alone. Decisions about whether to discharge a child from care were taken in a group – Family Team Conferences in which everyone involved in a child's life – including the child if over the age of 14 – would sit down together and reach "consensus". Mothers and fathers, foster parents, caseworkers, therapists, group home staff would all share their hopes and experiences, their plans and concerns.

But, most of all, these were kids who had already been taken from their homes. The mirror of that family's life had already been shattered. Now, it was just a question of how quickly you could put it back together – if it could be repaired at all.

Stevie walked up Jay Street and followed the morning throng into the sleek and modern office building that now housed Brooklyn Family Court.

Once every six months, after a child had been placed in foster care, a Family Court Judge was required to rule on whether the placement should be extended … or whether he could go home. Sometimes, for some children and families desperate to be reunited, these were the most important of days. They could end in shrieks of joy as Judges ordered the child to be discharged to his parent's custody, typically under some level of ongoing supervision by the

City or a nonprofit social service agency like BFS. However, these court sessions could also end in heart-wrenching despair as judges determined that parents were not yet ready to take their children safely home. There was that missed home visit; a dirty urine; the sudden loss of an apartment; an angry outburst at the caseworker.

All too often, however, a day at court ended with no ending at all. There was just the mind-numbing wait, hour after hour, on crowded, hard, wooden benches as the machinery of justice churned through case after case, family after family. A seemingly endless parade of attorneys, social workers, law guardians, kids and parents approached the judge in turn to plead their cases. What drama there was was disguised in the passionless protocols of generally acceptable court procedure – quiet, stilted, solicitously respectful. Confidentiality was maintained through the muffling din of a hundred impatient petitioners, each awaiting their own turn before the bar, shifting in their seats, rattling newspapers or engaged in hushed conversations.

Then, the moment of truth! Your case is called; the players shuffle to the stage. A quick review! Who is present; who is not? A missing attorney? An absent caseworker? No one representing the City? A crucial report not yet filed? The case is adjourned and rescheduled for two months! Three months? Four months? Legal paperwork stuck; lives in limbo.

Today, Stevie wouldn't even see this level of intensity. He was here to win a simple extension of placement for Saundra Whitehead – 16 years old, 11th year in care, second in a BFS group home. It wouldn't be hard. There was no tearful mother begging for her return; no law guardian battling on the girl's behalf. Stevie couldn't even get Saundra to show up. At 3:30, after a four-hour wait, young Miss Whitehead had her five minutes of judicial oversight – in absentia. A few probing questions from the judge, a few brief answers from BFS caseworker Stevie Corra, an agreement from the City's attorney, and it was over. Saundra would remain a ward of the state for another six months.

Stevie trudged down the court steps and headed back towards the BFS office. As he walked, he tried to shake off the combination of exhaustion and depression that only forced inactivity can create. He called Melody one more time without any hope that she would actually answer. He thought about trying Schwinn to hear what, if anything, the police might have learned about the break in at the apartment, but decided to wait.

Stevie slipped out of his tan, linen jacket and tossed it over his shoulder for the remainder of the 15-minute walk. The hot afternoon sun radiated off the concrete, asphalt and brick of downtown Brooklyn as he turned left on Atlantic Avenue and strode the last two blocks back to his office. Stevie was in a full sweat by the time he walked into the slightly dilapidated, 125-year-old community center that BFS called home.

The building was a tribute to another age, when some of New York's wealthiest families created large and stately settlement houses where their wives and daughters could do good works for the poor. It had all the turn-of-the-century features that seemed opulent and highly desirable by today's minimalist standards – a high-ceilinged lobby, assorted stained glass windows, fine woodwork, intricate wrought-iron staircases. Unfortunately, these were design elements now well beyond BFS' ability to maintain. Today's wealthy families and the foundations they created were more interested in measurable outcomes and tangible deliverables than mahogany moldings – or even paying utility bills.

As a result, the air in BFS' reception area was only marginally cooler than outside on the street. Stevie was relieved to find that a large and noisy window air conditioner in the second-floor office he shared with three other caseworkers was doing just a little bit better. Julie Shapiro was on the phone in one cubicle, apparently trying to calm a foster parent enraged by a child's refusal to be home by the 10:00 p.m. curfew. The other desks were empty. Robert Johnson was on vacation and Shelly Stackowski, who Stevie had met at court, was taking a child back to her Bay Ridge foster home before heading out for the weekend.

He hung up his jacket and settled into his own small cubicle to begin writing up his progress notes for the Saundra Whitehead court appearance. Paperwork, it often seemed, had become the most important – or at least most time consuming – part of social work. Every step, every action, had to be documented. Home visits, client interviews, court appearances, telephone conversations, service referrals, school visits, supervisory meetings, everything had to be recorded in exacting detail, according to a prescribed format to ensure that all essential and required elements of casework practice had been covered.

If it wasn't in the case file, it didn't happen! That was the mantra. It had been drilled into young caseworkers from their first day on the job.

Most caseworkers hated it. Stevie took it in stride. He had been filling out reports – arrest reports, interrogation reports, crime scene reports – his whole life. He only hated that it took up valuable time and kept him from seeing kids and families. There weren't enough hours in the day – certainly not paid hours – to keep up with all the paperwork and still see clients as often as you should... and were contractually required to.

Stevie had just begun filling out the report template on his computer screen when he heard someone call his name.

"Steve Corra?"

He looked up to see a young woman in her early 30s approaching his desk.

"Hi. Can I help you?" said Stevie, getting up from his chair.

"I hope so," said the visitor, offering a warm smile as she reached out to shake his hand. "I'm trying to locate Melody Saunders."

8

"Excuse me?" Stevie replied hesitantly, uncertain that he had heard correctly.

"I am trying to find Melody Saunders. My name is Lucy Montoya. I'm a caseworker with Safe Families. We're a domestic violence prevention agency. I'm sorry to just barge in like this but I was at court and I thought I'd take a chance that you might be in."

"Sure, no problem. I know Safe Families. Let's go find a better place to talk."

Stevie led Montoya to a small office that served as a conference room for client visits and counseling sessions. He motioned for her to sit down on one side of a table, closed the door behind them and sat down opposite her.

Lucy Montoya was short and trim with straight, black, shoulder-length hair, a hazel complexion and dark almond shaped eyes. She wore black trousers and a short-sleeved, burgundy-colored blouse, business-like yet casual, appropriate for the office, Family Court or the streets of any neighborhood in Brooklyn. She slipped a small black leather backpack that doubled as a briefcase off her shoulder and onto the seat next to her. From an inside pocket, she pulled out a business card and slid it across the table.

"I've been working with Ms. Saunders and she told me that you were the caseworker for her ACS case," said Montoya slowly, as if trying to lead Stevie to a predetermined outcome. "I was wondering if you have had any contact with her in the last couple of days."

"No," Stevie answered, shaking his head slowly. "I haven't. Why do you ask?"

The woman hesitated and studied him with soft but penetrating black eyes. Stevie understood the tension. Montoya was a domestic violence worker. Her main concern was the safety of her client. Stevie was a child welfare worker, charged with ensuring the safety of Melody's son. Anything Montoya told him might someday become evidence that could cost Melody custody of her child.

After a moment, as if an act of surrender, one eyebrow lifted above a slightly crooked smile. "Melody was supposed to meet me yesterday. She never showed up. I haven't been able to get hold of her since then."

Stevie eased back into his chair with a deep sigh. "That makes two of us."

"What do you mean?"

"I've been looking for Melody since yesterday morning. Her son Shaquan went AWOL from his group home some time Wednesday night or early Thursday morning. We assumed that he just went home to Melody, because that is what he has always done before. But..."

"She's not there?"

"No. Have you gone there to look for her?"

"No. That would be too dangerous... for her," Montoya added quickly, making sure that he understood the reason for her reluctance. "If I show up there, it could get her killed."

Stevie nodded knowingly, before asking some questions of his own.

"Why are you working with Melody? As far as I knew, she was living alone and not seeing anyone – or at least no one regular and likely to be a threat."

Montoya hesitated again before answering.

"How long have you had Melody's case?"

"Four years."

"Then you know about Levon Marbury?"

"Yes," Stevie nodded. He knew about Levon Marbury. Levon

was a small-time drug dealer who had strutted into the simmering chaos of Melody's life and brought it to a boiling crisis. He was the one who had handed out the beatings that first got Shaquan placed in foster care eight years ago. Marbury was worse than Melody's other men, who usually came and went after a month or two never to be seen or heard from again – if only because he kept coming back. Luckily for Melody and Shaquan, Levon had spent the last four years in an upstate prison.

"Well, he's back."

Stevie was stunned. "When? How?"

"He made parole back in April. Since he didn't have any place to stay, he looked up Melody and just moved in. She didn't have much say about it. He wasn't there all the time. He came and went as he saw fit."

Stevie was speechless… and embarrassed. He'd had no idea about any of this. Thinking back through the case notes in his mind, he recalled that it had been over a month since he'd met with Melody and even longer since he'd seen her at home. He'd never even been to the new apartment. They'd had a couple of phone conversations. It was a bad pattern, but not completely out of character for Melody. Worst of all was that she had cancelled two home visits for Shaquan. Clearly, Stevie should have been more concerned and active in pursuing the issue. Unfortunately, there had been any number of other crises with other kids to keep him busy.

He focused his attention back on Montoya.

"How did you get involved?"

"Melody contacted Safe Families early in June. Levon had been around for about a month and the honeymoon was over. He'd begun smacking her around. Then he told her he didn't want Shaquan in the house when he was there. When Melody objected, he beat her up pretty badly. That's when she called us."

"It all sounds pretty familiar."

"Yes, he'd already had quite a bit of practice; and so had she," said Montoya sadly. "Melody was justifiably afraid to tell him to leave and afraid to leave herself. He threatened to kill her if she tried to walk out. She was scared to death."

Montoya leaned over and pulled a bottle of water out of a side pocket on her backpack and took a small sip.

"I really give her credit," she continued. "Despite all that history; despite a lifetime of believing that she was just a pin cushion and punching bag, she reached out for help."

Lucy Montoya locked her gaze on Stevie. "It was Shaquan. She desperately wanted him back and couldn't deal with the fact that Levon was getting in the way."

Stevie nodded. He knew that Melody had made tremendous progress. She'd been in and out of drug treatment several times over the past few years. The most recent stint in a residential program designed only for women had really seemed to help. She'd graduated and looked to be staying clean. Stevie heaved a heavy internal sigh and kicked himself once again for failing to recognize the beginning of Melody's downhill slide when Marbury turned up in April.

"I started working with her around safety planning – how to recognize when she was in real danger; when and how to leave; what she needed to bring with her," Montoya explained. "The biggest problem was where to go. She really didn't have anyone."

"What about her mother and sister?"

"Melody wouldn't even consider it? I don't think they wanted anything to do with her. And, she was ashamed to ask them for help."

"Any friends?"

"None that could put her up." Montoya took another sip of water before continuing. "Last Saturday, Melody called me on my cell phone and told me that Levon had beaten her really badly. She sounded terrible and terrified."

Stevie shook his head and felt another wave of guilt. "Shaquan was supposed to go home for a visit on Saturday. When Melody called on Friday to cancel, I really read her the riot act. I told her that Shaquan had been looking forward to this for weeks; that she had already cancelled his last visit; and if she ever wanted to get her kid back she better get her shit together…."

"Christ!" he exclaimed, bursting upright from the chair in an explosion of frustration and inner rage. "I guess that explains that."

"Look," said Lucy, leaning back in her chair as she watched him pace towards the window. "It's not your fault. You didn't know."

"I'm supposed to know," said Stevie with an edge of anger directed at himself rather than Lucy.

"I understand. But you didn't know and it still isn't your fault. I wanted to go to the police right away but Melody wouldn't hear of it. There were drugs in the house. She was afraid of the cops and afraid that if Levon got arrested, he'd come back and kill her for sure."

She looked up, captured his gaze, and spoke softly. "It's not your fault. It's not my fault. We can only do what we can do. And, we can only do what they let us do."

Stevie nodded again and slumped back into his chair.

"What happened then?"

"The one good thing was that the beating helped her make a decision. She was ready to leave. I told her I would try to get her a bed in an emergency DV shelter. There aren't a lot of them so they're not easy to come by. If I got one, she'd have to leave right away and meet me. There was no turning back; once she left, she couldn't change her mind and go home. He'd kill her. She understood that."

Lucy took another sip of the water and leaned forward in the chair.

"On Wednesday I got word that Melody could have a shelter bed the following day. I called her and we made an appointment to meet in a place downtown at noon on Thursday."

She slumped back in her chair as a sudden weariness weighed upon her voice.

"She never showed. I waited for three hours. I tried her cell phone a half dozen times. She just never showed up. I haven't been able to reach her ever since."

The two sat in silence, staring at each other but lost in their own thoughts. What did this mean for Shaquan, Stevie wondered? How did his disappearance fit into this increasingly complicated story?

Montoya gave him a questioning look. "So, what do you think?" she asked.

Stevie took a moment to gather his thoughts before answering.

"Well, a lot happened between your phone call with Melody on Wednesday and the planned meeting on Thursday afternoon." He explained that a major local drug dealer had been gunned down right outside Melody's window and that, as a potential witness, the police were now looking for her as well. He also said that Melody had called Shaquan on Wednesday, the afternoon before he went missing.

"That's good," said Lucy. "At least we know she is alive."

"Or was then," Stevie answered, immediately regretting his words. "There may be other people looking for Melody too." He described how the apartment had been broken into and ransacked. "Whoever killed Rue James may think she is a witness."

"Oh, my God," said Lucy, clearly shocked by the developments.

"So, you don't have any idea where she might have gone?"

"None. That's why I came here. Do you think Shaquan is with her?"

"Yes," said Stevie without hesitation. "It is the only thing that makes any sense."

Once again, they sat together in silence.

"So, what do we do now?" Lucy asked with a combination of frustration and helplessness.

"I'm not sure. I'll check in with the police. I know the Lieutenant who is heading up the investigation."

Lucy nodded and reached across the table to take back her business card. "Here is my cell number and my home phone number," she said, writing on the back. "Please, call me if you hear anything."

"I will." Stevie answered as they rose together on either side of the small table and shook hands. "Let's stay in touch."

"Definitely," Lucy nodded as she turned to leave. He watched from behind as she walked down the narrow hallway towards the exit.

Julie Shapiro was gone and Stevie was alone when he returned to his office cubicle to finish entering his progress notes on the Saundra Whitehead court appearance.   It was another hour before he, too, walked out of the BFS offices and into the still stifling heat of a Brooklyn summer evening.

9

The Cumberland had long been home away from home for an eclectic and occasionally combustible mix of cops, firemen, nurses and emergency medical technicians who worked the nearby precincts, firehouses, hospitals and ambulances of northern Brooklyn. Whatever daylight that came through the large plate glass windows facing out onto the street was quickly absorbed by dark mahogany and tightly packed bodies before making it half way down the long bar. The murky twilight was an added convenience for couples tucked into a row of booths along the back wall, providing cover for steamy and often illicit liaisons.

Opposite the bar and closer to the front were a series of tables where larger groups gathered, some sitting, some standing as they cruised from one conversational island to another. This was a place where people knew each other – really knew each other from years, or even decades, of working together, often under the most stressful of situations. People either liked each other or didn't and they weren't afraid to speak their minds in either case. That could be unsettling in a place where almost everyone was a little drunk and half the clientele were carrying firearms.

Stevie Corra had spent a lot of time in the Cumberland, or places just like it. He often thought that if he hadn't, he would still be married and living with Sandy and Joey. But, that was a lie. They'd split up for a lot of reasons. The Cumberland was only one and surely the least important.

It now had been more than five years since Stevie had been inside the place. As he opened the door and walked in, it was instant déjà vu, a relic preserved in alcohol that flowed like water. He felt like he had never left. There were certainly new faces, lots of new faces, but plenty of familiar ones. Stevie instantly regretted his decision to come and felt an overpowering urge to simply turn on his heels and walk out. But, he didn't. Sooner or later he had to come back and face this part of his past. Now was as good a time as any. At least he had a reason to be there.

Just inside, Stevie stopped and scanned the crowd looking for Jack Schwinn. He had called ahead to confirm that Jack would be there. He quickly spotted him sitting with two other men at a table along the wall opposite the bar. Schwinn looked up, saw Corra and motioned for him to come over and take the free seat. Stevie didn't recognize the young, plainclothes cop next to Schwinn. But, as soon as he realized who had been sitting with his back to the front door, Stevie once again regretted his decision to come.

"Stevie!" said Schwinn. "It's good to see you. It's like old times." He reached out and grabbed the arm of a passing waitress – "Honey, get my friend a drink!".

"Dewars on the rocks, with a glass of seltzer on the side," Stevie said to the young woman. "Thanks," he added to Schwinn.

"You know Brian Finnerty," said Schwinn, nodding to the man at Stevie's right. "This is his partner Robby Calderone."

"It's nice to meet you," said Calderone, offering a friendly smile. "I've heard a lot about you."

"Good to meet you," said Stevie, nodding in return.

"So, how you doin', boss?" said Finnerty, his thick street accent exaggerated by what already sounded like one too many drinks. "How's the therapy going? You keep'n all the mopes out of trouble?"

Stevie turned his head and stared at the man sitting next to him. Yes, he knew Finnerty. Brian had been little more than trouble for the three years he'd been part of Stevie's unit. Corra had refused to recommend him for promotion and even tried to get him suspended once. No one had been happier to see Stevie leave the force than

44

Finnerty.

"It's all good, Brian," he said coolly. "It's all good." Stevie turned back in time to see Schwinn shoot Finnerty a dirty look.

"Brian and Robby are handling the Rue James case," Schwinn began. "I thought it would be good if we all talked together."

"That's great. I really appreciate it. What do you guys have so far?"

Finnerty glanced at Stevie with a look of weary hostility, then at Schwinn, but remained silent.

Calderone eyed the drama and spoke up. "Not a lot. Rue James was a worker bee who dreamed of bigger things. Over the past six or seven years he started building from one corner to the next along Utica and East New York Avenues. Two years ago he made a major acquisition when he took out Lonnie Marcellus and picked up his territory. We couldn't pin it on him. Things have been pretty quiet since then. Frankly, this came as a surprise."

"Was it a hit? Or, just some random trouble on the street?"

"It certainly looks like a hit. Two to the chest and one in the head."

"Any ideas on the shooter or who ordered it?"

"Could have been any number of people."

"Like who?" Stevie pressed.

Calderone glanced at Schwinn for approval before continuing. "The Santos brothers have been looking to expand. They control the territory on the other side of Atlantic. It also could have been someone on the inside."

"Don't forget about Pedro Townsend," added Schwinn.

"Yes," said Calderone, nodding slowly before taking a sip of his beer. "That's a possibility."

"Who on the inside might have wanted to step up?" asked Stevie. "How about that guy who runs the corner where it happened... Back Thompson?"

"You sound a lot like a cop," shot Finnerty, in an outburst of exasperation. "I thought you were just a social worker or something."

"Knock it off," growled Schwinn, flashing the detective a look that should have burned away any buzz he might be enjoying. "We're

45

just trying to help each other out."

Stevie ignored the exchange and remained focused on Calderone, who shrugged as he answered.

"It's possible; but I don't really think so. I always felt that Back had more muscle than ambition. But, hey, you never know!"

"Where was he when it happened?"

"Don't know! By the time I got to the scene there was nobody around and nobody in the neighborhood had seen or heard anything."

Calderone took another sip of beer before continuing. "The Lieutenant told us that Melody Saunders is the mother of one of your foster care kids. Her bedroom window looks right out at the alley where James got hit. If she was home, it is certainly possible that she could have seen the shooter. She wasn't home when I got there. We tried the apartment. Nobody in the building could tell us whether she had been home or not. We tried her mother and sister, but they said they hadn't heard from her. Then, today, after you called about the break-in, we went over to look at the apartment and asked around. Same deal. Nobody knows anything. The whole building just isn't talking."

Stevie nodded. He hadn't had much success with the neighbors either.

"So," said Schwinn. "That is what we know. What can you tell us?"

"Not much, unfortunately," Stevie answered, as he considered what to say and what not. The knowledge that Melody was planning to leave an abusive lover and head for a domestic violence shelter the day after the shooting had been given to him in confidence – and could be dangerous to Melody if it got back to Levon Marbury. The fact that Marbury had been living in the apartment, however, could be pertinent and helpful in the investigation.

"I haven't been able to track down any sign of either Melody or her son Shaquan…but, it turns out that a guy named Levon Marbury had been living with Melody on and off for the past couple of months after getting out on parole. He is a small time street dealer who has been in and out of her life for years. He went upstate a few years ago and got out in April. I don't really know any of the details. Any of you know him?"

One by one, the three detectives shook their heads.

"No," said Schwinn

"Never heard of him," said Calderone.

Finnerty remained silent.

"What about the boy?" asked Calderone. "You think he's with his mother?"

"Yes," said Stevie. "Based on his history, it's the only thing that makes sense. Every time he's gone AWOL, he's always gone home to Melody."

"What about other friends, relatives? There must be somebody he'd go to?"

Stevie shook his head, just as Finnerty's patience wore out.

"Let him find the kid; we've got a shooter to catch," he blurted, pushing back his chair and rising from the table. "I have to get going."

"Well, I guess I'm going too," said Calderone as he held up a ring of keys. "I'm driving. It was nice meeting you."

"Same here," said Stevie. "Thanks for your help."

Schwinn and Corra sat in silence as the two detectives left the bar. Stevie took a sip of his drink and felt the hard liquor burn across his tongue.

"Calderone's sharp," he said.

"Yes, he is," answered Schwinn. "He transferred up from Brooklyn South two years ago. And, as you can see, Finnerty is still a pain in the ass."

"Yes, he is," Stevie replied with a weary chuckle and took another hit of scotch. He absently scanned the familiar scene around him. The place was more crowded now than when he had arrived. The muffled din – a combination of shared war stories, raucous laughter and romantic come-ons – had grown even louder.

"It's good to see you in here again," said Schwinn. "How does it feel to be back?"

Stevie took a drink and shrugged. "The same… and different. It looks the same, sounds the same…. even smells the same. But, it's different. You know what they say. You can't go home again."

"Well, it is still good to see you. Let's do it again," said Schwinn as he started to rise from the table. "I should get going, too. We'll see what we have on Levon Marbury and let you know. If you hear anything about the Saunders woman and the kid, call me."

"I will. And Jack, thanks! I really mean it. Thanks for the help."

"No problem."

Stevie turned and watched Schwinn slip through the crowd, shaking hands and slapping backs like a successful politician, as he made his way to the door.

Stevie tossed back the rest of his scotch. The one drink had already made him feel good enough to begin thinking about having another. That alone, he knew from experience, was reason enough to get up and leave now.

10

It was almost 10:00 by the time Stevie got back to his apartment. There was one phone message from Sandy confirming that she would drop Joey off the following morning at 9:00. She almost always called on the house phone, making it less likely that she and Stevie would actually speak. It was a constant reminder of how painful their marriage and break-up had been for her.

Darkness had fallen over Brooklyn, but the night was still uncomfortably warm and muggy. He fired up the air conditioner in his bedroom, grabbed a beer and slipped outside onto the back patio. As usual, there was a slight breeze that funneled through the narrow valley of back gardens between the two rows of townhouses.

It had been a long day and Stevie suddenly realized how tired he was. In his mind's eye, he replayed over and over his visit to Melody's apartment; the conversation with Lucy Montoya with her news about Levon Marbury and Melody's plan to leave him; and the meeting with Schwinn, Finnerty and Calderone. Yet, when all was said and done, he was no wiser now than this morning. Where was Shaquan? Stevie had no idea, other than that he surely must be with Melody. His frustration welled up, battling his fatigue. Not a good combination! He was both exhausted and restless.

One image from the day came back to him again and again – the crime scene sketch of Rue James' body, outlined in chalk on the concrete alley outside Melody's window. Now, staring into the darkness, that white chalk silhouette seemed to glow like neon, burning itself into his consciousness, just as a similar image had done six years earlier.

Once more, Stevie found himself reluctantly called back to another urban battleground with its childlike stick figure of a fallen body – this time so much younger and more innocent – that had bled out its life onto the black asphalt of a Brooklyn street.

11

Sandy dropped their son off at 9:00 sharp the following morning. Joey threw his arms around his father's waist in a full body hug that simultaneously filled Stevie with joy and heartbreak. As usual, there was little in the way of conversation with Sandy, just a reminder about the time and location of Joey's soccer game and an agreement to return him back to her house the following day at 6:00 p.m. It was a fairly typical beginning for the time that Steve and Joey got to share every other weekend.

At ten, Joey was still a little short for his age and slim like both his parents. His dirty blond hair and fair complexion came from Sandy. The boy did well in school and rarely got into any kind of trouble. He struck almost everyone as polite, serious, and maybe even a little bit sad – something that flooded Stevie with guilt.

Today, he was already dressed for the game; with a red and white striped jersey and floppy black shorts that hung well below his knees, nearly touching the matching red socks and shin guards.

"You want something to eat?" Stevie asked.

"No, thanks. I already had breakfast."

"OK. You ready for the game?"

The boy just nodded in response before stepping up and throwing his arms around Corra's waist again. Stevie wrapped his son in a tight hug and they stood, silently clinging to each other.

"I love you, Joey," he said softly. He could have stayed like that all day. "Maybe we should get over to the field."

The two walked together, hand in hand, to Prospect Park and down to the Parade Grounds where Joey's AYSO summer league held its games. The scene, though lively, was nothing like the autumn when thousands of families with multi-colored kids in multi-colored uniforms swarmed over dozens of makeshift fields covering every inch of the park. Now, many children from prosperous "Brownstone Brooklyn" were away at summer homes or on vacation. Other families were headed for the beach or simply holed up at home with their air conditioners and video games. Only four fields were set up.

Stevie nodded to the parents of Joey's teammates, once again feeling guilty that he had not volunteered to coach. He watched as the kids chased the ball in one large mob, the concept of field position and passing still totally foreign. Two or three of the players stood out, their natural ability to control the ball as they moved seemingly a product of family tradition and backyard coaching sessions, most likely in Spanish or with a lilting Caribbean accent. Nevertheless, their goals still seemed more a product of pure chance than any particular soccer skills.

Joey played dutifully, almost always at the back of the chase or on the edge of the scrum. Even there, however, the laws of chaos ensured that he would get a fair number of whacks at the ball – once sending it far down field as Stevie and the other parents cheered.

When it was over, Joey's team had actually won, although it was unclear exactly why or how.

"Good game!" Stevie said as his son came off the field, sweating heavily from the heat and exertion. "Did you have fun?"

Joey just nodded, still out of breath as he reached for a bottle of water.

"How about some pizza?"

"Yeah," Joey answered between gulps. "I'm starving."

Stevie helped his son out of his cleats and back into his sneakers; then gathered up the rest of their gear in a small backpack. After waving goodbye to his coach and teammates, the two headed off as they had come, hand-in-hand, lost in conversation about the game and Joey's much improved play.

The mood was broken by the sound of Corra's cell phone.

Stevie didn't want to take the call, but knew he had to. The display told him that it was Joseph Otinga at the Flatbush Group Home.

"Hi! Joseph?"

"Good afternoon, Steve!" said Otinga in his usual relaxed yet still formal tone. "I'm sorry to bother you, but I know that you would want to hear right away."

"Sure. What do you mean? Hear what?"

"We've heard from Shaquan. He called Carlos this morning."

The news left Stevie momentarily speechless. "...Where is he? Is he all right?"

"We don't know where he is," Joseph said softly. "I didn't speak with him but Carlos said he sounded OK. Carlos is upstairs. I thought you might want to talk to him."

"I'll be right over."

12

Stevie took his son's hand once again and picked up speed back towards the apartment. On the way, they grabbed two slices of Sicilian to go that Joey ate in the car. Less than 45 minutes after Joseph's call, Stevie and his son walked in the front door of the Flatbush Group Home.

"Hello, Joey. It's nice to see you again," said Joseph Otinga as he let them in.

"Joey, you go with Mrs. Ramirez," said Stevie. "I'm sure she's got something in the kitchen that you are going to like. I have to go upstairs and work for a few minutes."

The boy eyed the surroundings uncertainly. A couple of the group home kids were watching TV in the living room. Joey had come to the home with him before and Stevie knew that he didn't like it. The older kids scared him a little; he didn't understand why they lived here and not at home with their parents. Somehow, his filthy little soccer uniform made him seem even more out of place among kids for whom the thought of a Saturday in the park with their dad was an impossible and long abandoned dream.

Joey looked at his father, who nodded reassuringly, then turned and walked hesitantly to the back of the house with Mrs. Ramirez.

Stevie bounded up the stairs and down the hall to Carlos' room, stopping to knock before entering.

"Hi, Carlos?" he said. The boy was laid back on his bed, the ever-present I-pod headphones booming in his ears. "Joseph tells me that you got a phone call from Shaquan?"

The boy nodded softly as he sat up and pulled out the headphones. "He called on the house phone a couple of hours ago. Pete answered it and then gave it to me."

"What did he say?"

"He said he was with his moms; that he was OK and we shouldn't worry about him."

"Did he say where he was?"

"No, I asked but he didn't answer."

"What did it sound like where he was?"

Carlos thought for a moment before answering. "It was quiet... I couldn't hear anything."

"So, you don't think he was on the street?"

"No, it sounded like he was inside someplace."

"Did it sound like a regular phone or a cell phone?"

"I'm not sure; maybe a cell phone."

"Did he say anything else?"

Once again, Carlos hesitated before answering. "He asked if anyone was looking for him."

"What did you say?"

"I told him that you had been here looking for him."

This time Stevie eyed Carlos for a moment before continuing. "So what did he say?"

The boy met his gaze. "He asked if there had been anybody else..." The words hung in the air for a few seconds before Carlos completed his report. "He asked if the police had been here looking for him."

"The police?" Stevie repeated questioningly.

Carlos nodded.

"Did he say why he was asking?"

"No. I told him no one had been here and he just said he had to go and hung up."

Stevie shook his head in frustration. "Thanks," he said, taking out a business card and scrawling on the back. "Here is my cell number. If Shaquan calls again, see if you can get him to tell you where he is or give you a phone number. At least, make sure he has

55

my number. Tell him I really want him to call me. I just want to make sure he is OK."

"I know," said Carlos. The obvious expression of trust was enough to give Stevie a sudden burst of hope. If Carlos felt that way, maybe Shaquan did too.

"The police?" Stevie wondered to himself silently has he turned to scan Shaquan's side of the bedroom. Once again, he looked at the posters and pictures hanging around the bed and over the desk. There were group shots with kids from the house; some with a couple of older boys who had aged out of care and others while out flying kites in Prospect Park.

"Why the police?" he questioned himself again. The boy had been AWOL enough times to know that while BFS would have filed a report, the police wouldn't actually have done anything about it.

"Thanks, Carlos," Stevie said to the boy who looked up at him with eyes that were both a little sad and a little frightened. "I sure wish Shaquan would come home."

"Me, too," answered Carlos softly. "I'm worried about him."

Stevie just nodded and headed downstairs where Joey sat at the kitchen table, staring wide-eyed at Rodney Davidson. The 17-year-old had the look and build of a 25-year-old prize fighter – six-foot one, rock solid with bulging biceps and a nose that had already been turned and flattened. For better and worse, the boy also had the temperament of a 10-year-old. Mrs. Ramirez was patiently explaining one more time why it was too late to have a sandwich; that they all would be having dinner soon.

Stevie turned to Joseph Otinga. "What do you think? Any of the kids have any ideas on where he might be?"

Joseph looked him in the eyes and just shook his head. "No. They all just knew he would be with his mother, but no one knows where they would have gone."

"Did Carlos tell you that Shaquan had asked if the police had been here looking for him?"

"Yes. That doesn't make any sense."

"No, it doesn't"

Stevie turned back to Joey and told him it was time to go. His son nodded and hopped up from the table.

"See ya, Joey," said Rodney.

"See ya," the boy answered quietly. "Goodbye, Mrs. Ramirez."

Stevie held out his hand for his son to take, but Joey ignored it. Then, he followed as the boy walked resolutely down the narrow hallway, past the now crowded and noisy living room, and out the front door.

13

"OK, let's go and see grandma and grandpa," said Stevie as he and Joey climbed back into the car. They pulled away from the curb and headed south along the bottom of Prospect Park and out onto Fort Hamilton Parkway.

Saturday afternoon barbecues with his family were a frequent part of Stevie's weekend schedule, particularly when he had Joey.

"Is Michael going to be there?" his son asked.

"Yes, I think so."

Stevie's brother Frank and his wife Jeannie usually made the weekly pilgrimage as well. Their son Michael was about a year younger than Joey and the two cousins, neither of whom had other siblings, were almost like brothers. Stevie loved to see the boys playing together. That and the chance to see his mother were the main reasons he came.

His parents still lived in the comfortable but surprisingly modest and tasteful corner house in Dyker Heights where Stevie and Frank had grown up. The still heavily Italian-American neighborhood – tucked between Bay Ridge on one side and Bensonhurst on the other – had been protected from the forces of change and progress by a distinct lack of mass transit. There wasn't a subway station for miles. That made the community particularly appealing to New York City cops and firemen – usually "brass" with salaries to match their rank – who commuted to work by car.

Stevie parked on the street, seeing that Frank's car was already in the short driveway in front of the garage. Joey was out the door and headed up to the house before his father had even turned off the engine.

By the time Stevie reached the front door, his mother had Joey locked in a grandmotherly embrace, rocking slowly from side to side, as if trying to get in a full week's worth of love and hugs during just one sporadic visit. Stevie realized that he knew exactly how she felt. It wasn't a comforting thought.

"Hi, mom," he said, as his mother gave Joey a final squeeze and turned to her oldest son.

"Hi, Steve. How are you?" She wrapped her arms around him and reached up to give him a kiss on the cheek. Stevie hugged her back and returned the kiss.

"I'm good, mom. How are you."

"Good! Good!"

Theresa Corra was still pretty and petite, her short black hair now streaked with silver highlights that betrayed the first signs of age as she entered her early 60s.

Even in a family solar system that completely revolved around his father as brightest star, Theresa always had been the main source of warmth and affection. She was the one who had offered praise and encouragement. It was on her shoulder that the boys would come to cry – always careful that their father wasn't watching – after childhood hurts and disappointments. Over the last few years, Stevie had come to realize that this type of unconditional and all-forgiving love could be just as comforting and valuable for adults as for children.

"Come on in," said his mother planting another kiss on his cheek. "Your father and Frankie are in the back."

Stevie dropped a backpack with Joey's change of clothing next to the couch in the living room. Along the back wall was "monument alley", as Stevie and Frank now referred to the display of portraits and honors recognizing their father's long and extremely successful career in the New York Police Department.

Over the course of 40 years, Joseph Corra had risen steadily through the ranks, eventually serving as Chief of Detectives – the job that most cops dream about. Stevie looked at his father's ornate gold shield – now mounted inside a Lucite frame – bearing the three stars of a full Bureau Chief. On the bookcase shelves were other personal mementos: his inaugural portrait as a newly appointed and fresh-faced young patrolman; his Sergeant's and Lieutenant's shields; the badges of Captain, Assistant Chief and Deputy Chief.

There were also the decorations. Joseph Corra had won two Medals of Valor – the first as a young rookie cop when he successfully and single-handedly disarmed a robber who had taken a storekeeper's family hostage. It was that case that had jumpstarted his career.

As a child, Stevie had loved to spend time with these symbols of his father's strength and courage. He still did, even now.

During the last two decades, Joseph Corra had shared space to record his sons' successes – and, therefore, more of his own. There were photos of Stevie on the day he joined the Department and of Frankie when he did the same two years later. There were framed clippings of news reports about their major cases and announcements of their promotions to Sergeant and Lieutenant.

For Stevie, this was as far as it went. While a family portrait marked Frankie's rise to his present rank of Captain, there were no framed newspaper reports of Stevie's disgrace; no embossed copies of his subpoena to testify before a special legislative commission or the announcement that he had resigned from the force.

"Come outside," his mother urged, her voice betraying that she knew what he was thinking and understood his pain. "We're going to start cooking."

Joseph Corra was already at the grill, which looked large enough to handle a busy night at TGI Friday's. There were two huge pieces of steak, chicken and burgers for the kids – or anyone else who wanted it. Even in his mid 60s, he was still a striking figure, tall, trim and ramrod straight. His brightly colored Hawaiian shirt and crisp jeans looked almost as sharp as his uniform always had.

"Hey, the prodigal son returns," he bellowed as Stevie came out onto the patio.

"Hi, dad! How are you doing?" Stevie responded, walking over and throwing an arm around his father's shoulders. "Got enough food there?"

"We'll get by."

Frankie was manning the bar, preparing a margarita for his wife. "Hey, Bro! What'll you have?"

"Just a beer! Thanks," said Stevie, sliding over to give his brother a similar hug. "How are you doing, Frankie?"

"Good."

Continuing his rounds, Stevie bent to give his sister-in-law a kiss. "Hi, Jeannie. You're looking beautiful as ever."

"I knew I married the wrong brother," she replied, raising her glass in a toast.

Quickly, the conversation fell into safe and familiar territory – updates on the kids, news about neighbors and family, commentary about the food, weather and vacation plans. As dinner wound down, Joey and Michael headed for the basement to plug in the Xbox. Jeannie and Stevie's mother cleared the table and went inside to do the dishes. None of the three men budged to help. Still pretty old school, thought Stevie. Nevertheless, he chose not to break the pattern. He'd already shattered enough traditions in this family.

With the women gone, Frankie settled in to share departmental news and gossip with his father. Joseph Corra had retired a couple of years earlier, once it became clear that he would never be getting a fourth star as Chief of Department, the NYPD's top uniformed position. Stevie knew that his own troubles had helped to end his father's career. It was a constant, gnawing source of unspoken anger for Joseph and irredeemable shame for his son.

Stevie sat quietly, sipping his beer and taking in the scene as they talked. Suddenly, Frankie turned to him.

"Hey, I hear you are back prowling your old haunts."

Stevie looked at his brother in puzzlement for a moment before making the connection. "Oh, The Cumberland? How did you hear about that?"

"I have my sources," Frankie replied slyly.

He certainly did. As a Unit Commander within Brooklyn Homicide, Frankie knew almost all the detectives in the borough, including most of the guys with whom Stevie had worked. With dozens of cases in the hopper, he was constantly in touch with cops all over Brooklyn.

"So, what gives? You hitting on one of the nurses... or somebody's wife?"

"No. One of our kids went AWOL and it turns out his mother might be a witness in the Rupert James murder. Did you hear about that one?"

"Sure. Narcotics caught the case because it's got to be drug related. It's your old unit...Jack Schwinn and a couple of his guys."

"Right. I wanted to ask Jack if they had any leads on the whereabouts of the mom. I'm pretty sure her son is with her."

As Stevie talked, his father rose silently from the table with a shake of his head and went into the house. Both brothers followed him with their eyes.

"Christ," Stevie muttered, as much to himself as Frankie.

"Hey, look. He doesn't mean it the way you think. He just feels bad for you."

Stevie was silent for a few moments before answering reluctantly and without any real conviction. "Yeah. I know."

"So, did Jack have anything?"

"No, but I had found out that she was living with a guy who had just come back from upstate a few months ago... a real scumbag named Levon Marbury... a doper and low level dealer... used to beat the shit out of her."

Frankie just nodded and the two brothers sat together in silence, sipping their beers. The late afternoon sun had lost some of its intensity and the light breeze almost felt cool.

"Hey, could you do me a favor," said Stevie suddenly. "Could you run Marbury's file for me? Maybe it will give me a lead on where he might be. And, if I can find him, maybe I can find Melody and Shaquan."

"Sure," said Frankie, staring at him with a touch of sadness. "No problem. I'll call you as soon as I have something."

Stevie couldn't help but see the irony. Two years older than his brother, Stevie had always been the golden boy, the rising star...

always one step ahead in terms of prestigious assignments, headline collars and promotions. He was the one on top; the one that Frankie had looked up to... ever since they were kids.

Now, suddenly, the tables had turned. Now, it was Stevie who was asking for help, hoping that his younger brother would use his rank and influence to obtain confidential NYPD information – information to which he, now just another citizen, was no longer entitled.

"Thanks."

Suddenly, the quiet of the moment was shattered.

"OK. It's time for desert," their mother announced in a voice designed to reach both the kids in the basement and her husband in the den.

The family quickly reconvened around the patio table for apple pie and ice cream – his father's favorite. There was more conversation about the same topics – as well as news about the Mets' latest loss.

An hour later, Steve grabbed Joey and repeated his round of hugs and kisses – this time in reverse.

"I'll call you," said Frankie.

"Take it easy, kid," said his father.

His mom gave them both an extra squeeze that said everything necessary. "Get home safe. I love you."

Steve and Joey climbed back into the car and headed home to catch a movie, some air conditioning and a good night's sleep.

14

Stevie woke early on Sunday morning and spent an hour or so sipping coffee while watching his son sleep peacefully on the cot set up for him in the corner of the living room. It wasn't his own room, but it was cozy and Joey seemed comfortable staying in the apartment.

At about 9:00 a.m., he began waking the boy so they could eat breakfast and get ready for church. That wasn't Stevie's idea. He had long since lost whatever faith he'd ever had. But, Sandy insisted. She was still a good Catholic and that was how she wanted to raise Joey. Stevie didn't have the heart to make an issue of it. He just went through the motions, knowing that soon enough his son would make up his own mind about what he believed and what he didn't.

After mass, the two raced back to the apartment. They jumped into bathing suits, grabbed towels and a blanket, and set out for the beach. Stevie had already stocked a cooler with sandwiches, soda and chips.

Riis Park was barely a 45-minute drive away, even in the heavy traffic of a summer Sunday in Brooklyn. It was one of many long and narrow sand spits guarding the southern tier of Long Island. Each, in turn, offered seaside respite to their own specific clientele, ranging from a distinctly urban ambiance on the Brighton Beach boardwalk to the oceanfront mansions of "jet set" Southhampton. Riis Park was definitely at the lower end of the food chain – but marginally more exclusive than Coney Island, if only because it was unreachable by subway.

Stevie grabbed a spot in the shopping mall-sized parking lot. Then came the harder job of finding space to squeeze their blanket in among the thousands of other New Yorkers out to enjoy a relaxing day at the beach. Father and son circled around the main throng and settled in about fifty feet from the water, surrounded by extended families of Haitians on one side and Russians on the other.

They dumped their stuff and headed for the water. The surf was a little rougher than usual, indicating that a late summer storm might be moving up the coast. Stevie had been teaching his son to body surf and the waves were just right for another lesson. The pair waded in, slowly, tentatively, letting the chill of the ocean ever so gradually strip away the heat of the sun... each step, each cold swell stinging another few inches of flesh... until, finally ready to take the plunge, they raced forward together and knifed into the soft underbelly of an oncoming wave.

For the next half hour, Steve and Joey bobbed and floated, watching and waiting for waves that could power them towards the sandy shore. Suddenly, with only an instinctive knowledge of exactly why or when, they would throw themselves forward in a maelstrom of flailing arms and kicking legs, struggling to find that perfectly invisible place where the surf itself would catch and throw them with strength far beyond their own. Bouncing along the salty froth, they steered as best they could around the hordes of other bathers.

Finally, Stevie decided he was ready for a break. Joey, as his father expected, wasn't. Stevie walked back to the blanket, toweled himself off, threw on a shirt and took a soda from the cooler. In the process, he also grabbed the waterproof pouch in which he had stashed his keys, wallet and cell phone. Then, he went back to the lip of the beach overlooking the water to keep an eye on his son.

Stevie watched as Joey continued to ride the waves, again and again, each time adding to his sense memory of when to lunge, when to let the swell pass. After good rides, the boy would pop up on the shore, smiling and waving to his father. After less successful attempts, he would simply turn and march back through the surf – resolute and focused – to try again.

As he waited, Stevie checked his phone for messages. There

were none. Suddenly, however, he remembered that he had never called Lucy Montoya to let her know that they had heard from Shaquan – and that he was with Melody. Lucy would want to know. It meant that Melody was safe, at least for the moment.

He looked towards Joey one more time. The boy was fine and showing no signs of coming out of the water. Stevie opened his wallet and found Lucy's card. He dialed the number and waited. After five rings, he got her voice mail message: "Hello, this is Lucy. I can't take your call right now. Leave your name and number and I'll call you back."

"Hi, Lucy," said Stevie, cupping his hands around the cell phone to shelter it from the sea breeze. "This is Steve Corra from Brooklyn Family Services. Sorry to bother you on a Sunday. But, I just wanted you to know that we have heard from Melody Saunders' son Shaquan. He is with Melody. We don't know where they are, but he says they are OK. I thought you would want to know. If you want to call me back today, my number is 917-555-3214. Or, I'll be in the office tomorrow. Bye."

Stevie popped the phone and wallet into his shirt pocket and once again turned his attention to Joey. The boy was finally beginning to look a little tired. Stevie signaled him to come out of the water and Joey strode up the bank of damp sand to his father.

"How'd I do?" he asked, the broad smile proving that he already knew the answer.

"Great," said Stevie, wrapping a towel around his son's wet shoulders. "You're really getting the hang of this."

"Yeah," said Joey with obvious pride. "It was fun."

The two worked their way back up the crowded beach and tossed themselves onto their blanket. Joey dried himself as Stevie pulled a plastic bag filled with sandwiches out of the cooler.

"Hungry?"

"Starving," said Joey, still shivering from the ocean's chill.

They sat together, shoulder to shoulder on the blanket, and ate, sipping their sodas and sharing the bag of chips. Stevie asked his son about his plans for the coming week. During most of the summer vacation, Joey attended a day camp run by the local community center. The kids went to parks, a local pool and on trips around the city. It wasn't exactly a day in the country, but at least it kept Joey busy and out of trouble. And, it was the only way both his parents could keep working when school was out.

After lunch, the two laid back on the blanket to catch some rays – once Stevie had ensured that Joey was sufficiently protected with sun screen. The boy's fairer complexion made him easy prey for a major case of sunburn. Stevie could almost feel, rather than hear, the sound of his son's slow and peaceful breathing against a background buzz of ocean waves and a thousand separate, wind tossed conversations.

Much too soon, the sun began to slide westward in the sky. It was time to join the slow but steady trickle of beach goers headed back towards the parking lot. Stevie roused Joey who had dozed off on the blanket and the two began to pack up.

For some reason – some immutable law of nature – the trek back across the beach going home was always much longer and far harder than it had been on the way to the water. By the time they got to the car, the pair were once again drenched in sweat which now mingled with sand and sea salt to create a particularly abrasive and uncomfortable body paste. The answer, Stevie knew, was a quick shower and a change of clothes. It was one of their few – and oh, so little – luxuries. He paid the $2.00 fee for use of the bathhouse where hot water on a summer day actually felt really good. A half-hour later, father and son were rinsed and dried, with clean T-shirts and cut-off jeans – ready for a trip to the mainland.

The drive back to Sandy's was always a little quiet. With so much to say – and so little time left – no one said much of anything. Whatever conversation there was seemed forced and artificial. The closer they got, the deeper they fell into silence.

Stevie pulled up along the curb, rather than swinging into the driveway as he used to when they all lived together and this was his home, too. That had been hard at first, requiring an act of concentration to overcome years of habit. He saw Sandy look out the window and knew that she would soon be standing at the front door, waiting for Joey.

Stevie pulled his son's bag out of the back seat and wrapped his arm around Joey's shoulder as they walked slowly up the path to the front steps.

Sandy swung open the screen door and stepped out to meet them on the small porch.

"How was the beach?" she asked.

"Great," said Joey.

"We had a real good time," added Stevie, sounding a little less upbeat than he'd hoped.

The weekend ended the same way it had begun. Joey threw his arms around Stevie's waist in a full body hug.

"Thanks, dad," he said, his face flat up against his father's stomach. "I'll see you next week."

"Joey…," Sandy said softly in words not meant to hurt, but painful nonetheless. "Remember that we are going to the country next weekend. You'll see your dad the week after."

Stevie gave his son another hug and tried not to sound disappointed. "It's OK, Joey. I'll call you and we'll plan something special. You have a good time and be a good boy. I love you."

"I love you, too," Joey answered as he turned and rushed into the house.

Stevie's heart sank as he watched his son disappear into a world, once familiar but where he now no longer belonged.

"I'm sorry," said Sandy. "But, we've been planning this for a month."

"I know. It's OK. He'll be fine."

He knew that Sandy had been seeing someone she'd met through work. It had been almost a year already and seemed to be getting serious. His family had a summer place in the Berkshires.

"He'll be fine," Stevie repeated, more to reassure himself than Sandy that things were going to be OK.

15

Stevie drove slowly west along Avenue Y and turned right on Ocean Parkway, which would take him almost directly back to his own apartment. In his mind's eye, however, he saw not the tightly packed, single family homes of southern Brooklyn, but only the back of his son as he walked out of his life for another two weeks. Stevie knew that he had no one to blame but himself. His own decisions had led to the break-up with Sandy. It wasn't that he had been unfaithful. He had never cheated on her – at least not with another woman. But he had never been completely honest either; never fully committed to her, to their marriage… or even to their son.

He had been a cop; and in love with being a cop. That had left far too little room for anything… or anyone… else. In the end, however, he would learn that his love had been an illusion and that it was he who would be betrayed by it. He had lost everything in his life that he had cared about… most importantly, Joey.

Now, Stevie was just a visitor in his own son's life, allowed only carefully prescribed periods of custody – every other weekend guaranteed, one evening a week if possible, two weeks during the summer. He was like those parents on his foster care caseload whose children had been taken from them due to abuse or neglect. The only difference was that they had the chance – through hard work and renewed commitment – to win back permanent custody of the children they loved. For Stevie, there would be no reprieve, no commutation of sentence. He would always be Joey's father, but never in the way he had always envisioned. His was fatherhood by appointment, each one with its own boundaries and limitations.

As he drove, the sun began to set almost straight ahead of him and twilight softly descended over Brooklyn. If Joey was lost to him now, at least Stevie knew that he was safe at home with Sandy. Shaquan was also with his mother, but where and whether they were safe remained a mystery.

Stevie felt far too restless to go directly home. At Church Avenue, he turned right and drove absent mindedly, past Flatbush Avenue, then up and around onto Linden Blvd., heading east. Suddenly, he recognized that he was unconsciously driving towards Brownsville and Melody's apartment. Somehow, the realization relaxed him, and he began to focus on the road and neighborhood around him. He still didn't know what he was looking for; but he was hoping that, like so many other things in life, he would know it when he saw it.

It took another 20 minutes before Stevie drove slowly up Utica Avenue where Melody's building was just off the corner of Livonia. From what he could make out, there was the same setup as his first visit. He recognized the tall player who had been wearing the Knicks jersey. He now wore some nondescript T-shirt with a baseball cap twisted sideways on his head and sat at the top of the steps. There was no sign of "Back" Thompson.

Stevie continued for another two blocks and then parked along the curb. He climbed out of the car and crossed the street to be on Melody's side of the avenue. Without really understanding what he was going to do... or why... he began walking slowly back towards the apartment.

While he approached, Stevie searched for the lookout who should be right off the corner watching for trouble coming from either direction along the avenue. It didn't take long to find him – a kid, maybe 15 or 16 years old, leaning against a gated and abandoned storefront on the opposite side of the street. The boy was locked in conversation with a girl his own age wearing a tight, blue tube top and amazingly short cut-off jeans. Every minute or two, he'd take a perfunctory glance in both directions but was clearly more interested in what he saw right in front of him. Stevie wasn't worried. There were still a handful of pedestrians heading to and fro. He just marched straight ahead, eyes down, looking like someone heading home on a Sunday night.

As he neared the alley behind Melody's apartment where Rue James had been shot and killed, Stevie snuck another quick glance at the lookout. Young Romeo was completely entranced, seemingly with no interest in who might be headed his way. Without any warning at all, Stevie turned abruptly into the alleyway and two steps later was out of view from anyone on the street.

Somehow, the little urban canyon, a mere six- or seven-feet-wide, seemed instantly quiet and protected. On one side was a sheer brick wall, four stories high with no windows at all. On the other was Melody's building, rising three stories above him. Stevie walked a little further into the alley, which ended at a solid wooden fence, maybe eight feet tall that separated the alley behind Melody's from the back yards of row houses further down the block.

The chalk outline of Rue James' body had begun to fade. Stevie stared down at it, and then looked up to see Melody's window, a bare seven or eight feet above the alley floor, directly overlooking where the shooting had taken place. There was no light in the window, but he could see that the curtain, which had been torn to one side when he was there last, was now drawn, blocking any view in or out.

Stevie stood silently and absorbed the scene around him. It was far darker in the alley than out on the avenue. The street light reflecting off dirty brick and dark concrete bathed the narrow space in a dim, yellowish haze. It was clear than Melody could easily have been the only person with a clear view of whatever went down here the night Rue James was killed.

At the end of the small alley, furthest from the street, was a steel door leading into the back of Melody's building. He stepped up and tried the knob. It was locked. Above the doorway, the outlet for a floodlight stood empty and rusted.

Stevie turned and once again stared down at the faint chalk drawing of where Rue James' body had fallen. For the second time, he imagined that he could see the young drug lord, thrown backward onto the concrete floor of the alley by the force of the shots that killed him, his right arm flung back above his head, his left arm lying limp by his side, his legs slightly twisted underneath him.

Now, however, Stevie realized that if this impression was correct, then James had been shot not from the street – as he had always assumed – but from the back of the alley… possibly by someone standing at the steel door where he himself now stood.

Suddenly, his thoughts were interrupted by the sound of steps coming into the alley.

Stevie looked up to see "Back" Thompson sauntering towards him. A loose, black tank top revealed a broad barrel chest, powerful shoulders and bulging biceps. The shock of his appearance jolted Stevie like an electric power surge. His stomach fell, his heart raced ahead at breakneck speed and his lungs locked into place, unable to either inhale or exhale. The narrow alley, which had seemed somehow safe and protected from the danger of Brooklyn street life only a few feet away, now felt isolated and threatening. People got killed here.

"What you do'in?" asked Thompson, in what was clearly a question not looking for an answer. "You got no business, here."

"I told you before," said Stevie, struggling to get control of his emotions. "I'm looking for Melody Saunders and her son, Shaquan. Any idea where they might be?"

"No, they're gone!" growled Thompson, taking a step closer, his cold black eyes focused on Stevie's. "And now it's time for you to be gone, too. I'm not going to *tell* you again."

As Thompson neared, Stevie felt an unexpected calm sweep over him. It was as if years of training and long-practiced habit suddenly allowed him to slip effortlessly into a once familiar, if recently forgotten, role.

"Are you threatening me, Back?" he said, taking his own step forward, never once losing his lock on Thompson's stare. "That's not really a very good idea. You should think again."

Stevie's sudden show of strength and confidence stopped Thompson in his tracks … but only for a second.

"You're not a cop anymore," said the young gangster in a combined sneer and humorless chuckle. "You best be picking up your skinny, little, fucking social worker ass and go on home."

Now it was Stevie who hesitated, but also for just a moment.

"Yeah, I'm not a cop," he began, before leaning forward until he was only inches from Back Thompson's face. "But, I still carry enough weight to make your sad, little fucked up life that much sadder … and way more fucked up."

He could almost see the mental and emotional churning in Back Thompson's eyes. But, the deadly game still wasn't over.

"You sure about that?" Thompson asked, eyebrows raised and head tilted slightly to one side.

This time Stevie showed no hesitation.

"Yeah, I'm sure. You want to take a shot and find out?"

Finally, Back Thompson remained silent.

"Well," Stevie said as he brushed past and headed toward the street. "It's been nice visiting."

Suddenly, he turned to look down at the chalk outline on the darkened concrete and then up at Back Thompson. "So, this is where your boss got killed? How's that working out for you?"

Once again, Thompson remained silent, staring at Stevie with eyes that understood the pleasures of first-degree homicide.

Stevie turned and walked back to his car, not once giving in to the fierce instinct to turn and see if anyone was following.

He climbed behind the wheel and pulled away from the curb. Finally, his eyes darted to the rear view mirror and scanned as much of the street behind him as possible. Romeo was just sticking his head out from behind a parked truck, undoubtedly noting the make, model and plate number of the car.

Why bother, thought Stevie. *"You're not a cop anymore!"* Back Thompson already knew who he was. How could that be? What did it mean?

He drove for another fifteen minutes through the side streets of central Brooklyn. As he did, the surge of adrenaline from his close encounter with a deadly drug dealer hit him like the delayed reaction to an automobile accident – the collision itself had occurred in almost calm slow motion; the paralyzing shock set in afterwards. Stevie broke into a cold sweat; his heart pounding; his consciousness somewhat removed from the reality around him – almost like an out of body experience.

He pulled to the curb along a dark and deserted stretch of road, and then reached back into the cooler for a bottle of water left over from his day at the beach. He suddenly realized that his mouth was parched… and his hand was trembling.

For more than a decade, Stevie had lived and thrived in this world on a daily basis. He'd developed and honed his ability to perform in each of the many roles required of a NYPD detective – good cop, bad cop, trusted protector, agent of revenge, blackmailer, extortionist, heavy hand of the law. He had practiced being alternately caring and cruel… all in the pursuit of justice.

Stevie had been stunned at how easily he had slipped back into character – relying on bravado and the implied threat of a force larger than himself – and how comfortable it had felt, like a protective armor that shielded him from the dangers of a very, very perilous world.

Yet he knew now, and had known for several years, that these persona were themselves a danger… that each and every role he took on left a little shadow on his soul…each ruthless threat, each act of callous indifference, every feigned denial of fear and loathing became a little more real, gradually crowding out his own true feelings and emotions until he was no longer sure whether he was acting or not.

Over the past five years, Stevie had worked hard to shed these false identities, to cleanse his character of the toxic residue they'd left behind. He had actually begun to believe he'd been successful.

Now, as he sat trembling behind the wheel, he knew that wasn't the case. His shock, he realized, was not delayed fear from meeting Back Thompson; it was the terror of seeing his former self – someone Stevie had been trying to escape for five long years.

16

Stevie climbed the circular staircase from the BFS lobby to the second floor offices at a little before 9:00 a.m. on Monday morning. It had been a restless night's sleep and he was just beginning to shake off the fog that still clouded his thinking. As he walked down the narrow hallway, he saw that Jackie Johnson was already in her office. Stevie stuck his head in while giving the door a gentle knock.

"Hi."

"Good morning," said Jackie looking up from the case file on her desk. It seemed as if she already had been at work for hours. "Any word on Shaquan?"

"Yes and no. We know he is with Melody, but we still don't know where they are," answered Stevie before giving a ten minute summary of almost everything that had happened over the past four days – the initial missing persons report to Jack Schwinn, the news about the Rue James shooting, Lucy Montoya's information about Melody's DV case and, finally, Shaquan's phone call to Carlos. He didn't bother to mention his visit with Back Thompson. Jackie had enough to worry about.

When Stevie had finished, Jackie just stared at him with weary amazement. "Not your typical AWOL," she said finally.

"No."

"Got any ideas?"

Now it was Stevie's turn to stare back blankly for a moment before shaking his head in frustration. "Not at the moment."

"OK, something will turn up. Right now you've got another dozen kids to worry about."

"Yeah! I'm headed to court for Richard Timmons," he said, actually feeling relief to be thinking about something else, something as routine and boring as a court appearance.

"Good. Let me know if you hear anything else."

"Sure."

"Stevie!" called Jackie as he turned to leave. When he glanced back, he saw his boss looking up at him with concern in her eyes – concern as much about Stevie as the boy who was missing. "Try not to worry too much. Shaquan is going to be all right. I just have a feeling."

"Thanks, I'll try," he responded and walked to his office.

Once again, the four cubicles were empty. Stevie tossed his jacket over a chair and fired up his computer while he searched the files for Richard Timmons' case record and tucked it in his bag. Bringing the document was a formality. Stevie knew Richard's life story by heart. Now 17 years old, he had been in foster care for ten years, after being largely abandoned by his parents. Since then, the boy had been through at least a dozen foster family homes, each one soon asking that he be removed after experiencing more and more troubling behaviors – angry and violent outbursts, self inflicted injuries, fire setting – as the extent of his mental illness became more and more apparent. Over the past five years, Richard had cycled back and forth between increasingly restrictive congregate residential programs and repeated psychiatric hospitalizations. Finally, it seemed, a new combination of psychotropic medications and intensive supports at a BFS group home specializing in seriously mentally ill youth had begun to create some stability in the boy's life and behavior. Stevie's job this morning was simply to present a psychiatric report urging that there be no change in current placement or treatment plans.

With case record in hand, he still had some time to check emails before making the 15 minute walk to court. Just as he began, Stevie heard and felt the low rumble of his cell phone vibrating in his pocket.

"Hello, Steve Corra," he answered.

"Hi, Steve. This is Lucy Montoya."

Stevie felt a slight flush of excitement as he recognized her voice. "Hi, Lucy."

"I got your message yesterday," she said. "Thank you for letting me know about the call from Shaquan. You said that he is with Melody?"

"That's right. That's what he told the boy he called – a friend of his at the group home."

"But he didn't say where they are?"

"No." Stevie felt a twinge of disappointment that he couldn't give her better news. "But he said that they were OK," he added attempting to sound a little more upbeat.

"That's good," answered Lucy, obviously trying hard to sound positive as well. There was a moment of awkward silence before she continued. "Have you been able to come up with any ideas about where they might be?"

"No," Stevie answered, once again feeling almost embarrassed at not being able to offer another lead. "No, I haven't. How about you?"

"Well… there is one thing that I wondered about," said Lucy. "I was going through my notes and remembered that Melody talked about a friend of hers that she had met in rehab. I think they had become close."

"In rehab?" said Stevie, surprised, but suddenly hopeful.

"Yes. Her name was Lakeisha. But, I don't know her last name. I don't even know which treatment program she was in."

"Hold on," said Stevie suddenly, putting down the phone and crossing to a file cabinet along the office wall. He dragged open a drawer and walked his fingers across the top until he found what he was looking for. Stevie pulled out another thick, brown file folder – identical in form to the Richard Timmons case record he had already placed in his bag. He returned to his desk and picked up the phone.

"I should have it here," he said, flipping through the wire-bound series of progress notes with his free hand. "Here it is. She went to New Beginnings Treatment Services in Flatbush. I know the Director of that program pretty well."

"Do you think he might know who Lakeisha is and how we could get in touch with her?"

"I would think so. I have to go to court now... and I have a Family Team Conference this afternoon that will probably go until about 3:30 or so. I could take a ride out there after that and talk to him."

"That's great," said Lucy, who hesitated for just a moment before continuing. "Can I go with you? I'm working at the Brooklyn Family Justice Center on Court Street today. It's right near you. I could leave whenever you are ready to go."

"Sure," answered Stevie. "If we can find Lakeisha, she may be more willing to talk to you than to me."

Lucy understood completely. As a child welfare worker, Stevie was part of the system that took Melody's son away and kept her from getting him back. Lakeisha could easily have had her own history and resentments when it came to Child Protective Services. Lucy, on the other hand, was just trying to help Melody. Hopefully Lakeisha would see that and help them find her.

"I know where the Brooklyn Family Justice Center is. Why don't I call you once I've got the car? I'll come by and pick you up out front," Stevie suggested. "Let's aim for 4:00."

"That works great. I'll see you then."

Stevie flipped off his phone and dropped it in his pocket. The dull depression that had been dogging him all morning was gone. He felt energized and hopeful. How much of this was due to finding a new lead in the search for Shaquan... and how much was the result of a sudden chance to spend some time with Lucy Montoya ... was unclear.

17

It was just a few minutes before 4:00 when Stevie worked his way through the congested traffic of downtown Brooklyn and pulled to the curb in front of 1220 Court Street.

The building was home to both the District Attorney's office and, less prominently, the Brooklyn Family Justice Center. The Center was one of a wave of innovative new programs popping up across the country designed to improve services for victims of domestic abuse. Dozens of public and private nonprofit agencies shared the facility to ensure that every essential service was readily available to women and children who literally might be running for their lives. There were both police and prosecutors specializing in domestic violence; legal services; shelter providers; immigration programs and medical and mental health practitioners. Every ethnic group in Brooklyn could find linguistic- and culturally-competent care – Haitians, Hispanics, Asians, Arabs... the list went on and on. The goal was to seal every crack that someone might fall through as they awaited referral to some critical but missing link in the chain of services. In these cases, those kinds of slips could wind up being fatal.

Stevie saw Lucy Montoya standing against the wall by the main entrance. He leaned over and waved through the open car window. She was dressed much the same as when he had first seen her – a short-sleeved, button-up blouse, now deep blue rather than burgundy, tucked into the waist of snug, black trousers; a black leather backpack slung over one shoulder.

As she spotted him, Lucy began to move quickly and gracefully, slicing through the throngs of pedestrians now headed towards homebound subway stations. Stevie couldn't help but smile at the sight. She was trim and athletic... a runner... a dancer... maybe both.

"Hi," she said, bending to look in with a bright smile through the passenger side window before swinging open the door and sliding into the seat next to him. "This is great. Thank you for doing this."

"No problem! Thanks for the tip. Maybe this will help us find Shaquan and Melody." Stevie suddenly realized that he was trying to sound formal and business-like.

They pulled away from the curb and headed south. The traffic was frustratingly heavy and their progress came in fits and starts.

"Sorry about the mess in the car," said Stevie pointing towards the pile of clothes, towels, beach blanket and cooler on the back seat that had never made it out of the car the night before. "And, the air conditioner has seen better days," he added in an even more apologetic tone.

"Don't worry," said Lucy with a smile as she settled back in the seat and rested her elbow out the open window. "I don't mind the heat and the breeze feels terrific.... How long have you been with Brooklyn Family Services?"

"A little more than five years. I mainly work with the older kids like Shaquan."

"They really need the attention. And, it's good for the boys to have a man in their life."

"I think that's true. Mostly they just need someone... anyone... to care about them."

They turned east on Atlantic Avenue towards Flatbush.

"Where did you work before BFS?" Lucy asked casually.

Stevie remained silent for a moment before answering. "That's kind of a long story," he said. "How about you? How long have you been at Safe Families?"

Lucy eyed him curiously for just an instant; then responded quickly. "About the same, I just finished my sixth year."

"How do you like it?"

"I like it a lot... at least most of the time. It's a good agency – well run and everyone really cares about the work. We help a lot of women and families. But, you can't help everyone. Sometimes they just aren't ready. Sometimes... a lot of times... they don't have any place to go and you can't get them a bed in a shelter. There really aren't enough shelters."

"Yeah...," said Stevie, offering a combination of agreement and sympathetic support. As she spoke, he could hear the slightest trace of accent hinting at the fluent Spanish – the language of home and family – lying just below the service. "Are you Dominican?" he asked cautiously.

"Yes," she answered, turning to look at him with surprise. "You have a good ear."

"It was just a guess."

"My family moved here when I was three-years old. I grew up in Washington Heights."

"Where do you live now?"

"Over in Prospect Heights. It looks like we are going to be driving right past my neighborhood," she said as they turned off Atlantic and headed south on Flatbush Avenue.

"Yeah," said Stevie. "I guess so. That's a nice area."

"It's OK."

They both settled into silence for a few minutes before Stevie spoke again.

"I called ahead to New Beginnings. I wasn't able to get hold of Roger Brown, the Director, but they said he would be in later this afternoon. I left a message that we'd be there around 4:30."

"Melody didn't have a lot of resources in the community," said Lucy, slipping into the social work jargon in which both she and Stevie were also fluent. "She wasn't on good terms with her family and she didn't have any other real friends. But I think that she and Lakeisha had grown pretty close this year. She told me that they had been visiting each other at home. But, she'd stopped having Lakeisha over to her place because Levon didn't like it. There is a real possibility that Melody would have gone to her for help."

"Let's hope so," said Stevie. Again, they fell into a silence that

felt surprisingly comfortable.   He turned left off of Flatbush onto
Empire Boulevard and then, five minutes later, swung south on New
York Avenue.

"We're almost there," he said. "Have you ever been to a
residential drug treatment program?"

Now it was Lucy's turn to hesitate before responding. Stevie,
with his eyes on the road, could feel Lucy's gaze turned towards him
as she spoke. "Yes," she said flatly. It was an answer that didn't
invite further questions. Stevie didn't ask any.

Corra eased the car into a parking spot on the avenue across
from their destination.

New Beginnings was housed in a four-story brick building
that once had featured two storefronts beneath three floors of
small apartments. Now, it was home to 24 men and women living
for periods of nine to twelve months in a therapeutic community
style residential program as they struggled to stay clean and
sober. Most had been "mandated" – ordered by the court to attend
the program as a condition of avoiding prison. As a result, not
everyone's commitment to a new drug-free lifestyle was absolute.
Others, however, had finally hit bottom and were now ready to
begin climbing out of the deep, dark hole their life had become.
Treatment, like chemotherapy, didn't always work the first time…
sometimes it didn't work at all… but when it did, it saved lives.

Steve and Lucy entered through an unmarked metal door and
were immediately standing at the New Beginnings reception counter.
The agency had all the down-market institutional ambiance of most
residential programs – a Plexiglas divider separating visitors from
reception staff; linoleum flooring from which all dirt and any trace
of original color had been scrubbed clean; blandly painted walls
covered by corkboards which themselves were filled with policy
bulletins, meeting notices, staff and client assignments and a host
of inspirational posters and quotations. Furniture of every type and
from every possible origin mingled in a way that the word "eclectic"
couldn't even begin to describe.

After a few minutes wait, Roger Brown sauntered down the
narrow hallway towards them, a broad, bright smile on his face.

Brown was a mountain of a man, at least 6'5" and 250 pounds, but all muscle, no fat, even now when he was closer to 60 than 50. Roger carried himself with a stately grace, straight and tall, as if wearing the dignity he had earned through the ups and downs of a hard, yet rewarding life – 15 total years in various state prisons, a successful battle with drug addiction and creation of a treatment program that had helped thousands of others do the same.

"Hello, Stevie," said Brown. "It's great to see you."

"Same here, Roger," Stevie answered, reaching out to shake Brown's hand. "This is Lucy Montoya. She's a case manager with Safe Families."

"It's nice to meet you. Come on back to my office so we can talk."

Brown led them along the hallway to his small and cluttered office in the rear of the building. "Have a seat," he said, pointing to two chairs on either side of a small conference table, which he quickly cleared of books and papers. He closed the door behind them and then pulled out a third chair where he sprawled out, stretching his long legs off to the side.

"So, what can I do for you today?"

"We're hoping that you can help us find one of your former residents," said Stevie.

Brown answered simply by tilting his head to one side and raising an eyebrow as if to question why he should breach a confidential relationship with one of his clients.

"We're worried about her…. and her son," said Stevie, beginning a brief history of Shaquan's AWOL, the "Rue" James murder and Melody's disappearance.

Lucy picked up right where he left off. "Melody was in an abusive relationship and was about to move out and into a shelter when she just vanished. She didn't seem to have a lot of options. I have to believe that she still needs help. I still may be able to get her a shelter bed where she will be safe and secure… at least for a while… as she tries to plan what to do next."

Brown looked from one to the other and then leaned forward to rearrange himself in the chair.

"O.K.," he said slowly. "I know Melody. She graduated from here about five or six months ago. She did good… or at least she *was* doing good. We have a group for past graduates that meets in the evenings. She came for a while, but then stopped after a month or so. I can look and see what contact information we have for her, but it sounds like you already know where she was living."

"Yes," said Stevie. "But, we actually think another one of your former residents might be in touch with her and could have an idea about where she is."

"Melody told me that she had become close to another woman while she was here... Lakeisha… I don't know her last name," said Lucy.

Brown sat up and leaned forward, nodding vigorously. "Sure, Lakeisha Smalls. They got very friendly. Lakeisha is really doing great. And, she was a big, big help for Melody. They both graduated right around the same time."

"Can you give us Lakeisha's address and phone number?" asked Stevie.

"Sure," said Brown with a chuckle. "But, if you just wait around for about a half hour, you can ask her yourself. She should be showing up any time now for that support group meeting I told you about."

"No kidding?" said Stevie, exchanging surprised glances with Lucy. "Are you certain she'll be here?"

"She hasn't missed a single meeting since she graduated. Like I said, she's really doing great." Roger Brown climbed out of his chair. "Why don't you two make yourselves comfortable? I have to do a few things around the house. I'll bring Lakeisha in once she shows up."

"That's great," said Lucy. "Thank you."

18

For the next half hour, Steve and Lucy passed the time by checking phone messages, returning emails and making a few calls. The 45 minutes after that passed more slowly as they waited impatiently, expecting Lakeisha Smalls to walk in at any moment. Roger Brown came back a couple of times; first to say that she must be running late and then to say that she still hadn't shown up.

At 6:30, a full hour after the meeting had begun, Brown came to the office one more time.

"I don't know where she is," he said, shaking his head in a combination of surprise tinged with worry. "This isn't like her at all. Like I said, she's never missed a meeting before. I tried her cell phone and got no answer."

"That's OK," said Stevie. "I'm sure she's fine. Something must have come up. Could you give us her address and phone number? We'll try to get in touch."

"Sure," answered Brown, bending over his desk to copy the information onto a note pad. "She lives pretty close to here; has a room in a building over on Courtland. It's sort of a SRO with lots of folks in recovery."

"Thanks," said Stevie, taking the information from Brown. "It was good seeing you again."

"Yes, and please tell Lakeisha that we missed her this evening," said Brown.

"It was nice meeting you," said Lucy.

Steve and Lucy made their way back down the narrow hallway, past the reception desk and out the front door.

"So near and yet so far," said Lucy. "That was a disappointment."

"Yes it was. Do you want to take a ride by her apartment? It is pretty close."

"Sure, I've got time," answered Lucy. Stevie felt somehow pleased to hear that she had no pressing commitments.

They crossed the avenue and climbed back into the Subaru which had been baking in the late afternoon sun. The air was thick with heat; every surface searing. They opened windows and added the AC for whatever relief it could offer. Stevie pulled away from the curb and raced up the boulevard, trying to generate as much breeze as possible. After a few minutes it was bearable again, if not quite comfortable.

"Do you know where the apartment is?" Lucy asked.

"Yeah, it's not far at all; another five minutes or so."

They drove together in silence, turning east along the south side of Holy Cross cemetery and then north up Utica.

"Do you think she'll be home?" Lucy asked.

"Probably not," Stevie answered wearily. "But, you never can tell."

The moment he turned right onto Courtland, Stevie hit the brakes. Ahead of them, midway up the block, were the unmistakable signs of an NYPD crime scene. A full array of official vehicles – patrol cars, vans, ambulances, unmarked cars – were scattered at all angles over the length of the street; dome lights flashing through the first hint of early evening twilight; radios crackling in quadraphonic static; uniformed officers idly keeping even more idle locals outside a perimeter created by yellow "NYPD Police Line" tape. It was the second time in less than a week that he had seen this stereotypical marker of murder and mayhem fluttering in the breeze.

Stevie took one look at the address on the house closest to them and did the rough math in his head. He knew instantly that the focus of all this official attention was Lakeisha Small's apartment building.

"Shit," he said, pulling the car into one of the few remaining spaces that vaguely resembled a legal parking spot. Simultaneously, Steve and Lucy swung open their doors, climbed out of the car and hurried along the sidewalk.

There was already a small crowd of onlookers, both bored and curious. Stevie brushed past a group of teenagers and approached the nearest police officer. His natural instinct was to flash a shield, grab the tape, slide underneath and take command of the scene. It was no longer a vision that matched reality; like the muscle memory of aging basketball players who no longer have the strength or agility for a drive to the hoop. Now, he was just another curious citizen to be held at a distance.

"What happened," he yelled to the uniform, a young African-American female in her mid 20s.

"Woman got killed," she answered, barely looking at Stevie as she casually strolled back and forth along the perimeter.

His heart seemed to stop.

"What was her name?"

"I don't know," she said, this time taking a little more interest in who was asking the questions. She looked at him and then turned to peer over her shoulder towards two detectives in plain clothes standing next to one of the cars. Stevie followed her gaze and recognized Tommy Quinn. This was his brother Frankie's squad.

"Tommy!" he called. "Tommy!"

Quinn looked up from his conversation, stared back at him and then began walking towards the crowd. "Stevie?" he asked. "What are you doing here?"

"Can we come over?" Steve asked, motioning across the barrier with one hand and reaching to take hold of Lucy's arm with the other.

Quinn nodded approval, first to Stevie, then to the uniform, who raised the tape barrier for them both to slip underneath.

"What are you doing here?" the detective asked again.

"We're looking for someone," Stevie answered. "Who's the victim?"

"A woman named Lakeisha Smalls."

Quinn's answer was punctuated by a shocked gasp as Lucy staggered at his side, the news literally knocking the wind out of her like a punch in the gut.

The detective looked at Lucy and then at Stevie with seeming irritation that he had not been let in on some important piece of information. "What's going on? Is this Smalls woman the person you are looking for? Who's this?" he added, nodding towards Lucy.

"Yeah," said Stevie. "We came here hoping we would be able to see her. We thought she could help us find a friend of hers who has gone missing with one of my foster care kids."

"Right," said Quinn, with a somewhat dismissive grunt. It was as if he had just remembered that Stevie was no longer a cop... just a social worker. "How well did you know her?"

"I didn't know her at all. We had never met, never even spoken."

"What about your friend, here?"

"This is Lucy Montoya. She's a case manager with Safe Families, the domestic violence agency. Lucy had never met Lakeisha either. She had only heard about her from one of her clients – Melody Saunders, the woman who had gone missing."

"Right," Quinn grunted again, now jotting down notes on a small pad.

"Is my brother here?" asked Stevie.

"No. Jimmy Williams is the lead. He's up in her room... on the third floor."

"Can I go up?"

"Sure, why not?" Quinn grunted again. "It's almost like old times."

Stevie nodded thanks and then turned to Lucy. "You stay here. I'll be right back." She looked back at him with a dazed expression and glazed eyes that were beginning to tear up. "OK," she nodded.

Stevie quickly walked up the stoop and then climbed the stairs, two at a time, until he found a small group of police, lab techs and coroner's men outside Lakeisha Smalls' room. He looked for Detective Sergeant James Williams and found him gingerly stepping over the human debris surrounding a bloody and badly beaten body. Stevie felt his stomach drop and a brief but powerful wave of nausea wash over him. It had been more than five years since he had seen a new corpse, freshly robbed of its life and soul. He was surprised to realize that he had lost his protective immunity to the natural shock and repugnance of the sight.

"Jimmy!" he called.

Williams looked up from the body and stared at Stevie with a total lack of recognition. Then, suddenly, he made the connection... a connection that made no sense.

"Stevie Corra? What the fuck are you doing here?"

"Quinn let me come up. I was on my way to see this woman. What happened?"

"What happened is that she got killed. Looks like a basic smash and grab. Somebody knocked on the door; she opened it with the chain still on to see who it was; he busted it in... took out half the door frame in the process; beat the shit out of her; stabbed her three... maybe four times... then took her money and split."

Once he'd finished his dissertation, Williams looked back down at the body and around the room, as if making sure it all fit together the way he thought, then, nodded quietly to himself once more as if to confirm his theory.

"So, what the fuck are you doing here?" he said turning to Stevie. "Aren't you some kind of social worker, now?" Williams shook his head in puzzlement as if there were some mysteries no one could solve.

"I was coming to see if I could talk to her," Stevie said slowly, hoping to rein in Jimmy Williams' racing thoughts. "I'm looking for the mother of one of my foster care kids who went AWOL last week. She is also a possible witness in the 'Rue' James homicide."

"Who? This one?"

"No, a friend of hers, Melody Saunders; she's the mother of my foster care kid."

"Hmmh... This looks pretty straight forward to me," said Williams, leaning over to pick up an empty purse lying on the bed. "It was definitely a robbery."

Once again, the detective seemed lost in thought, imagining a variety of possible scenarios, any one of which could have ended in the brutal death of Lakeisha Smalls.

"He was pretty rough on her. I'll say that for sure," Williams said as he came out of his trance. He leaned down and gently turned the victim's head to one side, revealing a long vertical slice and massive bleeding. "It looks like he cut her once straight down the edge of her face on the left side, from the hair line to the base of the jaw. No logical reason except to hurt her real bad."

"Or to scare her into telling him what he wanted to know... before he killed her," suggested Stevie.

"Yeah," said Williams, again temporarily lost in thought.

"Mind if I take a look around?"

"Go ahead. Just don't touch anything. And, for God's sake don't tell anyone we let you up here."

"I'll only tell my brother," Stevie said reassuringly.

"Yeah, thanks. That'll cost me my badge."

"Don't worry. You've got enough shit on Frankie that I'm surprised you're not the boss already."

"I don't need the aggravation," Williams answered absent-mindedly. Then he waved his arm around the room in a broad arc. "Have fun. Pretend you're a cop again. But let me know if you see anything I should know about."

"I will. Thanks."

Stevie stood for a moment and absorbed the scene in its totality. Lakeisha Smalls had lived in a very small room. There was just enough space for a single bed, a dresser and a small table and chair. She must have shared a bathroom with other tenants on the floor. The room itself had been thoroughly ransacked, her meager belongings searched and cast aside. It instantly reminded him of how Melody's apartment had looked after the break-in. Here, however, Lakeisha's personal possessions were splattered with her own blood.

Stevie stepped over to the dresser. On the wall above it hung a small mirror, its edges filled with family photographs, medical appointment cards and inspirational notes that had been tucked into its frame. He recognized a typed copy of the Serenity Prayer – "God give me the strength to" – a staple of every 12-step alcoholism and drug treatment program. He instantly felt a surge of grief for this woman – a woman he did not know at all – who had worked so hard to turn her life around, only to have it brutally snuffed out.

Lying scattered on the floor next to the dresser were a wooden tray, two shattered perfume bottles and some cosmetics. Mixed in among the debris were also a hairbrush and what looked like a home-made wooden pik – a long-toothed comb of rich black mahogany that Lakeisha would have used to preen her tight Afro.

Stevie stepped back over a small pile of clothes that had been tossed onto the floor and circled the body. He desperately tried to avoid the growing pool of blood that surrounded it. Williams was right. Whoever had killed Lakeisha Smalls had been pretty rough on her. There were cuts and bruising from punches to her left eye and lip. The perp wears a ring on his right hand, Stevie thought reflexively. In addition to the slash on the face, Lakeisha had been stabbed twice, once in the left side and another, probably fatal, thrust up under her rib cage into her heart.

"When did it happen?" Stevie asked Williams who had come back into the room from the hallway.

"The owner of the building found the body at about 4:00 this afternoon. He saw that the door had been busted in; says it wasn't like that earlier in the day. So, it had to have happened somewhere between noon and 4:00. Just from the look of the body and the blood, I'd say it was closer to the end of that range than the beginning."

"Anybody hear anything?"

"No. All the other tenants were at work or in different programs. Smalls worked weekends at the local restaurant. She had Mondays off."

Stevie and the detective looked at each other. "Shitty way to spend your day off… getting killed," said Williams, shaking his head.

Stevie just nodded silently. The passing years had also weakened his sense of gallows humor that serves to protect cops from the horror that normal people feel when in the presence of people who have just been brutally murdered.

"You want to talk about her friend, Melody Saunders, and the 'Rue' James homicide?" Stevie asked.

"Not right now," said Williams. "I'll call you. But, I have to say that I'm still thinking basic 'smash and grab'."

"OK," said Stevie wearily as he turned to leave. "Thanks."

19

Lucy was standing with her back against one of the police vans, arms wrapped tightly across her chest as if trying to hold herself together. She stared vacantly into space; her thoughts seemingly far from the scene around her. She didn't notice Stevie until he stepped up and placed a hand gently on her shoulder.

"Lucy, are you OK?"

She looked up with tear-stained and questioning eyes, before realizing who was speaking to her.

"Yes," she said softly. She wiped away another tear before continuing. "I'm sorry. I didn't even know her... I'm not sure why it hit me so hard."

"That's OK," said Stevie, stepping closer and draping his arm around her shoulders as if to shelter her from the pain. "It is always a shock."

"What happened?" She rested ever so slightly into the crook of his arm.

"Someone broke into her room and killed her. The police think it was just a robbery that turned fatal."

Lucy looked up at Stevie with eyes that were again beginning to brim with tears. "What do you think?"

He gazed at her for a moment before answering. "I don't know... We should probably go."

Stevie guided Lucy towards the perimeter of the crime scene, stopping for a moment to thank Tommy Quinn for his help. Back at the Subaru, he eased her into the passenger seat and then came around to climb behind the wheel.

"I'm sorry," Lucy repeated, staring straight ahead as Stevie turned the car and headed back across Brooklyn. "It's just... such a tragedy. It sounded like she was someone who really had begun to get her life together."

"You're right," answered Stevie, remembering that he would need to call Roger Brown to break this terrible news.

"What do you think?" Lucy asked again after a few more minutes of silence, this time turning to look across at him. "Do you think it was just a robbery?"

"I don't know. I just don't know what to think."

Stevie could feel that Lucy had not turned away and still was studying him intently.

"How is it that you knew all those cops... and that they let you go up to the apartment?"

It was a question that Stevie had known would be coming. The answer, he also knew, would lead only to more ... and more difficult... questions.

"I used to be a cop," he said, turning to look at Lucy briefly before shifting his gaze back to the road ahead. "I left the force about six years ago, just before I started working with BFS."

"Really? A cop?" She shook her head in puzzlement.

"Yeah," Stevie continued, surprised that for some reason he felt a need to explain. "Something happened. It's a long story... and complicated. Now is not the right time to talk about it."

"Sure," said Lucy slowly. Somehow, she was comforted by the implication that Stevie seemed willing to share this obviously painful piece of his past with her — maybe not now, but at some point in the future. Just as quickly, however, that sense of security morphed into anxiety as Lucy realized that she, too, would then have to share her own, equally painful story as well.

They rode in silence for another ten minutes, before Stevie pulled to the curb outside Lucy's apartment.

"Are you OK," he asked, turning to her with a soft and searching gaze.

"Yes," she nodded, "I'm OK." She reached out her hand and placed it softly on his arm. "Call me."

Stevie looked into her eyes and took her hand in his, holding it gently for a moment. He felt a warmth that he had not experienced for a long time.

"I will."

He watched as she slipped out of the car and walked quickly up the steps into her building. Then Stevie pulled away from the curb and headed home.

20

It was after 9:00 by the time Stevie got back to his darkened apartment. He grabbed a beer and braced himself for what would be the hardest call he would have to make. A young staff member who answered the phone told him that Roger Brown was no longer at the residence. He wouldn't give up a cell number but promised that he would relay a message immediately. It was only a matter of minutes before Roger called back.

Brown was used to hearing bad news about his former residents: they'd relapsed; they'd been arrested; they'd died of overdoses. It was part of the business. You had to know there would be many failures in order to achieve those wonderful successes – the men and women who got clean, stayed clean, found a job, finished school, got their kids back, had families; the ones who went on to live long, happy and productive lives.

Often, Roger could sense the bad news coming. It was the client who only had come to treatment because he was mandated by the court; or the one who hadn't quite hit rock bottom yet and still believed he could control the drug that actually controlled him. Other times, however, it was someone that you would never expect, someone who weakened for a moment, just a single moment, in the never-ending struggle to remain drug free. Addiction was a disease, like cancer or diabetes, and relapse was part of the natural course of the illness.

The murder of Lakeisha Smalls, however, came as a shock. In

a life filled with tragedies on an almost daily basis – many of the victims' own making – the violent death of this young woman who had come so far and had such strong hope for the future seemed extraordinarily unfair and exceptionally sad.

Stevie told Roger what he knew about the circumstances of Lakeisha's death and gave him the name of the detective in charge of the case. Brown thanked him for the call and prepared himself to begin notifying other members of her new and loving, recovery-based family.

Relieved to have this first conversation behind him, Stevie suddenly realized that he was famished. He took another beer and threw a few slices of ham and cheese onto a seeded hard roll that had grown even harder after two days in the refrigerator. As he chewed, he flipped through his cell phone directory to find the number for Lt. Jack Schwinn.

"Schwinn," Jack answered loudly, trying to talk over a dozen conversations in the background.

"Jack, it's Stevie Corra."

"Stevie! What's up?"

"Something happened in the Melody Saunders case that I wanted to talk to you about."

"Look, I can hardly hear you. It's a little loud here. I'm at The Cumberland. Do you want to come over?"

"No," said Stevie, too tired to go out and recoiling at the idea of seeing even more of his former colleagues in the same day. "That wouldn't work. How about tomorrow? Can I stop by at some point?"

"Sure," said Schwinn, almost shouting to make himself heard over the din of the crowd. "Can you come by in the morning? Maybe around 10:00? I'll see if Brian Finnerty and Robby Calderone can be there as well."

"Yeah, that would be great," said Stevie, once again trying to sound more enthusiastic than he actually felt. "I'll see you in the morning. Thanks."

The prospect of another conversation with Finnerty was bad enough; the thought that he and Calderone might be his best shot at finding Shaquan and getting him home safely was downright depressing.

However, Stevie didn't have long to dwell on his disappointments. Only minutes after hanging up with Schwinn, his cell phone rang again. The display showed that it was his brother Frankie.

"Frankie, hi!"

"Stevie, hey! How are you doing?" said his brother as a formality before immediately continuing. "Jimmy Williams told me that you showed up at one of our crime scenes tonight... that you were on your way to meet with the vic. What was that all about?"

"Remember I told you that one of my foster care kids, Shaquan Saunders, had gone AWOL and his mother, Melody Saunders, was a possible witness in the 'Rue' James murder. Well, it turns out that Melody was close to Lakeisha Smalls, the woman who got killed. We were hoping that she might have some idea where Melody and Shaquan had gone."

"Hmmm," Frankie mumbled. "Small world, huh?... You have any reason to believe that the Saunders woman and Smalls were in touch after she disappeared, or that they met?"

"No. But, the case manager from a domestic violence agency who was working with Melody thought it might be possible... that Lakeisha was the only person she could imagine her going to."

"Is that the woman who you were with?"

Frankie obviously had heard more about Stevie's visit than he'd first let on.

"Yes. Her name is Lucy Montoya. She is a case manager with Safe Families. Do you know them?"

"Sure."

"Melody had come to Lucy because her boyfriend – Levon Marbury – was getting more and more violent. You said you would run his sheet for me?" Stevie tried to make the reminder sound as benign as possible.

"Christ," his brother answered in a burst of apology. "I'm sorry. I forgot all about it. Today has been nuts. I'll get on it first thing tomorrow."

"Thanks. I'm hoping there may be something in it that can help me find Melody and Shaquan."

"Sure," Frankie answered again, followed by a few moments of awkward silence, before he continued. "Look, this connection between Smalls and your foster care kid's mom... it seems a little bit of a stretch. Jimmy still thinks this is just a smash-and-grab robbery that led to a killing when she fought back. That's the way we are going to approach this... unless something more substantial turns up."

Now Stevie hesitated before responding. "You don't think that it's something of a coincidence that a local drug dealer gets hit, a possible witness disappears and then her closest friend is murdered?"

"Look," his brother answered, the first signs of irritation adding an edge to his voice. "Like I said, it is a small world... and a very violent one. Shit happens. These kinds of robbery/killings happen every fucking day. You know that. I'm not saying there's no connection, but right now I don't have anything to base it on except for you and your girlfriend's imagination."

"She's not my girlfriend," Stevie shot back, suddenly sounding more defensive than necessary. "She's a DV caseworker."

"I'm sorry," Frankie answered, taking his tone down a notch. "I didn't mean that the way it sounded. Look, I'm keeping an open mind. If we find anything more solid, we'll follow up."

"OK," said Stevie. "I do have a meeting with Jack Schwinn and his guys tomorrow morning to let them know about the link between Melody and Lakeisha Smalls. Maybe they'll come up with something."

"Why are you going to Schwinn about this?" Frankie fired back, the irritation instantly returning.

"Because they are working the Rue James case," said Stevie with his own level of impatience rising. "And, they *are* looking for Melody Saunders. Maybe they will think there is a connection actually worth pursuing." He couldn't keep his last comment from sounding like an accusation that his brother wasn't doing his job. He knew instantly it had been a mistake.

"I don't know why the fuck they got that case to begin with," Frankie said angrily. "It's a homicide. It should be ours... The Lakeisha Smalls case is *definitely* ours."

Turf wars for jurisdiction over high profile cases were a constant theme inside the department. All cops... his brother, Schwinn, even Stevie in the old days... were like dogs continually peeing on the same tree stump to claim it as their own. He understood immediately that he might have just started a new pissing contest.

"Look," he said, trying to sound as conciliatory as possible. "I don't know anything about that. I don't work there anymore.

"Frankie..." he continued softly. "I'm just trying to find my kid... and get him home safe. Like you said, it's dangerous out there."

"OK," said his brother, seeming to accept what he considered an unspoken apology before changing gears entirely. "You going to dinner at mom and dad's next weekend?"

"I don't know," answered Stevie, caught off guard. "Joey's going to be away with Sandy. I'll let you know later in the week."

"Good. Everything else OK?"

"Yeah," said Stevie. "Everything is fine." Then, just before breaking off, he added one more thing. "And, Frankie... you'll get me that stuff on Levon Marbury, right?"

"Sure," Frankie answered with a mix of resignation and weary reluctance. "I'll call you tomorrow."

Stevie hung up and put the phone down on the table. He took another sip of beer, feeling even more depressed after the conversation with his brother than before. He looked out across his patio and could almost feel the darkness blanketing the streets and back alleys of Brooklyn. It had been five days since Shaquan first left the Flatbush Group Home. In that time, Stevie had stumbled across two murders, domestic violence, open drug dealing and Melody's disappearance; he'd been threatened by Back Thompson and apparently was starting a bureaucratic battle within the NYPD – a war in which one of the combatants was his own brother. And, despite everything, he was no closer to finding Shaquan.

As a wave of fatigue washed over him, Stevie leaned back in his chair and closed his eyes. Once again, there was an image in his head that he could not escape. This time, however, it was the face of Lucy Montoya as she looked across at him in the car.

Stevie smiled to himself as he recalled the soft warmth of her touch as they held each other's hand for that brief moment. Then, the pleasure of the memory was shadowed by a sense of guilt. *Where was Shaquan?* That's what he needed to be focusing on.

21

Stevie rose early on Tuesday morning and went for a three-mile run around Prospect Park, the events of the previous day replaying over and over in his head. He cooled down during the walk back to his apartment and ate breakfast on the patio while reading the news on his laptop. After a shower, he dressed for the day and called Jackie Johnson's secretary to say that he would be meeting with NYPD on the Shaquan Saunders case before coming into the office.

At 9:00 a.m., just before leaving the apartment, Corra picked up his cell phone and dialed Lucy Montoya's number.

"Hello," she answered.

"Hi. It's Stevie," he said. "I just wanted to check in and make sure you are OK. That was a pretty rough day yesterday."

"Yes… it was," said Lucy, her voice a little unsteady as she seemed to recall the details. "But, I'm OK. How about you?"

"I'm all right. I've got a meeting this morning with the detectives who are looking for Melody. I'm going to tell them about the connection to Lakeisha Smalls and what happened."

"That's good. Maybe it will help."

"Yeah, I hope so," said Stevie, hesitating before he continued. He was surprised at the sudden nervousness he felt. "Lucy… I was wondering if you would like to get together. Maybe have a drink or dinner and talk?"

There was no hesitation at all on the other end.

"Sure. I'd like that. When did you have in mind?"

Stevie's anxiety was washed away by a wave of relief that was quickly turning to euphoria. "How about tonight?"

"Oh…" Lucy chuckled in response. "O.K. That would be great…. Look, do you want to come over here? If you bring a bottle of wine, I'll make us a little dinner… nothing fancy."

"That sounds wonderful. Red or white?"

"Do you like fish?"

"Definitely!"

"OK, then make it white. Does 7:00 work?"

"Yes, that would be terrific. I'll see you then."

Stevie hung up, picked up his brief case from the chair next to him and left the apartment. It suddenly seemed like it was going to be a good day.

22

It took Stevie about 20 minutes to make his way through heavy morning traffic to the outer fringe of Bedford Stuyvesant. Brooklyn North Narcotics was housed in the 79th Precinct, a fortress-like, dirty-grey, brick and concrete structure that occupied nearly half of a full city block. He cruised past the long lines of patrol cars, vans and private vehicles, each with an NYPD placard or PBA card strategically placed in the windshield to indicate that normal rules regarding double parking, hydrants or even being in the middle of a sidewalk no longer applied. In days gone by, Stevie would have simply slipped into any available free space. Now, he continued on for another block and a half to find a legal spot.

Inside, Stevie stopped to check in at the elevated and imposing front desk. He was surprised when, after a brief phone call, the gently aging uniformed sergeant simply handed him a visitor's pass and waved him towards the long hallway.

"You know how to find Lieutenant Schwinn's office?" he asked.

Stevie nodded and set out through the maze of narrow hallways that would lead to his own former squad room.

"Hey!" Jack called out as Stevie appeared at the office door. "Come on in."

Schwinn shuffled a pile of papers to one side as his former boss slid into a chair on the opposite side of the desk. "Sorry about last night. I could hardly hear a word you said. The Cumberland was packed... and very loud."

"No problem," said Stevie. "I really wanted to come in and talk to you anyway. This worked out perfect. Thanks for taking the time."

"Sure. We need all the help we can get. Let me find Finnerty and Calderone." Schwinn picked up his phone, punched a pair of buttons and mumbled a few words. "They're on their way."

Within minutes, the two detectives sauntered into their boss' office and squeezed into two extra side chairs along the wall next to the desk. Finnerty was like a training poster for passive-aggressive behavior. He sat scowling, head tilted to one side, legs crossed and arms folded. Calderone was more relaxed. He smiled at Stevie and reached out to shake hands.

"So, what do you have for us?" Schwinn asked.

"Well, this could be a coincidence… but I don't believe in coincidences," said Stevie, looking at each of the detectives in turn, "…especially when they involve two murders that could be related."

Shwinn leaned forward, his interest growing instantly. "Go ahead."

"It turns out that Melody Saunders, who you are looking at as a possible witness in the Rue James killing, was about to leave her boyfriend, an abusive scumbag named Levon Marbury, because he was getting more and more violent. After the murder, Melody disappears… together with her son Shaquan who went AWOL from one of our group homes. I know they are together because Shaquan called the house a couple of days later to say they were OK and ask if anyone was looking for them."

Stevie hesitated briefly to see if his small audience was following the story; they were, even Brian Finnerty.

"It seems that the only person who Melody might have been able to go to for help was a woman named Lakeisha Smalls, who she had met during a stint in residential rehab a few months back."

Stevie paused again, this time for effect.

"Last night, Lakeisha Smalls was killed in her rooming house out in Brownsville."

"No, shit," blurted Schwinn, sitting up straight behind the desk. Finnerty and Calderone were both silent but clearly following every word.

"Someone busted in through the half-open doorway, worked her over pretty bad, slashed her and stabbed her twice."

"Who caught the case?" asked Schwinn.

"Jimmy Williams in my brother Frankie's Homicide Squad."

"Have you talked to him about this?" asked Calderone.

"Yeah… I was there while he was still working the scene," said Corra. "We were on our way over to try and talk to the Smalls woman."

"No shit," said Schwinn again, this time with an ironic laugh. "What does Jimmy think?"

Stevie sat back in his chair and sighed as he answered. "He thinks it is a smash-and-grab robbery that turned bad…. I know Jimmy and he's a good cop, but he's one to believe that the simplest explanation is usually the right explanation."

"Most of the time that's true," said Calderone, also sitting back and shaking his head in amazement at the new turn of events. "How sure are you that Melody Saunders went to this woman for help? What was her name, Lakeisha Smalls?"

"Look, I don't have anything solid," said Stevie. "But, it all seems like too much of a coincidence. And, we can't think of anyone else she could have gone to."

"You keep saying 'we'," interjected Schwinn. "Who is the 'we'?"

"Melody had been seeing a domestic violence caseworker from Safe Families. Her name is Lucy Montoya."

"Christ," mumbled Finnerty in disgust. "Now we got a whole fucking squad of social workers on the case."

"Save it," Schwinn spat angrily to Finnerty, before turning his attention back to Corra. "What does your brother say?"

Stevie sighed again, before answering slowly. "He's backing Jimmy's theory… until something more substantial turns up to prove there's a connection." Then he turned to look squarely at Jack Schwinn. "And, he says it's definitely *their* case. He's not all that pleased with the fact that you guys kept the Rue James case."

"Yeah," Schwinn chuckled again, temporarily lost in thought. "I'm sure he's not that pleased. Well, we'll give Jimmy Williams a call and talk things over with him."

"You said that Melody's son called the group home and said that he and his mother were together?" said Calderone.

"Yeah," said Stevie. "He called on Saturday morning. He talked to one of the other kids in the group home, his roommate Carlos Martinez. He said they were OK; wanted to know if anyone was looking for them. He even asked if the police had been there."

"Hmmh," mumbled Calderone. "I take it he didn't say where they were?"

"No."

"Did the other kid have any ideas where they might be?"

"No, none!"

"Does the son… Shaquan… have anybody that he might have gone to who would put them up?"

"No, not that I can think of," said Stevie. "He's been in foster care for a long time. He's really got no connections to family or anyone else in the neighborhood. The only place he ever wanted to be was with his mom."

"Hmmh," mumbled Calderone again. "This isn't getting any easier."

After a moment, Stevie broke the silence. "What about Levon Marbury? Has there been any sign of him?"

"Nope," said Calderone. "Do you think he's with Melody and her son?"

Stevie shook his head slowly. "I can't say for sure, but I wouldn't think so. Shaquan hated Levon … for what he had done to both his mother and to him. I just have to believe that he and Melody took off and left Levon behind."

The four sat quietly, each seemingly working the various facts over in their minds. Stevie broke the silence.

"Did you guys ever run Levon's sheet? Was there anything there that could be helpful?"

"There's nothing," answered Calderone. "The guy just did a few years up in Otisville on a low-level drug charge. He had a few earlier busts, nothing of note. The guy's a zero. Nobody knows anything about him; there's nothing worth knowing."

Stevie took in Calderone's response without comment. He'd love to get a look at the criminal history report himself, but no one was offering. He looked from Calderone to Finnerty to Schwinn and decided not to ask.

"What about Back Thompson?" Stevie asked.

"It looks like he's running the show now," said Calderone. "He's off the corner and overseeing the rest of his spots."

"I had a little conversation with him the other night."

"What?" Schwinn blurted in shock. "What the fuck were you doing talking to him?"

"I was over taking a look at Melody's place on Sunday night and he took exception to my visit."

"What the fuck were you doing over there?" Schwinn asked again, his agitation visibly rising. "You could get yourself fucking killed over there."

"Yeah," said Finnerty. "You could get yourself seriously fucking hurt. You should be careful." Stevie thought he could detect just a hint of actual concern in Brian's voice.

"Look, I'm fine," said Stevie. The statement appeared to carry no weight whatsoever with the three detectives.

"Just do us all a favor and stay away from there," said Schwinn, his voice flattening out and turning several degrees cooler.

The change in tone failed to calm or deter Stevie. "Look, I have a kid I need to find," he said. His own voice was now edged with irritation ... and frustration at his obvious powerlessness in dealing with his former colleagues.

"Don't worry," said Robby Calderone with a heavy dose of reassurance. "We'll find him for you."

"Yeah, we'll find him," echoed Schwinn, his manner relaxing only slightly. "But stay away from Melody's place. I mean it."

"Yeah," added Brian Finnerty. "We don't need any social workers getting whacked. We have enough problems already."

Stevie didn't answer. He stared at Finnerty with cold eyes that could not mask his pent up anger. Then he turned to face Schwinn. "Well, if you are looking for him, then maybe you need to try a little harder. Otherwise, I've got a feeling he and Melody are going to wind up just like Lakeisha Smalls."

Without waiting for a response, he rose, shoved the chair roughly to one side and stormed out of the office.

23

Stevie was still boiling when he got to the car. He couldn't imagine going back to his office. Instead, he decided to head straight out to the Flatbush Group Home, where he had an afternoon meeting scheduled with Rick Jones, one of the more difficult kids on his caseload.

Jones was 17 years old and extremely challenging. He'd come to BFS eight months earlier after multiple foster boarding home placements and three years in an upstate residential treatment center. Whatever the system was trying to do for this kid just wasn't working. The City's decision to bring him back into a smaller community-based setting looked like a serious mistake. After transferring into the local high school in mid-semester, Rick quickly got himself thrown right back out for a series of escalating confrontations, first with other students, then with his teachers. Stevie's efforts to get him into a new "Transfer School" specially designed for "over age, under credited" students got things back on track, but only for a brief period. Over the course of that spring, Rick had begun creating problems both inside and outside the house. Now, he'd gotten himself suspended again.

There weren't a lot of options left. As troubled as Rick was, he wasn't suffering from any diagnosable mental illness. Psychotropic drugs or psychiatric hospitalization weren't the answers. He was just angry and hurt, traumatized by the painful path his life had followed up to this point, silently fearful of where it might lead in the future.

Stevie was certain that Rick should not remain at the Flatbush group home or any other. The boy needed a higher level of care with more structure, regular focused therapy and stronger safeguards to protect him from a chaotic community with which he was not yet ready to cope. Stevie knew of several agencies that were using a new "Sanctuary" model of treatment, specifically developed to serve seriously traumatized youth such as Rick.

However, getting approval to step Rick back up to a residential program, and then finding an actual placement, would be next to impossible. New York City's child welfare policy was now firmly committed to moving kids towards lower – not higher – levels of care… out of larger congregate programs and into individual homes with loving foster families. It sounded good on paper. And, for many, many kids it was good – but not for everyone.

Rick, Stevie believed, was one of those kids who needed more. Unless he got it, the boy would soon be gone. Rick would run, like so many other failed foster care kids before him. He would go AWOL, like Shaquan, but to an even more dangerous and less forgiving world of gangs, drugs, violent crime and prison.

The group home was quiet when Stevie arrived. Most of the kids were off at school or to specialized vocational programs. Joseph Otinga was at a meeting outside the house. Rick was in the kitchen getting lunch and some heavily-accented, homespun wisdom from Mrs. Ramirez.

Stevie waited until they were finished and then took the boy back to a small office that he and other staff used for private meetings and counseling sessions. He spent the next hour talking to Rick – and trying to get Rick to talk to him – about the latest school incident and problems in the house. The boy was sullen and quietly hostile. The more Stevie pressed him, the angrier Rick became. Stevie gradually backed off. His only desire now was to keep a lid on the boy's simmering emotions in hopes that a new and better placement would come through before they boiled over.

After their conversation, Stevie made a series of calls. One was to the school social worker in an attempt to get Rick's suspension lifted. She suggested that they schedule a face-to-face meeting with the principal and the teacher who had thrown the boy out of class. It was exactly what Stevie had expected, but not what he wanted to hear. Now Rick would be hanging around the home 24/7 for at least several more days, his boredom and angry frustration rising, gradually filling the house like an explosive gas. One spark – one wrong word, any perceived insult from staff or another kid – and Rick would erupt, taking himself and God knows who else with him.

Next, he phoned Jackie Johnson and urged that she make a personal call asking the City to approve Rick's transfer back into a residential treatment center. Jackie agreed, adding that she would reach out to some friends at residential programs to see if she could line up a bed in advance. When she asked if there were any developments in Shaquan's case, Stevie decided to spare her the news about Lakeisha Smalls' murder. He said he'd fill her in when they met for supervision later in the week.

Finally, he wrote up his progress notes for the case file, carefully documenting his conversation with Rick and the phone calls to the school and his director.

It was almost 3:00 when Stevie emerged from the small office. The house was still almost empty, quiet in that special way that only a family home can be during the middle of a workday. It wouldn't last long. Kids would begin returning from school any minute now, bursting with energy pent up from hours confined to a classroom desk.

Without thinking, Stevie climbed the stairs and walked down the second floor hallway to the room that Shaquan and Carlos shared. He knocked softly on the door twice, knowing there would be no response; then he let himself in.

Stevie had been coming to the group home for five years and had been inside this room dozens of times. Yet, it was only now, after Shaquan's disappearance, that he felt he was beginning to know it, becoming familiar with its two sets of mismatched beds, desks and dressers on either side, each a distorted reflection of the other, each revealing at least to some extent the personality of the child who lived there at this moment in time. He crossed to Shaquan's bed and sat down, once again studying the boy's relatively meager collection of personal possessions. There were some books, magazines and CDs. There were the photos of himself with Melody and with friends from the group home tacked up on the bulletin board above the desk. His rap posters and the kite he had made with Joseph Otinga hung on the wall over his bed. It wasn't a lot to show for 16 years of childhood.

Stevie looked across at Carlos' side of the room and saw little more – just different posters and photos of his own family and other friends, a similar collection of schoolbooks, paperbacks and magazines.

He rose and crossed back towards Carlos' bed. As his gaze scanned along the top of the boy's dresser, it struck him. There, amid a hair brush and some personal toiletries, was a pik – the same type of home-made, long-toothed wooden comb he had seen on the floor at Lakeisha Smalls' apartment. The carved decorations and coloring were different, but the basic design was the same.

Stevie reached down and picked it up. At that same moment, the door swung open and Carlos walked in, his silent surprise at finding someone looking at his things filling the room.

"What are you doing?" asked the boy.

Stevie turned to him, holding the pik in front of him with two hands. "I was looking at Shaquan's things, hoping I would get some ideas on where he might be," he said, still half lost in his thoughts. "Where did you get this?" he asked, looking down at the pik.

"I made it," said Carlos uncertainly, as if concerned that he was in trouble for some unknown reason. "They taught us to do it in shop class."

"Did Shaquan make one?" Stevie asked, continuing to stare at the wooden pik in his hands.

"No, but I made one for him that he could give to his moms. He liked it."

"Was it darker than this one? Did it have little crosses as decorations on the handle?"

"Yes," said Carlos, even more hesitant. "How did you know?"

Stevie ignored the boy's question and asked another of his own. "When did you give it Shaquan? And, do you know when he gave it to his mother?"

"I finished it last week," said Carlos, looking at his caseworker suspiciously. "I gave it to Shaquan on Wednesday afternoon."

"That was the day before he went AWOL?" asked Stevie, as if to confirm his own understanding of what this meant.

Carlos just nodded. Then, he asked again. "But, Stevie, how did you know what it looked like?"

"I saw it yesterday."

The boy just looked at him, trying to understand something that seemed to make no sense. "Where? Where did you see it?"

"I'll explain later," said Stevie, struggling to come to grips with what this latest piece of the puzzle meant. "Look, Carlos, I have to go. But, thanks, this helps a lot."

24

Stevie left the group home, his mind reeling from the realization that it was Melody's pik, a gift from Shaquan, which he had seen among the debris in Lakeisha's apartment. Did it really mean what seemed so obvious, that Melody… and perhaps Shaquan… had been there at some point before Lakeisha was killed? Did it prove that the woman had been murdered because of her friendship with Melody… and that the killer was still out there, searching for Melody…and Shaquan?

Back in the car, Stevie drove as if in a daze. At one moment, he stared out the windshield at the streets of Brooklyn. At others, he saw only the alternating images of two wooden piks – one lying proudly atop Carlos' dresser, the other cast to the floor in a heap, only inches from the widening blood pool surrounding Lakeisha Smalls' dead body.

Impossible as it seemed, Stevie struggled to rein in his racing thoughts. He still had another home visit scheduled for this afternoon. This one was with a 14-year-old girl who had recently been discharged back to her mother after three years in foster care. Stevie's job now was to ensure that the reunification was going smoothly. There would always be bumps – some very big bumps – along the way. Both mother and daughter had seriously troubled pasts, personal histories scarred with poverty, drugs, domestic violence and neglect. But, Stevie was optimistic. These two, it seemed, had each stared into the abyss and turned back. They realized that they wanted and needed each other. They were really trying to make it work.

For the next hour, Stevie forced himself to focus on their lives. He talked to them together and separately, studying the ways in which they spoke to each other, sensitive to any unstated anger or hostility that might reveal itself in a facial expression or physical gesture. He asked about home, school, work, discipline, friends and family. As discretely as possible, he searched the apartment for any signs of drugs, alcohol or violence. He looked for positive signs of home cooked meals and clean laundry. He found nothing to give him concern. He promised to come back again for one final visit next month and urged them to call if they needed help… with anything. This was one of those times when Stevie felt like the system was actually working.

It was after 5:00 when he got back to the car. There was just enough time for him to go home, take a shower and change before going to Lucy's for dinner.

As he drove, his thoughts once again turned back to the latest information he had uncovered in his search for Shaquan. What should he do with it? This was evidence? Should he call Jimmy Williams, the detective investigating Lakeisha Smalls' murder… or his own brother who was Williams' boss? Or should he call Jack Schwinn who was looking for Melody?

Yet, his most recent conversations – with Schwinn this morning and with Frankie the night before – made him reluctant to call either. For the moment, he unconsciously chose to do nothing. Instead, he pulled to the curb outside his local liquor store and bought a bottle of dry Sicilian white wine that he knew was both very good and reasonably priced.

25

At a few minutes past 7:00, Stevie climbed four flights of stairs and knocked at Lucy's apartment. Moments later, the door swung open.

"Hi, Steve," said Lucy, offering a friendly smile as she stepped back to invite him in.

"Hi," he answered with a shy smile of his own.

Lucy was wearing a colorful sundress that looked loose, cool and comfortable. It made a markedly different impression than the black trousers and short-sleeved blouses he had recognized as her regular work day "uniform" for the streets of Brooklyn. While both outfits emphasized her petite figure and natural grace, the dress was both relaxed and casually stylish. Cut off just above the knee, it also gave Stevie a chance to appreciate Lucy's shapely legs.

"Come in," she said.

Lucy lived in a small one-bedroom on the top floor of a brownstone townhouse in Prospect Heights. The rear half of the apartment was an open, L-shaped space with a small kitchenette and wooden dining table along the back wall of the building. Three large windows looked out over a row of rear gardens four stories below. In front of the dining area in the center of the apartment was a small living room with couch, armchair and TV. A doorway leading to the bathroom and Lucy's bedroom at the front of the building was to Stevie's left.

The height of the apartment and its three tall, southward facing windows, which reached nearly from floor to ceiling, gave it an extremely bright and airy feel.

"Nice apartment," said Stevie. As he walked inside, the delicious aroma of sautéed garlic and olive oil sizzled towards him from the kitchen stove. "The food smells great."

"Thanks," said Lucy. "It's nothing very fancy. I hope you'll like it." She handed him a corkscrew and pointed to a pair of glasses on the counter. "Why don't we start with a glass of wine?"

As he opened the bottle, Lucy glided along the narrow kitchenette and came back with a plate of crostini, small pieces of toasted Italian bread topped with a succulent mixture of finely chopped orange, onions, celery, garlic and herbs, all drenched in olive oil and a little lime juice. They looked like the very image of Mediterranean summer. Stevie expected to gaze out the window and watch the sea lapping at a rocky shoreline.

He handed Lucy a glass of wine and they looked at each other silently for a moment. Somehow, there didn't seem to be a toast appropriate to the situation. They each took a sip of wine before Stevie spoke.

"How are you feeling... about last night?" he asked softly. "It was quite a shock. I was worried about you."

A shadow seemed to fall across Lucy's eyes and her smile faded as she recalled the events surrounding Lakeisha Smalls' death.

"Yes," she said, shaking her head. "It was terrible... I don't know what to say... or what to think. It was just awful."

"I know," said Stevie, reaching out to place his hand on her shoulder. His grip was firm, his touch comforting. "I'm sorry you had to be there for that."

"No," said Lucy in protest. "We went because we thought it would help us find Melody and Shaquan. It made sense to be there." She hesitated before continuing, her expression growing darker, her eyes once again beginning to moisten. "It's just...."

"What?" asked Stevie. "What is it?"

"It was ...," Lucy began, seemingly lost in her own thoughts as she moved slowly over to sit in one corner of the couch. "It was just everything... all the police, the patrol cars with their lights flashing, the sounds of the radios." She looked up at him as he crossed over and sat in the arm chair opposite her. "It made me remember something I had been trying hard to forget… remember it in a way as if it was really happening all over again."

Stevie watched as Lucy struggled to control strong emotions that were welling up inside her. "What was it," he asked.

She looked at him for a moment, seeming to brace herself for what she knew would be an emotional ordeal.

"When I was 17…," Lucy began, before hesitating. Then, closing her eyes tightly as if to block out a painful vision from her past, she continued. "When I was 17, my father killed my mother."

The jarring horror of that simple, matter-of-fact statement took Stevie's breath away.

"He was a violent man. He beat her… he beat all of us… often. He would drink, and the anger and the frustration and the resentment would start to rise up inside him. He would look at my mother, my sister and me as if he hated us… as if we had taken something from him… as if we were the reasons why his life was so hard and so different than he had hoped. He would drink and it would start with insults and complaints. Why wasn't the food ready? Why was the food cold? The house was dirty! Me and my sister were ugly and would never find husbands. My mother was stupid or lazy. Then someone would say something or do something… anything… and he would start. He would reach out and smack one of us. Usually it was my mother, but it could be me or Maria, my sister. Whoever he hit first was the one he would keep hitting. No one could stop him."

Lucy hesitated for just a brief moment, unable now to hold back this story that somehow needed to be told.

"It was horrible. We were all terrified all of the time. We never knew when it would begin…who would be the one. He wasn't like that every night; it could go days or even weeks without happening. There could be weeks of peaceful dinners. He'd joke and tease; be the loving father we all wanted him to be.

"But we were terrified every day," she said, her voice rising, her eyes imploring Stevie for understanding. "Do you know what that is like? To be frightened every single day of your life, never knowing if

118

this was when it would begin again? If this was the night when you would see your father suddenly transformed by rage, feel that first sudden sting of his hand across your face, knowing that there would be another, and another, and another? Or, was this another night when you would have to watch helplessly as he lashed out at your mother... or your little sister? Sometimes, that was even worse.

"I wanted my mother to save us – to save herself – to take us and run away so we could live somewhere else and he would never find us. But, she couldn't do it... she didn't know how."

Stevie listened in silence, making no effort to respond, knowing that Lucy had more she needed to tell.

"One day I came home from school. And, it was just like yesterday. The street was closed off; there were cops and cop cars everywhere. At first I didn't know what had happened. I thought there had been a robbery, that maybe one of the neighbors had been hurt. I had no idea that it was our building... that it was my family... that it was ... my mother!"

Lucy's voice broke softly and Stevie watched as full-bodied tears rolled down her cheeks.

"Once they found out who I was, that I was her daughter, they took me aside with one of the detectives. I wanted to go and see her. I cried and pleaded with them to let me see her. But, they wouldn't. They just kept asking me questions about my father and my mother, why did they fight and why would he kill her.

"Why would he kill her?" she cried. "They asked me why he would kill her, as if there is some kind of answer to that question that makes any sense at all. As if a 17-year-old girl can explain why her own father would strike out and kill her mother?"

"Lucy!" Stevie said, reaching out to take her hand. He could find no other words that might offer comfort or solace.

"I'm sorry," she said, looking up at him with tearful eyes. "Last night just brought it all back to me. I'd have never thought it would hit me like this... not after all these years."

"No," said Stevie, shaking his head. "Don't..." Once again, he was at a loss for ways to express his sense of how painful this must have been.

"What happened," he asked after a moment, "...to your father?"

"He went to prison," Lucy answered, her expression suddenly emotionless. "He died there. Nothing dramatic! He got cancer and died."

"What happened to you and your sister?"

"We went to live with my aunt... my mother's sister. It wasn't easy. They tried very hard to make us feel part of their family. I'm very grateful for everything they did and I love them all. But, it wasn't easy."

"What about your sister?" asked Stevie. "Maria?"

Lucy's face darkened again. "It was very hard for her; very, very hard. She was devastated; we both were. But she was four years younger than me. I was already rebellious and angry with my mother. Maria was still my mother's 'little girl'. They loved each other in an extra special kind of way because of how things were at home. When my mother died, it just destroyed Maria. It was as if my father had killed her too."

"Where is she now?"

"Right now? I can't say for sure." Lucy's voice grew heavy with sadness. "After we moved in with my aunt, Maria started getting in trouble – doing drugs, hanging with a really bad group of kids. It didn't take long before the drugs took over. I tried to stop her. I've tried to help. She's been in and out of rehab, in and out of jail."

Lucy turned and looked into Stevie's eyes. "Yesterday you asked if I had ever been to a residential drug treatment program before. The answer is yes." She took a sip of wine before continuing.

"A few years ago, Maria relapsed for what seemed like the 100th time. She had been staying with me for about a month, then she suddenly just disappeared. For the first time in my life, I didn't go looking for her. I just couldn't do it. It had hurt too much, too many times before. I also started to feel like maybe I wasn't good for her... that I was a constant reminder of everything that had happened when we were kids... that it was too painful to be with me. So, I just let her go... but I still hope that she'll come back."

"Maybe she will," said Stevie. "It's really true what they say. You have to hit the bottom of the hole before you can start climbing out."

Lucy just nodded hopefully.

"Is what happened to your mom the reason you work at Safe Families?"

"I think so," said Lucy. "My mother might be alive today if someone had helped her to get us away from my father. I guess I wanted to be there for other families that need help. I have a pretty good idea of what these women and kids are going through. That makes it easier for me to talk to them and for them to trust me. I understand what it means when they tell me they're afraid of what their man might do to them if he finds out they are planning to leave. No one has to remind me to be careful.

"And," Lucy added, turning to him as she wiped away the last of her tears, "as hard as it might be for you to believe right now, I can be very objective when working with clients. I can focus on their situation without having it bring up a lot of my own emotional baggage. Tonight was very unusual. I don't usually get this upset."

"Don't worry. I believe you," said Stevie, now drawing on his own experience. "We try to put the painful memories in our lives behind us, but they never really go away."

"That's the truth," said Lucy, reaching out to grasp his hand for just an instant. "Hey, I promised to make you dinner. I guess I better get started."

26

Stevie stood at one end of the kitchen counter and watched as Lucy effortlessly sautéed two fillets of sole in butter and wine. Pasta bubbled in a pot of boiling water. Another covered pan rumbled on the burner next to it; and a tossed green salad stood ready to be served.

He was surprised by the power of his attraction to this woman whom he had met just four days earlier. Their shared horror at finding the murder of Lakeisha Smalls – and Lucy's emotionally charged revelation of her own family tragedy – only heightened the sense of intimacy that was growing between them.

Within minutes, they sat down to two plates of perfectly cooked and exquisitely seasoned fish with linguini and steamed vegetables. As they ate, Steve and Lucy dialed down the intensity of their conversation, allowing themselves to enjoy the "getting to know you" small talk that creates the building blocks for any relationship. They chatted about apartments, neighborhoods, food, music and movies. Stevie explained that he was divorced and had a ten-year-old son who stayed with him at least every other weekend, more often if possible.

It wasn't long, however, before they once again found themselves talking about their work… and the case that had brought them together in the first place – the search for Melody and Shaquan. Stevie was stunned to realize that he had yet to tell Lucy about his discovery earlier in the day regarding the wooden pik he'd seen at

Lakeisha's apartment. In a sudden burst of excitement, he described what he had found at the crime scene and then how he had seen a similar home-made wooden Afro comb on Carlos' dresser at the group home. Finally, he explained that Carlos had made a pik – just like the one at Lakeisha's apartment – for Shaquan to give as a gift to Melody.

"What do you think it means?" Lucy asked with a gasp.

"I can't be 100% certain, but I'm pretty sure it means that Melody was at Lakeisha's apartment at some point after she disappeared and before Lakeisha was killed."

"Oh my God," said Lucy, covering her mouth with one hand as if to keep from saying what now seemed ever more likely to be true. "Did someone really kill Lakeisha because he was looking for Melody?"

"It's a definite possibility," said Stevie, running the facts through his mind once again. "But, who could it have been? Who would have even known that Melody and Lakeisha were friends?"

"Levon," Lucy answered flatly. It wasn't a question, an idea, or a suggestion. It was a statement of fact. "It would have been Levon. He knew all about Lakeisha. And, he didn't like the fact that she and Melody were close. Melody told me that herself. It's typical for an abusive relationship. The batterer doesn't want his victim to have outside relationships. They can lead to exposure of the abuse. And, they give the victim hope and opportunities to escape.

"Oh, my God," Lucy repeated, this time closing her eyes tightly and shaking her head as if to deny the tragic injustice that had befallen this woman, just because she had reached out a hand to a friend in need. "It had to be Levon. He certainly knew about Lakeisha and that she was the only one Melody would turn to. There was nobody else. He probably even knew where she lived. I think Melody told me he had driven her there once."

Stevie studied Lucy as she made her case. Once again, she was the domestic violence professional who had walked into his office the previous Friday, now going over the elements of Melody's risk assessment and safety planning – this time in an effort to solve a crime, rather than prevent one.

"But, do you think Levon would have killed Lakeisha? Why would he kill her?" Stevie asked, instantly recognizing the absurdity of his question – the same question that Lucy had been asked so painfully once before.

If Lucy caught the irony, she gave no indication. "I don't know," she answered after a moment's thought. "Who knows? It certainly wouldn't be unusual for a batterer to assault his victim's friend or a family member who was trying to help her escape – especially a female friend."

Stevie sat silently, reviewing in his mind the Lakeisha Smalls crime scene. Then, he shook his head. "Something doesn't fit. I think the person who killed Lakeisha wanted to kill her. It didn't look like an assault that got out of control. She was stabbed twice… by someone who knew how to use a knife."

Lucy shuddered involuntarily at the raw brutality Stevie described. He worried that her own traumatic memories once again would unleash a wave of painful emotion.

"I don't know," she said, her words expressing helplessness in the face of a much deeper mystery than who in particular had killed Lakeisha Smalls. "I just don't know.

"What are you going to do?" she continued after a moment. "Have you told the police?"

For the second time this evening, Stevie was stunned to realize that he had yet to act on this new and critical piece of evidence. "No," he said almost sheepishly, shaking his head in disbelief. "No, I haven't told them. But, I should."

He checked the time and saw that it was a little past nine. A wave of sadness washed over him. "Lucy, I really want to stay. But, I actually should call the detectives working this case and let them know what we've found."

She looked at him questioningly. "It's late. Will they be working now?"

"Yeah, they'll be working," Stevie answered. "And, they'll want to know this. I should have called them earlier."

Lucy just nodded. "I understand."

Together, they rose and started towards the door.

"The dinner was great. Thanks," said Stevie. Then, he reached out for her hand. "Lucy, I... I want to see you again. Can we do that?"

She looked up at him and stepped forward, their bodies just touching. "Yes," she said. "We definitely can do that." Then she rose on her toes, brought her lips up to his, and they kissed, gently and only for an instant. It was a moment that he would remember for a long time. "Call me," she said.

Stevie smiled. "I'll call you in the morning. Good night."

27

Hearing Lucy's door close behind him was almost physically painful. Stevie could still sense the lingering touch of her lips on his. Yet, he felt a certain relief that he was leaving now. He wasn't sure what would happen if he stayed. His feelings for Lucy were different and much stronger than he'd had for any woman since he and Sandy split up. And, he was certain, Lucy felt something special as well. This was all happening fast...very fast. As powerful as this new relationship was beginning to seem, Stevie knew that it was still fragile. He didn't want it to shatter before it had a chance to fully develop.

Once in the car, Stevie pulled out his cell phone and, for a second time that day, wondered whom he should call. Jack Schwinn? Jimmy Williams? His brother? All three should be interested in this new piece of evidence. He wondered if they would be.

The logical first call was to his brother, Frankie. It was his unit that was investigating the Lakeisha Smalls case and the pik, which Stevie now knew had been Melody's, was evidence from that crime scene.

He tapped in his brother's cell number and raised the phone to his ear. Seconds later, he heard Frankie's voice, along with the unmistakable background noise of a crowded bar.

"Stevie, what's up?" asked Frankie.

"Frankie, I need to talk with you. Where are you?"

"You want to talk now? I'm at The Cumberland. Do you want

to come over?"

"Yeah," said Stevie. "I can be there in about 15 minutes. Is that OK?"

"Sure. It'll give me a good excuse to tell Jeannie."

Less than a quarter hour later, he walked through the front door of The Cumberland. After years of absence, it was his second visit in just five days. This once all-too-familiar cop bar was starting to feel familiar again. Yet Stevie knew – could sense it right to his very soul – that he was an outsider now. And, he always would be.

The Cumberland catered to a clientele who worked all manner of rotating, round the clock shifts. Theirs was a 24/7 world, impervious to the natural rhythms of larger society where people were governed by such concepts as workdays, weekends and school nights. As a result, the place was still relatively crowded for 10:00 p.m. on a Tuesday.

Frankie was planted on a stool midway down the long bar, nursing a bottle of beer. Stevie strolled over and slid onto the stool next to him.

"Hey," he said, reaching out to give his brother a pat on the shoulder.

"Hey, bro," said Frankie, raising a hand to get the bartender's attention. "What will you have?"

"A beer," said Stevie, pointing to the bottle in front of Frankie. "Thanks."

The younger Corra turned and placed his own hand on Stevie's shoulder. "Listen… about last night… on the phone... I'm sorry if I got a little hot. You know how this shit works."

"Believe me, I understand," said Stevie, waving away his brother's concerns. "Don't worry about it. I'm sorry if I'm making this more complicated for you."

"You're not making it complicated…" Frankie began; then hesitated as he studied his brother. "Are you? … What was it you wanted to talk about?"

"Look," said Stevie, taking a sip of his freshly poured beer. "When I was up in Lakeisha Smalls' apartment… it was when Jimmy was working the scene…I saw something. It was a homemade

127

wooden pik, one of those Afro-combs black women use for their hair. It didn't mean anything to me then. But today I learned something more and I think it proves that Melody Saunders, my foster kid's mother, was at the apartment sometime after Rue James was shot on Tuesday night and before Lakeisha Smalls was murdered yesterday. Remember that Jack Schwinn is looking for her as a possible witness to the Rue James shooting!"

Frankie turned and focused his attention on Stevie. "O.K., explain this to me again."

Corra ran through the way he had first seen the pik at Lakeisha's apartment and then found a similar one today at the group home. He explained how Carlos told him that he had made it for Shaquan to give to Melody – and that Shaquan still had it when he went AWOL on Wednesday night.

"So, you think this proves Melody was there between Wednesday and Monday?" said Frankie, working the new information over in his own mind. "Maybe... but it still doesn't prove that it had any connection to the murder."

"No, it doesn't," Stevie admitted. "But it sure is a hell of a coincidence for a woman on the run after one murder to show up in advance of another one only a couple of days later."

"Yeah," nodded Frankie, as he took a drink of his own beer. "It has a certain ring to it... for sure!"

The two brothers sat in silence for a few moments, before Frankie again turned to Stevie. "So, how do you think these things are connected? Do you have anyone in mind as the do-er?"

Stevie chuckled a little sheepishly. "Look, Frankie, I don't know exactly how these things all fit together. It could be that the Lakeisha Smalls murder had nothing to do with the Rue James hit. Lucy Montoya... the domestic violence worker from Safe Families I told you about..."

"Ah, Lucy," Frankie interrupted, teasingly. "When do I get to meet Lucy?"

"Hopefully never... for her sake," said Stevie, trying to get back on track. "Anyway, she thinks it could have been Melody's boyfriend, Levon Marbury.... You may remember that I've been asking you to run his sheet for me?"

"Yeah, sorry," Frankie said, sounding only a little embarrassed. "I've been busy."

"I can see," said Stevie, staring at the beer sitting on the bar in front of his brother. "But Lucy says that Levon would know that Lakeisha was the only place Melody could have gone for help... and that he probably knew where she lived."

"So, you... and Lucy... think that Levon killed Lakeisha?"

"I don't know," said Stevie. "But, he is a mean son of a bitch; that's for sure. It just seems like something worth checking out."

"Yeah, it does," Frankie responded, even now seeming somewhat resistant to accepting his brother's viewpoint. "I'll pass it along to Jimmy. He'll probably give you a call... maybe tomorrow."

Again the two sat in silence at the bar until Frankie continued. "What about Jack Schwinn? Have you given him this latest tidbit as well?"

"Not yet," said Stevie. "I will, though. Don't you think I should? They are looking for Melody."

"Sure," Frankie answered without enthusiasm. "Sure, that makes sense."

Now the silence between them seemed a little more awkward. Stevie made an effort to break the mood.

"Are you going to mom and dad's this weekend?"

"Yeah, probably," Frankie answered. "What about you?"

"I don't know. I can't remember if I said, but Joey is going to be away with Sandy."

"That's a reason to stay away?"

"No. It's just one less reason to go."

"So...." Now it was Frankie's turn to change the subject. "Tell me about Lucy?"

"What?"

"There's something about the way you talk about her!"

"She's just a DV caseworker," Stevie lied. "Melody Saunders is her client."

"That's it?" Frankie probed, his eyes lighting up as he playfully pressed for more. "It's just business?"

"Yeah," Stevie answered. Then, realizing his brother could see right through him, his façade cracked into a sly yet innocent smile. "But, I did have dinner with her tonight."

"OK," said Frankie, satisfied at having gotten to the truth. "Why not bring Lucy to mom and dad's?"

"No," Stevie answered flatly. "Absolutely not!"

Frankie just chuckled. "O.K., I need to get going. At least I can tell Jeannie that you wanted to meet to talk about your new girlfriend."

"Frankie!" Stevie commanded sternly.

"Don't worry," his brother laughed again. "Don't worry."

The two rose together and gave each other a quick man hug, complete with brotherly back slaps.

"See ya," said Frankie.

"Yeah, see yah. And, Frankie, please get me what you can on Levon Marbury?"

His brother stared back at him for a moment. "O.K.," he said with a ring of commitment in his voice. "I'll get you whatever we have."

28

Stevie emerged from the dimly lit bar onto the now even darker streets of northern Brooklyn. It was past 11:00 and he was feeling a surprising combination of elation and fatigue after what had been a long but exhilarating day.

Stevie walked the two blocks back to his car, his thoughts continually returning to dinner with Lucy. He slid behind the wheel and literally forced himself to focus on the process of driving himself home. He started the engine, buckled his seat belt and checked the rear view mirror before pulling out from the curb. He made a right turn off of Flushing and onto Thompkins. It was a trip Stevie had made hundreds of times and he knew by heart the twisting combination of side streets that eventually would bring him back to his apartment in Windsor Terrace.

As he drove, Stevie recalled almost word for word Lucy's terrifying description of her life as a young girl, the fear of her father's violent rages, and the ultimate horror of her mother's death. Once again, he felt the extraordinary sense of intimacy that only comes when two people share their most personal, and often most painful, secrets. It was an emotional bonding which he had not experienced with anyone, not even Sandy, for a very long time... perhaps ever.

Yet, Stevie also felt a lurking anxiety mingled with this newfound joy. Tonight, it was Lucy who had shared her terror and shame, trusting that he would accept, if not fully understand, what this trauma had meant for her and what it had taken to survive. Soon, very soon, it would be his turn to reveal the truth about who he was… and what he had done.   Could he trust her to accept, understand and forgive? And, with his feelings already yearning for her, how could he possibly go on if she did not?

Stevie abruptly pulled his thoughts back from this painful prospect, suddenly aware that he had mindlessly driven half way home without even realizing what he was doing, his subconscious guiding him through a maze of familiar streets and avenues. He quickly looked around, searching for street signs and accustomed landmarks, to see exactly where he was. Instantly he recognized that he needed to make a sharp left turn onto Clinton off DeKalb. His eyes flashed to the side mirror, checking for any cars coming up in the turning lane. The only other vehicle was a half-block behind him. With room to move, Stevie darted over; then swung the car into a full 90-degree left turn.

As he continued south along Clinton, however, Stevie was suddenly filled with a deep unease. Something was wrong.   Just as his subconscious had found his normal route home, it now recognized that danger was near at hand.

Stevie's eyes flashed again to his rear view mirror, just in time to see the car behind him on DeKalb Avenue make its own left hand turn onto Clinton. A coincidence? Probably, he thought. Still, there was something about that car. Had he been watching it in his mind's eye for the entire drive?

Stevie continued straight up Clinton for five blocks, past Lafayette, Greene, Gates and Fulton. Behind him, the headlights followed, always a consistent half-block's length behind.

At Atlantic, he turned right. Then, gliding smoothly across three lanes of traffic, he stopped at the light, preparing to make another immediate left turn onto Vanderbilt Avenue. As he waited, Stevie's eyes scanned the mirror to study the scene behind him. He watched as the car – a late model black SUV with darkened windows – quickly snuck its nose into the intersection; then hesitated before beginning a slow right hand turn. It was following his every move, but clearly trying to keep its distance.

When the light changed to green, Stevie made the turn and drove straight up the avenue, shifting his gaze back and forth between the road ahead and the mirrored image from behind. His stomach dropped and his heart skipped a beat when he saw the SUV repeat his maneuver and pursue him up Vanderbilt.

Who was following him? What did it mean? Was he in danger? Stevie's mind raced through dozens of questions as he fought back against a slight, but still unsettling, sense of panic. He must be imagining things, he told himself.

There was one way to find out.

At the corner of Prospect Place, Stevie made a quick right turn. A hundred feet behind him, the SUV did the same. At the intersection with Flatbush Avenue, he now made a left, back up towards Grand Army Plaza. No one could be following this route by pure chance.

Once again, Stevie stared into the rear view mirror to see what happened next. Behind him, the SUV raced past the changing traffic light just in time to stay with him; then the driver slowed quickly, struggling to maintain a discrete distance as he tracked his prey.

Stevie felt his heart begin to race, the blood pounding in his temples. Who was it? What was this all about? This was an entirely new sensation. Even as a cop, it was he who had done the tailing, not the other way around.

Suddenly, however, the instinctual memories of a hundred long forgotten stakeouts began to reassert themselves. Stevie sensed a certain calm come over him, as he assessed the situation, evaluating his tracker from a professional perspective. Clearly, the SUV was working alone. If he had been part of a surveillance team, they would have handed him off from one to another several times already. Nor was this guy a pro. He wasn't bad, but obviously had never been trained in the art of the tail. Once Stevie had begun his last zig-zag maneuver, the SUV surely should have known that he'd been spotted. The smart move would have been to stop at Flatbush or continue straight across without turning, leaving Stevie to go about his business wondering if he'd imagined the whole thing.

Who was it, Stevie asked himself again, checking the mirror

as he entered the sweeping circle around Grand Army Plaza. One quarter of the way through the arc, he swung right onto Prospect Park West. Behind him, the SUV followed suit.

Now, he felt anger rise up in place of fear. Who the fuck was this? It was time to end it. Stevie stomped on the accelerator. His aging Subaru struggled to respond, haltingly picking up speed along the broad avenue, Prospect Park on his left, the posh townhouses of Park Slope on his right.

As he sped up, so, too, did the SUV. In tandem, they raced block by block past President, Carroll and Montgomery. At Garfield, without warning, Stevie braked suddenly and turned sharply to his right, tires squealing as the Subaru barreled down the narrow side street.

Behind him came the SUV.

Together, they flew down Garfield, heading towards 8th Avenue. With the light luckily still green, Stevie shot through the intersection, maintaining his speed as he continued down the side street, his eyes now watching for the moment when the SUV, too, made it across. At that instant, already half way down the block, Stevie slammed on his brakes, screeching to a halt next to a long line of parked cars and just before the spot where Polhemus Place, a tiny, alley-like side street cut for one block to his right.

Stevie's erratic driving had left his pursuer with few options. What would he do? It was too late to stop at any reasonable distance behind the Subaru. If he did brake, Stevie was prepared to force a confrontation and find out who was following him… and why? The only other alternative was for the SUV to slow down and pass him… either hoping to pick him up once Stevie continued… or give up for the night.

He watched through his side mirror as the SUV shuddered and swerved from side to side as the driver's first reaction was to hit the brakes. Then, the truck-like car seemed to regain control, moving slightly to its left as it slowly rolled passed the double-parked Subaru.

Stevie felt his previously suppressed panic begin to surface once again as he stared without success into the darkened windows of the

SUV... unable to see whomever it was staring back at him from the other side.

As the SUV continued straight down Garfield, Stevie quickly turned to his right onto Polhemus Drive, then only seconds later swung right again up Carroll back towards the park. Less than fifty yards further, he once more turned to his right onto Fiske Place, another small alley where he raced back to Garfield... hoping against hope that the SUV would have already turned on 7th Avenue in an effort to catch up with him heading west.

It had.

He turned again back down Garfield, crossed 7th Avenue and made a left on 6th, continually searching for any sign of the black SUV back on his tail. There was none.

Stevie felt his heart pounding, adrenaline racing through his body, as he forced himself to hold the Subaru to a reasonable speed. Relief at being free of his pursuer swept over him, only to be followed quickly by another surge of anxiety. Whoever it had been, his follower certainly knew who he was and where he lived. Stevie had only spotted him coming home from the Cumberland. Had he been followed before that? From home? To Lucy's apartment? Another wave of panic arose at the thought that he might somehow have put Lucy in danger.

Who was it? Stevie turned the question over again and again in his mind as he headed home. There was only one possibility that came back in response. Back Thompson! Or, one of his boys! It had to be that. Who else could it be?

At least Stevie would have hoped to gain one piece of vital information. He might not have been able to see through the SUV's darkened windows, but he'd been a cop far too long not to spot and memorize the SUV's plate number. Not this time! The vehicle's plate had been purposefully muddied... and the small bulb designed to illuminate it had been blacked out.

29

"Are you shitting me?" Frankie's response on the other end of the phone was an equal mixture of shocked surprise and sudden concern for his brother's safety.

"I wish I was," Stevie answered.

"So, go over it one more time," Frankie directed.

Stevie sighed. He was beginning to understand how frustrating it was for witnesses and suspects to answer the same questions... again and again.

"Someone followed me back from The Cumberland. It was a black SUV... a Dodge Durango... I don't know what year. It had darkened windows. I couldn't see anyone inside. I spotted them about half way home. I made a few turns to see if they'd follow me and they did.

"Fuck!"

"Exactly"

"And, you couldn't get a plate number?" Frankie asked, as if questioning a less than intelligent child.

"No," Stevie repeated, torn between embarrassment and an urge to explode in rage. "It was too dark... and they'd broken the plate lamp and blackened out the number."

"Hmmh," Frankie grunted. "You really have gotten yourself into the middle of something!"

"That's what I've been trying to tell you." If nothing else, Stevie felt a sense of satisfaction that at least someone was finally taking him seriously.

"Do you really think this has something to do with your missing kid?"

"What else could it be?"

There was a brief silence on the other end of the line. "I don't know," said Frankie. "So... who do you think it was?"

Now it was Stevie's turn to hesitate. "I don't really know. My first thought is Levon Marbury. If he is looking for Melody, he might think I could lead him to her."

"How would he find you?"

"He's been living with Melody for a couple of months. She could have told him that I was Shaquan's caseworker."

"Maybe," his brother said thoughtfully. "So how long do you think this guy was following you? Was he on you before you got to The Cumberland?"

"I don't know. I didn't see anyone... but I certainly wasn't looking." Stevie thought for a moment. "He must have followed me from home. How else could he have picked me up?"

"Could he have spotted you coming out of your office? If he knew you were Shaquan's caseworker, he could have waited for you to turn up there and then followed you?"

"I never even went into the office today. I was in the field all day."

"But, how would he know where you live?"

"I'm in the book."

"You're in the book?" Frankie spat back disbelievingly.

"Yeah, I'm in the book," Stevie answered defiantly. "I don't go around arresting people anymore. I don't need to hide."

"Hmmph," his brother grunted. There was silence on either end of the phone line for a few moments before Frankie continued. "All right, I'll get Jimmy to look up Levon Marbury. He'll call you in the morning. Tell him whatever you know."

"Thanks."

Again, there was a brief hesitation before Frankie spoke again.

"You said that your 'first thought' was Levon Marbury. Who else are you thinking about?"

"I wonder if it could be Back Thompson or someone working for him."

"Who?"

Stevie swallowed hard, gathering whatever patience he had left. Then, he slowly recounted the sequence of events, beginning at the encounter with Back Thompson during his first visit to Melody's apartment; the subsequent conversation with Jack Schwinn about the Rue James murder; then his second confrontation with the drug dealer in the alley behind the apartment on Sunday night."

"Are you fucking crazy?" This time his brother's voice rang with a combination of worry and anger. "You can't be wandering around out there on your own in the middle of the night! You're going to get yourself killed! Remember… you're not a cop anymore."

Frankie's words stung…like a cold, hard, slap across his face. Stevie stood holding the phone in stunned silence.

"Come on," Frankie continued, his tone softening. "That neighborhood is dangerous… all the time. To go into a back alley behind that building…at night…by yourself… that's crazy! You know that. You wouldn't even do that when you were on the job."

"I'm fine," said Stevie flatly, unable to admit that Frankie was right.

"Then why are you on the phone telling me that some scumbag just followed you home? That doesn't sound 'fine'." The younger Corra waited a few moments before continuing, again softening his tone. "OK, let's start at the beginning. Why do you think Back Thompson wants to have you tailed?"

"Same thing, maybe he thinks I'll lead him to Shaquan… and Melody? She might have seen Rue James get shot… and who shot him."

"OK, that's a possibility," his brother acknowledged. "So how do you think they would have found you?"

Stevie thought for a moment before answering. "On Sunday night, after I ran into Back, one of his kids followed me to the car. He could have gotten the license and traced me through that."

"That's possible."

"It's the damndest thing," Stevie said, recalling the confrontation in the alley with its exchange of words and implied threats. "It's like 'Back' knew who I was. Like he knew that I had been a cop… but wasn't anymore…."

The thought hung for a moment in the silence between them. Then, Stevie voiced another more immediate, and more troubling, concern.

"Frankie, I stopped at the apartment and took a shower before going to Lucy's for dinner. If someone followed me from here, that means they followed me to her house…."

"Don't worry," his brother said reassuringly. "Whoever it is – Levon, Back – these guys are following *you*. If you're right about the reasons why, they won't have any idea at all who Lucy is and she won't mean anything at all to them.

"Just be careful," he concluded. "If you see them again, you call me… right away. We'll find out who it is once and for all."

"Thanks," said Stevie, feeling surprisingly comforted by this conversation with his younger brother. "Give Jeannie my love and tell her I won't bother you any more tonight."

"I certainly hope not," said Frankie with a light chuckle. "Get some sleep, bro."

Stevie hung up and walked to the glass door overlooking his back patio. His thoughts were still preoccupied with the possible danger he might have brought to Lucy's doorstep. And, he heard his brother's words – *You're not a cop anymore* – echo again and again in his head. It was true. He was now a civilian…just another citizen…unable to protect himself or those he cared about… calling the police for help.

He stood there, looking into the darkness… and thinking. Finally he turned, walked to the hallway closet and reached up to take a heavy metal container from the top shelf. Stevie carried it back to his kitchen table and placed it to one side. On top was a numerical keypad. He punched in 1,9,6,3,2 – the numbers of his father's patrolman shield, a Lucite-encased icon hanging in Monument Alley that he had studied for years while growing up. There was a muffled click as the electronic lock released and the gun safe's lid sprang free.

Inside, a Glock 19 automatic pistol sat snugly in its foam bed. Deep black with a matte finish that seemed to absorb all light, this was the weapon that Stevie had carried for most of his ten years on the force. During that time, unlike most cops, he had drawn it repeatedly and even fired it on several occasions. It was one of these that had been the defining moment in his life.

Stevie stared at the gun with a cold detachment. It had been more than five years since he had last seen it. He had hoped that he would never see it again. Nevertheless, for reasons he couldn't fully understand, he had kept it – along with the "concealed carry" permit that was available to virtually all, former NYPD officers…even Stevie Corra.

He reached in and picked up the pistol. Physically, its weight and balance felt like a natural and somehow familiar extension of his right hand. Emotionally, however, the weapon seemed distant and threatening. Stevie sensed that he was watching someone else as he turned it awkwardly from side to side. Then, gripping one hand with the other, he pointed it towards the wall, sighted down the barrel and panned the weapon from left to right. Suddenly, he recoiled in horror as he found himself aiming at a framed photograph of his son, Joey. Clamping his eyes shut, as if to block out that vision…and others… Stevie lowered the gun. Then he turned, laid it on the table and walked to the glass door, where, once again, he stared into the darkness. Images of what might happen – to Lucy, himself, possibly even to Joey – battled with other, painful memories of what actually had happened years before.

After a few moments, Stevie walked back into the living room. He unlocked a desk drawer, took out a box of 9mm ammunition, and carried it back to the kitchen table. He reached into the metal gun safe and picked up a standard 15-shot Glock magazine. Then, cartridge by cartridge, he clicked the bullets into place and slid the magazine up into the handle of the pistol.

Joey wasn't going to be in the apartment for at least a week, so he stuck the Glock into a clip holster. For the first time he could remember, Stevie was about to sleep with a loaded pistol next to his bed.

30

Stevie awoke early after a restless night's sleep. The events of the previous evening had weighed heavily on his subconscious mind. The first thing he saw was a holstered handgun lying on his night table. The sight was both reassuring and unsettling.

He climbed out of bed, walked to the bedroom window, which offered only a limited view of the street, and peered out between the blinds. At least there was no black Dodge Durango with darkened windows parked in front of his house.

At a little past 6:00, he set out for his morning run around Prospect Park. As he left the apartment, Stevie discretely scanned the street in both directions searching for any signs of last night's pursuer. There were none. Forty-five minutes later he returned, dripping with perspiration and catching his breath. He looked up and down the street again. Still nothing.

Stevie slipped inside; ate a quick breakfast as he cooled down; then showered and dressed. It was barely 7:45 before he gave in to the urge to call Lucy.

"Hi," he said as soon as she answered. "I hope I'm not calling too early?"

"No, not at all," she said. Her voice was soft and warm. "I'm getting ready for work. I'm glad you called."

"I just wanted to say thanks for last night. The dinner was great and I really enjoyed being with you."

"Thanks. I enjoyed it too…very much. Did you talk to the

detectives?"

"Uh…," Stevie hesitated. "Yeah. It's kind of a long story. Is there any chance we could get together later? Maybe I can make dinner for you tonight? I could pick you up."

"Sure, I'd like that," Lucy answered.

"Would a couple of barbecued steaks work? You're not a vegan, are you?"

"No," she laughed in response. "I'm definitely not a vegan. Steaks would be terrific. Do you want to just pick me up at the office after work? Say about 5:30?"

"That sounds like a plan. I'll see you then," Stevie said enthusiastically as he hung up. His mood already had improved dramatically.

A half-hour later at 8:30, he walked into his office at Brooklyn Family Services. Stevie had a long day of meetings and a family team conference scheduled. As usual, Jackie Johnson was already at her desk, going over case files. She looked up as he knocked gently on her open door.

"Good morning," she said. "How are you today?"

"I'm still here," Stevie answered.

"Good! Any news on Shaquan?"

"Yes and no. Can I come in?"

Jackie nodded, pushed her papers to one side and prepared herself. Stevie dropped into one of the chairs facing her desk. He quickly reviewed the information his boss already had heard, beginning with the home visit to Melody's apartment and ending with Lucy Montoya's news that Melody was trying to escape an abusive relationship with Levon Marbury. Then, he told her what she didn't know. When he described how he and Lucy had tried to meet with Lakeisha Smalls, only to find that she had just been murdered, Jackie gasped in shocked disbelief. Finally, Stevie explained that he had found a pik which Carlos had made and given to Shaquan at the crime scene – meaning that Melody, and perhaps Shaquan, had likely been there at some point during a five-day period between the two murders.

"Oh, my God," Jackie stammered. "This is just terrible."

"Yes," said Stevie dejectedly.

"And the police know about all this?"

"Yes. And, I think they are finally starting to take it seriously." He once again decided to spare Jackie the details about his encounters with Back Thompson and the fact he had been followed home last night. "And, the worst is that we still don't have any idea where Shaquan is, other than that he and Melody are probably together. Right now, that could get him killed."

"No other leads? No friends; no family?"

"Nope. Melody's not in touch with her family. Lucy Montoya says that the only friend she might go to for help was Lakeisha Smalls. Shaquan hardly knows anyone outside the system other than Melody."

"Christ," Jackie groaned, her face contorting into one enormous, painful frown. "It's been a week. Shaquan is going onto suspended payment tomorrow. We can keep his spot for a while, but pretty soon there is going to be pressure for us to take another referral and fill the bed."

Stevie just nodded. He understood the system. Under normal circumstances this was the beginning of the end for many kids who went AWOL. The City stopped paying for their care seven days later and agencies moved to accept other kids to take their place – particularly in congregate settings like group homes or residential treatment centers where the loss of a hundred dollars a day could quickly break an agency that was already spending more on care than it received in government reimbursement. Sure, both Stevie and BFS were expected to continue searching for Shaquan. But, those efforts would soon fade to just an occasional phone call and carefully worded entries in the case file. The ever present, in your face demands of 18 other kids and families would take precedence. Before long, Shaquan would become just another open "suspended payment" case and a vague recollection about a kid who used to be in care.

"Keep looking," said Jackie emphatically.

"I will," he answered with equal determination. Neither of them wanted to see Shaquan disappear onto the streets of Brooklyn... or, in this case, turn up as part of a drug-related, double homicide.

Stevie headed back to his cubicle. It was a busy day in the office. Each of his three colleagues were at their stations, completing progress notes, updating case files and preparing for a series of supervisory meetings and case conferences. As soon as he sat down, his cell phone rang. It was Jimmy Williams, the lead detective on the Lakeisha Smalls murder.

"Jimmy!" he answered.

"Stevie! Good morning! Your brother suggested I give you a call. It sounds like being a social worker is more exciting than I would have thought."

"It has its moments."

"Frankie said that you saw something at the Lakeisha Smalls crime scene that makes you think your foster kid's mother was there sometime before the killing… and that someone tailed you home last night?"

"That's right."

"Can you come in and talk about it? I'd like to get all the details." Jimmy actually sounded sincere. Stevie knew Williams was a good cop who would want to hear everything he could about a case he was working on… even if it did conflict with his original theory about what had happened.

Stevie looked at his schedule. There were two meetings and one family team conference he absolutely had to attend. On the other hand, suddenly having an excuse to get out of a mid-afternoon staff meeting on new ACS reporting procedures was more than he could have hoped for.

"How about if I came over at around 3:00?" he asked.

"That works. I'll see you then."

31

Jimmy Williams worked out of a Homicide Squad at the 67th precinct, no more than a mile from where Lakeisha Smalls had been murdered. The building was another three-story, poured-concrete fortress, this time overlooking a row of small, ramshackle, wood frame houses on the opposite side of Snyder Avenue. Blue and white patrol vehicles and unmarked cars jutted outward from the precinct across the sidewalk and onto the street in a line of makeshift parking spaces.

Inside, Stevie went through the familiar drill – announcing himself to the desk officer and waiting for Jimmy to come and get him. Rather than go back to Williams' desk, the detective led him to a small, bare interview room with one gray, metal frame table and a few well-worn chairs. Tommy Quinn was already sitting at the table with a notebook, a case file and a large manila envelope. Stevie had spent what must be years in rooms just like these, questioning suspects, witnesses and victims. Now, he was on the other side of the table – providing information, taking questions and asking for help.

"So, Stevie, let's start at the beginning," said Jimmy. "Tell me about this kid and his mother and why you think she's mixed up in the Lakeisha Smalls murder."

For what seemed like the umpteenth time, Stevie recounted the events of the last week, beginning with Shaquan's disappearance and ending with his realization that the Afro comb had been a gift from Shaquan to Melody.

"This one?" asked Williams, taking a carefully marked plastic bag out of the brown envelope. Inside was the wooden pik Stevie had last seen on the floor in Lakeisha Smalls' apartment.

"Yeah, that's the one."

"How do you know it's the same one that Shaquan gave Melody?"

"Carlos described it perfectly, even the type of markings he had carved into it. They had been making them in woodworking class."

"What's the kid's full name," asked Quinn. "And, where could we find him if we wanted him to ID the comb?"

"Carlos Martinez," said Stevie, a little defensively. "He lives at our Flatbush Group Home. Look, if you need to talk with him, I can bring him by. That would probably be better."

"OK," Quinn nodded, carefully noting the information.

"So, you think this means that Melody Saunders was at Lakeisha Smalls' apartment sometime in the last week?" Jimmy Williams continued.

"That's right. Shaquan went AWOL last Wednesday, the night Rue James was shot and Melody Saunders went missing. He still had the pik then. If Melody took it to Lakeisha's, it was when she was on the run, maybe hiding from Levon Marbury…or somebody else."

"And you think Marbury could have tracked Melody Saunders to Lakeisha Smalls?"

"It's possible," said Stevie shrugging his shoulders. "Lucy Montoya, Melody's DV worker, says that Levon would have known Melody had nowhere else to go for help… and he knew where Lakeisha lived."

Again, he watched as Tommy Quinn carefully noted Lucy's name and contact information.

"And, he's a mean son of a bitch," Stevie continued. "He could have roughed Lakeisha up trying to find out where Melody was. Then, maybe it got out of control… or, maybe, he decided to tie up any loose ends."

Williams sat in silence for a moment, once again going over the facts in his head. Then he looked at Stevie with a weak smile of resignation. "Well, who knows? We certainly don't have many other leads. This should keep us entertained for a while.

"You got any ideas on where Melody Saunders and the kid are?" he added.

"No," Stevie answered. "I wish I did."

"OK," said Williams as he started to rise from the table. "We'll let you know if we want to talk to that kid, Carlos. We also may get in touch with Lucy Montoya."

"Thanks."

"And," Williams added, sliding a thin brown manila envelope across the desk. "Your brother wanted me to give you this…. But, remember, you didn't get it from me."

"Sure," Stevie chuckled, picking up the envelope. "Thanks."

Stevie made his way out of the precinct house and back to his car. He slipped in behind the steering wheel and opened the envelope. Inside was Levon Marbury's rap sheet – a listing of his prior arrests and convictions. Before he could even begin to read it, his cell phone rang. It was Jack Schwinn.

"Stevie! What's the matter? You don't love me anymore?"

"What are you talking about?" Stevie asked, tossing the envelope onto the seat next to him.

"Jimmy Williams in Homicide just called me. He said you had new information on the Lakeisha Smalls murder that might involve Melody Saunders. It sounds like you've been holding out on us?"

"Come on, Jack," Stevie said with irritation. "I told you yesterday that I thought Melody might have gone to Lakeisha for help…and maybe that had something to do with her murder. You didn't seem all that interested."

"Yeah, but Jimmy says that now you have some evidence to back it up."

"That's right."

"Some wooden comb that one of your foster kids made?"

"Yeah. I saw it at the crime scene and yesterday I found out that Shaquan had given it to Melody sometime after Wednesday night? So, she must have been there – or at least seen Lakeisha – at some point during the last few days."

"And, you're thinking this points to Levon Marbury as the

killer?"

"It could certainly fit."

"Look, Stevie, if you come up with anything else let me know, OK? Remember, we're the ones looking for Melody."

"Yeah... sure."

"None of your kids has any idea where Shaquan and Melody might be?"

"No," said Stevie, again feeling irritation rise in his voice. "How about you? You're the ones looking for her, right?"

Schwinn hesitated a moment before answering. "We're working a couple of leads."

"Like what," Stevie pressed.

Again, Jack hesitated a moment. "... Nothing all that solid. I'll let you know if anything pans out."

"Good."

There was an awkward silence on the line before Jack Schwinn continued.

"...Jimmy told me someone was tailing you last night?"

"Yeah."

"Any idea who it was?"

"Not really," Stevie answered, suddenly struggling with a surprising reluctance to share his thoughts with Schwinn. "Maybe it was Levon Marbury or one of Back Thompson's guys."

"Maybe," Jack said. "Remember, we told you yesterday that you need to be careful. It's dangerous out there."

To Stevie's ear, it sounded as much like a threat as a concerned warning.

"Yeah," he said flatly before hanging up. "I'll remember."

Stevie checked the time on his phone. It was almost 5:00. He would need to hurry if we was going to pick up Lucy by 5:30.

32

Stevie drove up just in time to see Lucy come out of the building. Once again, she had exchanged her more conservative blouse-and-trousers workday outfit for a loose and comfortable summer dress that highlighted her trim and shapely figure.

"Hi," Lucy said as she opened the door and slipped into the passenger seat. She reached across, took Stevie's hand, and then leaned over to give him a soft, brief kiss on the cheek.

"Hi," Stevie answered as their hands lingered in a gentle embrace. "You look great."

"Thanks," Lucy responded with a surprisingly shy smile. "How are you?"

"Right now, I feel great," he said with a broad smile of his own. "But, I haven't had lunch, so I'm starving. I hope you are too."

"I can't wait to eat. I've been looking forward to this all day."

Stevie pulled out from the curb and they enjoyed some pleasant small talk as he headed south, out of downtown Brooklyn with its government office buildings into the residential neighborhood of Cobble Hill. Along the way, they stopped at Luccio's Pork Store, a now beyond old-fashioned Italian butcher where he bought two steaks, some fresh provolone rolled in prosciutto, and a large pasta salad tossed with roasted vegetables. Ten minutes later, they walked into his apartment.

"Make yourself comfortable," he said, dropping his briefcase in the hallway and escorting Lucy into the combination living room and kitchenette. Stevie opened the sliding glass door overlooking the patio. "This is my estate," he said with a wave of his arm.

"It's really nice," said Lucy. "It's great to have some outdoor space. And, the apartment has a warm and cozy feel."

"Well, right now, it has a *hot* and cozy feel," Stevie corrected. "It'll be cooler outside. How about a glass of wine?"

"Thanks," said Lucy as she cruised slowly around, looking at his books, posters and pictures. She stopped at a large framed photograph at one end of the couch. "This must be your son?"

"Yeah, that's Joey. It was taken a couple of years ago when he was seven."

"He's a great looking boy."

"Thanks. He's a great kid. I love him to death."

Stevie handed Lucy a glass of wine. "Let's sit outside. I'll get the grill started."

The backyard patio offered both shade from the late day sun and a gentle breeze that flowed up the line of back gardens between the two- and three-story homes on either side. Lucy eased into one of the canvas director's chairs at the patio table, tossing her jet-black hair from side to side as if to shake off the stress of the day and cool her slender neck and shoulders. She watched as Stevie piled charcoals and old newspaper into a cylindrical metal container sitting on the bottom of a black kettle barbecue. Seconds later, flames were licking upwards around the coals and grey smoke began to pour out the top, only to be carried away by the steady breeze.

"Works like a charm… sometimes," said Stevie with an ironic smile as he joined Lucy at the table.

"How long have you lived here?" she asked.

"About five years," he answered, taking a sip of wine.

Lucy nodded. "About the same time you started working at BFS?"

"Yeah," Stevie said, raising an eyebrow. Then he got up and went to the kitchen. A few moments later he came back with the mozzarella and some Italian bread. "Here's a little something to keep us going until dinner's ready." He cut a thin slice of the soft cheese with its colorful swirl of rolled, deep burgundy prosciutto and slid it onto a plate for Lucy.

"Thanks," she said taking a bite with a piece of bread. "It's delicious."

They sat together in silence, enjoying the early evening air ... and each other's company ... without any need for unnecessary conversation.

"You actually have a garden," said Lucy with delighted surprise, studying the bed of plants running along one side of the back yard, "... with tomatoes ... and fresh herbs."

"Absolutely," said Stevie with a laugh. "I'm Italian. We don't believe in flowers. If I didn't grow at least some vegetables, my family would disown me."

"That's wonderful! Where did you grow up?"

"In Brooklyn... Bensonhurst...then Dyker Heights. That's where my folks live now."

"Did you have a big, Italian family?"

"No," he laughed again, "just me and my brother, Frankie."

"So, you're the older brother?"

Stevie looked at Lucy in surprise. "Yes, he's two years younger than me. How did you know?"

Now it was her turn to chuckle. "It was just a guess. But, there was something in your voice when you talked about him. Are you close?"

Stevie was surprised that he actually had to think about the question. "Yes, I guess we are. We get along fine... usually. There certainly have been some times when we didn't. We used to be very close. But, as we've gotten older, we've each changed a little. We don't always see eye to eye on everything."

"What does he do?"

"He's a cop," Stevie answered, putting his glass down as he rose to spread the glowing coals in the barbecue.

The clipped tone of his answer and the sudden timing of his move away from the table gave Lucy the distinct impression that this line of conversation had come to an end. It was time for a tactical retreat.

"So, how are the tomatoes doing this year?"

Stevie laughed with what was almost audible relief. "Fine. It's

151

certainly been hot enough. But, we could do with a little more rain."
He walked over and studied the line of plants, softly caressing two or
three of the largest, carefully judging their feel and deep red color. "A
couple of them are ripe. We can have them with dinner."

Lucy watched as he twisted them off the vine and turned back
towards the kitchen.

"I'll get the steaks," he said.

"Need any help?"

"No, you just relax."

Lucy leaned back, closed her eyes and savored the lingering
warmth of the summer evening, no longer oppressive, now only
soothing, as it gently melted away any remaining tensions from a day
focused on domestic violence.

Stevie returned, carefully placed two steaks on the grill and
nodded at the first sounds of sizzle. "OK," he said, smiling to Lucy.
"I'll be right back. Don't go away."

Lucy watched as he headed into the kitchen. There was an air
of peace and simplicity that surrounded Stevie here in his home…
really from the first moment she had met him. He seemed grateful for
even the smallest of pleasures…the joy of his modest urban garden, a
quick but easily elegant dinner of grilled steaks and store-bought pasta
salad, and … even being here with her. Lucy felt herself blushing at
the unspoken thought. She knew that he felt something special for her.
She felt the same.

Lucy had been in a number of relationships over the years…some
that seemed serious at the time… a couple that actually were. There
was one that had been "right", but ended for the wrong reasons – her
past trauma and lingering fears over what committing your life to one
man could mean; what it had meant for her mother. There were others
that had been "wrong" and ended for the right reasons. It had been a
while since she'd felt both attracted to and comfortable with any man
in particular. She was starting to feel that way now.

Stevie returned, set two places at the table with plates and
silverware, brought out a bowl of pasta salad and checked the steaks.
Lucy liked the way he moved; quick without rushing, sure of what he
was doing; agile and graceful in black jeans and a loose, blue, short-

sleeved shirt. He hovered over the grill for another moment or two, gently prodding and probing the steaks with a pair of metal tongs. Then, based on some invisible sign, he quickly plucked them from the sizzling barbecue and slid them onto a small wooden cutting board. A piece of pre-cut, perfectly-creased foil stood ready to shelter the deliciously charred meat as it rested before its moment in the spotlight. Lucy found herself admiring both his cooking skills ... and his sense of planning.

"OK, we'll just give them a few minutes," said Stevie who once again disappeared into the kitchen, only to return with a bottle of red wine.

"Who taught you to cook? Your mom?"

"My mom and my dad," he answered, plating the two steaks and handing one to Lucy. "He was the grill master in the house."

"Wow," said Lucy, savoring the first cut of her meat. "These are delicious."

"Thanks. It's hard to ruin good meat."

"Not that hard," Lucy chuckled. "I do it all the time."

"I doubt that." He poured a glass of red wine for each of them and raised his glass. "I'm glad you could come."

"I'm glad you invited me." They each took a sip and then ate silently, enjoying the simple but tasty food.

"Tell me about Joey," Lucy said, after a few minutes.

Stevie nodded and chewed for a moment before picking up a napkin and wiping his mouth. "He's a great kid. He lives with his mom in Sheepshead Bay. He's ten. He stays with me every other weekend. I'd love to have him more often, but that's all I got in the custody agreement."

"That's tough," Lucy murmured in sympathy.

"Sandy, my ex-wife, is actually pretty good about it," Stevie shrugged with an air of resignation. "The truth is, she gets pretty busy, so there are a lot of weeks when I can come over one night and take Joey to a soccer practice or go out for pizza. But, it's still up to her. I can't just plan it."

"What, is he in the...fifth grade?" Lucy asked, doing the calculations in her head.

"No," Stevie answered, an extra note of sadness entering his voice. "He's only in the fourth grade. Sandy and I were splitting up six years ago... just when Joey was about to go into the first grade. He took it really hard. So, we decided to hold him back a year."

"That probably was a good idea," Lucy said reassuringly.

"Yeah," said Stevie, now weighed down by his own familiar guilt. "He's the oldest kid in his class. So, that probably makes things a little easier for him. He gets good marks in school. But, the divorce has been really tough for Joey. It was as if he couldn't be a kid any more. He always seems a little sad and very serious."

"Hey, it's true. Divorces are hard for the children. But, so are bad marriages." Her comment was spontaneous, born of the most painful personal experience. At once, she looked up at Stevie, as if to acknowledge that she could never imagine his marriage being anything like her own childhood. "I'm sorry..."

"Don't worry," he said. "Look, my marriage hadn't been very good for a while. I wasn't a very good husband ...or father. It wasn't like I was cheating or running around," he added hurriedly. Stevie didn't want Lucy to think he was worse than he actually was. "But, I was really caught up in my work. I wasn't around a whole lot. Joey and Sandy should have been the most important things in my life. Instead, it was like they were the least important. I felt like as long as I was bringing in the bucks, I was doing my job. I had no idea. I got my priorities all mixed up. It all started to fall apart between me and Sandy. Then, at one point, things really turned sour."

Lucy could hear the pain as Stevie recounted his past mistakes.

"Was that when you were a cop?" she asked.

"Yes," he sighed, a hint of resignation in his voice

"So," Lucy continued, softly and cautiously, nervous in the knowledge that her next question could either take this new and fragile relationship to another level... or destroy it. "How does a cop wind up becoming a caseworker?"

Stevie took another sip of wine and stared briefly into the depths of the garden before turning back to Lucy. He looked directly into her eyes, his gaze both honest and anxious.

"I killed someone."

33

"Oh my God," Lucy gasped. Stevie's statement struck her like a blow. Her heart raced; she couldn't breathe; her mind swirled as she suddenly began to recall hazy fragments of old newspaper articles and TV broadcasts. "That kid?" she stammered. "You... shot..."

"Jamal Watson," Stevie answered flatly, not cold but deliberately drained of emotions that had already taken their toll... and could easily overcome him once again. "He was 14. We were doing a 'buy and bust' over on East New York Avenue... not far from Melody's apartment. I was the Lieutenant in charge."

"Oh, Stevie!" Lucy cried again, this time in response to the anguish she recognized he was feeling.

"Jamal was there... on the corner," Stevie continued, no longer looking at Lucy, his gaze focused inward. "We pulled up in force. There were a dozen of us, six of my guys and six uniforms. As soon as we jumped out, all hell broke loose; everyone running in different directions. That wasn't unusual. It was always like that."

Lucy watched in silence as he took a breath before going on.

"Jamal ran... up along the side street. He was carrying a black gym bag over his shoulder. We were sure that he had the corner stash. I went after him along with one of my detectives and a uniform...." Stevie hesitated for only a moment as the emotion began to well up once again.

"Half way up the block he cut into one of the alleys alongside a building... We turned and followed him in..."

His eyes begin to moisten, but could not wash away the remembered horror.

"Stevie," Lucy tried to interrupt. "Don't... You don't ..."

"Yes... I do," he said, his eyes again fixed on hers. "I have to tell you. You have to know."

Stevie once more faded back into his memories.

"The alley was fenced off... at the end of the building... about 20 yards in from the street... Jamal tried to get over, but couldn't. He fell back down and dropped the bag."

Again, there was a momentary pause as Stevie seemed to brace himself for what was to come.

"I yelled... 'Stop! Police! Stop!' It was already dark... and at the end of the alley, where Jamal was, there was hardly any light at all..."

Stevie swallowed hard; then continued.

"Jamal had fallen and was still down, but facing the fence. Suddenly, he grabbed the bag and turned, reaching out towards us with his right hand... There was a flash of light... What happened next is still a blur to me."

Lucy watched as tears began to stream down Stevie's cheeks.

"Somebody yelled 'Gun!'," he continued. "That shout...and the flash of light in Jamal's hand... was all it took. I fired...and so did Jim Kelly, my detective. We each hit Jamal. He flew back against the fence, his arm still pointing out towards us, the muzzle of his gun still flashing in the darkness. I fired again... and again. So did Jim. In that alley, the gunshots echoed off the brick walls over and over. They drowned out everything. You couldn't hear; you couldn't think. It sounded like a battlefield."

Stevie clamped his eyes closed, helplessly trying to shut out a vision that had already imprinted itself on his soul.

"When it was over, I thought I had fired three times. I had actually fired seven shots. Jim Kelly had fired five. Robert Peterson, the patrolman, hadn't fired his weapon at all. He just froze, thank God. In all, we hit Jamal eight times. He was dead by the time he slid down the fence onto the ground."

"Stevie," Lucy murmured. She could feel the anguish as he

relived for another countless time the one fatally tragic act he could never un-do.

"And," he continued, turning his tear-filled eyes to hers, "of course, he didn't have a gun... It was his cell phone."

Lucy nodded; then asked, "What about the flash?"

Stevie looked at her, a hint of bitter irony in his misty eyes. "He got a call! At that exact, God-forsaken, split second, he got a call... and the phone lit up...and kept lighting up. We couldn't hear it ring. We couldn't hear anything except shots...our own gun shots... over and over again."

He heaved a pain-filled sigh and reached out to take a sip of wine before continuing.

"It was his mother," he said. "She was calling to find out where he was... and when he would be home." His voice broke as he completed the sentence and the stream of tears returned.

"Stevie," Lucy pleaded again. "You don't have to ..."

His look interrupted her.

"Yes," he said, staring deeply into her eyes. "I almost never talk about this. But I think about it every day... every single day. It's what I did. It's part of me. It's the answer to almost every question that you've asked me... It's who I am... You need to know that.

"And I need to know if you will still have me," Stevie asked, surprised at his own words, as his questioning gaze searched Lucy's soul for an answer.

Lucy just nodded. She tried to speak but couldn't as Stevie's emotions ignited hers. She felt tears begin to well up in her own eyes.

"Yes," Lucy said. "Yes."

She leaned across and took his face in her hands; then bent forward and began kissing away his tears.

"Yes," she said again, moments before her lips found his. "I'll have you."

34

Lucy woke a little before 7:00. Stevie was already up. She could hear him padding around the apartment. Lucy pulled the sheet tight around her naked body and savored memories of the night before. Their love making had been like a refuge, a combination of passion and tenderness, powered by an extraordinary intimacy that had grown so quickly between them. This was not casual sex, no one-night-stand. It was, she knew, something special; something she hoped might endure.

Lucy climbed out of bed and slipped into the light cotton robe that Stevie obviously had left for her. She found him at the kitchen counter.

"Good morning," she said, reaching up for a soft and lingering kiss that was simultaneously exciting and comfortably familiar. "Thanks for dinner."

"You're very welcome," Stevie answered with an almost shy smile. "Thanks for everything else." They kissed again.

"How about some breakfast?"

"Sure. How great is this? A man who never stops cooking," Lucy chuckled, "…except to take care of other important business." She reached up and kissed him once more. "Can I help with anything?"

"You want to set the table?" Stevie nodded. "I thought we could eat on the patio. It's still nice and cool outside."

"That sounds wonderful?"

"How much time do you have?" he asked while pointing Lucy towards the plates and silverware.

"I'm good. I don't have to be in until 10:00 or 10:30. But, I'll have to go home first."

"I'll drive you."

Ten minutes later, they sat down to goat cheese omelets, fresh fruit salad, toast and coffee.

"Now, this is the way to wake up in the morning," Lucy said.

"It wasn't a bad way to go to sleep, either," Stevie answered with a smile, before his tone turned more serious. "Thanks for listening last night... and thanks for still being here."

Lucy just nodded and reached out to take his hand. "Hey, I'm not going anywhere."

It was a moment before she continued. "I know it must have been awful for you. It must still be. But you were never charged with anything. Why did you leave the police force?"

Stevie chewed on his breakfast for a moment before answering. "No, I wasn't charged. The Department did an internal investigation. They determined that it had been 'a tragic accident'; that there had been 'unique extenuating circumstances' which resulted in our use of deadly force. The family filed a lawsuit against the City, but we were effectively cleared of all wrongdoing."

He took a sip of coffee and then continued.

"It certainly didn't help my career any. They put me behind a desk while they did the internal review and it probably would have delayed any further promotion. But, that wasn't it."

Lucy could see hints of the prior night's emotion simmering just beneath the surface, but Stevie seemed more in control now.

"I had always loved being a cop. I told you that my brother, Frankie, is a cop. But, my father was a cop too – a real hero, rose all the way up through the ranks to become Chief of Detectives. I had wanted to be a cop as long as I can remember. I bought into the whole idea, the whole image. I wanted to be out there keeping the streets safe, protecting people from murderers and criminals."

He took another sip of coffee.

"And, it was great. I loved it. I had lots of success; made some high profile arrests; got promoted quickly; led some major investigations; and made Lieutenant as fast as anyone in Department

159

history. I was Joe Corra's son; I was destined for great things.

"But, over time, something happened. It started to sour for me. Me and my guys were out there on the streets busting kids for nickels and dimes, hoping to build cases against guys who were running things further up the food chain. These kids never had much of a chance to begin with, but once we sent them to Rikers or prison upstate a couple of times, they were done. They were just ex-cons with criminal records who'd never get hired for a straight job in the real world. The only thing they could do from that point forward was work corners... or something worse. Instead of taking 'bad guys' off the street, we were producing a whole new generation. Shit, there were blocks in my district where it seemed like every kid in every building had done time.

"It just started to get to me. It didn't make any sense. At one point, I learned that some of my guys were stealing drugs from dealers in order to feed their CIs – their Confidential Informants. I didn't *really* know; I certainly didn't *want* to know; but I *knew*. That just killed me. What were we doing? Half of the people we were arresting were actually victims, either of their own addictions or the poverty they grew up in. We were turning them into criminals. And, now we – the cops – were actually dealing drugs."

Stevie paused for a moment, organizing his thoughts.

"I wasn't really all that clear about this back then. Being a cop is a lot like being in combat. You can't spend a lot of time wondering if you are doing the right thing. You just have to go out there and do it. But, I knew something was wrong... and it was bothering me. I started drinking more than I had before. In hindsight, I realize I was depressed and I wasn't processing my feelings. There wasn't anyone on the job I could talk to... and I wasn't sharing any of this with Sandy.

"After the shooting, things just fell apart completely. Half of the department looked at me like I was damaged goods. The other half gave me all this gung ho support. People were telling me it wasn't my fault; it was a freak accident. There were even guys saying that it didn't matter; the kid was just another mutt who was going to wind up dead on the streets anyway. I couldn't stand it. Once they pulled me out of the field and put me in a desk job, I really started drinking.

"That's when things got worse at home. Sandy and I hadn't been doing too well for a while. She started talking about leaving...and, at that point, I didn't care... I didn't care about anything. I told her that they could keep the house and I would go. I moved in here."

Once again, Lucy saw the same pain etched on Stevie's face as the night before.

"As soon as I did that, I knew that I had hit bottom. I had lost my family, hated my job which had meant everything to me, and might even be going to jail. I started looking for help.

"Jim Donnelly, who runs BFS, was an old family friend. I had gotten to know him better myself over the years when we tried to run some programs together. He was someone who I felt I could talk to ... and would understand what I was talking about. I called him and he was great. He spent a lot of time with me himself and hooked me up with a therapist. Between the two of them, they helped me sort out my feelings about the job. I realized I just couldn't do it any more... didn't want to do it any more... and decided to leave."

"That was a pretty big step," said Lucy.

"Yes, it was. Jim actually offered me the job at BFS. He convinced me that I had some skills and personal experiences that could be useful in working with kids."

"So, that's how you got to BFS. It seems like it was a good decision."

"I think it was," Stevie nodded. "The money sucks... I'm barely making a third of what I was making as an NYPD Lieutenant. But, I like what I do... most of the time. I feel like I'm helping kids rather than locking them up. I wish the system worked better... but that's always true wherever you are.

"My father has never forgiven me for leaving," he continued, a tone of regret clear in his voice. "He feels like I'm a quitter; that somehow it was like admitting I was guilty in the shooting. He's never understood why I want to do what I am doing now."

"You're no quitter," Lucy offered. "You've just finally found your own way."

"That may be true, but my father had a plan... for his life... and for mine and Frankie's. Part of it is that my leaving just reflected badly on him. He retired a couple of years later. I'm pretty sure he thinks it's my fault that he never got promoted to Chief of Department."

"What about your marriage," she added, a little hesitantly.

"The therapist helped me deal with that as well. The marriage had really been over long before it finally ended. A lot of it was my fault… but not entirely. I had always blamed our problems on the job; so did Sandy. But it was more than that. Relationships take two people to make them work. We just grew apart. By the time we split up, there was no going back.… I just feel bad about Joey. Like I said, it's been really hard on him."

Lucy nodded understandingly. They sat together in silence, as the morning sun slowly warmed the garden air. Stevie watched as Lucy eased back in her chair, the loose cotton robe sliding along her bare, olive skin.

"Maybe we should think about getting ready for work?" he suggested reluctantly.

Lucy eyed him mischievously with one arched brow; then rose, circled the table and took his hand. "There's something else I think we should do first."

Stevie simply smiled. "You know how to cheer a guy up," he said; then followed her back into the apartment.

As they walked towards the bedroom, the mood was shattered by the sound of his cell phone ringing on the kitchen counter. Stevie looked at Lucy with a grimace and picked up the phone.

"It's my brother, Frankie. I need to take it."

Lucy nodded with shrug of disappointment.

"Frankie, what's up?" he said, his eyes still focused hopefully on Lucy. Instantly, she saw Stevie's gaze turn away as he concentrated his full attention on the phone call. "Christ! … How? …Where? …Why? …Sure, I can be there in about…45 minutes. Yeah, I'll see you soon."

"What is it?" Lucy asked as he hung up.

He looked at her in a stunned silence before answering.

"It's Levon Marbury. He's dead."

35

Fifteen minutes later, they drove north on Flatbush Avenue towards Lucy's apartment. As they dressed, Stevie had relayed the skimpy details gleaned from the phone call. Levon Marbury had been found dead in a parked car not far from Melody's apartment. He had been shot three times. While still too soon to be certain, it looked like he had been killed within the past few hours, as Wednesday night prepared to become Thursday morning. Frankie wanted his brother to come and look at something; he wouldn't say what it was.

Steve and Lucy rode together in near silence. Any ideas about further lovemaking had been displaced by news of yet another murder, this one even more closely linked to Melody and Shaquan. Now, their thoughts were focused on what this might mean for their respective clients. Were they safer now that Levon had been killed? Or, did this mean that mortal danger was even nearer?

"I'll call you as soon as I know anything," Stevie said as he pulled to the curb in front of Lucy's building. She nodded. He once again recognized the fear that had crept back into her eyes.

"I'll keep my cell phone on."

They leaned towards each other and kissed, their lips briefly locked in a reluctant farewell. Then, Lucy climbed out of the car and hurried into her building.

It was just another 15 minutes before Stevie pulled up at the address Frankie had given – a vacant lot at the corner of Pine Street and Saratoga Avenue that had been commandeered as makeshift parking for a rag tag fleet of delivery trucks, vans and private cars. The perimeter of the lot had been sealed off with the seemingly ubiquitous yellow and blue NYPD "Police Line" tape and surrounded by the usual collection of Department vans and patrol cars. A handful of detectives – including Frankie and Jimmy Williams – focused their attention on a black SUV that was wedged between a bread truck and a well-worn gypsy cab.

He climbed out of the car and called to his brother, who nodded his approval for a watchful patrolman as Stevie crossed the line. It was a step he had taken thousands of times and, surprisingly, was becoming all too familiar once again.

He slipped past a team from the Coroner's Office waiting for the call to load the body onto their still empty gurney. Frankie stood talking to Tommy Quinn near the back of the SUV. A crime lab tech was up next to the open driver side door, taking photos of the body as Jimmy Williams hovered behind, pointing at details and asking for specific shots.

"We've got to stop meeting like this," Quinn said as he approached.

"That's for sure," Stevie answered and nodded a greeting to his brother. "So, Frankie, what do you guys have here?"

"Well, it looks like your old friend Levon Marbury pissed somebody off. One of the drivers got an unpleasant surprise when he came to pick up his truck this morning at about 6:00. It looks like someone capped him from the passenger side of the car… maybe three times… twice in the torso and once in the head."

Stevie nodded at the information, then pointed to that side of the car. "Do you mind?"

"Go right ahead," Frankie answered with a wave. "But don't touch anything."

The older Corra tossed his brother a dirty look. "Gee, thanks, I'd almost forgotten."

The passenger side door was already open. He peered across the front seat and studied the bullet-riddled body of Levon Marbury slumped forward against the steering wheel. Stevie was stunned by the sudden realization that he'd never actually seen Levon before. Marbury had played a major role in the tragedy that was Shaquan's life. It was his beatings of both Melody and Shaquan that had led to the boy's removal and placement into foster care in the first place. Stevie had heard the stories; read the reports; even seen the pictures that served as proof of Levon's vicious brutality. He felt like he knew the man. Yet, they had never met. Stevie had never set eyes on him until this moment as he stared at Levon's lifeless body.

He visually examined the gunshot wounds that Frankie had described. The shots to the torso were both on Levon's right side. The kill shot had entered just above the right eye and exited, taking bits of skull and brain with it, at the back of Levon's head. There was blood everywhere. To Stevie, it seemed obvious that Marbury had been killed by someone in the passenger seat – the first two shots coming as a sudden and deadly surprise; the head shot, a finishing touch as Levon turned in horror to face his killer.

Stevie studied the passenger seat and the floor around it for any visible signs of who might have used it last. There was only the usual collection of dirt and bits of debris – gum wrappers, a fast food container, crumpled napkins and an empty coffee cup – littering the floor of the SUV.

"Any prints?" Stevie asked, as he returned to the small group of detectives.

"We're not sure. The lab guys aren't finished yet," said Jimmy Williams who had left the photographer to complete his work without further supervision. Jimmy mopped his black brow, already sweaty from his exertions and the morning's rapidly rising humidity.

"So," said Frankie, focusing his gaze on his brother. "See anything familiar?"

Stevie stepped back to take in the entire scene. He looked at the tinted windows and recalled the mental image of the car that had followed him home on Monday night. "It could be. It's hard to be sure," he said.

Then, he bent down and stared at the plate. Some bits of tar and dirt had been carefully splattered across the numbers, making a clear reading almost impossible. "That looks right," he said, turning back to the group. "If the plate bulb is out, then I'd say it's probably the one."

"Good," said Frankie. "So, it looks like it was Levon who was tailing you."

"Is it his car?"

"Yeah," answered Quinn. "We just ran the plates. Levon was the registered owner."

Stevie nodded. He was surprised by the sense of relief that swept over him. Someone who had already hurt Shaquan and Melody – and could still have been a threat to them … as well as to himself and Lucy – was dead. The possibility that Levon also might have been involved in another recent murder came back to him almost as an afterthought.

"Where are you on the Lakiesha Smalls case?" Stevie asked.

Jimmy Williams chuckled softly. "Maybe this closes that case."

"Really?" Stevie shot back, his voice rising with an edge of sarcasm and anger. "Now isn't that just so convenient?"

"Hold it," Frankie interrupted. "Jimmy had already been coming over to your point of view. He told me yesterday afternoon that he was starting to like Levon for the Smalls murder."

The older detective nodded in agreement. "After we talked, I went back and looked at Levon's sheet. He'd had a couple of busts involving use of a knife. There was one where he had sliced a girl up and down the side of her face, just like Lakeisha."

"O.K. Sorry," Stevie said with a hint of an apologetic smile. "What about this one? Got any ideas on who might have done Levon?"

"No, not yet," said Williams.

"Anyone see or hear anything?"

"No, of course not," Jimmy answered.

Stevie looked at the car again; then scanned the rest of the lot and the surrounding buildings. "This wasn't Levon's regular spot, was it?"

"No, we don't think so," said Quinn. "The driver who found the body said he had never seen this car parked there before."

"So, Stevie, you got any ideas about this one?" Frankie asked.

"You seem to have been one step ahead of us on this all along."

Stevie looked at his brother and then at the other two detectives before shaking his head. "Not really! Levon was living with Melody at the building where Rue James got shot. Maybe he saw something... or somebody thought he saw something."

The group nodded in unison.

"Any leads in that case?" Stevie asked.

Again the three remained silent until Frankie spoke. "It's not our case," he said, an undertone of bitterness in his voice. "We'll check with your buddy Jack Schwinn."

Stevie started to respond, but thought better of it.

"I'm done here," the photographer interrupted. "If it's OK with you guys, I'll have them take the body."

Jimmy nodded his approval and turned back to Stevie. "Any luck in finding your kid or his mother?"

Corra's heart sank at the question... and the answer he had to give. "No. There is no sign of them." He watched as the Coroner's men bundled Levon's body out of the car and into a body bag that had been laid out on the folding gurney. For the first time, Stevie felt a pang of concern that Shaquan and Melody may have already met a similar fate.

"I need to get going," he said.

"Yeah, sure," Frankie answered. "Thanks for coming over. I'll call you if we get anything more."

Once again, Stevie was just another witness, a civilian being dismissed.

36

Stevie sat for a moment in his car, absorbing the crime scene activity stretched out before him. The shock of Levon Marbury's murder was only just settling in. Stevie certainly felt nothing for the man. He had only brought tragedy and heartache, violence and perhaps death, to those people Stevie did care about. However, his killing was another step in a path of human devastation that seemed to be leading relentlessly towards Shaquan and his mother. Yet, at the same time, Stevie still had absolutely no idea where Melody and the boy could possibly be. They had, with the exception of a single phone call, completely disappeared.

Stevie started the car and pulled away, his thoughts still lost in a maze of unanswered questions. For the second time in days, he suddenly found himself unconsciously driving towards Melody's apartment – only blocks from where her former lover and abuser now lay stretched out inside a Medical Examiner's body bag. He had no idea what he expected to find. His actions, he suddenly realized, were simply an instinctual response to having lost Shaquan's trail, no different than a dog circling back to pick up a lost scent at the last place he'd found it.

Only minutes later, Stevie was approaching Melody's building, driving up the same side street along which he had walked on his first visit. It was still early, only a little past 10:00 a.m., and the stoop and sidewalk were empty. The corner, it seemed, was not yet open for business.

He cruised by slowly, carefully studying the building for signs of life. There were none. Most of the windows in the four-story structure were sealed off by drawn curtains in a hodgepodge of drab and mismatched colors. The inhabitants apparently wanted neither to see nor be seen by those who did business on the street below.

At the corner, Stevie turned left onto the avenue and slipped into a parking space directly opposite the back alley where Rue James had been killed. Deep inside, below the window to Melody's apartment, was a parked car facing out towards the street. The vehicle was another black SUV, standard G.I. – Ghetto Issue – with darkened windows and polished chrome. With the look and feel of an urban armored personnel carrier, it was virtually indistinguishable from the one in which Levon Marbury had just been murdered; an identical twin to that which had tried to follow him home two nights before.

Stevie suddenly realized that a driver, possibly sitting unseen behind the SUV's tinted windshield, could be staring right at him. He quickly slid down and reclined the seat back as far as it could go so that he was peering, almost unnoticeably, through the very bottom front corner of the Subaru's rear driver-side window. Stevie watched and waited, hoping against hope that no pedestrian would stroll down his side of the street and bring attention to the strange white man sprawled out inside his car.

Stevie didn't have long to wait. Suddenly the heavy metal door leading out into the alley from the back of Melody's building swung open. Three men emerged. The first, he recognized as young "Romeo" who he had seen on his last visit. The second was a stranger, tall and trim; someone who obviously knew how to handle himself. The third was Back Thompson.

Back was the picture of an urban street boss. He wore a brightly colored, short-sleeved silk shirt open over a tight black tank top that accentuated his broad and muscular chest. He carried himself with an air of power and authority. Romeo dashed around the front of the SUV and climbed behind the wheel. Back slipped up into the passenger seat. Number three sat in the back, undoubtedly ready to open fire in any direction at the first sign of trouble.

Stevie struggled to make himself as small and as invisible as possible. It seemed incomprehensible that they would not spot him. He lay back in his seat, tucked as low as he could get below the car windows, almost afraid to breathe. At any moment he expected to hear the sounds of surprised and angry shouting, then perhaps shots. At first, he heard nothing. Then, to his indescribable relief, the SUV engine roared to life as it pulled out of the alley and turned sharply to the left, as far away from the Subaru as possible under the circumstances.

Stevie waited until the sound of the SUV had completely disappeared before he rose up in the driver seat and gave himself permission to breathe again. That had been a close call. Stevie had survived his last encounter with Back Thompson through a combination of bluster and bravado. He wasn't looking forward to trying it again – particularly if Back felt the need to make a show of strength in front of his crew.

Clearly, this was not the entourage of just another gangsta who ran a single corner. Back had stepped up in the world since his boss had been killed. The question, Stevie wondered, was whether Back had taken it upon himself to make that promotion possible.

Despite his very real concerns about another confrontation with the drug dealer, Stevie felt a nearly irresistible urge to go back into the building. He understood that there was no possibility whatsoever that Melody would be back in her apartment, sitting down to a late breakfast with Shaquan. Nevertheless, there was something drawing him to go inside.

After a few minutes hesitation, he stepped out of the car and walked slowly up the avenue to the corner opposite Melody's building. There were still no signs of any business activity – no lookouts on the corner, no kids with a stash next to the stoop, no one at all.

Stevie waited for the light to change and crossed the avenue, continuing to study every detail of the block in front of him. Everything looked clear.

When he got to Melody's building, he quickly climbed the steps and hit the buzzers, one by one, until he got a buzz back that unlocked the front door. With a last look up and down the street behind him, Stevie stepped inside and carefully closed the front door. Once again, he heard an apartment door open on one of the upper floors.

"Leroy, is that you?" someone called.

"No," he answered brusquely. "I hit the wrong buzzer."

After a muttered insult came the sound of a firmly closed and locked door.

Stevie climbed the same rickety staircase to the dimly lit second-floor landing. At the back of the hallway, where he had last seen the shattered doorway to Melody's ransacked apartment, was a freshly installed steel door. The wooden door jam, which had been ripped almost entirely off of the walls, was now replaced with a new single-piece, heavy-duty, metal frame.

Against his better judgment, Stevie rapped his knuckles on the metal door. There was no answer. He waited a moment, then knocked again, this time pounding his fist on the door. The sounds reverberated through the old building.

As if déjà vu, Stevie was stunned to hear the apartment door nearer the front of the building open, ever so slightly and the same, elderly woman eyed him once again through the narrow opening.

"Hello," he said softly. "Do you remember me? I'm looking for Melody Saunders and her son, Shaquan."

The woman nodded, just barely, her eyes fixed on Stevie and her hands poised to close and lock the door.

"I showed you his picture last week," he coaxed. "I'm trying to find out if they have been back?"

"No," the woman whispered. "They gone. They didn't come back."

"You told me that Shaquan was here a lot."

She nodded again.

"Was he here the night the man was shot in the alley?"

Stevie could see the flash of fear in her eyes as she began to close the door.

"No! Please, it may help me to find him. He's just a boy," he pleaded. "Was he here that night?"

Again, Stevie waited as she studied him in silence. This woman

171

hadn't lived for almost a century in this neighborhood without understanding the rules of the street. See nothing; say nothing.

"Please," Stevie asked again. "You told me he was a nice boy."

"Yes, he was a nice boy," she nodded. Her eyes softened, perhaps as they thought of other nice boys whom she had known, perhaps her own sons or brothers, and what had happened to them. "Yes," she said, her whisper falling even lower, barely making any sound at all. "He was here that night."

Then, the door closed and the familiar sounds of locks being bolted began; first one, then another.

Stevie stood stock still, absorbing this startling new information and what it could mean. Then, in an instant, his attention turned to the building entrance and the sounds of someone opening the front door. He didn't hesitate. He had no idea whether this might be Back Thompson or one of his crew, but Stevie saw no reason for sticking around to find out. At the rear of the narrow hallway, directly opposite Melody's apartment and hidden behind the staircase rising up to the third floor was another doorway. Stevie assumed it was some type of utility closet. He grabbed the handle and was stunned to find it unlocked. Once inside, he was even more surprised to see that it was short set of stairs that led down to the back alley doorway where Thompson had exited only a few minutes before.

As quietly as possible, Stevie tiptoed down the stairs, listening with one ear for sounds from the hallway behind him, and with the other for any noise in the back alley below. There was nothing. After a final momentary hesitation, he flipped the deadbolt and swung the heavy steel door open. To his immense relief, there was no fully manned SUV positioned in the alley. There was no one.

Stevie closed the door quietly behind him, walked quickly to the end of the alley and peered both ways up and down Utica Avenue. It looked like any other quiet thoroughfare on a summer morning in Brooklyn. A few pedestrians were scattered in either direction; some kids were playing on the corner; but there were no signs of Back Thompson, his drug dealers or lookouts.

Stevie took a deep breath, casually crossed the avenue, climbed into the Subaru and drove away.

37

"Where the hell have you been?" said Jackie Johnson as she stormed into the office where Stevie Corra was unpacking case records from his shoulder bag. "We were supposed to have supervision an hour ago!"

Shelly Stackowski in the next cubicle looked up in surprise from the telephone where she apparently had been placed on semi-permanent hold by some government bureaucrat.

"Christ, I'm sorry," Stevie said apologetically.

"Leave the Lord out of this," Jackie shot back. "Where have you been?"

"At another murder scene," he answered slowly. "Levon Marbury, Melody Saunder's boy friend, was just found shot to death in his car over in Brownsville."

"Jesus," gasped Jackie.

Shelly looked up in surprise once more; then hung up the phone so she could devote full attention to eavesdropping on their conversation.

Stevie's supervisor was silent for a few minutes as she absorbed the news; then looked at him quizzically. "Why were you there?"

"The police called and asked me to come." He didn't bother to add that it was his brother who was leading the investigation. This was complicated enough already. "Remember I told you that Melody's friend, Lakeisha Smalls, was killed on Monday? …"

Jackie just nodded, as Shelly almost choked on her coffee at this new piece of the story.

"Well, Lucy Montoya from Safe Families and I told the police that we thought Levon could be a possible suspect in Lakeisha's murder…"

"And…?" Jackie prompted, seeing that Stevie was having trouble getting out another, and perhaps even more unpleasant, bit of news.

"And…someone tried to follow me home the other night. The police wanted me to look at Levon's car and see if it was the same one."

"Oh my God," Shelly muttered in amazement.

"What do you mean, someone was following you?" Jackie said, her voice suddenly showing real concern.

Stevie shrugged a deep sigh, before beginning to explain. "On Monday night, I met my brother Frankie for a drink over at this cop bar on Willoughby Avenue. You know, he's an NYPD Captain in Brooklyn Homicide. I've told you about him. It was his unit that got the Lakeisha Smalls case. I went to tell him about the wooden pik that I had seen at Lakeisha's apartment and that Shaquan would have given it to Melody only a couple of days earlier…remember, I told you on Tuesday?"

Jackie nodded.

"Well, on the way home, I suddenly realized that this black SUV seemed to be following me. I made a couple of sudden turns to see if it would stay with me…and it did. It was definitely tailing me."

Shelly just stared at Stevie, her mouth slightly open, hanging on his every word.

"I made a couple of more moves, tried to see if I could find out who it was or get a plate number, but couldn't. Then I lost them and went home… Don't worry," he added, trying to allay the fear and concern he saw in his boss' expression. "Nothing happened. I'm fine."

"What do you mean, don't worry?" Jackie said angrily. "People are getting killed left and right in this case… and someone was following you… at night… on your way home? This thing has gotten way out of our league. This is a matter for the police."

"The police are on it," Stevie said, again trying to reassure his boss. "I told them about it right away. That's why they called me this morning. They wanted to know if I thought it was Levon's car that had been following me."

Jackie nodded before answering. "So, what do you think? Was it Levon's car that you saw the other night?"

He hesitated briefly. "It could have been," he said, thinking back to the morning's events. "But there are a lot of people out there driving those kinds of SUVs." Stevie went no further. He saw no need to share his morning's visit to Melody's apartment and his close encounter with Back Thompson.

"Do the police have any idea where Shaquan might be?" Jackie asked.

"No, not that I know of."

"Are they looking for him?"

"Only because they think Melody might be a witness in the Rue James murder."

Shelly put down her coffee cup and leaned forward into the conversation. "Excuse me, but I'm losing track. Is that two... or three ... murders all together?"

"Three," Stevie clarified.

"Good," Shelly nodded with a deadpan smile. "I just wanted to be sure."

Jackie Johnson turned on Shelly with an intentionally exaggerated look of exasperation. "I thought you were supposed to be on the phone."

Shelly just laughed, waving towards the two of them. "You've got to be kidding... and miss this?"

Jackie shook her head and turned back to Stevie. "Look, I want to find Shaquan as much as anyone. But this is starting to seem really dangerous. I don't want you getting killed in the process. Let the police take the lead on this one. Promise me you'll be careful."

"I promise," he offered, trying to flash his most winning smile.

"Hey, it's not easy finding caseworkers who'll do this for what we pay," she added with a touch of sarcasm.

"That's for sure," Shelly chimed in, now playing the role of

175

Greek chorus.

"Do you want to do supervision?" Stevie asked as Jackie turned to leave.

"I can't now. I'll get back to you to reschedule," she said; then continued. "I may have a spot for Rick Jones in an RTC upstate. I'll know for sure later today. If it comes through, and ACS approves it, you'll have to drive him up there tomorrow. OK?"

"OK!" Stevie responded enthusiastically. Anything that got Rick out of the group home – and into a more appropriate level of care – before he had a complete meltdown was good with him. He'd drive the boy wherever he needed to go. "Just let me know what I have to do."

"I will," said Jackie as she left.

At his desk, Stevie turned back to see that Shelly had never taken her eyes off of him.

"How about lunch," the young woman suggested with a broad smile. "I just have to hear the whole story.

"I'd love to," he answered, "but not today. I'm buried and very far behind… as you might have gathered from that conversation."

Shelly nodded appreciatively. "OK. I'll let you off the hook today, but I'm going to hold you to your promise. Do you want me to bring you back anything?"

"No, thanks," he said, surprised to see that it was already after noon. "I'm good. See you later."

Shelly rose from her desk and headed for the door.

Suddenly, Stevie was alone in the office. He looked at the pile of case records and pushed them to one side; then picked up the phone.

"This is Lucy Montoya." The now familiar sound of her voice as she answered instantly brought back a cascade of emotions from that morning and the night before.

"Hi, Lucy. It's Stevie."

"Hi. How are you? What happened?"

He quickly explained what he had seen and learned after dropping Lucy off several hours earlier. Levon was dead, shot three times by someone as yet unknown. The police had begun to accept Steve and Lucy's theory that Marbury was the likely suspect in the killing of Lakeisha Smalls. And, separately, he'd learned from one of Melody's neighbors that Shaquan had been at his mother's apartment the night that Rue James was shot.

As Stevie finished his narrative, there was only silence. Despite a rapidly escalating spiral of fatal events, there was still no clue as to the whereabouts of either of their clients – Melody or Shaquan.

"What did your brother want you to look at?" Lucy asked.

"Levon's car…" Stevie answered, choosing not to go into detail. "It's complicated. I'll tell you more when I see you."

"I've got a support group that I run on Thursday nights, so, I can't today," Lucy said, a hint of sadness in her voice. Stevie's own disappointment was offset by the realization that Lucy, too, obviously wanted to get together again as soon as possible. "How about tomorrow night?" she suggested. "Would you like to come over for dinner?"

"I'd love to," he said enthusiastically. "I'll give you a call in the morning. Have a good night."

"Thanks. You too," Lucy answered. "And call me if you learn anything new."

"I will. Bye." The joy of hearing her answer the phone was now matched by a twinge of sorrow as she hung up.

Stevie looked at the pile of case files on his desk and then checked the time. It was already close to 1:00. He had a lot of catching up to do this afternoon.

38

Stevie was still entering casework progress notes into the State's "Connections" system when Jackie strode back into his office at a quarter to four.

"O.K, we have a bed for Rick at Taconic Valley's 'hard-to-place' program," she said, dropping a small pile of forms and yellow sticky notes on his desk. "The City has already approved it. You can take him up there tomorrow."

"All right," Stevie exclaimed. It felt like the first good news on any of his cases for weeks. "What did you have to do to get that?"

"You don't want to know," Jackie responded, eying him warily. She quickly walked him through the details of the boy's transfer. "Give Joseph a call and fill him in. He should tell Rick tonight. How do you think he will react?"

"Badly, at least at first," said Stevie. "But, he will be OK once it settles in. He's really not doing well in the house; and he knows it. He's been at Taconic Valley before. I think he actually liked it."

"Let's hope so."

"I'll take a ride out to the house now so I can tell him myself."

"Joseph will appreciate that," Jackie nodded in approval. "When can you leave in the morning?"

"If it's all right with you, I'll go directly to the house and drive him straight to Taconic Valley. It will take most of the day anyway."

"That's fine," Jackie said, turning back towards her office.

"Call and let me know how it goes."

"I will."

Stevie watched his boss leave and picked up the phone to call the group home.

This would be good news; good for Joseph, good for the staff, good for the other kids, but most importantly good for Rick. The Taconic Valley campus with its on-grounds Special Ed school and a dozen residential cottages was nestled in the rolling hills of eastern Dutchess County. It felt and truly was isolated; far from and fundamentally foreign to the world in which its residents had been born and raised. Most kids found their way to Residential Treatment Centers like Taconic Valley through a haphazard path marked by failed foster boarding home placements, multiple AWOLs, psychiatric hospitalizations and a stint or two in Non-Secure Detention while awaiting formal court certification as Juvenile Delinquents or Persons In Need of Supervision.

Too many of the kids – and unfortunately even some staff – viewed RTCs as "kiddie jails", the first stage of basic training for a life that would ultimately lead from one bigger and tougher institution to the next, until the mountains of upstate New York could only be seen through the hazy sheen of coiled razor-wire.

Yet, Stevie knew that Taconic Valley, and RTC's like it, offered some kids – often very, very troubled kids – a chance to work out their problems in the comparative safety and security of an all encompassing world with a 24/7 therapeutic focus. It certainly wasn't any "Ivy League" prep school, but, for an awful lot of kids, it was the best option – at least for a while. Stevie knew in his heart that Rick was one of them.

*   *   *

An hour later, he pulled his Subaru to the curb a half block from the Flatbush Group Home. He had spent most of the drive preparing in his head for what was certain to be a difficult conversation with Rick Jones. As Stevie sat for a moment, gathering his thoughts, he suddenly realized that there was some type of altercation taking place

179

further up the street.

Stevie quickly climbed out of the car and peered along the sidewalk. To his horror, just outside the group home, he saw Mrs. Ramirez and Roger Barnwell, another child care worker, blocking an obviously enraged Rick Jones from going out onto the street. Stevie heard a torrent of screamed curses and violent threats. It took him a moment to realize that Rick was not directing his abuse at the group home staff, but rather past them towards another confrontation taking place still further down the avenue.

Stevie picked up speed and began to jog towards the group home, carefully studying the street before him as he ran. Then, all at once, he saw them. Joseph Otinga stood, his left hand holding Carlos by the arm, pulling him away from a tall, well-muscled man standing next to the open door of a black SUV. Stevie's heart sank. It was the second time that day that he had seen this man... and that car... Back Thompson's car.

"Joseph!" Stevie yelled, as he raced towards the group. "Carlos!"

His sudden shouts interrupted the intense standoff taking place in front of him. The young gangster looked up through aviator sunglasses under the peak of his slightly crooked baseball cap. He stared into the eyes of this foolhardy stranger on the street, and then, after making the connection, just smiled.

Joseph took immediate advantage of the distraction to pull Carlos backwards along the sidewalk, away from the open SUV door.

Again, the dark glasses flashed from Carlos to Joseph and back to Stevie. With another sinister smile, the young man twirled and leaped back into the car. The SUV pulled sharply away from the curb, forcing its way into the traffic on Church Avenue, made the first left and disappeared from view.

"Carlos! Joseph!" Stevie yelled again as he ran towards them. "Are you all right? What happened?"

The boy looked up with lingering terror. Blood trickled from a small patchwork of scrapes and bruises near the edge of his left eye.

"Let's go inside," Joseph suggested. Stevie could hear the forced calm in his voice, but saw a slight trembling as he held out his hand.

"Yes," he answered, wrapping a protective arm around Carlos' shoulders as he led him towards the group home. He couldn't help but look back over his own shoulder to where the SUV had stood just moments before.

Inside, Roger Barnwell continued trying to calm Rick Jones. "I'll trash that mother fucker," the boy shouted, still waving his arms in the direction of the street outside. "He best not be fucking with my man Carlos."

"It's all right," said Mrs. Ramirez, her heavily accented voice soft and soothing. "They are gone now, Rick. They are gone."

Stevie and Joseph led Carlos past the living room and into the kitchen where they settled him into a seat at the large table. Mrs. Ramirez soon followed, grabbing a damp rag and a heavy metal first-aid kit. As she began ministering to Carlos' cuts and bruises, Stevie focused his attention on Joseph.

"What happened?" he asked, feeling uneasy that he might understand more about the incident than Otinga.

"I'm not really sure," Joseph answered, suddenly seeming a little shakier himself as the shock of the encounter began to sink in. "We were inside. Most of the boys were still on their way home from school when we suddenly heard shouting outside. The man in the car had grabbed Carlos and was hitting him…"

"He wanted to know where Shaquan is," Carlos said, turning away from Mrs. Ramirez for the moment. "I told him I didn't know nothing. Then he grabbed me and punched me in the face. He told me I better tell him, or he'd fuck me up." Stevie looked into the boy's eyes. Tears of pain and fear couldn't mask his angry defiance. He knew from Carlos' long case record, that this wasn't the first time the boy had been beaten. He'd been through much, much worse.

"Did you know him?" he asked, cautiously. "Have you ever seen him before? Maybe with Shaquan?"

"No! Never! I've never seen him before." Mrs. Ramirez handed Carlos a tissue so that he could clean away the tears and blow his nose.

"Did he know that you were Shaquan's roommate?" Stevie ask, perplexed.

"I don't know," the boy answered, still surprised and unsure of what had happened and why. "He asked me if I was Carlos and did I know Shaquan."

"Did he say anything else?"

"Just that I better tell him where Shaquan was or he was going to fuck me up good. Then, Rick came out and started yelling. That's when Joseph came, just before you got here..." Carlos began to tremble and his voice dipped into a whisper. "I thought he was going to take me in the car..."

Stevie reached out and placed his hand on Carlos' shoulder. "It's OK," he said, trying to believe what he was saying. "You're OK. He's gone now. You're safe here with us."

"But what if he comes back," Carlos asked, once again looking up with tear streaked eyes.

Stevie studied the boy in silence as he felt a wave of his own anger well up within him.

"He won't be coming back," he said flatly.

"But..."

"He won't be coming back," Stevie interrupted with quiet assurance. "Trust me. He won't be back."

He turned to meet the searching gaze of Joseph Otinga. The House Manager stared at him in silence for a moment, as if attempting to determine what it was he had just learned about his co-worker. "We will need to report this," Joseph said after a moment.

"Yes, we will," Stevie answered. "But, we have 24 hours to file the report. Let's let things settle down."

"Are you sure," Joseph asked, one eyebrow rising in uncertainty.

"Yes," Stevie said without hesitation. "I'll take care of it." Then, he turned and looked back distractedly toward the living room. "I need to talk with Rick."

"I can do that," Joseph said.

"Are you sure?"

"Yes. That's not a problem. Rick will be fine."

"O.K.," Stevie said, looking down at Carlos once more before turning back to Joseph. "Then, I'm going to take off."

"O.K," Otinga said slowly as he followed Corra back down the hallway. "Steve, I'm not exactly sure what it is you are going to do. But, I think you should be very careful."

Stevie forced a soft laugh. "Don't worry, Joseph. I'll be careful." He reached out and touched his friend's arm as he saw the worry etched on his dark, round face. "I'll see you tomorrow morning. Good luck with Rick."

39

The trip from the Flatbush Group Home to Melody's apartment in the heart of Brownsville seemed to take almost no time at all. Stevie drove as if powered by an inner fury, yet one he knew must be kept in check as he prepared for the encounter to come. Surprisingly, an odd calm settled over him as he drew nearer to what potentially could be a fatal confrontation.

At a stop light on the corner of Powell and Vernon, he reached over into the canvas backpack on the passenger seat. Pushing aside a collection of notebooks and case files, he pulled out the Glock 19 which he had retrieved from his gun safe two nights earlier. Stevie didn't think he'd actually need it, but it was nice to know the gun was there. He slid the clip holster onto the waistband of his jeans and tucked it underneath the bottom of his loose shirt.

He drove towards Melody's building from the south along Utica Avenue. As he slowly crossed Livonia, Stevie looked to his left into the side street and saw that the corner was up and running. The tall dealer who had been working with Back during his first visit a week earlier now lounged on the top step, seemingly in command. A teenager was at the bottom of the stoop talking to a customer who would soon be directed to an even younger accomplice across the street where he'd pay his cash and get his vials.

Stevie continued through the intersection and up the avenue. At the end of the building, he saw the black SUV once again backed into the alley, neatly parked on the spot where Rue James had been murdered. He felt a jolt of anxiety mixed with rage at the realization that Back Thompson and the young punk who had just roughed up Carlos would likely be in the building, unaware that they were about to have a surprise visitor.

He made a left at the corner and drove slowly up to the next avenue where he made another left, gradually circling the block. As Stevie approached Livonia from the opposite end, he began a series of slow and steady deep breaths, forcing the carbon dioxide out of his lungs, slowing his heartbeat and focusing on what was about to take place.

Stevie made the final left onto Livonia, now approaching the building from the west. For the first quarter of the block, he maintained a steady speed. Then, all at once, he stamped his foot onto the accelerator, instantly hurling the car forward as fast as the aging Subaru, its engine screaming as if in pain, could manage. Stevie watched as the sudden appearance of a car hurtling up the street towards them roused the players into a near panic. The new boss at the top of the stoop looked around in alarm. His assistant on the sidewalk made an instinctive move to break and run; then froze, uncertain of what to do next.

No sooner had he hit the gas than Stevie just as suddenly stomped on the brake, bringing the car to a squealing, skidding stop directly in front of Melody's building. He threw the door open before the Subaru had even stopped moving.

"Don't anybody move!" he shouted, using a voice he hadn't heard for more than five years, as he leaped out of the car. "Nobody's going to get hurt! Nobody's going to jail!" He held his two hands up and out in front, palms facing the building as if to stop the crew in their tracks. The hands were empty and unthreatening; no gun, no badge.

Stevie knew that he could dominate the first critical seconds through a combination of bluster, feigned authority and carefully created confusion. He watched as the dealers grappled to understand who this crazy white man was who had burst in on their lives. Was he a cop? Was he a rival? Was he alone? Did he have back up?

"I need to see Back," Stevie said calmly, striding past Number Two on the sidewalk and focusing on the young hoodlum at the top of the stairs.

"I don't know what you're talk'n 'bout," he answered, quickly trying to shake off the shock of this sudden development.

"Don't bullshit me, asshole," Stevie shot back. "I want to talk to Back. I know he's here. Tell him it's Stevie Corra."

The lanky young gangster strutted forward in an exaggerated show of defiance, but remained silent. Stevie could see that he was trying desperately to decide what his next move should be. Luckily, the decision was made for him when the front door to the building swung open and Back Thompson stepped out onto the top of the stoop, followed closely by the Aviator Shades who had most recently been outside the Flatbush Group Home.

"What the fuck do you want," Back said threateningly. "I told you to stay away from here."

"We need to talk! You sent your punk here to rough up one of my kids." Behind Thompson, Stevie saw the tall hoodlum shift from side to side. He could feel the angry glare coming from behind the darkened lenses. "You're looking for Melody Saunders and her son. Well none of the kids in that house have any clue where they are. If they knew, I'd know. And, if I knew, Shaquan would be safe at home now."

Back Thompson simply shrugged, staring at Stevie with cold, black eyes, his lips tightening into a grimace as hard and sharp as a knife edge.

"So, stay away from my kids."

"Who the fuck are you to be walking into my house, telling me what to do...what not to do," Back exploded, spitting out the words in a torrent of rage.

"You know exactly who I am," Stevie countered, leaning forward into the eye of the fury.

"I know who you *waaaas*," Thompson sneered, stretching out the word to stress that Stevie's past power had been lost long, long ago. "You ain't *nobody* now. Nobody! I ought to just cap your shitty, little, social worker ass and be done with it."

"I don't think so," Stevie answered, stepping up till he was toe to toe with Thompson, their faces only inches apart. "Once a cop; always a cop. You know the drill. It's just like the Bloods or the Crips. It's a gang, Back, the biggest gang in the City.... 30,000 strong. My brother's a Captain in Homicide; my father was Chief of Detectives... *CHIEF OF DETECTIVES*...You don't get any higher than that. I've got cousins and uncles in every precinct, every bureau in the Department. I practically ran Brooklyn North Narcotics, and I still have plenty of friends there. You cap me and I bleed NYPD blue all over you, until you drown in the shit that rains down.... you and every one of your sorry little crew." He paused and looked slowly from Back to each of his men, making it clear that he was burning their faces into his memory for future reference.

"So, like I said," Stevie continued, slowly releasing his words with sizzling menace. "Stay away from my kids. They don't know anything. Don't fuck with them! Don't fuck with me! It's only going to get you into a world of hurt."

He had no need to wait for a response. None was coming. Back Thompson stood in angry silence, seething at the realization that Stevie was beyond his grasp... and always would be.

Their eyes met once more as Stevie confirmed for himself that his message had been received. Then, he turned, strode down the steps, climbed back into his car, and pulled away.

40

Stevie drove for three blocks, heading north on Utica, before it hit him. Shudders racked his body as he began to crash off the adrenaline overdose that had fueled his street theater performance. The toxic residue of all-too-reasonable fears, fears that Stevie had successfully suppressed during the confrontation with Back and his crew, resurfaced now, sending his heart racing and erupting in a cold sweat. He knew at this moment, just as he had known beforehand, that any miscue, any sign of weakness or self-doubt, could have been fatal.

Stevie resisted an urge to pull over and continued driving mindlessly north towards Atlantic Avenue. Gradually his nerves began to settle once again. Suddenly, the sound of his cell phone, its harsh ring exaggerated within the close quarters of the Subaru, shattered the calm.

"Hello," he answered, picking up the phone without bothering to check who it was.

"Stevie," his brother Frankie said at the other end of the connection. "Where are you?"

"I'm in the car. I'm on Atlantic Avenue…," he hesitated for a moment before explaining further. "I'm on my way back from a home visit. What's up?"

"Are you busy? I'd like to talk with you."

"That works. I've got nothing I need to do," Stevie answered. There was something in his brother's tone that sounded strange. "Is anything wrong?"

"No! No," Frankie repeated reassuringly.

"Is it something to do with the Levon Marbury killing?"

"Yes. But let's get together and talk. Why don't we meet at The Cumberland? I'm ready for a drink."

"Me, too," Stevie answered, surprised at how appealing the thought of a scotch on the rocks suddenly seemed. "I can be there in about 15 minutes."

"Same here," Frankie confirmed. "See you there."

*   *   *

Stevie got to the bar even faster than he'd expected. It was a Thursday night, and the crowd – reinforced by folks already in a weekend frame of mind – was a little thicker than when he'd met his brother on Tuesday. Luckily, a pair of nine-to-fivers who had stopped in for a couple of quick ones were just heading home for the night and Stevie grabbed two stools at the far end of the bar. Minutes later, he saw his brother walk through the front door.

"Hey," said Frankie as he slid onto the stool next to Stevie. He nodded to the bartender who lumbered into action. "Johnnie, Black, on the rocks."

"I'll have the same, with a seltzer on the side," Stevie added, as he laid a $20 on the bar.

"So," he continued, turning to his brother. "What's going on?"

"We're starting to get lab results back on the Levon Marbury case," Frankie said. He waited for the bartender to finish pouring the drinks before he continued. "We were able to get three different sets of prints from the passenger side of the car … on the dash and the door handle."

The two brothers each paused to take a burning, yet soothing sip of their liquor.

"So, what did you find," Stevie prompted.

"We were only able to get a match on one of the sets," Frankie answered slowly, taking another hit of his scotch before turning to face his brother squarely. "It was your boy, Shaquan Saunders."

The words took Stevie's breath away.

"What?" he gasped. "Shaquan?"

"Yeah," Frankie nodded, his voice flat and factual. "He had been arrested on assault charges about a year ago. So, his prints were in the system."

"Yes," Stevie said, his mind spinning. "He had gone after one of Melody's boyfriends with a knife. The guy had been abusing her. Christ, Shaquan was only 14 at the time. He got the shit kicked out of him. In light of the circumstances, we were able to get it knocked down to simple assault with an adjournment in contemplation of dismissal. He had to go to therapy."

"So, what do you think Shaquan was doing in Levon's car?"

"Shit," Stevie muttered. "I don't know…I mean it was his mother's boyfriend's car. Maybe he had been in it earlier."

"I thought you said that Shaquan and Levon weren't exactly on the best of terms."

"They weren't," Stevie acknowledged. "Shaquan hated Levon. The prick had beaten the boy senseless a bunch of times before he went into foster care. For all practical purposes, Levon was the reason Shaquan went into care. And Levon was still abusing Melody…"

Stevie hesitated for a moment and then turned his searching gaze onto Frankie. "You're not thinking Shaquan killed Levon, are you?"

The younger Corra just sighed. "Why not? You've already told me that he hated Levon. He's got a history of assault with a deadly weapon… against another one of Melody's boyfriends, for that matter. And, his prints are in the car." Frankie paused to let the facts add themselves up. "What's not to like?"

"No," Stevie shot back, feeling a surprising anger rise up inside him. Shaquan was one of his kids. He almost felt like someone was attacking his own son. "Shaquan didn't do this! He couldn't have done this!"

"Why not?" Frankie repeated, an edge of anger in his own voice, before he toned it down a notch. "Look, I know that you can't believe your kid did this. And, if that's what you believe, then I believe you. But, we certainly have to consider Shaquan as a candidate for this. You know that."

Stevie just shook his head, still refusing to accept that anyone would think that Shaquan might have killed Levon Marbury.

"Frankie, there's got to be a lot of people who might have wanted Levon dead. He was a long time drug dealer. Shit, he lived in the building where Rue James got shot. Whoever did Rue, might have done Levon. What about Back Thompson?"

"Yeah," Frankie nodded thoughtfully. "That all makes sense. The only problem is that I don't have Back Thompson's prints in the car. The only prints I get belong to Shaquan Saunders."

"This is bullshit," Stevie barked back. "There's no fucking way that Shaquan did this. I know the kid. He's not a killer."

"Like I said, I believe you. But I still need to find him and talk to him. Do you have any idea at all where he could be?"

"Christ," Stevie said, shaking his head angrily. "Have you listened to a word I've said for the past week? I don't know where he is. I've come up completely empty. I've got nothing."

"Yeah, all you keep finding is dead bodies."

"That's right," Stevie shot back. "But Shaquan didn't kill any of them."

"If you say so," Frankie answered, his own anger returning, "if you say so. But you're not going to be the only one looking for him from this point forward."

The two brothers sat in silence, each washing down the increasing bitterness of their exchange with a sip of scotch.

Suddenly, their private conversation was interrupted by the sight of Jack Schwinn making his way through the crowd towards them. Behind him, came Brian Finnerty and Robby Calderone.

"I thought I'd find you here," Schwinn said to Frankie, before turning to Stevie. "But, I didn't expect to see you as well."

Corra just nodded.

"Jack," said Frankie, raising his glass towards the Narcotics Lieutenant in a casual greeting. "What can I do for you?"

"We understand that you guys caught the Levon Marbury case this morning," Schwinn said coldly. "You know that we've been looking for Levon and his girlfriend, Melody Saunders, in connection with the Rue James murder. It seems to us that these two cases must be related, so we'd like to take it off your hands."

Frankie gave a short, dismissive laugh. "Well, thanks for your thoughtfulness, but we're OK. We'll take care of this one."

There was a strong negative energy between Jack Schwinn and his brother that Stevie couldn't miss, but didn't understand. Was it just bureaucratic competition? Or, was there something more?

"Come on, Frankie. You know that this is an extension of our case."

"I don't know any such thing," Frankie said, turning the full force of his anger on Schwinn. "There are a lot of ways Levon could have gotten himself killed. And, as for the Rue James case, you never should have pulled that one in the first place. It's a *murder*, right? Doesn't that mean *homicide*?"

"It was a *drug-related* murder," Schwinn shot back. "*Drugs!* That means *Narcotics*. Come on, Frankie, give it up already. Don't make me fight you for it."

"You go do whatever it is you feel you have to do," Frankie said. "I couldn't give a shit."

"Hey, Stevie," Brian Finnerty interjected, his voice dripping with its usual vicious sarcasm. "I hear your foster care kid's prints turned up at the Levon Marbury murder scene; that he's top of the list for potential do-er."

"That's bullshit," Stevie answered, trying to contain his contempt for Finnerty. "Shaquan didn't kill anyone."

"That's not what we're hearing," said Robby Calderone, piling onto the conversation.

"What are you talking about," asked Stevie.

"There's some talk on the street that it's your kid and his mom who did Rue James," Calderone said. "That they took him down for the drugs he was carrying in the alley right behind her apartment."

"You've got to be kidding. Who told you that?"

Jack Schwinn stepped in before anyone else could speak. "Stevie, you know that we can't tell you that. These are C.I.s. It's all confidential."

"It's all bullshit," Stevie exclaimed. "You're telling me that a

16-year-old kid and his little, battered, ex-addict mom took down a major Brooklyn drug boss? That's fucking nonsense."

"It's what we're hearing," Finnerty said again. "And now it looks like he did the Levon Marbury killing... maybe to cover their tracks."

"This is pathetic," Stevie answered. His tone made clear that he would have nothing more to say on the subject.

Schwinn turned his attention back to Frankie. "I'm going to be requesting that the Levon Marbury case be consolidated into our investigation."

The younger Corra turned and held up his glass towards Schwinn once again. "Like I said, you do whatever you want. But I'll fight you on that. As far as I'm concerned you guys are already investigating too many homicides. Now, if you'll excuse me, I'm trying to have a drink with my brother."

Schwinn just stared at Frankie in silence, before turning to make his way back through the crowd and out through the front door.

"See what I mean," Frankie said softly to Stevie, without taking his eyes off the glass on the bar in front of him. "I'm not the only one who thinks that Shaquan's a good fit for the Levon Marbury murder. If he didn't do it, he better come in and prove it."

Stevie just nodded.

Then, Frankie turned and stared into his brother's eyes. "Can I ask you something else?" He reached down and tapped the heavy, metal bulge beneath the shirt on Stevie's right hip. "Why are you carrying a gun?"

41

Stevie awoke at 7:00 on Friday morning, groggy from a poor night's sleep. His final conversation with Frankie had gone about as badly as he could have expected. At first, he had been reluctant to reveal that he'd been out to see Back Thompson – and that he had brought along a loaded gun for the meeting. He felt that his little performance had established an unspoken understanding between himself and the drug dealer. If Back stayed away from the kids in his care, Stevie wouldn't do anything about that first visit and the assault on Carlos. It wasn't necessarily fair or even legal, but he believed that it would keep his kids safe. Right now, that was his first priority.

At the same time, however, Stevie knew that withholding information about Back Thompson's active interest in Shaquan's whereabouts would be totally unforgiveable for Frankie – particularly now that the boy was a "person of interest" in the Levon Marbury murder.

So, Stevie came clean. He fully described the day's events, beginning with the incident at the group home and then his confrontation with Back. Not surprisingly, Frankie exploded. First, he reamed Stevie out for not reporting the initial assault and taking matters into his own hands. "You're not a cop anymore," his brother had screamed. "When are you going to realize that? You're going to get yourself killed." Then, he immediately wanted to haul the drug dealer and his crew in for questioning. The only way Stevie had been able to dissuade him was to point out that Back had to be a suspect in the Rue James case and Frankie would need to coordinate his actions with Jack Schwinn. That was like pouring salt on an open wound. Once again, his brother railed against the injustice – and downright stupidity – of having Brooklyn North Narcotics detectives investigating homicides in his district. It had become something of a pattern, and he didn't like it. In the end, Frankie agreed to hold off on going after Back Thompson, at least until there was a final decision on Schwinn's request to take over the Levon Marbury case.

Stevie had spent the rest of the night tossing and turning in worry over where Shaquan was and exactly how much more danger he'd gotten himself into.

He climbed out of bed and immediately decided to skip his usual morning run around the park. He was sitting down to coffee and breakfast when his cell phone rang. Half expecting to hear from Lucy, Stevie was surprised to see that it was Sandy on the phone.

"Hi," he answered.

"Hi," his ex-wife said, a little awkwardly. "I hope I'm not calling too early."

"No. I'm just having breakfast. Is everything OK? "

"Something's come up," she said, her voice sounding a little strained. "We're not going away to the country. So, I was wondering if you'd like to take Joey for the weekend."

"Uh, sure," Stevie answered, surprised by the sudden change in plans. "What happened?" he asked; then immediately regretted the question.

"It was… Something just came up. We had to cancel." Sandy clearly didn't want to discuss her personal life any further. "Can you pick up Joey tonight?"

"Uh…" Stevie hesitated, thinking through the day's schedule … and his date to meet Lucy for dinner. "I don't think that will work," he continued. "I've got to take a kid upstate. I'm not sure what time I'll be back. And…I've got some plans for later."

"Oh," Sandy said with a mixture of surprise and irritation.

"I'll pick him up in the morning," Stevie said quickly. "What time is good for you?"

"Why don't I drop him at your place at 9:30?" Sandy suggested.

"I am going into the office."

"Sure, that sounds great. There's a soccer game. So Joey will be able to play. Bring his uniform and equipment."

"I will," Sandy answered before quickly moving to get off the phone. "Look, I need to go. I just wanted to make sure I caught you."

"Yeah, sure, I'll see you tomorrow."

Stevie hung up, feeling a twinge of guilt that he had backed out of picking up his son so that he could see Lucy that evening. The plans had already been made, he told himself, trying to put it out of his mind. They'd have a good time for the rest of the weekend.

*   *   *

An hour later, he pulled up to the Flatbush Group Home. All the kids, with the exception of Rick Jones, were already up and off to school. Stevie checked in first with Joseph Otinga.

"How did it go with Rick?" he asked.

"He is OK," Joseph confirmed. "He put up an argument at first, but I think it was a bit of a show. He will be happier on a bigger campus with more kids and more staff. He did all right the last time he was at Taconic Valley. He has some friends there and he likes some of the staff."

"That's what I was hoping," Stevie said, relieved that the transfer had not posed more of a problem.

"How about Carlos?" he continued. "Was he OK after the incident yesterday afternoon?"

"Yes," Joseph said. "He was a little bruised up but there were no other problems. Carlos is a pretty tough little guy."

"He sure is."

"Stevie," Otinga continued, eyeing him warily. "We need to file an incident report."

"I know," Stevie answered reassuringly. "I'll take care of it and I'll make sure you have a copy for the files. There won't be any more problems."

"OK," Joseph said cautiously. "I trust you."

"Thanks. I guess I should find Rick and get going."

"He's finishing packing. I'll help him down with his things."

A few minutes later, Rick appeared in the living room with one large duffle bag and a canvas backpack. It certainly wasn't much in the way of personal possessions for a 17-year-old in the richest country on earth. Yet, Stevie took at least some satisfaction in the fact that BFS didn't send the boy off with his clothing stuffed in a black plastic garbage bag. He had seen far too many kids arrive that way, carrying what seemed like a symbol of how society viewed the children themselves.

During the first hour of the trip, as they drove through Brooklyn and Queens, over the Triborough Bridge, and then north out of the Bronx, Rick had maintained a stony silence, passively acting out his anger at just one more sudden detour in the path of his young life – a change of direction over which he had no control whatsoever. Gradually, however, Stevie had been able to chip away at the defenses, asking about his prior placements at Taconic Valley, whether they had any friends in common among the campus staff. Kids who had been in foster care as long as Rick were like lifers in the army; they'd spent time at institutions and group homes all over the City and much of the state. They knew their way around the system. Sadly, it was the thing they knew best, a set of coping skills that had helped them to survive. It didn't take much to get them talking about it.

The second hour of their drive was probably the most productive conversation Stevie had ever had with Rick. Enclosed together inside the humming Subaru, with brick and concrete gradually giving way to green forests and open fields, the two had settled into a "road trip" frame of mind. Rick had shared some stories of his prior placements, friendships he had made and lost, things he liked to do and some he definitely didn't. Looking out onto the passing countryside, he'd even talked about a trip he thought he'd made down south once with his own mother, a woman who now existed only in the haziest reaches of his childhood memory.

It was only as they neared the Taconic Valley campus that Rick fell back into silence, emotionally preparing to prove himself once again among an entirely new group of kids and adults, establishing that he was no one to fuck with, but rather a force in his own right. Stevie understood what he was going through and gave the boy the space he needed.

Upon their arrival, they were directed to the administration building, a two-story, gray stone structure nestled on a hillside that rose gradually eastward towards the Connecticut border. To the left, was a large, modern-looking high school that easily could fit in any suburban community; to the right, scattered over a half dozen acres of grassy fields, were a collection of long, low cottages, each housing 22 troubled teenagers.

Rick took a seat on a long wooden bench in the reception area while Stevie went in to meet with the Taconic Valley intake worker. They had met before on a number of occasions. The middle-aged, yet still trim and athletic, social worker quickly sorted through Rick's file, assuring herself that all required documents were on hand. She and Stevie briefly discussed Rick's history, conversing in a mixture of professional jargons that bridged the clinical and legal worlds of psychiatry, social work and juvenile justice. Once satisfied that she had everything that was needed, she called in Rick and welcomed him back to Taconic Valley.

BFS would continue to have "case management" responsibility for Rick Jones. So, Stevie assured the boy that they would see each other again soon. Despite the openness and intimacy of their recent drive, he could see Rick's stare glazing over with a mixture of fear and self-protective defiance. It was a sight that almost brought tears to Stevie's own casework-hardened eyes. He reached out and gave the boy a brief hug, urging him to make the most out of the services at his new home. Then, he turned, walked out to his car and began the two-and-one-half hour drive back to Brooklyn.

42

It was almost 4:00 before Stevie saw the rooftops of the Bronx mark his arrival back in New York City. During the drive, he had called Lucy to confirm their dinner date for 7:00 at her apartment. The mere sound of her voice continued to bring a smile to his face.

He had also checked in with Jackie Johnson to report that Rick Jones was safely residing at Taconic Valley Residential Treatment Center. That news, he was sure, had also provoked a smile, although one of relief rather than anticipation.

After that, there had been little to do but sit back, listen to the radio and enjoy the drive. Midway through the Bronx, however, the mood was shattered by the sound of his cell phone.

"Hello," he answered, unable to check in advance to see who was calling.

"Stevie!" It was his brother, Frankie, but it didn't sound like he was smiling.

"Yeah, Frankie, what is it?"

"Well, I've got bad news and I've got bad news. What do you want to hear first?"

"Frankie!" Stevie said impatiently, his disposition sinking rapidly in response to his brother's tone. "What's happened?"

"OK. To begin with, we got the ballistics report back on the Levon Marbury case this afternoon." Frankie paused, partly for effect, partly in an apparent effort to control his anger. "It was the same gun that was used in the Rue James killing."

"No, shit," Stevie exclaimed.

"Correct," Frankie continued. "There's no question about it. The match is perfect."

"OK," Stevie responded, unperturbed by the news. "So, the same person who hit Rue hit Levon. That makes sense. We've been saying all along that Levon and Melody could have seen the shooting, and that the killer would want to take them out. This fits."

"Yeah, but you're not going to like who they are casting for the part of 'perp' in both killings."

"What…"

"Your kid, Shaquan," Frankie answered before Stevie could finish. "And maybe his mom."

"That's bullshit," Stevie exploded. "That's the same crap they were handing out last night. There's no way that Shaquan did this. There's no reason why he would have done this."

"Jack Schwinn says that his guys, Robby Calderone… and that asshole Brian Finnerty … have a CI who claims that Shaquan and Melody have been on the street selling crack… that they got it from Rue James… that they killed him in the alley behind her apartment and took a package he was delivering for his corners."

"That's bullshit. There's no way…"

"Look," Stevie continued, his tone taking on a more plaintive tone. "You and Jimmy Williams don't buy that shit, do you?"

"It doesn't matter what Jimmy and I think," Frankie responded, his voice flat with a combination of dejection and anger.

"What do you mean?"

"I mean it's not our case anymore. I mean that Jack Schwinn made his argument that the Levon Marbury killing was an extension of the Rue James case and that they should take over. And…" his voice began to rise in volume, driven by his growing rage. "And… I mean the fucking brass gave them the case."

"What?" Stevie couldn't believe what he was hearing.

"That's right. It's not our case anymore. So, if you have any complaints about the way NYPD is handling this investigation, you'd better take them to your buddy, Jack Schwinn, and his pair of assholes, Robby Calderone and Brian Finnerty."

"I can't believe it," Stevie said in shock.

"Well, believe it," Frankie shot back, his voice dripping with anger ... and a bitterness that Stevie felt might be directed partly at him.

"And, you should know one other thing," Frankie continued. "You are one of the reasons why they decided to transfer the case."

"*Me*? Why *me*?"

"Schwinn made the argument that since Shaquan was your foster care kid... and since you are *my* brother... I had a conflict....*I HAD A CONFLICT.*"

"That's crazy," Stevie said, before realizing that he had put his brother in an extremely difficult and embarrassing position. "Frankie... I'm sorry... but that's really crazy."

"I know," Frankie said, his voice dialing down several notches. "I know, but, they bought it. Christ, I'm pissed.... You know that I've never really liked Schwinn....and I guess the feeling is mutual. But this really pisses me off."

"Frankie, I'm really sorry if..."

"Don't worry about it," his brother interrupted. "This is just life on the job. You know that. But, there's not much I'm going to be able to do to help you on this one anymore."

"Sure...," Stevie said, feeling increasingly guilty about having placed his brother in any kind of professional jeopardy. "Thanks for everything you've done already... and I'm sorry about all this."

"Don't worry about it," Frankie said. "Look, I've got to go. Let's talk over the weekend."

Stevie heard the connection go dead. During the conversation he had driven across the Bronx, almost all the way to the Tri-Borough Bridge. He was only about a half hour from home.

Moments after paying the toll, his cell phone broke the silence again.

"Hello."

"Steve, it's Joseph Otinga."

Stevie's heart sank at the sound of his voice. "Joseph, what is it? Did something happen? Did they come back?"

"No," Joseph said, trying to sound reassuring. "Not the guys from yesterday. But the police were here."

"What? Who?"

"Two police detectives. Their names were Robert Calderone and Brian Finnerty. They wanted to question Carlos."

"About what?"

"About where Shaquan is? They said Shaquan is wanted for questioning in two murders. They wanted to know if Carlos had any idea where he might be."

"Christ," Stevie exclaimed. "I can't believe this. Is Carlos OK?"

"I don't know," Joseph said, his voice finally losing his practiced optimism. "They took him in for questioning. I asked to go with them, but they said that wouldn't be possible. They said I could come to the station... the 79th Precinct. So, I called you right away."

"That's OK," Stevie said. "I'll take care of it. I know where the precinct is and I know the two cops..."

"You know them?" Joseph interrupted.

"Yes, they are the detectives who have been looking for Shaquan.... And I know them from before..." He didn't need to say more. "But they shouldn't have come to talk to Carlos... and they definitely shouldn't have taken him to the station..."

"I'll take care of it," he concluded. "I'll go to the precinct and get Carlos and bring him home."

"Thanks. That would really mean a lot. I'm sure that Carlos is very frightened."

"I'm on my way."

Stevie hung up and immediately scrolled through the cell phone's long list of contacts and phone numbers. He stopped at Lieutenant Jack Schwinn and hit send.

"Schwinn," he heard as Jack picked up.

"Jack, it's Stevie Corra."

"Stevie," Schwinn answered, a tone of surprise and caution in his voice. "What can I do for you?"

"You can stop harassing my kids."

Jack's tone lost any sense of caution and took on an edge of irritation. "Right now, we think one of your kids may be the do-er in two, maybe three, murders. So, I wouldn't call this harassment; I'd

202

call it doing our job."

"Your job is to find whoever actually killed Rue James and Levon Marbury…" He hesitated for a moment, trying to regain control of his own anger and rebuild the sense of friendship and trust he'd once had with Jack Schwinn. "Look, Jack, Shaquan didn't do this. I know the kid. He didn't do it."

"Maybe not." Stevie's plea seemed to have touched a chord, if only slightly. "But, Robby Calderone has a CI who says that Shaquan and Melody are out there selling Rue's dope and that they got it by killing him."

"I just don't buy it."

"Well, that's not your decision," Schwinn said, a hint of exasperation returning. "Look, if your kid didn't do this, he needs to come in so we can talk about it."

"I understand that; I just don't know where he is… and neither does Carlos," Stevie added.

"Who's Carlos?" Schwinn asked, sounding puzzled.

"He's the kid in my group home that Shaquan had called after he went missing. Remember, I told you about the call. Calderone and Finnerty just went and picked him up. They told my staff that they were taking him to the 79th Precinct for questioning…"

Again, Stevie paused before continuing. "They shouldn't have done that, Jack. We had an agreement. I told you that if you needed to talk to him, I'd arrange it. These kids all have problems. Getting hauled off by the cops doesn't help."

He heard Schwinn grunt into the phone. "I didn't know that they picked this kid up." The irritation in his voice now seemed to be focused on someone other than Stevie. "I'll talk to them."

"I'm coming in to the station. I want to bring Carlos home."

"O.K.," Jack said, capitulating. "I'm not going to be here. I've got to leave for a meeting downtown. But I'll call Calderone and clear it…" Again, there was a brief hesitation before Schwinn continued. "In case you need it, here is Robby's phone number…" Jack waited while Stevie fumbled for a pen and paper. "…917-555-3617. And, deal with Calderone on this… not Finnerty. He's a real asshole when it comes to you."

"He's a real asshole all the time," Stevie replied, just before he heard Schwinn hang up.

Fifteen minutes later, he walked into the front desk area of the 79th Precinct. The same, aging patrol sergeant he had seen on Tuesday was manning the front of the house. Stevie asked for Robby Calderone and was directed to take a seat. Today's wait was considerably longer than his earlier visits. It was a full half hour before the detective appeared from the back of the precinct. Behind him, Brian Finnerty guided Carlos up the narrow hallway with a right hand planted firmly in the small of the boy's back. Carlos walked slightly ahead of Finnerty looking like a frightened animal being led to an uncertain fate.

"Stevie," Calderone said, approaching with hard eyes and a smile that was all business. "I'm sorry about the wait, but we had to finish up a few questions. Carlos is free to go."

"I thought that we had an agreement," Stevie said in turn, struggling to keep his own anger hidden and in check. "If you wanted to talk to Carlos, all you had to do was call me. I would have arranged an interview. You didn't have to do this."

Calderone brushed off Stevie's concern. "Well, there have been a lot of developments in this case over the last day or two. Under the circumstances, we felt we needed to talk to Carlos as soon as possible."

"What circumstances might those be," Stevie asked, his tone pointed, bordering on sarcastic.

"That your foster care kid looks to be the shooter in two murders," Finnerty blurted, leaning forward to insert himself into the conversation.

"I told you last night," Stevie said, turning an angry glare on his former colleague. "Shaquan didn't do this. I know the kid. He didn't do it."

"This isn't about you… not anymore," Finnerty muttered in response. His words were filled with personal animosity and bitterness born of prior perceived grievances. "It's time you let the real police handle this case."

"You couldn't…" Stevie started to explode with his own torrent

204

of angry abuse when, looking down into Carlos' surprised and frightened eyes, he checked himself.

He turned back to Calderone. "You're looking for the wrong man. If you find him, be careful. You don't want to hurt an innocent kid."

"I guess you'd know all about that kind of thing," Finnerty jabbed.

"Yeah, I certainly would," he answered, then turned a searching gaze once more to Calderone. "I would hate to see it happen to anyone else."

The detective took Stevie's stare full on for several moments. Then he spoke, his voice steady and cold. "Hey, I just want to bring the kid in for questioning. He's not going to get hurt... unless he does something stupid."

43

As they left the precinct, Carlos wore the same expression – that all-too-familiar mixture of fear and defiance – that Stevie had last seen in the eyes of Rick Jones. Carlos, like many of the kids with whom he worked, had his own long and difficult history with the police. They usually had grown up in neighborhoods where the combination of being a teenager *and* black or Hispanic appeared to be justifiable cause for a "stop and frisk" pat down or a few threatening words by a passing patrol car. It didn't make for good community relations or a warm and fuzzy feeling towards the police on the part of many New York City youth.

"Are you OK?" Stevie asked as soon as they got back into the relative safety of the Subaru.

Carlos just nodded.

"What did they say to you?"

"They think Shaquan killed some people," the boy answered with a combination of disbelief and horror. "That's crazy!"

"Yes, it is," Stevie agreed. "What did they ask you about?"

"They wanted to know where Shaquan is. I told them that I didn't know, but they said they didn't believe me; that me and Shaquan were homies; that I had to know where he was…"

Carlos paused for a moment as he recalled the interview.

"They knew that he had called me."

"Yeah, I told them that Shaquan had called and that he had talked to you…" Stevie felt the need to explain and apologize.

"Those are the detectives that were looking for Shaquan. When I talked to them, they thought that he and his mom might have been witnesses to a murder... and that they might be in danger."

"That's not what they think now," Carlos said quickly, his eyes flashing with anger.

"I know. It doesn't make any sense."

The boy just shook his head sadly.

"What else did they ask?"

"They wanted to know what Shaquan had said on the phone? I told them that he said he was OK and he was with his moms, but he wouldn't say where he was. I told them he wanted to know if anyone had been looking for him. That he asked if any police had been looking for him."

"Did they say anything about that?"

"No, they just listened and kept asking me questions."

"What else?"

"They kept asking if I knew where Shaquan could be? Did he have any friends or relatives he might be staying with? I told them no, there was no one I could think of?

"Then they started to ask me if Shaquan talked about going to visit his moms, if he ever talked about her boyfriend, Levon? They said they knew that Shaquan hated Levon; they wanted to know if he had ever talked about wanting to kill him?"

"What did you say?"

Carlos shot a quick and almost angry look at Stevie as if he had accused the boy of being a rat. "I told him that, yeah, Shaquan didn't like Levon none, but he never said nothing about killing him."

"I know, Carlos. You would never say or do anything to hurt Shaquan. But, between us, did he ever talk about wanting to kill Levon?"

Once again, Carlos studied Stevie, assessing whether he should disregard most of his life experience and actually trust an adult in a position of authority.   "Yeah," he said, "Shaquan really hated Levon bad. Levon had fucked up his mother and he had fucked up Shaquan lots of times. Shaquan said that if he ever did it again he'd kill him for sure."

"So, you think there is a chance that Shaquan could have done it?"

This time, the boy answered slowly, reflecting his own ambivalence over whether it was praise or criticism. "I think Shaquan would really want to kill Levon…. but I don't think he actually would do it."

Stevie nodded his own agreement with Carlos' reading of his friend's character. "Go on. What else did they ask you?"

"They asked me about the place where Shaquan's moms lived. They wanted to know if he ever talked about what went on there; any of the people he saw? They asked if I had ever gone there with him? I told them no, he never talked about that place at all."

"Is that the truth, Carlos?" Stevie asked. When the boy remained silent, he pressed a little harder. "I'm only trying to help him."

"I know. He had told me that there was a lot of shit going down over there. That there were some real gangstas running the building and that he hated that his moms lived there."

"Did he say anything about anyone in particular?"

"No, just that the place was a real shit hole with a lot of really bad people; that he wanted to keep his eye on his moms to make sure she was OK."

"Did the detectives ask you about anything else?"

"They wanted to know about what happened yesterday, when that guy in the car grabbed me and hit me?"

The question took Stevie by surprise. "Had you said anything about it first, or did they already know about it?"

"I didn't say nothing; they knew all about it. They wanted to know if I knew who it was; if I had ever seen the person before? I told them no. They wanted to know what the person had asked me and what I had said?"

Their conversation had consumed much of the drive back to the group home.

"I'm sorry, Carlos. They never should have taken you into the station house." Stevie's remorse was both personal and shared on behalf of the department he had been part of for so long.

"That's OK. It was nothing," the boy answered, once more trying on his protective streetwear of defiant bravado. Then he turned to Stevie again. "So, you used to be a cop?"

"That's right," he answered. "I was a cop for about ten years."

"What was all that talk about hurting a kid?"

"That was an accident, but it was something that I feel really bad about. It's a long story. I'll tell you all about it at some point when we have more time."

"Is that the reason you're not a cop anymore?" Carlos asked, his tone cautious, knowing that he was venturing beyond the normal boundaries of his relationships with a caseworker.

"No, that's not the reason," Stevie answered, turning to the boy. "The reason is that I'd rather be here with you."

44

Stevie delivered Carlos safely back to the group home and waited as the boy described his experiences at the police station to Joseph Otinga and Mrs. Ramirez. By the time he had finished his second rendition, the interrogation had begun to seem more like a badge of honor than a frightening personal ordeal. As Carlos moved out into the living room to share his story with the other group home kids, the boy had already graduated to full-fledged street gangsta status, having taken everything the cops could throw at him without giving up Shaquan.

Joseph and Stevie agreed that no formal report on the incident was necessary. They would simply add a note in the boy's case file stating that Carlos had been questioned with regard to the case of another kid who'd gone AWOL.

Hanging over their conversation, however, was a growing concern about Shaquan's safety and worry over exactly how much greater danger he might be in now that the police considered him a murder suspect.

"This is just terrible," Joseph said, for once giving voice to his fears. "It is not possible that Shaquan did these things. I simply cannot believe it." The group home manager was feeling guilty that he was about to leave for a long-planned and well-deserved weekend in Baltimore to attend a family wedding. Stevie reassured him that there was nothing he could do at the group home. They simply had to wait until Shaquan turned up… or the police found him.

It was almost seven by the time Stevie climbed back into the car. He called Lucy to say that he was running a little late but was on his way. They would have a lot to talk about when he got there.

*   *   *

Lucy already had the apartment door open when he reached the top of the stairs.

"Hi," she said with a warm and welcoming smile that somehow managed to convey both her happiness to see him… and her own surprise at just how happy she was.

"Hi," Stevie answered with a broadening smile of his own as he stepped into the apartment and dropped his backpack in the hallway. They turned to face each other and he bent to take her in his arms. Lucy reached up and leaned into him, cradling his face in her hands as they kissed, tenderly at first, then with growing passion. Together, they let their kiss play itself out, but stopped before going further.

"God, it's good to see you," Lucy said, flushed from their embrace. She was wearing a deep burgundy tee shirt over a pair of loose, khaki shorts – another cool and comfortable 'look' that highlighted the silky olive skin tones of her bare limbs.

"Yeah, it feels like forever." Stevie almost couldn't believe his own schoolboy words. It had been a day and a half since they had last been together, sharing their most personal and painful secrets, making love for the first time, and agonizing over the ever more complicated and dangerous circumstances of their two clients – Melody and Shaquan.

"A lot has happened," he said as Lucy took him by the hand and led him to the living room. She poured them each a glass of chilled white wine and tucked herself onto the couch facing him from the opposite corner.

There was no need for her to ask. Without hesitation, Stevie ran through the details of the Levon Marbury crime scene; then described Carlos' confrontation with Back Thompson's goons at the group home.

His first inclination was to skip any mention of his own visit to

211

Back and his crew at Melody's old apartment. But Stevie decided that he didn't want to be keeping secrets from Lucy. It had been just those kinds of secrets, the difficult and sometimes messy details of his day-to-day-life he'd refused to share with Sandy, always with the best of intentions, that had gradually undermined the foundation of their relationship. Like dry-rot, they had left gaping holes in the base of their marriage. In the end, there were large sections of his life that she knew nothing about and didn't understand. It wasn't her fault; it was his.

So, he told Lucy about the trip to Brownsville and the exchange he'd had with the drug dealer and his men – admittedly going out of his way to present it in as matter-of-fact manner as possible. The sudden look of fear on Lucy's face as he told her almost made him regret his new-found honesty.

"I was fine," he comforted her. "I've been in hundreds of situations like this. I know guys like Back; how they think, what makes them do what they do and what keeps them from doing other things. I knew that Back couldn't hurt me. You don't have to be afraid."

Lucy was surprised to find that she believed him; but it still didn't quell the fear of losing him.

Stevie moved on to describe the news that Shaquan's prints had been found inside Levon's car … and that the gun which had killed Levon was the same one that had killed Rue James.

It was only then that he told Lucy that the police now considered Shaquan and Melody to be suspects in both murders; that a confidential informant reportedly was claiming that they had killed Rue James for his drugs which they were now out selling on the streets.

"That's nonsense," Lucy shouted, flying to the defense of her client. "Melody has spent her whole life as a victim of abuse, being beaten and battered without ever defending herself. There is no way that she could suddenly, out of the blue, bring herself to kill a drug dealer so she could steal his drugs and start dealing herself. It is completely out of line with her personality and what she is capable of."

"That makes sense," Stevie answered. "And, I know that

Shaquan couldn't do this. That boy is no killer."

"And, the police wouldn't believe you?"

"No."

Stevie went on to explain that the Levon Marbury case had been taken away from his brother and transferred to Calderone and Finnerty. Finally, he described how the two detectives had picked Carlos up and taken him in for questioning. And, he told her of the angry – and even menacing – conversation he'd had with Robby Calderone to end the day.

They sat together in silence, facing each other from their respective ends of the couch, lost in thought. After a few minutes, Lucy crawled over to Stevie and gave him another long and lingering kiss. "Come on, let's have something to eat," she said.

He just smiled. "How about we go right to dessert?"

She smiled back, and kissed him again. "Dinner first; we'll save room – and time – for dessert."

While Lucy brought a pot of water to a boil and sautéed thin slices of chicken breast, Stevie continued to sift through the facts of the case as they swirled around in his head.

"You know, one of the things that I still can't figure out is how Melody wound up renting an apartment in that building," he said. "The place is like a drug fortress and Melody's apartment has a really key location, right opposite the stairs leading out into the back alley, where Rue got shot and where Back Thompson parks his car."

"It wasn't her apartment," Lucy answered, focused on her sizzling chicken. "It was Levon's."

"But, I thought you said that Levon had come to Melody after he got out of prison and didn't have any place to live?"

"That's right," Lucy said, looking over from the stove. "But, then he found that apartment and got Melody to move in there with him. She didn't want to go, but she was afraid to refuse."

"Did she ever say how he got it? Did he know people there?"

"She didn't say. She never really wanted to talk about the building at all."

"I'm not surprised," Stevie muttered, turning this new piece of information over in his mind. It was the latest in what was beginning to feel like a long list of stray facts that bothered him for one reason or another. They were like a series of dots that he had yet to connect before seeing the whole picture.

"Voila," Lucy said with flair as she placed their dinner – sautéed chicken, topped by a brightly colored salsa of finely chopped orange, celery, onions and cilantro, with a side of pasta – on the kitchen table.

"This is delicious," Stevie said after taking his first bite. The dish was light, fresh and summery. "You're really a good cook."

"Thanks. Coming from you, I'll consider that a real compliment."

The rest of the meal passed with conversation about ingredients, recipes, favorite restaurants and places they'd like to travel, but hadn't … at least yet."

"What are you doing for the rest of the weekend?" Stevie asked, wiping his mouth after finishing his meal.

Lucy washed down the chicken with a sip of wine. "I have to work tomorrow. I've got a client who is going to be leaving her boyfriend. I have a place for them…her and her daughter… in a DV shelter out on Long Island. A friend of mine works there. I'm going to pick her up in the late morning and drive her out, help her get settled. I'm not sure what time I'll be back. What about you?"

"It turns out that I will have Joey this weekend after all. I guess Sandy's plans to go away fell through. I'll take him to his soccer game in the park and then we'll just hang out together."

He hesitated briefly before continuing. "If the weather holds, we'll probably go out to the beach on Sunday… Riis Park… Would you like to come with us?"

Lucy looked up at him with questioning eyes. "Are you sure?"

"Yes. If you want to? I'd like you to meet him."

She reached across the table and gave his hand a gentle squeeze. "I'd love to. Thanks."

Stevie sat with a growing feeling of contentment as Lucy cleared the table and carried the dishes to the sink.

"What time do you have to pick up Joey in the morning?" she asked.

"Sandy will drop him off at my place about 9:30."

"So," she asked, tilting her head provocatively to one side, her jet black hair dancing gently as she moved. "Can you stay the night and go home in the morning?"

Stevie felt the smile spread across his face. "Yes," he nodded.

"Good," Lucy answered, returning his smile as she crossed the kitchen, took him by the hand and drew him to his feet. "Then, it's time for dessert."

45

Stevie walked back into his apartment just a few minutes before 9:00. It had been a wonderful night, filled with rounds of lovemaking and intimate conversation; then, finally, a peaceful, satisfied sleep. Now, there was just time for a quick shower before Sandy showed up with Joey.

At 9:30 on the dot, he heard the door bell. He opened it to find Joey standing alone, in his soccer uniform with a backpack slung over his shoulder. Sandy stood in the street, next to her double parked car, as if unwilling to come any closer. Stevie could almost see the tension in her stance. Something bad had happened to put off her trip.

"What time tomorrow night?" he called.

"How about 6:00?"

"Great, I'll have him home then."

Sandy was in the car and gone by the time he turned his attention back to his son.

"Hi, dad," the boy said, lunging forward to hug his father.

"Hi, Joey. I'm really glad you were able to come after all." Stevie returned the embrace with equal fervor.

"Me, too."

Eventually, Joey released his grip and followed his father into the apartment.

"I thought we could drive over to the game; then go up into the park and have a picnic," Stevie offered. "After that, we'll just play it by ear. Maybe we can go to a movie tonight."

"That sounds great," Joey said enthusiastically. Stevie was certain that this would have been the boy's response to any suggestion.

Joey dived onto the couch and they caught up on the week's events while Stevie packed a small pile of sandwiches into a cooler. He covered all his bases, adding both apples and peeled carrots as well as bags of chips and pretzels. There was water for during the game and soda for afterwards. At 10:30, they scrambled into the Subaru and headed for the soccer fields, only a few minutes away.

The game was a videotape replay of the prior week, indistinguishable to any but the most attentive parent closely monitoring their own child's progress. Amazingly, Joey almost scored a goal. His kick was just wide of the wooden frame. Stevie could see the painful mixture of excitement and disappointment on the boy's face. In the end, Joey's team won again. He, along with all the kids, received copious praise from their coach for good play and a great game.

By 12:30, they were back in the car, headed towards the opposite end of the park. Stevie found a spot on Prospect Park West, the broad avenue that seemed to run like a spine through this section of Brooklyn. To one side, Park Slope lived up to its name as tree-lined streets filled with fashionable townhouses dropped off towards the west; on the other, behind a long, low, grimy stone wall, the broad expanse of Prospect Park began its own gradual descent towards the east.

Stevie involuntarily shuddered, suddenly recalling that he had just been here on Tuesday night, racing to elude a black SUV with darkened windows. If Levon Marbury had been behind the wheel, then his pursuer was now dead. For some reason, Stevie was no longer certain it had been Levon. Could it have been Back Thompson, or one of his boys? He wasn't sure... and had no way of really knowing.

Stevie and his son grabbed the cooler and a blanket and headed towards the Long Meadow. On any summer Saturday, this large field attracted throngs of Brooklynites –families of every color and configuration; kids of all ages; occasional pairs of quiet young lovers, oblivious to anything outside their own romantic bubble. Stevie found that he suddenly viewed these couples with renewed sympathy and understanding.

Joey picked a spot midway between a Frisbee game and a large group of Caribbean families, seemingly out for a church picnic. Stevie spread out their blanket, planting the cooler at one end. Joey dived straight in, pulling out a sandwich, chips and soda.

"I'm starving," the boy said, his face and legs still grimy from the dusty soccer field.

"Yeah, I'm hungry too," Stevie nodded in agreement. He took a sandwich, but decided on carrots instead of chips and water instead of soda.

It was another in what seemed like an endless series of hot summer days. Stevie felt the warmth of the sun bake into his body. Luckily, there was a gentle breeze that swirled up the slight incline of the park. It was one of the reasons he and Joey liked this spot for a picnic lunch.

"I'm glad you could come this weekend after all," he said again, giving his son a loving clap on the back. Stevie was curious about what had happened between Sandy and her boyfriend to derail their plans for the weekend, but knew he couldn't ask Joey.

After lunch, both father and son stretched out on the blanket. Stevie closed his eyes and savored the memories of his night with Lucy. He could feel the silky touch of her skin on his; the gentle brush of her hair against his face as she turned to taste his lips. And, he remembered the ease with which they could talk and the comfortable silences when they didn't. Things were moving fast; faster than he ever could have imagined. And, he liked it.

He turned to look at his son. Joey was quietly watching the Frisbee game, a group of young men in their early 20s weaving among the picnickers to track down and catch a soaring blue plastic disk as it floated down to earth. Then, without losing stride, they would suddenly spin and launch it back towards another of their friends. Stevie admired their skill and athleticism, but knew this was likely to end badly when either the Frisbee, or one of the players, wound up in someone's lunch.

The park was being put to full use on this beautiful July weekend. Stevie gazed at the scene before him, scanning the broad expanse of the meadow. In addition to Frisbee, there were makeshift games of soccer and whiffle ball; food and drink were everywhere; and the sounds of scattered guitars and drummers mixed with hints of marijuana in the air. In the distance, Prospect Park Drive wrapped up and around the meadow. Closed off to normal traffic on weekends, it was now the sole province of runners, bicyclists and roller-bladers – plus the occasional official vehicle maintaining order and services.

Stevie lay back on the blanket once more and stared up at the almost cloudless blue sky. High above, he watched a squadron of kites dancing in the breeze that had swept up from the west. There were kites of every description – graceful three-dimensional box kites with their lattice-like wooden frames; multi-ribbed parafoils; and those good old-fashioned diamond kites, with their slightly elongated bodies and long fluttering tails.

And, the colors! They were a rainbow of reds and blues, deep purples and bright yellows. There were dragon head designs and geometric patterns, and...

Stevie's eyes opened wide; then focused tightly, studying just one of the dozen kites overhead. It was a diamond kite, with broad diagonal panels of black and green. Overlaid, at an opposing angle was a tight red oval, itself crisscrossed by thin shafts of white. It was like a personalized version of the Kenyan flag.

He had seen this kite before. It was a kite that Joseph Otinga had helped make for one of the boys in the Flatbush Group Home.

Stevie sat bold upright, keeping his eyes glued to the hovering shape in the sky.

"What is it, dad?" Joey asked, surprised by his father's sudden movement.

"Nothing," Sevie answered absently. "I'm just looking at the kites."

He tried to judge where the kites were being flown from. It was impossible to see the thin strings, stretching hundreds of yards to the ground below, which controlled their movements. Stevie watched the kite's fluttering maneuvers, imagining in his mind's eye how and from where it was being held taut against the wind. Gradually, he realized that there was a small group of young men and boys behind him and far to their left staring upward, their own bodies dancing in distant unison with the kites high above.

"I'll be right back," Stevie said to Joey as he rose and turned towards the group. The kite flyers were at the western most part of the meadow, almost at the edge of Park Drive as it turned to circle back towards the south.

He carefully weaved through the scattered checkerboard of picnic blankets and folding lawn chairs, his eyes locked on the group of young men. There were more than a dozen of them spread out over a corner of the grassy field. Most were intently focused on their kite's movements, holding sticks of coiled string in one hand, the other suddenly pulling the taut line in one direction or another. The crowd was as diverse as the kites they flew; different shapes, sizes and ages; almost as many shades of color, if more muted in tone.

Stevie was about 20 yards away when he stopped dead in his tracks. There, toward the far edge of the group was a young African-American boy of about 16. He was dressed in a black tee shirt and ragged jeans. His newly maturing muscles were just beginning to harden beneath a thinning layer of baby fat.

Shaquan, like those around him, was entirely focused on his brightly colored diamond kite as he coaxed it ever higher towards the afternoon sun.

46

Stevie stood in stunned silence, staring at the boy for whom he had been searching throughout the past week. He could not believe that this was possible. He had... despite every fiber of his being... begun to doubt that he would ever find Shaquan... or, at least, before he was falsely arrested as a murderer... or gunned down by someone who truly was. Yet, there he stood, less than ten yards away, totally oblivious to Stevie's presence.

Stevie struggled to keep his emotions in check. A burst of adrenaline surged through his body. He was surprised that Shaquan didn't hear the pounding rhythms of his racing heart. He took a cautious step forward, then another, circling one of the kite flyers. Still, Shaquan did not notice his approach. He paced forward again, then stopped, only a few feet from the boy whose eyes were still locked upward on his distant craft.

"Shaquan," Stevie said softly.

The youth reacted as if to the sound of a gunshot, spinning to face him, fear in his eyes, unable for several seconds to make out from where this sudden threat had come.

"Shaqan! It's me, Stevie."

He watched as the boy's chest heaved, gasping for air to replenish the oxygen consumed by his terror. Shaquan now lived in a world where it was unhealthy for someone on the street to suddenly call you by name.

"Stevie!" Shaquan said, as if to confirm what his eyes were

telling him, that his caseworker was now standing right next to him

"It's OK," Stevie said softly, trying to calm the boy who still seemed ready to burst out of his skin. "It's OK."

He waited another moment to let the initial shock of his appearance subside, if only a little; then tried to lock onto Shaquan's frightened gaze. "Are you all right?"

Shaquan nodded first; then answered. "Yeah, I'm OK."

"What about your mom? Are you still with her? Is she OK?"

The question only raised the boy's anxiety. "Why do you think I'm with my mom?" he asked warily.

"Because I've known you for four years," Stevie said softly, deciding not to mention Shaquan's phone call to Carlos. "You're gone and she's gone; where else would you be?"

"Yeah, we're fine," Shaquan acknowledged reluctantly.

As they spoke, the youth's kite string had begun to go limp, allowing the kite itself to begin spinning out of control. Stevie nodded up to it, as if in warning, and Shaquan turned back to reel it tight again. As he did, the multi-colored diamond righted itself and began a rapid climb back up to its former heights.

"Shaquan, there's a lot of scary stuff going on. You really need to come home."

"What do you mean?" The youth's voice was filled with feigned ignorance, like a chocolate-stained child denying that he had eaten the cookies.

"Come on, Shaquan," Stevie prompted. "You were at the apartment the night that guy got shot in the alley. There are a lot of people looking for you and your mom."

Again, the boy turned to him with a flash of terror in his eyes. "Who...? Who is looking for us?"

"Well, the police are...and the guys who run that building where your mom lived."

"Those guys?"

"Yeah," Stevie answered. "They even came to the group home and tried to get Carlos to tell them where you were." As soon as he said it, he knew it was a mistake. He saw Shaquan's eyes widen in fear.

"Is Carlos OK? What did he say?"

"Carlos is fine," Stevie answered, again trying to calm the boy. "He told them he didn't have any idea where you are. He doesn't know where you are? Does he?"

"No," Shaquan insisted quickly. "He doesn't know where we are. Nobody knows."

"Come home, Shaquan. Please!" Stevie pleaded.

The boy shook his head, less a statement of defiance than an effort to strengthen his own resolve. "I need to take care of my mom," he said.

"Shaquan, you can't do this on your own... It's too dangerous. Look at what happened to Levon."

Once more, the boy looked up at him in panic. "What about Levon? Is he looking for us too?"

Stevie just stared at Shaquan in silence, studying his reaction. "No, Levon is dead. He was shot to death early Thursday morning."

The news clearly stunned the boy. He staggered as if taking an unexpected blow. There was no way he could be faking this reaction, Stevie thought.

"Levon's dead?" Shaquan asked, as if unable to believe what he'd just heard.

"Yes," Stevie nodded, waiting for him to adjust to this new reality.

"Do the police know who did it?"

Again, Stevie hesitated. "Well... right now the police are thinking that maybe you did it." Once more, he saw the boy's eyes open wide in fear. "It's crazy. I know. But, you really need to come in so we can straighten all this out."

As they'd talked, Shaquan had again lost control of the kite. This time, he seemed not to care. The boy's body stiffened as his gaze focused on something behind Stevie and to his right.

Corra twisted around to see two NYNP patrol cars pull up along the edge of Park Drive, only a few yards from the spot where they were standing. As they stopped, the doors of both cars swung open and four uniformed officers climbed out.

Stevie turned back just in time to meet Shaquan's accusatory glare... and hear him drop the coiled ball of line attached to his kite.

"No," Stevie said, shaking his head in denial and disbelief. "Shaquan! No!"

It was too late. The boy had already spun away, first jogging; then running along the Drive and up a path towards the park exit.

"Shaquan," he called again, beginning to race after the teenager. "Shaquan, come back!" he shouted.

By the time Stevie got to the park exit, he could just make out Shaquan as he disappeared around the edge of a building at the corner of Union Street. Suddenly, he heard the unmistakable jangle of NYPD equipment belts – guns, flashlights, nightsticks and ammunition, all bouncing in unison as two of the patrolmen jogged up from behind.

"Are you all right?" one asked, radio in hand. "Did that kid get something? We can put out a call for another car? They'll pick him up further down the slope."

"No," Stevie answered in puzzled disbelief. "No. Everything is fine. He's just a kid I know. I was trying to tell him something... I'm sorry to have bothered you," he added in response to the sudden look of irritation written on the faces of both officers.

"We had just pulled over to grab a couple of hot dogs from that vendor when we saw the kid take off and you started screaming," said one of the cops. "We figured for sure that he had grabbed your wallet or something."

"Sorry," Stevie said again, his attention focused on the corner where he had last seen Shaquan. Finding him today had been one chance in a million; what would the odds be of ever doing it again.

Stevie turned and made his way dejectedly back into the park. As he crossed the Drive he looked over to the spot where Shaquan had been only a few minutes earlier. There, standing stock still in the middle of the crowd, was his son.

"Joey," Stevie said, rushing up to the boy. "I'm sorry I ran off. It was one of the kids from the group home. Are you all right?"

"Yes," Joey nodded. "I saw him run away. He dropped his kite. Here it is."

Stevie looked down to see his son hand him a coiled ball of

string; string that was attached to a red, black and green diamond kite laying somewhere on the fields of Prospect Park. It was a kite that Joseph Otinga had helped make for one – and only one – of the kids at the Flatbush Group Home.

"Thanks, Joey," his father said with a sudden smile. "Thanks a lot." He was hoping that the odds of finding Shaquan one more time had just increased dramatically.

47

"Come on," Stevie said. "Let's go find Shaquan's kite."

Together, father and son began to track their way across the Long Meadow of Prospect Park. Joey walked ahead following the twists and turns of the kite line as it had fallen to earth; Stevie was right behind, winding up the ball of string as fast as he possibly could. Along the way they received more than a few angry stares and muttered comments from picnickers who had suddenly found a kite string slicing down onto their Saturday afternoon lunches.

On and on, the string played itself out; through the field and across Park Drive where it curved around beneath the meadow, and then over towards the woods on the opposite side. Fifteen minutes after beginning their search, they looked up to see the kite – majestic in its bright African colors – dangling from the tip of a branch mid-way up an aging maple tree.

Stevie and Joey eyed each other with a matching pair of mischievous smiles.

"Don't ever do this," Stevie said as he sprang upwards and grabbed hold of the lowest branch. Years of training for a life fighting crime on the streets of Brooklyn – and a healthy disdain for donuts – had given Corra an unexpectedly strong and wiry frame. Branch by branch he pulled himself up the tree until he was sitting on the limb where Shaquan's kite was resting.

"Walk back away from the tree and pull hard on the string when I tell you," he shouted to Joey who nodded excitedly in response and ran to his assigned position. Then, Stevie began to inch his way out towards the kite, hoping against hope that the thinning branch wouldn't break beneath his weight. Amazingly, he was able to just grab a tip of the kite, twist it free and call for Joey to yank it back away from the tree. He watched as the kite fluttered peacefully to the ground; then hurriedly made his own way back to safety.

"That was great," Joey shouted, his face alight with excitement from this very special, shared adventure. "I've never seen you do anything like that, Dad. You were great."

"You were great too," Stevie answered, giving his son a full-body hug. "If you didn't pull that string as hard as you did, we never would have gotten the kite down. We did it."

"Are you going to give it back to Shaquan?" Joey asked.

Stevie sighed. "Well, Shaquan had borrowed it from another boy. I'm going to try to return it for him."

Joey looked slightly perplexed, but still radiated a glow of excitement from having retrieved the kite. Stevie unhooked the bowed wooden cross-pieces used to form the kite's diamond shape: then wrapped the material up around them into a long thin roll.

"Let's go back and get a soda," he said, draping his arm around his son. "I'm parched."

Forty-five minutes later, after gathering up their blanket and cooler for the drive home, the pair walked back through the front door of the apartment. Stevie dispatched his son to take a reluctant shower and wash off the lingering grime from the morning's soccer game. As Joey followed orders, Stevie quickly tried Lucy's cell phone. In response, he heard only the recorded sound of her voice. Rather than leave a long and sure-to-be confusing message about having found Shaquan and then lost him again, he simply said that he had news and that she should call him as soon as she had a chance.

Stevie looked down at the rolled up kite that they had retrieved; then spread it out across the top of the kitchen table. There was no doubt that it was one which Joseph Otinga had made together with one of the boys from the group home. Stevie recognized the style, but that was all. He was confident that Joseph would remember precisely which of the kids had been the proud owner of this particular model. And, since Shaquan had just been flying it in Prospect Park, that meant the two boys were in contact; possibly even staying together. This was, he hoped, the clue that would lead him to Shaquan a second time.

Unfortunately, Joseph was away for the weekend, attending a family wedding in Baltimore. He wouldn't be back in the group home – and able to examine the kite – until Monday morning.

Stevie tried to search his memory in an effort to recall who the owner of the kite might be. Rather than coming up empty, he found too many possibilities. There had been dozens of kids who had passed through the group home during the four-year-period that Shaquan had lived there. Some had stayed for months or years; others only weeks or even days. Otinga would have used kiting as a way to build relationships with many of them, but Stevie wasn't certain about which ones. And, he realized with a sharp twinge of professional and personal guilt, he really didn't know which of the boys – other than Carlos – had developed lasting friendships with Shaquan.

Joey emerged from the shower, an oversized bath towel wrapped around his slight and now considerably cleaner body. He went over to the corner where a camping mattress and a backpack served as his "room" in Stevie's apartment and quickly slipped into a pair of cutoff jeans and a Mets tee shirt. Joey turned back to see his father staring absently at the kite on the kitchen table.

"Why did Shaquan run away when you were talking to him?" the boy asked with a cautious tone signaling that he knew this was a serious question.

"Well," Stevie began slowly, wanting to keep this very complicated and frightening situation as simple and unthreatening as possible. "Shaquan had run away from the group home because he thought his mom was in trouble… and he wanted to help her. He ran away today because he got frightened. He thought the police were coming to take him back."

Joey nodded in that special way children do after they've heard something they don't understand at all.

"Can you help him…and his mom?"

Now it was Stevie's turn to nod, more out of hope than any sense of certainty. "Yes. I can help him. But he has to come home first. I am trying to find him so I can bring him home."

Joey nodded again, a look of intense seriousness etched on his face. Suddenly his mood changed. "Want to play 'Call of Duty'?" he asked excitedly.

"Sure," Stevie said, relieved that Joey had already moved on… and that he, himself, might find some diversion after his depressing failure to engage with Shaquan in the park.

For the next two hours, father and son teamed up in front of the Xbox he had purchased as an added enticement for his son's visits. Together, they fought their way through an endless series of similar looking combat situations, killing countless terrorists while repeatedly being killed and wounded themselves. For Stevie, it now seemed like the height of peaceful and innocent relaxation.

At about a quarter past six, he suggested that they go out for some Mexican food. Their favorite restaurant on the circle near the corner of Prospect Park was only a few blocks away. As Joey turned off the Xbox, Stevie gathered up his wallet and keys.

Then, his cell phone rang. Stevie expected it to be Lucy, but didn't recognize the incoming phone number that appeared on the display.

"Hello," he answered.

"Hello?"

Stevie couldn't believe his ears. "Shaquan? Is that you?"

"Yeah," the boy answered hesitantly. "I called Carlos… I wanted to make sure he was OK. He told me I should call you. He gave me your number."

"That's great," Stevie said, stunned by the boy's sudden and totally unexpected phone call. "I'm glad that you called…" He paused for a moment, trying to find the best way to proceed. "I know that you thought those cops were coming for you this afternoon… but they were just stopping for a hot dog. I wouldn't call the cops on you, Shaquan."

"I know." He could hear the trust returning to Shaquan's voice. "Carlos told me how you had told those detectives that they were crazy… that I never killed nobody."

"I know that you would never do that," Stevie said encouragingly. "But, you need to come home so we can get this straightened out. We need to talk to the police together so you can tell them what really happened; so we can convince them that you didn't have anything to do with it."

"I can't do that," Shaquan said. Now Stevie could hear the boy's voice harden in response to the fear he was feeling. "I can't come home. They'll kill me… and they'll kill my mom."

"Who will kill you?"

"Them dealers…those cops. They're saying I'm a murderer… that I killed that guy in the alley… and Levon. They'll kill me."

"Nobody's going to kill you," Stevie said, struggling to convince the boy he'd be safe. "We'll protect you. I'll get the police to protect you…" Try as he might, Corra heard his words go flat. He suddenly realized he had offered the same empty assurances hundreds of times to victims and witnesses, hoping to coax them into statements that might send someone to prison… but could just as easily send them to their own death.

"What did you see…" Stevie asked with renewed intensity. "What did you see that someone would kill you for?"

"I didn't see nothing," Shaquan shot back. "We don't know nothing. You got to leave us alone. You're gonna get us killed."

"You're not safe out there," Stevie pleaded. "You can't do this on your own, Shaquan. Please, come home. Where are you? I'll come and get you…and your mom. I'll protect you. Just tell me where you are."

"I can't," he heard the boy answer, just before the line went dead.

Stevie found that he had been staring blankly out into the back garden during the conversation. Now, in his mind's eye, he saw only the image of Shaquan standing before him, that same look of terror etched onto his face, just as it had been in the park earlier that afternoon. Stevie was devastated. He could not believe that he had found Shaquan, and then lost him again, for the second time in the same day.

He looked at the phone that lay silent in his hand. Just moments ago, it had been his one link to the boy; a boy entrusted to his care and now in mortal danger. Suddenly, Stevie's eyes focused on the display. All at once, he realized that his link to Shaquan might have been temporarily broken – but it had not been cut completely.

There, emblazoned on the electronic display, was the incoming number of the phone Shaquan had used to make the call.

48

Joey offered no arguments when his father told him to fire up the Xbox and play another couple of games before going out for dinner.

Stevie grabbed a pen and pad from the kitchen counter and copied down the number of Shaquan's phone. Then, he flipped through the contact list on his own phone and hit send.

"Stevie," his brother Frankie answered as soon as the connection went through. "How are you doing?"

"I'm fine," Stevie said hurriedly, cutting through the formalities. "I need you to help me with something."

There was only silence for several moments before his brother spoke. "What kind of help?

"I need you to run down a phone number for me; find out whose phone it is and get me a list of incoming and outgoing calls for the last few weeks."

"I can't do that," Frankie exploded. "Whose phone? Where did you get the number?"

Now it was Stevie's turn to pause before answering. "It…it was Shaquan…the foster care kid I've been looking for."

"What?" his brother shot back again.

"He called me a little while ago. I got the number on my cell phone. If I can find out whose phone it is and maybe some of the calls that have been made recently, I'm pretty sure it will help me find him."

"Maybe it will help Jack Schwinn and his guys find him as

well," his brother broke in quickly. "They're looking for the kid too... as a suspect in two separate murder cases. Remember?"

"Frankie, come on. If I can bring the kid in, I can clear this whole thing up. If they bring him in..." Stevie hesitated for a moment, feeling his anxiety rise. "I just have a feeling that something bad is going to happen."

"Stevie... I can't just do this on my own. You know that. There's a process. It's got to go through channels. I need justifiable cause to get phone records; and I have to get a judge to sign off."

"Frankie, please! I'm not some rookie Legal Aid attorney. I know how this works. You can get Judge Greene to sign off on anything you want. Just tell him you need the phone records to locate a material witness, not a suspect; that it will never come back to contaminate the case."

"Christ, Stevie, I don't even have a case," Frankie blurted.

"What about Lakeisha Smalls? Did Schwinn take that one as well?"

"No," Frankie answered. Stevie could hear that his brother had begun to turn the possibilities over in his mind. "No, they didn't take that one."

"Well, you can make the argument that Shaquan is a 'person of interest' in that case. That's certainly true."

"Yeah, I guess that is true," Frankie said, clearly weakening. Then he continued. "But, whatever I get, I'll have to share it with Schwinn."

Stevie knew his brother was right. Frankie was fully aware that the Brooklyn North Narcotics detectives were looking for Shaquan. There was no way he could hold back information that might help them find him.

"I know," Stevie said with a sigh. "But, you don't have to do it right away. Just give me a day or two. I've got some other leads that also might help me find Shaquan."

"OK," Frankie answered with a pained sigh of his own. "I'll talk to Jimmy Williams. He's not going to be happy; he'll have to do the paperwork on this."

"Jimmy will be fine; he's a stand-up guy. When do you think

you can have something for me?"

"If I can get a hold of Judge Greene tonight, I might be able to have it tomorrow. I'll let you know." Suddenly Frankie's tone brightened. "Hey, are you going to Mom and Pop's tomorrow?"

"I...wasn't planning on it," Stevie answered a little sheepishly.

"Well," his brother said, once again all business, "if you want this stuff, you better be there."

"Frankie, I've got a date," Stevie pleaded.

"So do I; I'm going with Jeannie. Just bring her. Who is it, that social worker?"

"Yeah," Stevie acknowledged, his own tone now sounding as pained as his brother had only moments before. "Lucy...Lucy Montoya. I was kind of hoping not to scare her off too soon. I don't think this is going to help."

"Don't worry about it," Frankie chuckled mischievously. "Tell her it's a field visit. She's working this case too, right? Besides, it'll be fine. You know Mom and Dad. They'll put on a real show for her: *The illustrious NYNP Chief of Detectives Joseph Corra with his beautiful and charm ing wife Theresa.*" His brother paused briefly, and then continued in a more serious tone. "It's been a long time since you brought a girl home. It'll be good."

"OK," Stevie gave in, sounding far from convinced. "I have to talk to Lucy... and I'm not sure how long we'll stay."

"Good," his brother said, starting to break off. "Let me call Greene and Jimmy."

"Frankie," Stevie interrupted, suddenly remembering something that had been bothering him. "Did you tell Schwinn... or Calderone and Finnerty... that Back Thompson's guys had been out to the group home to talk with Carlos?"

"No."

"What about Jimmy? Did you tell him... and could he have told them?"

Now, Frankie was beginning to get irritated. "No, Stevie. I didn't tell anyone. We had an agreement. Why do you ask?"

"Because they knew about it!"

"Hmmh," Frankie said thoughtfully. "That's odd."

"Yes, it is," Stevie agreed.

"Look, if you want those phone records tomorrow, I need to make some calls. I'll see you tomorrow afternoon."

Stevie was still lost in thought when he turned back to Joey and said it was finally time to go for dinner.

They walked to the Mexican restaurant and had to wait only a few minutes before a table for two with a window overlooking the circle became available. Joey ordered his favorite chimichanga. The deep fried burrito – crispy, golden brown, and filled with beef, rice, and refried beans – looked to be roughly the same size as his son's stomach. Stevie had a tangy shrimp burrito that he knew was a house specialty. They shared an order of guacamole and chips.

After dinner, the pair strolled around Park Circle towards the 'multiplex' movie theater on the next corner. They were just in time for the 8:00 p.m. showing of the latest "Fast and Furious" sequel. For the next two hours, Joey sat enthralled by the roar of muscle cars, hurtling along the freeways of Southern California, often defying the laws of gravity and general physics to go airborne at great heights over long distances. Amazingly, their horrific crashes back to earth generated masses of fiery sparks, but no serious damage that might prevent them from doing it all over again in the very next scene. Stevie couldn't help but find his mind wandering back to the conversations with Shaquan.

Following the film's action-packed conclusion, the two Corras completed a Saturday night ritual by picking up soft-serve vanilla ice cream cones with multi-colored sprinkles. Then, they made their way back to Stevie's apartment.

Joey was settling in to play a video game version of the movie they had just seen when Stevie heard his cell phone ring tone. This time it was Lucy.

"Hi," she said. "I saw that you had called before but I couldn't call back until now."

"That's OK," Stevie said. "How did it go with your client?"

"It was hard. That's why I couldn't call. She was scared; wasn't sure what was going to happen next in her life. She'd been with this guy a long time. Even though it had been really bad, at least she had a man in her life. Now it was going to be just her and her daughter. She was afraid of being along; afraid that he would find her; just afraid of everything. It took a long time to help her work through this and then get her settled in at the shelter."

"Are you back?"

"No, I'm still in the car on Long Island. I'll be home in about an hour." Then Lucy hurriedly changed the subject. "You said that there had been some news. What happened?"

Stevie took a deep breath and began the story of the day's events. "That's amazing," Lucy said excitedly when he described how they'd found Shaquan in the park. "Oh, no," she cried at word that he had run off again only moments later. Nevertheless, Stevie could hear her relief at knowing that Shaquan and Melody were still together, and that they were still unharmed.

Then, he told Lucy that Shaquan had called again. And, although he hadn't been able to talk the boy into coming home, he had learned the number of the phone Shaquan was using … something they now might use to help locate him. His brother Fankie was working on identifying the phone's owner and a history of calls it had made over the last several weeks.

"That's great," Lucy said. "You've really made a lot of progress. I'm sure you will be able to find them." Then, changing the subject once more, she continued. "Are we still on for tomorrow?"

Again, Stevie took a deep breath. "Sort of," he said hesitantly. "Don't take this the wrong way, but how would you like to meet my family?"

"What?" Lucy said in surprise; then shifted her tone to one of mock seriousness. "Isn't this a little sudden?"

"Yes, it is," Stevie agreed, and then began to fumble through a series of awkward explanations. "It's not really my idea… Not that I don't want you to meet them, or them to meet you… but it is a little soon."

"That's OK," Lucy offered reassuringly.

"It's my brother, Frankie. He's sort of holding us hostage. He said if we want those phone records, we've got to come to my folks' for dinner. I think he wants to meet you."

"You've told him about me?"

"A little; he heard from one of his detectives that you were with me at the Lakeisha Smalls crime scene. I think he's figured out that this has become more than just a professional relationship."

"I didn't realize that," Lucy chuckled on the other end. "I thought this was just business."

Then, her tone changed again. "Stevie, I'm a big girl. I'm not afraid to meet your family, now or whenever. I don't know what is going to happen in our relationship. All I know is that I like you... I like you a lot. And, if I have to go to your parents for dinner just to spend the day with you... and meet Joey... then that is fine with me. It's really up to you. Do you want me to come?"

"Yes, I definitely want you to come. Bring your appetite; my dad likes to cook. Why don't you come over here around noon? You can meet Joey and we can relax for a while before we go over."

"That sounds wonderful. How should I dress?"

"Like a human sacrifice! Seriously, it's a backyard barbecue. Anything that I've seen you in would be perfect."

"Thanks," Lucy said sarcastically. "That was really helpful."

"Don't worry; you'll look beautiful. You always do."

Stevie thought he could actually hear Lucy blushing on the end of the line. "OK, you're forgiven. See you tomorrow at noon."

"Great. Get home safe."

49

Stevie woke early despite it being a Sunday morning. He came out and saw that Joey was still sound asleep on the mattress in his corner of the living room. He quietly made a pot of coffee; toasted a roll; then added a slice of cheese with a dab of apricot jam. While waiting for the coffee to brew, he went to the hallway and pulled a manila envelope out of his backpack. It was the NYPD criminal history for Levon Marbury that Jimmy Williams had given him on orders from Frankie. With all that had happened since Wednesday afternoon, including Levon turning up dead Thursday morning, Stevie hadn't even looked at it. He tucked the envelope under his arm, grabbed a cup of coffee and his breakfast; then slipped out the sliding glass door onto the patio.

It was another warm and sunny day, perfect for a trip to the beach that had now been cancelled. Instead, he would be taking Lucy Montoya, a woman he'd known for little more than a week, to his parents' house for Sunday dinner. Stevie shook his head in wonder. How absurd was this? Still, he was surprised to find himself looking forward to the day? He knew that Joey would be happy for the chance to see his cousin Michael. And, he felt this strange surge of pride at being able to show off Lucy to his family. Frankie was right. It had been a long time since he'd brought a girl home. It's not that Stevie hadn't dated during the past five years. But there hadn't been anyone he wanted to take home to meet mom and dad. Partly, that was a natural reluctance to make commitments after the divorce.

Partly, it was that he hadn't met anyone who made him want to commit. Lucy, he was starting to believe, was someone different.

Stevie took a bite of his breakfast and a sip of coffee; then looked down at the manila envelope lying on the table. There were a lot of questions about Levon Marbury's role in the events of the last weeks and months that troubled him.

Lucy believed it was Levon who had found the apartment where he and Melody lived; where Rue James had been killed; and where Back Thompson now made his headquarters. How had Levon penetrated the security of that particular drug den to get that particular apartment? Was he part of Rue's crew? Or, Back's?

Had it been Levon who killed Lakeisha Smalls? And, if so, why?

If it was Levon who'd followed Stevie home from the Cumberland on Monday night, how had he been able to find him?

And, perhaps most important of all, who was it who had killed Levon? If Stevie was to prove that Shaquan was innocent, he'd need to find the real killer.

He slid the report out of the envelope and began to read. It came as no surprise to find that Levon had a long history of involvement with the NYPD. There were arrests and convictions dating back almost twenty years to when Levon was just a teenager. Petty larceny, shoplifting, assaults, and multiple drug charges, including possession and intent to sell; Levon's rap sheet was fairly typical for a small time career criminal living on the streets of Brooklyn. What did come as a surprise, however, was the fact that Levon's most recent bust – which had earned him a four-year stint in Otisville – had not been for a drug crime, as Stevie had been led to believe. It was "Assault with a Deadly Weapon"; undoubtedly the knifing of a woman that Jimmy Williams had mentioned at the crime scene.

Just as interesting was the name of the arresting officer in that particular case. It was Artie Schwartz, a veteran detective who had worked the precincts of Brooklyn South for more than 30 years. Artie had been Stevie's first partner – and mentor – after Corra was promoted to carry the gold shield of a Detective. During their one year together, Schwartz had passed on a career's worth of hard-earned street smarts to the up-and-coming young son of then Deputy Chief Joseph Corra. His assignment to work with Artie was no random chance. His father's guiding hand had been at work. It hadn't taken long for Stevie to move on, rising up and away from Artie in terms of rank and grade. Still, however, they remained close and there was no one in the Department for whom he had more respect.

Artie had retired a little over two years ago, hoping to spend more time with his wife Celeste before she died of cancer. Now, Artie was living with his daughter Rochelle and her family in Jersey.

Stevie re-read the criminal history report, knowing that it was just the barest outline of Levon's criminal past. If he wanted to know more, he would need to reach back and talk to those who had actually been there and understood the nature and circumstances of the crimes. No one could possibly be more helpful in this regard than Artie Schwartz.

He looked at his cell phone. It was a few minutes after 9:00. Artie was an early riser. He wouldn't mind a call, even on a weekend morning. Stevie went into the apartment and dug out a tattered and dog-eared address book from a shelf next to his desk.

Back on the patio, he sat looking at Artie's phone number. It had been years since they'd spoken. Stevie had sent flowers after Celeste's death, but had skipped the funeral which would have been filled with his former NYPD colleagues.

After a moment's hesitation, he took a deep breath and punched in Artie's number.

"Hello." Stevie would have recognized that Queens accent anywhere.

"Hi, Artie. It's Stevie Corra."

"Stevie!" He could hear the surprise in Artie's voice. "How are you? It's been a long time."

"Yeah, I know. I'm fine. I know it's been a while. I'm sorry about Celeste."

"We got your flowers, Stevie. Thanks."

"I wanted to come to the funeral, but…"

"I understand," Schwartz interrupted. "It's OK. So, how about you? I hear that you're a social worker? I bet you're good at that."

"Thanks," Stevie said. The two former partners spent a few minutes catching up before they got down to business.

"So, Stevie, you didn't call me at 9:00 on a Sunday morning just to say hello. What can I do for you?"

"I want to pick your brain, Artie. You made a lot of collars over the years; I'm hoping you might remember one of them."

"My problem is that I remember almost all of them. I wish I could forget," Schwartz said. "Which one are you interested in?"

"It was back in 2007; a guy named Levon Marbury. You busted him for Assault with a Deadly Weapon. I think he knifed some woman. Do you remember any of the details?"

It didn't take long for Artie to go through the case files in his head. "Yeah," he said. "I remember all the details on that one."

"Christ, you are good."

"No," Artie said a little more seriously. "I remember some cases better than others. This one I remember for two particular reasons. First of all, it was a pretty heinous crime. There were also some issues on the job about it."

"Can you give me some details?"

"First, you tell me why you're interested in that case."

"Fair enough," Stevie answered. "Levon Marbury was living with the mother of one of the foster care kids on my caseload. He's a real bastard; used to beat her and the boy pretty bad. He was the reason the kid got removed and placed in care in the first place. The kid went AWOL last week, right about the time his mother went missing. There is a chance that she might have been the witness in a drug murder. I'm not sure where Levon fits into all this, but he turned up dead on Thursday morning."

"No, shit?" Artie interrupted. "It couldn't have happened to a nicer guy. Like I said, one of the reasons I remember the case was because it was so brutal. Marbury had beaten up this girl he was seeing something terrible; then he took out his knife and sliced her up; really fucked up her face. He was one vicious little turd..."

The phone went silent. Stevie could imagine that Schwartz was remembering the sight of the girl's bloody wounds and the emotions he had felt, and fought to suppress, at the time."

"I think he did something similar to a friend of my kid's mom while he was looking for them," Stevie explained. "This time he killed the woman. I can't say for sure it was him; but it all seems to fit."

"So, who caught the lead on his killing?"

"Initially, it was one of my brother Frankie's Homicide squads. You know Jimmy Williams, right?"

"Sure, Jimmy's great."

"Yeah, but a couple of days later Brooklyn North Narcotics got the case transferred, claiming it was an extension of this drug-related murder they were already working?"

"Hmmh," Artie muttered, immediately grasping the departmental politics involved in the case. "So, who in particular has the case now?"

"It's a couple of Jack Schwinn's guys; Robby Calderone and Brian Finnerty."

Stevie could almost hear the air go dead on the other end of the connection. "Robby Calderone? Really?" It was less a question than an expression of disgust.

"Yeah," Stevie asked cautiously. "Do you know him?"

"Yes, I know him," Artie responded, his voice tinged with bitterness. "Like I said, there are two reasons I remember that particular case. The other is that after I made the collar, Robbie Calderone approached me. He was working out of Brooklyn South Narcotics at the time. He told me that Levon was a snitch, not an official departmental CI, but a regular source of information for him personally. He asked me to drop the whole thing and let Marbury walk. I told him that after what Marbury had done to that girl, I didn't give a shit if he knew where Jimmy Hoffa was buried and who killed him. I told Calderone that if he wanted to make a pitch up the line, go ahead; I'd fight him every step of the way. After that he just backed off. I never heard another word about it."

Stevie couldn't believe what he was hearing. "Robby Calderone knew Levon Marbury?"

"That's right," Artie replied. "You sound surprised."

"I am… only because Calderone told me personally that he had never heard of him before."

"He was lying," Schwartz shot back. "Look, I don't really know Calderone. But there was something about him that I didn't like. The whole thing with Marbury as his snitch just didn't sit right for me. On the one hand, Marbury was a real scumbag… not the kind of guy you're going to go out and fight for no matter what kind of info he's giving you. Then, as soon as I suggested he take it up through channels, he just dropped it. It all just left a real bad taste in my mouth."

"Yeah," Stevie said, still stunned by this new insight into Robby Calderone's history and his relationship with Levon Marbury. "So did you have any other dealings with Calderone?"

"No, not really; we never ran in the same circles. This was only a year or two before I retired. Like you said, at some point he transferred up to Brooklyn North."

"How about Levon? Is there anything you can tell me about him? What he was doing? Who he was hanging with?"

"There's not that much to tell. He was just your average worthless street punk, with an unpleasant penchant for beating up his women. He was part of the crew running the drug trade in Marlboro Houses; never got that high up. As I recall he wasn't all that tight with anyone. He was a little older than most of the kids working the projects."

Stevie waited while the retired detective searched the recesses of his memory. "There was a kid, a few years younger, that he had sort of partnered up with. He was a mean son of a bitch too. He had some kind of odd street name… 'Bike'… or 'Back'. That was it, 'Back'… 'Back' Thompson…"

"Back Thompson," Stevie almost shouted. "Levon and Back Thompson were tight?"

"Yeah," Artie shot back. "You know him?"

"Yes," Stevie said in amazement. "Back was running the corner at the building where Levon and this foster care kid's mom were living. It's the building where Back's boss, a guy named Rue James, was killed about a week and a half ago. That's the killing where they

243

think the mom might have been a witness."

"Really?" Artie said, sharing Stevie's surprised tone. "This is getting pretty interesting."

"It sure is. Now, with Rue James dead, it looks like Back has gotten himself a promotion running a whole series of corners up and down Utica Avenue."

"Isn't that nice," Schwartz offered sarcastically.

There were a few moments of silence as the men on both ends of the conversation tried to sort out the new information.

"Artie, do you think that Calderone knew Back Thompson as well?"

"I can't say for sure, but if he was working Brooklyn South Narcotics, there were certainly opportunities for them to run into each other. And, if he was as tight with Levon Marbury as he claimed, that might be another connection. But, I honestly can't say for sure."

After another few moments of silence, Artie continued. "So, you're telling me that Robby Calderone is the lead investigator on the murder of Levon Marbury and a murder that cleared the way for Back Thompson to take over his boss' business."

"That's right."

"Does he have any suspects?" Artie asked, his tone now overflowing with bitter sarcasm.

"Yeah," said Stevie. "My foster care kid and his mom."

"Now, isn't that great? I just love police work."

"Me too! Listen, Artie, thanks for everything. You've been a huge help."

"No problem," the older man responded, his tone softening. "Let me know if I can do anything else to help. And let me know how this plays out. Let's stay in touch, kid."

"Will do," Stevie answered as he broke off the connection.

He took a sip of coffee that had gone cold, his mind trying to comprehend the meaning of what he had just learned. Then, he looked at his watch. It was after 9:30. He and Joey were going to be late for church.

50

They were back from mass soon after 11:00. Stevie couldn't help but be a little anxious over how his son would react to Lucy. They had talked about it the night before when he had explained that a friend of his would be coming to the house on Sunday and going with them for dinner at grandma and grandpa's.

"Is she your girlfriend?" Joey had asked in an especially serious tone.

"No," Stevie had answered after a moment's thought. "Not exactly; she's a friend. We're just getting to know each other. But I do like her a lot."

It took a while before he realized that this was a bigger deal for him than it was for Joey, who was used to the fact that his mother dated and had been seeing her current boyfriend Richard for almost a year.

At the stroke of noon, the doorbell chimed. Stevie hopped out of his chair, strode quickly up the hallway and opened the front door.

"Hi," said Lucy with a slightly mischievous smile. "How's this?" She held her arms stretched slightly out to the sides, modeling her short-sleeved silk blouse, its floral pattern a bright bouquet of rich blues, golden yellows and deep purples. Loose and comfortable, she wore it tucked at the waist into a pair of neat khaki shorts. The rest was just those legs, trim and tanned, delightfully descending into a pair of cork-soled sandals. It was an outfit both casual and elegant.

"You look perfect," Stevie nodded in approval.

"Thank God," Lucy answered with mock relief; then leaned forward and gave him a quick kiss.

Stevie took her by the hand and led her into the living room where he introduced her to his son.

He could not have wished for a better beginning to what he hoped might be a long lasting relationship. Lucy talked to Joey in a way that was neither patronizing nor inquisitorial. She asked about his soccer game, where he went to school, if there were any particular subjects he liked more than others. She made sure to draw Stevie into a three-way conversation about the movie they'd seen last night and whether it was better or worse than the prior versions of "Fast and Furious". Once they had settled in for a few rounds of video games, with Lucy more than able to hold her own, he knew that his worries were over… at least for the moment.

The butterflies returned when the three packed into the Subaru – Joey automatically opting for the back seat – and began the drive to his parents' home in Dyker Heights. For once, Stevie actually wished it was longer than just a 20-minute trip.

When they pulled up outside, Stevie could see that his brother's car was already parked in the short driveway. Joey threw open the door, leaped out of the car and raced up to his grandparents home. He disappeared inside with the metallic clatter of a slamming aluminum screen door.

"Are you ready," Stevie asked.

Lucy just looked back and smiled. "I'll be fine. How about you?"

"Do you know CPR?"

"Come on; let's go in before you start making me nervous."

As usual, his mother had taken up her post at the front door.

"Hi, mom," Stevie said giving her a warm hug and a kiss on the cheek. Then, he turned. "I'd like you to meet my friend Lucy."

"Hello, Mrs. Corra," Lucy said, extending her hand. "Thank you for having me."

"Please, call me Theresa," his mother said with an appreciative look. "I'm glad you could come. Let's go inside."

Together, they followed her into the house, through the kitchen and out onto the backyard patio. There, the rest of the family had assumed their usual positions. Joseph Corra quickly adjusted the grill-full of sizzling meat one more time; then turned toward them.

"Hi, Lucy," he said, focusing his attention on Stevie's date. "I'm Joe. It's nice to meet you." The older Corra held her hand for just an extra split second after their initial greeting, long enough to convey warmth without being awkward. "I hope you brought your appetite. We like to eat in this family."

"Don't worry about that, dad," Stevie said reassuringly.

"I can't wait," Lucy said. "I've been looking forward to seeing where Stevie learned his grilling skills

"Hello Lucy. It's great to meet you," Frankie said, rising out of his deck chair. "I'd like to say that Stevie has told us a lot about you, but this guy can be pretty tight lipped. He does get a sort of wistful, happy look on his face when he mentions your name, though. Can I get you a drink and pump you for information?"

"The drink part sounds good," Lucy said with a defensive laugh. "How about a glass of white wine?"

"Ignore these guys and come sit here," Jeannie said tapping the chair that Frankie had just vacated. "I'll try to protect you. I'm Jeannie; the big lug's wife."

Lucy laughed again and then took the offer of a safe haven.

"So, I understand that you and Stevie work together?" Jeannie said.

"Sort of," Lucy said. "We both are caseworkers, but we're at separate agencies." Then she explained the different types of work they did, and how their paths had crossed over the past couple of weeks.

As Lucy introduced herself in more detail, Stevie approached his brother by the bar.

"Got anything for me?"

"Christ," Frankie glared back in mock indignation. "Don't I at least get dinner and a kiss first?" Then he glanced at his watch. "Jimmy's working on it. It should be another hour or so. Once he gets it he'll call me and then fax a copy of the report here."

"Thanks," Stevie said sincerely. "I really mean it."

"That's OK," Frankie answered, his tone turning serious as his eyes focused on Stevie's. "But remember, I need to cover myself on this. I'm going to have to share it with Jack Schwinn pretty soon.... tomorrow or the day after at the latest."

"I understand," Stevie replied. "That will be fine. If things go like I'm hoping, I'll have Shaquan back in the group home by then."

"I hope you're right," Frankie answered as he headed off to deliver another round of drinks.

For the next hour and a half, Stevie watched with delight as Lucy fit right in at a Corra family dinner. She chatted about recipes and clothes with his mom; about work and the kids with Jeannie; deftly sidestepped questions from Frankie about how long they'd been dating; even talked baseball with his dad. At various points during the meal, Stevie had received discrete nods of approval from everyone at the table. Amazingly, even his father, who hadn't had much good to say about his oldest son's life choices in recent years, suddenly flashed him a warm and encouraging smile.

Midway through dessert, Frankie reacted to a muffled buzzing from the phone on his hip. No one, except for Stevie, seemed to notice. With a retired Chief of Detectives and two sons who had reached NYPD command rank, the Corras were used to sudden interruptions at the family dinner table, or anyplace else for that matter. Frankie grabbed his cell phone with one hand and wiped a napkin across his mouth with the other. Then he rose from the table, walked back across the patio and slipped into the house.

Lucy threw Stevie a quick questioning look from across the table. He just nodded once, indicating that Frankie should soon be giving them Shaquan's phone records. Stevie could hardly contain his impatience as he waited for information that he believed might lead him to the boy.

It didn't take long. Moments later, he heard the screen door to the kitchen open as his brother stepped half way out of the house. Frankie looked to Stevie; then signaled silently for him to come inside.

"Excuse me," he said to the family as he rose and walked towards Frankie. The look on his brother's face suddenly filled him with dread.

"What is it?" he said as soon as they got inside. "Has something happened? To Shaquan?"

"No," Frankie shook his head; then focused his gaze firmly on Stevie. "But, Bro, you've got what looks to be a real problem here. Your boy looks to have a very, very real problem."

"What? What is it?" He asked, unable to understand what it was that Frankie was trying to tell him.

"The phone that Shaquan called you on yesterday... It was Levon Marbury's phone."

"What?" Stevie cried out. "Levon's phone? That's.... that's impossible."

"Well, it's definitely Levon Marbury's phone. Jimmy got the basic billing information from Verizon. But he won't be able to get the recent call history until tomorrow."

"Why not?" Steve asked impatiently.

"I don't know," Frankie shot back. "Maybe because it's Sunday! Look, we'll get them tomorrow."

The two brothers stood in silence for a few moments before Frankie continued. "Stevie, this is starting to look very bad for Shaquan. His prints were in the car where Levon was killed. Now, he's making calls with his cell phone. Come on, this is all circumstantial, but it's starting to add up."

"No," Stevie insisted. "I just can't believe that Shaquan killed Levon. It's not possible. I can't explain how Shaquan got his cell phone or how his prints wound up in Levon's car, but I am positive he didn't kill him."

Frankie stared at his brother in silence for a moment; then spoke in a more forceful tone.

"Look, you're reacting with your heart, not your head... Now, maybe that's the way you're supposed to react. You're the kid's caseworker... But, I'm a cop. I'm just looking at these facts and I'm thinking this kid definitely is starting to look like the one."

"Bullshit," Stevie looked up at this brother angrily. "Bullshit. Yeah, these facts don't look good, but there has to be an explanation. Frankie, when you work a case, you don't just work it with your head. You work it with your gut, too. Sometimes your gut just tells you that something doesn't fit, that something is wrong. Well that's all I'm saying. I know this kid. My gut, my heart… and my head… tell me that he's no killer."

"Well, my gut tells me that you had better hurry up and find an explanation for all these very damaging facts. This kid has gotten himself into some serious trouble."

Stevie nodded, acknowledging the raw truth in his brother's words.

"And, Bro," Frankie continued. "I can't sit on this. It's a critical piece of evidence in a homicide investigation. I need to pass this on to Schwinn right away."

Again, Stevie nodded. "When?"

"Tomorrow morning! First thing! If I don't, it could be my badge." Frankie's eyes met Stevie's. "And I like being a cop… I don't want to be a social worker."

"And one other thing," Frankie added. "If I were you, I definitely would not call Shaquan and let him know that NYPD will soon be tracking the location of his cell phone. If that ever found its way back to you… and to me… we'd both be in deep shit."

51

When Stevie and his brother returned to the dinner table, most of the family reacted as if they had never left. His mom and dad were busy retelling the story of how they had met. Joe was a young rookie cop, as was Theresa's brother, Anthony. It had definitely *not* been love at first sight. Theresa knew from personal family experience what it meant to be a police officer's wife. She wasn't interested. However, Joe Corra had pursued her with the same dogged determination that would make him a legendary detective and eventually win him one promotion after another. Within a few months, Theresa succumbed. A year later they were married. And, soon after that, the new Mrs. Joseph Corra gave up her job as a teacher in the local Catholic school to begin raising their own family.

"That's wonderful," Lucy said appreciatively.

"How about you and your family," Stevie's mom asked. "Do your parents live in New York?

"No, they're both dead," Lucy answered without going into any details; then turned the conversation back to her hosts. "How long have you lived in this house?"

For the next half hour Stevie struggled to focus on the "getting to know you" back and forth that accompanies the arrival of any new face at a family gathering. Once the last dessert and coffee had been served, he nodded to Lucy and then announced that they would have to get going. It was getting close to his deadline for driving Joey back to Sandy's house. The whirlwind of "goodbyes" confirmed what he already knew; Lucy had been a hit.

"You make Stevie bring you back again soon," his mom said, giving his son's girlfriend a warm embrace.

"Forget about Stevie; leave him home and just come on your own," his father suggested.

"Thanks a lot, dad," Stevie responded sarcastically. Then he turned to his brother. "Thanks for the help. I really mean it."

Frankie just nodded, his demeanor serious again. "It's OK. But, remember what I said about tomorrow morning."

"I will," Stevie said. Then, he gathered up Joey. The three left together and climbed back into the Subaru.

"What happened?" Lucy asked as soon as they were inside the car. "Did you get the phone records?"

"Yes and no," he answered with considerably less enthusiasm than she had expected.

"What is it? What's wrong?"

"It was Levon's phone?"

"What?" Lucy exclaimed in disbelief.

"Yeah," Stevie answered, turning to face her with grim eyes. "I need to drop Joey off. Do you want to ride over there with me? It's about 20 minutes away?"

"Sure."

A heavy silence hung over the car for the trip to Sheepshead Bay. Joey almost always grew quieter as his weekend with Stevie came to an end. For his father and Lucy, their thoughts were completely occupied with this most recent news in their hunt for Shaquan and Melody.

When they pulled up outside the simple raised ranch where Stevie's son and ex-wife lived, Lucy turned to face Joey in the back seat.

"It was nice meeting you, Joey."

"It was nice meeting you, too," the boy answered with enough sincerity to raise his father's spirits. "See ya."

"I'll be right back," Stevie said as he hopped out of the car and walked Joey up to the door. When he got there, Sandy came out to greet them.

"Hi Joey," she said.

"Hi, Mom." Joey turned to give his father an all consuming hug. "Bye, Dad. I'll see you next week."

"Bye, Joey. I'll call you. Have fun at camp."

Stevie felt the same inevitably repetitive heartbreak as his son disappeared into the house.

"So who's your friend?" Sandy asked, nodding towards the car.

"Just a friend," Stevie answered.

"Is it serious?"

He shrugged, uncertain of the real answer. "I don't know. It's a little early to tell; but, maybe."

"Well, good luck then," Sandy replied, with just the slightest hint of bitterness. Then, she too turned and disappeared into Corra's former home.

When Stevie got back into the car, Lucy turned to face him. "Are you OK?"

"Yeah," he answered with a tone that wasn't particularly convincing. "I always get a little down when I take Joey home."

"That makes sense. It's got to be hard. Your ex-wife is very attractive."

"Yeah, I guess so." Then he turned to face Lucy. "Do you want to come home with me?"

"God, I thought you'd never ask," she answered with a smile; then reached across to take his hand and gave it a warm squeeze. "One condition, though; you have to promise not to make me eat anything else. I'm stuffed."

"It's a deal."

On their own, they could now voice what they had each been thinking.

"So," said Lucy, her voice filled with concern and confusion. "What do you think this thing with the phone means?"

"I don't know. But, Frankie thinks it means Shaquan is a very likely suspect in Levon's murder."

"You don't believe it?"

"No," Stevie answered, with a shake of his head. "But I have no explanation for how Shaquan wound up with Levon's phone or how

253

his prints came to be in the car where he was killed."

"What are you going to do?"

"There's not much I can do, other than try to find Shaquan and bring him in before Calderone and Finnerty get to him. Tomorrow morning I'll go to the group home to see if the house manager recognizes the kite Shaquan was flying. That might give me a lead on where he is."

For the rest of the drive, Stevie forced himself to focus on Lucy and the day they'd just shared with his family.

"So what did you think?" he asked.

"I had a wonderful time. They're great, all of them. Your mom's a real sweetheart. Your dad's a little intense but not anywhere near as bad as I had expected. Frankie comes on a little strong, but it feels like he's just trying too hard to live up to what he thinks his dad wants. And, I liked Jeannie a lot."

"Well, everyone was on good behavior today. It goes downhill from here," Stevie said with a half laugh – because he was only half joking.

"So, how did I do?" Lucy asked.

"Are you kidding? You were great. They loved you. You heard my father. He wants you to leave me home next time and go back alone."

"Oh, don't be so sensitive," she replied with a smirk. "They won't mind if I bring you along."

It was just past seven when they walked back into Stevie's apartment.

"Would you like a glass of wine?"

"I'm fine," Lucy said, gliding gracefully across the floor to wrap her arms around him as she pressed her body against his. "I was kind of hoping we could go into the bedroom and work off some of those calories from lunch." Then she kissed him, warmly and deeply.

Two hours later, Stevie looked across the bed at Lucy as she slept, blissfully spent, naked except for the light sheet that wrapped around her, covering her breasts then slanting down to reveal the trim and taut, yet silky soft, contours of her bare back.

Stevie decided to let her sleep. He got out of bed; slipped on a pair of shorts; went outside into the kitchen; and poured himself a glass of wine. Lying on the table was the brown manila envelope containing Levon Marbury's criminal history report. Instantly, his conversation with Artie Schwartz replayed itself in his head. Stevie sat for several minutes, sipping his wine and staring blankly at the envelope, his mind lost in a maze of twisting, turning paths, each one leading to an inevitable dead end. Then, he picked up his cell phone and punched in a speed dial code.

"Christ, Stevie, what do you want now?" It was a fairly typical Frankie greeting. This time, however, there was an added edge of irritation that seemed closer to the truth.

"I need to talk to you about something."

"About the kid? You know I've got to go to Schwinn with…"

"Not that," Stevie interrupted. "I understand all that. Do you know anything about Schwinn's guy on the Marbury case, Robby Calderone?"

"No, not much," Frankie answered immediately. "What are you getting at?"

"Well," Stevie sighed before beginning. "I finally looked at Levon's rap sheet that Jimmy had given me. And it was pretty interesting. It turns out that Levon's last bust had been for assault. It was the case Jimmy talked about the other morning. Levon had cut up some girl he was seeing. Well, Calderone had told me that Levon had gone upstate on a drug charge."

"So, what?" Frankie asked, the irritation in his voice becoming more apparent.

"I'm not exactly sure. But, the arresting officer in that case had been Artie Schwartz."

"No kidding," his brother answered a touch more softly, mellowed by his own fond memories of the retired detective. Their father had arranged for Frankie to benefit from a year working with Schwartz as well.

"Yeah… and Artie told me that after he busted Levon, Calderone, who was working out of Brooklyn South Narcotics at that point, had asked that they drop the charges. He told Artie that Marbury was a snitch for him… totally off the books, but valuable as a source. Artie refused and Calderone backed off entirely."

"OK," Frankie said, still unsure of the point his brother was trying to make.

"So," Stevie pressed on. "Calderone knew Levon. A week ago, when I asked him flat out if he had ever heard of Melody's boyfriend, Levon Marbury... this was before the killing... before Levon figured in the case at all... he told me no... never heard of him."

"OK," Frankie began again. "So, he lied to you. If Levon was his snitch, he's not going to walk around telling people. Shit, I know a lot about my cases that I don't necessarily share with anyone."

"Yeah," Stevie acknowledged. "But, now Levon's dead. Wouldn't the fact that he was a snitch for Calderone be an important piece of evidence? Did Calderone tell you or Jimmy when you were working the case?"

"No," Frankie said. "But, we didn't have the case that long. Maybe he's shared this information with his partner and with Jack Schwinn."

"Yeah, maybe. One more thing; Artie said that Levon knew Back Thompson from when he was living down in the Marlboro Houses... that they had sort of partnered up."

"And once again," Frankie interrupted, "so what?"

"Shit, they were in the middle of investigating the Rue James murder. Back's got to be a suspect. If Levon was close to Back, that makes him even more a person of interest, but Calderone acts like he's never heard of him."

"Same answer: so what?" Frankie shot back, his voice starting to rise. "Maybe Calderone's protecting his informant; maybe Levon's giving him information on Back Thompson and he doesn't want you to fuck it up."

The more he went on, the angrier he became. "What are you trying to say, Stevie? You think Calderone is behind this whole thing? You're so turned around trying to protect this kid that you're trying to pin this on a cop? Come on, that's bullshit."

"Look," Stevie continued. "I'm just saying there are some interesting questions here. How is it that Calderone and Finnerty knew Back Thompson's boys had been out to the group home to put the arm on Carlos? You didn't tell them, right? Neither did I. How could they have found out?"

"I don't know," Frankie replied, his patience wearing thin. "Maybe he's got another snitch in Back's operation. Maybe he knows everything that these guys are doing... he's just not telling *you*."

Stevie's brother took a deep breath to regain control before continuing. "Look, Stevie, it's your kid whose prints were in the car where Levon was killed. It's your kid who is walking around with Levon's cell phone. It's your kid who has a long list of very personal reasons to want Levon dead. This stuff about Calderone; it's just some kind of harebrained scheme. If you really want to help your kid, stop chasing conspiracy theories and find out how he can explain away the evidence that is piling up all around him."

Stevie remained silent, unable to counter Frankie's arguments. When he voiced his still unformed concerns about Robbie Calderone out loud... to another cop... they sounded absurd. He decided to take a different tack.

"Frankie, let me ask you something else. You really have a hard-on for Jack Schwinn. Why?"

Stevie could hear his brother searching for an answer through the silence on the other end.

"I don't know, really," Frankie said hesitantly. "Maybe part of it is that he's the guy who took your place after you left. Maybe in some strange way I feel like that was disloyal. I know that's bullshit, but I think that's part of it.

"Then there's just the department politics," his brother continued. "A couple of years ago, Jack started poaching homicides that had occurred in my zone, claiming that they were drug related. There have been at least four or five. He argues that if he's going to have any leverage on the crews working his sector, he needs to follow up on the killings as well as the dealing. I suppose there is some truth to that, but it still pisses me off."

"Does he close them?" Stevie asked.

"Sometimes yes; sometimes no; his record is about average, I'd say."

"So, it's not like you think there's anything wrong with Jack?"

"You mean do I think he's on the take? Do I think he's a crooked cop?" Frankie fired back, his voice rising in anger once again. "The answer is no…NO! I told you to drop that shit. I don't want to hear it. Christ, you're really starting to piss me off."

Again, Stevie remained silent in the face of his brother's rage.

"I have to go," Frankie said, beginning to break off. "I'll talk to you in the morning."

As he hung up, Stevie saw that Lucy had come out from the bedroom. She was wearing the same white cotton robe he had left for her the other night.

"I can't believe this, but I'm actually hungry again," she said. "What does a girl have to do to get something to eat around here?"

"You already did it…twice," Stevie answered with a smile as he rose to open the refrigerator door.

52

"Can you stay for breakfast?" Stevie asked the next morning as Lucy emerged from the bedroom, once again dressed as she had been the day before.

"No," she answered with obvious disappointment. "I've got a couple of early meetings so I need to get going. Are you going to the group home?"

"I will as soon as I know that Joseph is there. I need to go into the office first and clear out my calendar for the rest of the day."

Lucy nodded and then leaned forward to give him a quick kiss. "Call me as soon as you know anything. If you find out where they are staying, maybe I should come with you. It might help to convince Melody that you are trying to help her as well as Shaquan."

"That makes sense. Hopefully I'll be able to call you soon."

They kissed again, this time lingering in their farewell, before Lucy left.

A half hour later, Stevie walked out of the apartment and climbed into the car for the 20-minute drive to BFS' downtown Brooklyn offices. As always, Jackie Johnson was already at her desk when he arrived.

"Good morning. Can I come in?"

"Sure," she answered, slightly startled by his sense of urgency. "What's up?"

"I need to reschedule my supervision meeting with you today." Stevie immediately recognized the mix of irritation leavened by concern that appeared on his boss' face. Before she could interrupt, he quickly described selected events from the weekend, focusing on his surprise meeting with Shaquan in the park and the fact that he now had the kite the boy had been flying. As a result, it now seemed likely that Shaquan was staying with… or at least had been in contact with… a prior resident of the Flatbush Group Home. Stevie wanted to drive out to the house as soon as Joseph arrived to see if he could identify both the kite and the boy who owned it. From there, he was hoping to quickly to locate Shaquan and bring him home. Stevie decided to skip the fact that NYPD now considered the 16-year-old foster child a prime suspect in two homicides.

"Do what you have to do," Jackie said warily. "But, Stevie, you need to be careful. And, after this… if you don't find him today or tomorrow… that's it. You'll need to leave it to the police. You've got another 18 kids to worry about. They need you just as much as Shaquan."

Stevie stared back in silence, reluctant to make such a final commitment. "OK," he said after some hesitation. "I'll find him." Then he turned and walked back to his own cubicle in what was still an empty office.

At 8:30, he dialed the group home phone number. To his extreme frustration, the morning supervisor told him that Joseph Otinga was still on his way back from Maryland and would be in the house at noon. For the next half hour, Stevie made one call after another, cancelling home visits with biological parents and a planned meeting at BFS' supervised independent living "SILP" apartment where two older kids now lived on their own in preparation for aging out of foster care once they turned 21. As soon as Shelly Stackowski arrived, he implored her to appear for him at a court hearing that afternoon. In return, he promised a complete blow-by-blow account of everything that had happened over the past few weeks as soon as Shaquan was safely back in the group home.

An hour later, once Shelly had left for court – and was safely out of eavesdropping range – Stevie grabbed his cell phone and punched in a familiar number.

"Hello, Stevie," Jack Schwinn answered. "Anything wrong? I

understand that you picked up your kid from Calderone and Finnerty on Friday afternoon. Look, I know that they shouldn't have brought him in before talking to you, but he was OK, right?"

"Yeah, he's OK," Stevie replied. "Jack, I have to ask you one thing." He waited a moment, partly for effect, partly to make sure that he had Schwinn's full attention. "Why didn't you tell me that Levon Marbury was Robby Calderone's snitch?"

The puzzled silence on the other end of the line told him everything he needed to know even before Schwinn answered. "What are you talking about?"

"Levon Marbury was Calderone's CI. At least that is what he told Artie Schwartz a few years back when he was working Brooklyn South."

Again, there was a moment's silence before Schwinn regrouped. "Look, Stevie, I know you were a great cop, but you're not on the job anymore. I give you as much professional courtesy as I can... for old time's sake... but we don't talk about our confidential informants with anyone. I've really got nothing more to say about this subject. I've got to go?"

"Jack," Stevie interrupted. "Just one more thing; you know Levon and Back Thompson used to be partners down at Marlboro Houses... the same time that Calderone says he was getting info from Levon, right?"

The brief hesitation repeated itself; then Jack Schwinn spoke with finality. "Like I said, I have to go." Stevie heard the line go dead.

He stared blankly at his computer screen, his thoughts focused on the conversation with Schwinn. While he couldn't be certain, Stevie's gut told him that this was the first Jack had ever heard of Robby Calderone's connection to Levon Marbury.

His musings were soon interrupted by the sound of his cell phone. It was his brother.

"Frankie," Stevie answered.

"Hey," the younger brother began, his tone flat and stiff. "I'm going to email you a pdf of the call history on Levon Marbury's phone. If this gives you information on how to find Shaquan, you'd better hurry up. I'm going to be bringing the whole package to Jack Schwinn right after I hang up. It will take them a few hours, but by late this afternoon, they should be able to get phone company tracking reports on the location of the phone. The kid doesn't have to be making calls. As long as the phone is on, Verizon can identify its approximate location as it reaches out to nearby cell towers looking for calls. They'll be right on your kid's ass before you know it."

"OK," he answered a little meekly. "Thanks."

"And, Stevie… like I said yesterday… under absolutely no circumstance should you call Shaquan to let him know about this. It would be both our asses."

"Understood," Stevie repeated. Then, he continued. "Frankie, you should know one other thing. I just called Jack Schwinn and told him about Robby Calderone's history with Levon Marbury. I'm pretty sure it was news to him."

He could hear his brother's anger under the silence on the other end of the phone. "You just called Schwinn and told him that?"

"Yeah!"

"Stevie," Frankie spat in range. "I told you to drop that crazy idea. Don't ever ask me to help you with anything like this again. You're going to cost me my shield… and my pension. And… for that matter… don't call me at all for a while! If I want to talk, I'll call you."

Again, Stevie found himself staring mindlessly at his computer screen. This time, however, he saw an incoming email from Frankie. There was no message, just an attachment. He clicked on the link and opened what appeared to be a pdf of the call history, both incoming and outgoing, on Levon Marbury's cell phone for the past month. Stevie quickly printed out two copies and downloaded the original document into a file on his hard drive. He placed one of the printed copies into a random file folder in his desk drawer for safekeeping; then picked up the other copy and grabbed a pencil.

Stevie scanned down the list of phone calls. Almost all of the activity had taken place before Thursday July 19th, the morning Rue James was murdered and Shaquan had gone missing. There were dozens of calls during the first half of the month. And, while there were lots of calls to lots of different numbers, several turned up again and again. He quickly recognized Melody's number which showed up day in and day out. He had called it often enough himself during those first days of searching for Shaquan.

After July 19th, the number of calls dropped off dramatically. The phone had not been used for any outgoing calls on the afternoon of the 19th or Friday the 20th. On the other hand, there were almost a dozen incoming calls on both days, all from the same number. In each case, the call duration was only a matter of seconds, leading him to conclude that they had not been answered but simply went to voice mail. According to the record, these calls had never been returned, at least not from this cell phone.

On Saturday, July 21st, there was one outgoing call – and to a number that Stevie did recognize. It was the Flatbush Group Home. Clearly, this was the phone Shaquan had used when he called Carlos to let him know that he and Melody were safe... and ask if anyone was looking for them.

After this, the outgoing and incoming activity picked up again, but only slightly. There appeared to have been several calls back and forth between Shaquan and his mother, at the phone number Stevie had recognized previously.

On the afternoon of Saturday, July 28th, after he had confronted Shaquan in the park, he saw another phone call to the Group Home – Carlos again – and then the call that evening to Stevie's own number.

He was almost surprised to see that Shaquan had continued to use the cell phone afterwards. He twice received a call from his mother and made one to her during the course of the day on Sunday. Clearly, the boy didn't know that his location could be tracked if he carried a powered-up cell phone. Or, he thought with a twinge of guilt, Shaquan never imagined that Stevie would report his phone call to the police.

Gradually, Stevie worked his way back up through the list, eventually focusing on the night and early morning hours leading up to the murder of Rue James. Interestingly, there were just three outgoing calls from this phone during the period from 9:00 p.m. on July 18th to 2:00 a.m. on July 19th – all to the same number, 917-555-

3617. Any incoming calls during that same period had been allowed to go to voice mail.

Stevie stared at the number – 917-555-3617 – that had been so popular on the night of Rue James' killing. It had showed up on only one or two other occasions earlier in the month. Despite the fact that his head was now swirling with phone numbers from Levon's call history, Stevie felt that there was something familiar about this one.

Suddenly it hit him. This was Robby Calderone's cell number; the number that Jack Schwinn had given him on Friday when he was trying to pick up Carlos from the 79th Precinct.

Stevie couldn't believe it. Could this really be true? The scrap of paper on which he'd written Calderone's number had long since disappeared. There really was only one way to check for sure. He hesitated for a moment; then reached out and picked up his BFS desk phone. He took a deep breath; then dialed.

"Yeah!" Stevie heard as the connection went through. While it sounded like Calderone, there was no way he could be certain.

"Robbie?" Stevie asked. "Robbie Calderone? This is Stevie Corra."

"Stevie?" the detective answered slowly with a mixture of surprise and caution. "How did you get this number?"

"Jack gave it to me on Friday," he said, struggling to maintain a façade. "You probably know by now that I heard from Shaquan over the weekend. I reported it to my brother; I thought he still had the case."

"Yeah, sure," Calderone answered slowly. There was an eerie, threatening calm that overrode the obvious tension in his tone. "Your brother just sent over some phone records from the call. Did he show those to you?"

"No," Stevie lied easily. "Frankie would never do anything like that."

"It turns out it was Levon Marbury's phone that the kid used to call you. That doesn't look to good for your boy."

He couldn't get over Calderone's self-control. The detective was obviously looking at the same document Stevie had just studied; proof that his own phone had figured prominently during the hours

264

leading up to a major drug slaying.

"So, what did the kid say?" Calderone asked.

"Not much," Stevie answered, struggling to match Robby's cool pretense. "He said he was OK but he wouldn't tell me where he was. I told him that the police were looking for him as a suspect in Levon's murder and he should come home and straighten everything out. He told me he was afraid to do that; that he thought the police … or Back Thompson… would kill him. Why would he think that?"

"You know the way these kids are," Calderone answered. "They think we're the enemy. Nobody is going to hurt Shaquan…unless he does something stupid."

The detective's threat – an echo of their conversation on Friday – touched a raw nerve in Stevie's soul. He understood why Shaquan might fear being taken into custody.

"That wouldn't be good… not for him… not for anyone," Stevie replied. He didn't know whether Calderone heard his words as a counter threat; that was certainly how they were intended. If anything happened to Shaquan, he would know who was responsible… and make him pay.

"Yeah," Calderone said dismissively. "I've got to go." Then the line went dead.

Once more, Stevie sat, phone in hand and lost in thought. He knew that he didn't fully understand how all these bits of fact and suspicion fit together. Yet, he was somehow certain that Robby Calderone was at the heart of all the events which had taken place during the last two weeks. And he was absolutely positive that Shaquan was in mortal danger; that if Calderone found him before Stevie did, the boy would never make it back to the police station alive.

Stevie hesitated for a few moments more; then braced himself to make a call he'd been avoiding for the past five years.

"Dad," he said as soon as his father answered. "It's me, Stevie. Can I come out there and see you? I need your help."

53

It was almost 1:00 when Stevie walked out of his parents' house in Dyker Heights. The conversation with his father had gone better than he ever could have imagined. Despite some initial skepticism, Joseph Corra had gradually begun to accept Stevie's suspicions as reasonable. The sketchy collection of facts – evidence would be too strong a word – was only part of it. Stevie realized that the opportunity to once again involve himself in a homicide investigation, albeit unofficially, was too tempting for his father to pass up. And, he was surprised to learn, Joseph Corra still had a lingering respect for his son's skills and instincts as a detective. The former NYPD Chief agreed to make the two calls his son had requested; and suggested a couple of other paths they also might pursue. Joseph Corra still had the juice and the contacts to reach deep into the heart of the department and call in favors owed.

Now, Stevie turned his attention back towards tracking the one lead he hoped would help him find Shaquan. He drove the 15-minute trip to the Flatbush Group Home and was pleased to see Joseph Otinga's aging but carefully-maintained Volvo station wagon parked nearby.

"Hello, Stevie," Joseph greeted him as he got to the front door. "I understand that you have been looking for me."

"That's right," he answered, holding out the tightly wound roll of multi-colored material in his right hand. "I'm hoping you will remember this kite and the boy who owns it."

Together they went into the dining room where Joseph unrolled the kite and laid it out flat on the table. Stevie watched anxiously as the group home manager studied the design in silence. After a moment, he turned towards Corra. There was a look of embarrassed uncertainty on his face.

"We've made a lot of kites here," Joseph said a little sheepishly. "While they are all a little different, they are also very similar. It's a little hard for me to remember exactly whose kite this was."

Stevie felt his heart sink like a stone. This was the lead he had been counting on. Could it really be that it would take him no further?

"Keep trying," he urged Otinga. "Maybe it will come to you."

Together, they studied the fabric with its bright Pan African colors – the broad diagonal panels of black and green, the tight red oval shield with its crossed, spear-like shafts of white.

"I'm sorry," Joseph said. "I just can't remember."

"It's OK," Stevie answered in muffled disappointment, still focusing his attention on the kite. After what seemed like hours of staring at it on his own kitchen table over the weekend, it was as if the image of its design had already burned itself into his memory. Yet, as he looked at it here, in the group home itself, there seemed to be some additional connection; some other competing image that called out for his attention.

"Damn," Stevie shouted, startling Joseph. It was not a cry of anger, however; it was one of surprise. "Damn," he said again, suddenly turning and bounding up the stairs to the second floor bedrooms. With Otinga right behind him, he unlocked the door and walked into the room that Shaquan had shared with Carlos.

There on the corkboard hanging above the desk was what Stevie had suddenly remembered. It was a photo, one that he had seen dozens of times without thinking and had noticed during his last visit to this room. It was a snapshot from one of the group home outings. Shaquan stood to the right, holding his own diamond kite which still hung on the wall over his bed. Next to him were two other boys from the group home, both older, each holding his own personally designed kite.

Stevie reached out and plucked the photo off the wall; then turned so that he and Joseph could study it together. In the center, standing right next to Shaquan, was a taller boy, also African American, beaming with pride as he displayed his kite – the same, personalized version of a Kenyan flag that now lay on the dining room table downstairs.

"Raymond," said Joseph, the memories falling into place. "That's right, it was Raymond."

"Raymond Watkins," Stevie said, mentally sorting through the case files in his mind. Raymond was 19, probably three years older than Shaquan. He had left the group home more than a year ago after being discharged into the custody of his older half-sister.

"Were they close?" he asked.

"Yes," Joseph answered thoughtfully. "Raymond was older, but they were very friendly. They were probably here together for two or three years. Shaquan sort of looked up to Raymond and I think Raymond liked that. He watched out for Shaquan... made sure that none of the other kids gave him a hard time."

"Did they stay in touch after Raymond was discharged?"

"I didn't think so," Joseph said, again searching his memory for any clues. "But a couple of months ago... when we had those 'Alumni Nights' and invited some of the older kids to come back and see their friends... Raymond came to those... and I do think that he and Shaquan talked a lot."

Stevie stared at the photo again, almost sensing the bonds that may have already begun to develop between them.

"This must be it," he said excitedly to Joseph. "Shaquan and Melody must be staying with Raymond."

"Let's hope so," said Otinga, his voice ringing with sudden optimism. "Do you have his address?"

"Back in the office; do you have it here?"

"Yes," Joseph nodded.

Together they went back downstairs. As Joseph found

Raymond's address in the files, Stevie popped the photo into his shirt pocket and gathered up the kite into a tight roll.

"I'm going to try and return this," he said to Otinga.

"Good luck," Joseph answered. "I really want Shaquan to come home again."

54

Back in the car, Stevie thought about how best to proceed. The address Joseph had given him was in Sunset Park, not more than 15 minutes away and only a few miles or so southwest of his own home in Windsor Terrace. He remembered visiting the apartment many times both before and after Raymond's discharge from foster care.

Janelle Watkins, Raymond's half-sister, was in in her late-20s. She had been about eight or nine when her father, Robert Watkins, ran off with another woman who'd then given birth to Raymond. To the dismay of her mother, Janelle's father had kept in touch with their daughter and helped to create a bond between the two half-siblings. A few years later, however, Robert was arrested for armed robbery and sentenced to 15-to-20 in an upstate prison. That's when Raymond's world began to fall apart. His own mother spiraled downward into a life of crack and prostitution. The boy wound up in foster care and, as far as Janelle was concerned, effectively disappeared. A half dozen years and an equal number of failed foster boarding home placements later, Raymond arrived at the Flatbush Group Home. Stevie learned about Janelle and set out to re-establish the relationship.

It was easier than he could have hoped. Janelle's own mother – whose instinctive hatred for Robert's bastard son had been a major barrier to their reunion – was dead. Raymond was now the only family the young woman had. The two reconnected emotionally almost immediately. For the troubled teenager, his older half-sister, with no husband or kids of her own, now became almost half-mother, really the only loving and responsible mother he'd ever had.

It had been more than a year since Janelle was awarded custody of Raymond by the Family Court. She worked as a Licensed Practical Nurse and was studying for her RN. He enrolled in a special Department of Education High School for kids who were "over age and under credited". Stevie had made a series of follow up visits in the first few months after the discharge and everything seemed to be going well. That, however, was almost a year ago. He hadn't seen or heard from them since.

Stevie picked up his cell phone and dialed Lucy's number.

"I think we've found them," he said as soon as she answered. He explained about the kite, the photo and the likelihood that Shaquan and Melody were staying with Raymond Watkins and his sister.

"I'll come with you," Lucy said immediately. "Can you swing by the office and pick me up?"

"Sure. Be outside in 15 minutes."

Then he made a second call. As a condition of gaining his father's help, Stevie had promised to keep him informed of everything -- absolutely everything – that happened…*as soon as it happened.*

"Give me the address," Joseph Corra commanded when his son told him he was on his way to pick up Shaquan. "I want to know where you are and where you'll be." Then, he gave Stevie a quick update on the calls he'd been making since they'd met a couple of hours earlier.

By the time he'd hung up with his father, Stevie was approaching the downtown building where Safe Families was based. There, standing by the entrance, was Lucy, once again, in her working uniform of black trousers and a deep blue, short sleeved blouse.

As soon as he pulled to the curb, Lucy raced across the sidewalk and slipped into the passenger seat.

"Hi," she said, reaching out to place her hand briefly on Stevie's arm. It was the only sign of intimacy in what was now important business for both of them.

"Do you really think they might be there?" Lucy continued, her tone a mixture of hope and worry.

"I don't know. At the very least, Shaquan has had to have been in touch with Raymond. And, I don't know that there is any other place they could have gone. This is certainly our best bet."

Lucy just nodded in response. "I can't believe how nervous I am," she said a few moments later.

"I feel exactly the same way."

For the next ten minutes, as they drove up Atlantic and then turned south on Fourth Avenue, Stevie told Lucy about Raymond Watkins and how Janelle had helped him get out of foster care and get his life back on track.

"She sounds like someone who might take in Melody and Shaquan just because they were in trouble," Lucy offered.

"Yes," he agreed. "I think she would."

They continued south on Fourth Avenue until they reached 44th Street, then made a left.

"That's it," Stevie said, pointing to a tired looking four-story grey brick apartment building at the end of the block just off the corner of Fifth Avenue. Then, he pulled into one of the several free parking spaces and turned to Lucy. "Are you ready?"

"I guess so," she said. "Do you think they'll let us in? Or, try to run?"

"I don't know," Stevie said uncertainly. "I have to believe that Shaquan trusts me... and that Melody trusts you... Let's go."

Together they walked up the sidewalk towards the building entrance. The list of names and buzzers showed seven apartments, one on the ground floor and two on each of the others. Janelle and Raymond Watkins were #5 on the third floor towards the rear.

Stevie decided it was worth trying to get inside the building before letting Shaquan and Melody know they were there. He placed his fingers over the buzzer buttons for each of the apartments except Janelle's and pressed them all simultaneously. Corra knew from long experience that the tenants in each unit would only hear the sound of their own door bell. With luck, someone would simply let them in.

This time, they were lucky. Moments later, some trusting tenant triggered an electronic connection and the front door to the building rattled open. Stevie and Lucy slipped inside and, quickly and quietly, began climbing the two flights of stairs.

On the third floor, the entrance to Janelle's apartment was at the rear of the building. The muffled sounds of a daytime TV talk show could be heard from the other side of a rickety wooden door. Melody was watching *Oprah*.

Once again, Stevie looked at Lucy to make sure that she was ready. She nodded in response.

Then, he knocked on the door, as gently and unthreateningly as he could.

If anything, Stevie could almost hear Melody's shocked silence as she held her breath, attempting not to make a sound, afraid of who was at the door and uncertain of what she should do.

"Melody," Lucy called out through the door. "It's me, Lucy Montoya, from Safe Families. I'm here with Steve Corra, Shaquan's caseworker. We want to help you. You two are in danger. We need to get you out of here."

Again, there was nothing. No sounds of sudden panic; no doors slamming or windows opening. Stevie knew that there was a fire escape at the rear of the building, but was certain he would hear if someone tried to use it.

"Shaquan," Stevie cried. "Please let us in. We can help you. We can keep you safe."

Together, he and Lucy stared at the closed door. After a few moments, just seconds that seemed like hours, they heard footsteps, then the sound of the peep hole being used. Finally, the door opened.

There, standing before them, was Shaquan. Further back, against the living room wall was Melody.

"Com'on in," Shaquan said, his voice steady, his eyes wary and alert, like a hunted animal instinctively judging the level of danger. "How did you find us?"

"The kite," Stevie answered. "We figured out it was Raymond's. I've got it in the car so he can have it back."

"Thanks," Shaquan mumbled.

"Melody, are you all right?" Lucy asked. Shaquan's mother stood shivering from shock and fear. Still in her early-thirties, she looked like an old woman, frail and thin in a way that only comes through a

273

diet consisting mainly of drugs and alcohol.

"Yeah, I'm OK," she mumbled; then focused a hollow, questioning gaze on Lucy. "Shaquan says that Levon's dead?"

"That's right. He won't be able to hurt you anymore." Lucy watched as a few lonely tears formed a track down the edge of Melody's cheek. She understood the mix of emotions that had come with the news; relief that she might finally be safe from his abuse, yet also a lingering sense of loss for that once imagined lover, kind and caring, who had only been a cruel illusion in her life.

"Shaquan, we need to get you out of here," Stevie broke in. "The police are close to finding you. They could show up here any minute."

"How? How could they find me?" The boy's eyes opened wide with renewed fear.

"Your phone. They know you have Levon's phone. They can track your location."

"How did they find out about the phone," Shaquan asked, his eyes now angry and accusing. "Did you tell them?"

"Yes," Stevie confessed, another surge of guilt rising up inside him. "I thought it would help me find you first. But once it turned out to be Levon's phone, they had to pass the information on to the detectives on the case."

"Those cops? Those cops will kill us," Shaquan spat back in anger as Melody let out a painful wail, something between a cry and a whimper. "They know we were there; they know we saw it.

"What?" Stevie pressed. "What did you see?"

Shaquan stared back in silence, unsure of whether he should speak, whether telling what he knew would make him safer or more at risk. After a moment, he heaved what seemed a great sigh of surrender.

"We saw them kill that guy… that drug dealer."

"Who?" Stevie almost shouted. "Who killed him?"

"Those cops… and Levon… they shot him in the alley behind the apartment. We saw it from the window."

"You mean it was the cops who shot Rue James… the drug dealer…the cops shot him?"

"Yeah," Shaquan continued without hesitation, having finally

274

freed himself of the secret he'd been guarding for the past two weeks. "It was those cops… Levon's friend… the little one with the scar on his face… he was the one who shot the guy. Levon helped to set it up. The other cop was there but didn't shoot him."

"Robby Calderone," Stevie said flatly, his memory playing back his last conversation with the detective, and the image of a knife wound that stretched across his right cheek. "Robby Calderone and Brian Finnerty."

"I don't know their names," Shaquan said struggling to contain his rising panic. "But we saw them do it and they'll kill us for sure."

"They won't," Stevie shot back, shaking his head in emphasis. "We can protect you."

The boy just stared, his skepticism fueled by a lifetime of disappointment and betrayal by the adults around him.

"You know that I used to be a cop," Stevie pressed. "I have a lot of connections in the police… a lot…I've already arranged for your case to be taken over by a whole different unit…detectives we can trust."

He knew that this – the idea that the police would protect him – was probably impossible to believe for a kid like Shaquan,

"Trust me! You've got to trust me."

Shaquan stood silent, staring deep into Stevie's eyes. Corra could see that he was fighting his natural instinct to believe the worst.

"O.K.," he said at last. "I trust you."

"O.K.," Stevie echoed, nodding with a relief that almost brought him to tears, "O.K."

No sooner had they completed their exchange than the momentary sense of peace in the room was shattered by the sound of Stevie's cell phone. To his complete amazement, the digital display showed that it was Jack Schwinn. He let it ring two more times while he gathered his thoughts and decided whether to answer.

"Jack?" he said questioningly into the phone.

"Stevie, where are you?"

"What do you want?" He replied, brushing aside the question.

"If you have any idea where your kid is, you need to tell me… right away."

"Why?"

"Calderone and Finnerty are getting close," the NYPD Lieutenant said. "They just got a general location from the phone company. It's not exact but they are going to be able to start closing in."

"So, isn't that what you want?"

"Look, " Schwinn continued. Stevie could hear the anxiety in his voice. "After you called, I started to think about things. Calderone never told me he knew Levon Marbury. There have been some other things… things that have nothing to do with this case… that never made sense. Suddenly you got me thinking. I'm worried that if they get to your kid before I do, he might get hurt."

"Why don't you just call them off?"

"I tried. But, they're not picking up. Not Calderone; not Finnerty. I don't like it."

"Yeah," Stevie answered flatly. "I don't like it either."

"So, do you have any idea where the kid is? I'll go personally with another team and bring him in. I'll make sure he's safe."

Stevie stood with the phone to his ear and looked across the room to Shaquan. Like the boy, his natural instinct was to think the worst. Yet, he knew that Schwinn was right. A location report from Verizon on Levon's cell phone could easily have brought Calderone and Finnerty right to their doorstep.

"Yeah," he said flatly. "I'm here with Shaquan right now. We're at 432 44th Street, between 4th and 5th Avenues, in Sunset Park. It's apartment #5. If you're coming, hurry up."

"No shit," Schwinn blurted. "You're there with him now?"

"Yeah," Stevie answered. "You coming?"

"Yes. I'm in the car and not that far away. I can be there in five minutes."

Stevie looked from Shaquan to Lucy and on to Melody, each standing in puzzled and anxious silence. "That was the police… a friend… they're coming to pick us up."

55

Stevie walked towards what served as a dining area at the rear of the apartment. He slid the backpack he was still carrying off his shoulder and onto one of the chairs next to the table. Then he raised his cell phone again and scrolled through the contact list.

When the connection went through, he heard only his father's voicemail.

"Dad," he said leaving a message. "I'm here with Shaquan; the same address I gave you earlier. Jack Schwinn just called to say that he was worried about Calderone and Finnerty too and was coming out to make sure we got in safe. Call me as soon as you get this."

"It's going to be OK," Stevie said, turning back to Shaquan. "We've got a lot of people on our side."

"I hope so," the boy answered with little if any conviction.

Stevie put his cell phone down on one end of the long dining table; then walked back to the others. Lucy was trying to calm Melody who continued to sob quietly at the end of the sofa.

"It shouldn't be long," Stevie said, as much to himself as anyone else. "Jack said he was only a few minutes away." There was no response from the other three.

"Do you know why they shot the drug dealer?" he asked Shaquan.

"It was the money," the boy said. "He had a major stash of cash because he had just sold off part of a shipment. The cops were going to take the cash and Levon was going to take the rest of the dope.

Levon had called the cop to let him know when the dealer was going to be coming."

"How do you know all this?" Stevie asked.

"My mom," Shaquan said, nodding towards Melody. "Levon told her that he was about to make a major score."

That explained the repeated calls from Levon's phone to Robby Calderone the night of the murder, Stevie thought to himself.

"Why were you at the apartment that night?" he asked.

"My mom had told me that she was going to leave Levon once and for all," Shaquan said. "She had made an appointment to meet her caseworker …" He hesitated and nodded towards Lucy. "But, then she called to tell me about what Levon was planning and that maybe she should stay. That's when I decided to go and get her and take her out of there. I had no idea what was going to happen that night."

"So, what happened when you got there?" Stevie pressed.

"My mom was in the apartment by herself. Levon was gone. I told her we had to go right away; that this big plan would just be big trouble and that she would get herself killed if she stayed. Then, all of a sudden we heard some people come in the front door of the building and walk up the stairs towards the apartment. I went into the back bedroom to hide."

Shaquan hesitated for a moment as he prepared to continue his tale.

"From the bedroom, I could hear Levon come into the apartment. He told my mom that she should stay in the living room and away from the bedroom; that this was going to be it and that he would be back in a while.

"I could hear them in the hallway," the boy continued. "There was a few of them… not just Levon… they went down the back stairs to the door that led out to the alley. That's when I heard a car pull up behind the building. I snuck over to the window and peeked out. There was a big SUV that had pulled into the alley. I saw the drug dealer get out and start towards the back door. All of a sudden, the door swung open. The guy stopped and then started to back up. Then I heard shots… three of them… and the guy went down on his back. It was that cop, Levon's friend, who had shot him."

"Oh, my God," said Lucy who had been following the boy's story while consoling his mother.

"Yeah," Shaquan said with surprisingly little emotion. "When she heard the gunshots, my mom came running into the bedroom and saw me looking out the window. She ripped the curtain to one side. We saw the two cops and Levon standing over the body... then they looked up and saw us."

"What happened then?" Stevie asked.

"The cop who had done the shooting... the one with the scar... he just stared at us for a minute; then he said something to Levon. Levon was all flustered and nervous. He kept looking back and forth from us to the cop; then he waved us away from the window and turned around and headed back towards the alley door.

"I told my mom we needed to get out of there right away or they'd kill us for sure," Shaquan continued. "We ran out of the apartment and started to head down the stairs..."

Stevie looked skeptically from Shaquan to Melody. "And Levon couldn't catch you?"

The boy shook his head and a shy – yet sly – smile appeared on his lips. "Old Mrs. Greene in the apartment next door suddenly stuck her head out and said we should come in to her real quick... and be real, real quiet. Nobody ever paid her no attention at all. Levon just thought that we had run down the stairs and out the front door. He hadn't even thought to check in her apartment."

Stevie shook his head in amazement, the image of the wispy grey-haired woman instantly appearing in his mind. *"Yes, he was here that night,"* she had said of Shaquan during his last visit to the building.

"We waited there until things quieted down. The shootings had cleared the boys off the corner. Then, when it looked like no one was around, we slipped out and took off. We needed to get out before the cops... the real cops... came."

"And you came here... to Raymond's house?" Stevie asked.

"No, first we went to my mom's friend, Lakeisha," Shaquan explained. "But, they were afraid that Levon could find us there, so I called Raymond. His sister came and picked us up."

Stevie simply nodded in response and then exchanged silent glances with Lucy. This was not the time to tell Melody that she had been right in her assessment... and that her friend Lakeisha was now dead.

"How did you wind up with Levon's cell phone?" Stevie asked instead.

"He left it in the apartment. I grabbed it thinking it was my mom's."

Suddenly, their conversation was interrupted by a knock on the door.

All four of them turned towards the sound; then Shaquan, Melody and Lucy looked back to Stevie. He breathed deeply to calm the sudden racing of his heart as he crossed to the door. He peered through the tiny peephole and saw the face of Jack Schwinn. With a sigh of relief he swung the door open.

"Hi, Jack," he said. "Come on in." Then he turned to introduce the Police Lieutenant to Shaquan Saunders.

The moment he saw the look of terror once more etched on the boy's face, Stevie understood that he had made a terrible, and possibly fatal, mistake.

56

Stevie turned back and stared at Schwinn in disbelief. It was only then that he saw the pistol in Jack's hand, rising from his side and aiming into the apartment.

"Thanks for helping us find them, Stevie," Schwinn said as he waved the four back towards the far end of the room. As they moved towards the dining table, Stevie saw Robby Calderone and Brian Finnerty follow Schwinn into the room, also with guns drawn, then close the door behind them.

At the sight of them…the cops she'd last seen murder someone right before her eyes… Melody broke down into tearful hysteria.

"Shut up!" Schwinn commanded. Then his gaze – and the barrel of the gun – moved from Stevie to Shaquan, Melody and finally Lucy. "I expected to find the kid and his mother. Who are you?"

"Lucy Montoya," she answered, struggling to get the words out as a rising sense of panic left her breathless.

"Right," Schwinn said, understanding immediately. "Stevie mentioned you. OK, this is great. We've got everybody here."

"I can't believe that you are mixed up in this, Jack," Stevie said with disgust. "I always trusted you."

"Yeah," Schwinn shot back. "You always were a little *too* trusting."

"What's he talking about?" Brian Finnerty asked; his voice filled with unexpected questions.

"Nothing you need to worry about," Robby Calderone answered.

Then, he turned and leveled his own weapon – a Colt automatic with a bright stainless steel barrel; not the dark matte finish of a NYPD service handgun – and fired two shots into his partner's chest.

The roar of gunshots was amplified by the confined space of the apartment. That, together with the sight of Finnerty being thrown backwards against the door, his body erupting in a mist of blood spatter, unleashed a chorus of terrified screams from Melody and Lucy.

Despite the surge of adrenaline pounding through his veins, Stevie found himself impossibly calm and focused on the events occurring before him, as if in slow motion, frame by frame.

The two cops, he thought. *The two cops* were not Calderone and Finnerty; they were *Calderone and Schwinn*.

"The gun that killed Rue James… and Levon?" Stevie asked, looking at the shiny silver automatic in Calderone's right hand.

"That's right," Calderone answered turning the weapon back towards Corra. "It's the gun that Shaquan used to kill them both… and that he will have used to kill you and your girlfriend when you came here to bring them in…."

"Just before we got here and killed them both in a raging gun battle in which Detective Brian Finnerty was also killed," Schwinn added with chilling menace.

A heavy silence fell over the room as the four – Stevie, Shaquan, Melody and Lucy – recognized that their own deaths might be just moments away.

Suddenly, however, that silence was shattered by the sound of Stevie's cell phone at the far end of the dining table, its ringtone seemingly as loud and unnerving as the gunshots which had preceded it.

All eyes in the room turned at once toward the unexpected sound. Stevie reacted instinctively to the momentary diversion and launched himself in a low horizontal dive behind the back of the table, grabbing the open backpack off the chair where he had placed it. By the time he hit the ground, Stevie had already reached in to take hold of the pistol he had been carrying around with him for the past week.

Calderone, his attention instantly refocused, fired a shot in Stevie's direction that chipped the edge of the table just above his head. Behind him, Stevie could hear a scramble as Shaquan, Lucy and Melody all dove for cover in different directions. Then, he heard another shot – this time fired by Jack Schwinn at Shaquan – but to no effect.

Still partially hidden from view by the dining table, Stevie pulled the pistol from its holster and flicked off the safety with his thumb.

Another shot rang out from Calderone's gun, downward through the tabletop and only inches from Corra's ear.

Stevie, his own vision equally obscured, struggled to place Calderone's location by the sound of approaching footsteps. It seemed that the detective was simply walking slowly in his direction, making no effort to take defensive precautions, unaware that Corra might also be armed.

Stevie sprawled along the floor behind the table and prepared for what might be his only chance. He coiled his right knee up along one side while reaching out his left arm and digging the elbow into the carpet; then in one desperate move, he lunged forward, coming out from beyond the end of the table, the pistol in his outstretched right hand turning towards the approaching Calderone.

Stevie heard…then felt the searing pain… of a third shot which tore into his left shoulder. Thankfully, the off-center impact of the bullet helped roll him onto his back, freeing his right arm for a clear shot of his own. Stevie's first bullet caught Calderone near the top of his left thigh; his second, square in the center of his chest. The detective's body buckled as he fell backward, firing a final and wild shot that buried itself harmlessly in the wall.

Suddenly aware that Stevie was now armed and very dangerous, Schwinn turned his aim toward him as he still lay stretched out on the floor next to the table. At that instant, Lucy sprang up from her defensive crouch and grabbed hold of the detective's right arm, driving the pistol away from its target just as he fired a first shot. A split second later, Shaquan dove into Schwinn with all his might, tackling him at the knees. Despite Schwinn's considerable size and strength, the combined and unexpected impact of both of them together knocked the detective to the floor, where Lucy clung to his right arm in a desperate attempt to keep him from taking aim again.

Stevie scrambled to his feet, the pain in his now useless left arm dulled by an overdose of fear and adrenaline. As he rose, he saw Jack struggling to free his gun hand from the full weight of Lucy's body. In spite of Shaquan's hold on his legs, Schwinn twisted his prone torso and landed a powerful left hook to the side of Lucy's face, loosening her hold on his arm. A second later he jerked completely free of her grasp; then swung his elbow violently backwards into the other side of her face, knocking her to one side and clearing himself to shoot again.

Stevie's own shot preceded Schwinn's by the slimmest of margins, hitting him high in the left shoulder and throwing off his aim just enough for the bullet to whizz past – rather than into – Corra's head. However, Schwinn, fueled by an equally powerful surge of desperation, fought through the burning pain and steadied himself to fire one more time. He never got the chance. Stevie's second shot was just a touch lower and more centered; right in the heart.

Schwinn's eyes opened wide in shock and surprise at the deadly blow. They remained open, even after the life drained out of them a split second later.

57

Stevie took one look at Schwinn and immediately turned his attention back to Calderone who lay in a rapidly spreading pool of his own blood. He was still alive, taking weak, shallow breaths, which were echoed by a hissing gunshot wound that was also sucking air into his chest. Even more serious, Stevie's first shot into Calderone's thigh looked to have nicked the detective's femoral artery and, without attention, it would only be minutes before he bled to death.

Brian Finnerty appeared to be dead already.

None of the other three seemed to be hurt, at least not seriously. Lucy was still dazed from her struggle with Schwinn. Shaquan was unharmed and Melody remained in the corner of the room whimpering softly.

"Get some towels," Stevie said to Shaquan. "Hurry!"

He removed the belt from Calderone's trousers; wrapped it around the detective's thigh, above the pumping wound, and pulled it as tight as possible. Then, he tied it back to create a tourniquet. When Shaquan got back, Stevie pressed one towel on Calderone's thigh and the other on the chest wound.

"Hold these in place," he told Shaquan. "Apply steady pressure. I don't know if he's going to make it, but we want to keep him alive if we can."

The boy nodded and took Stevie's place trying to save the man who had just been trying to kill him.

"Are you OK?" Stevie asked as he bent down to check on Lucy.

She was bruised and swollen around her left eye and bleeding from one corner of her mouth where Schwinn's elbow had nearly knocked her teeth out.

"Yes," she said, still a little woozy from the blows and the delayed shock. "I'm OK. What about you?" She reached out towards Stevie's torn and bleeding shoulder.

In the panic of the moment, he had almost forgotten about his own wound. "I'll be fine," he said. "Can you find some more towels that we can use as bandages?"

"I'll get them," Melody said as she stood up, beginning to regain her composure.

"I've got to make some calls," Stevie said as he walked to the table and retrieved the cell phone that had helped to save their lives. First, he dialed 911 and simply asked for an ambulance in response to a shooting. He ignored all requests for more information; just gave the address and hung up.

Then, he dialed his father.

"Stevie, I tried to call you," Joseph Corra said as soon as the connection went through. "Are you all right?"

"Yeah, we're OK," Stevie answered. "Jack Schwinn showed up together with Calderone and Finnerty. Schwinn and Finnerty are both dead. Calderone is pretty close. I just called 911."

"Christ," the senior Corra muttered in stunned surprise. "Was it you?"

"I shot Jack and Calderone," Stevie answered, the first hints of any emotional response to what he'd done beginning to simmer inside him. "Calderone shot Finnerty as soon as they walked in. I guess Finnerty wasn't in on the deal."

"Nobody else got hurt?"

"I took a bullet in my shoulder and Lucy got beat up a little. She and Shaquan tackled Schwinn. If it wasn't for them, he would have shot me."

"Christ," his father repeated. "Look, Tommy Peterson from Internal Affairs is on the way. When you didn't answer, I told them to get their asses in gear and get over there. I'm going to call him again now. I'll call you back."

Stevie and his father had agreed earlier that morning that they needed to bring in IA. For someone who was unquestionably "a cop's cop", Joseph Corra had always maintained a surprisingly good relationship with the NYPD unit that investigated police corruption. The former Chief of Detectives was a lot of different things – not all of them positive – but he was absolutely honest. Throughout his career, he'd go to the mat to defend his men from any unnecessary harassment or second guessing, but he was equally supportive of IA's effort to nail any cop that was dirty.

"OK, help is on the way," Stevie said to no one in particular after putting down the phone. He walked across the room, stepping around Calderone and over Brian Finnerty's lifeless body. He opened the apartment door as wide as possible and made sure it would stay that way.

Then, Stevie made his way back the through field of human debris towards the dining table. He took a fresh towel from Melody, pressed it against the wound in his shoulder that had already soaked his entire left side in blood, and slumped into one of the dining room chairs. As he sat down, Stevie was overcome by a powerful wave of fatigue and what he recognized as the first signs that his body was going into shock.

For the next several minutes, they sat together in stunned silence, all four of them physically and emotionally spent. There was only a soft but labored rasping as Robbie Calderone struggled to keep breathing. Then, in the distance they heard the sounds of sirens, faint at first but growing louder as police cars and ambulances raced towards them.

"They're going to be coming in here prepared for anything," Stevie told the others. "Just stay where you are. Don't make any sudden moves and keep your hands still and in plain sight. Just do whatever they say. Everything is going to be all right from here on. We're all safe now."

At that moment, his cell phone rang once more. It was his father.

"Tommy Peterson and the IA team are almost there," he said. "They'll take the lead. How's the shoulder?"

"It hurts… but not so bad. I'll be fine."

"Yeah, you'll be fine." Stevie heard something in his father's voice that he hadn't heard for a while. "Now, hang up, put the phone down and wait for them to get there."

"I will. And, Dad… thanks."

Stevie slid the phone away from him towards the center of the table – next to his pistol – just as a swarm of screaming sirens converged on the street outside. He heard the sounds of the building entrance being forced open; then, the pounding of heavy soled shoes storming up the stair case.

"Remember, just stay where you are and don't say or do anything other than what they tell you," he instructed once more.

Four sets of eyes were focused on the open door and the hallway beyond where the sounds of footsteps were approaching.

"Police! Police!" cried out a disembodied voice from around the edge of the doorway. "Put down your weapons and put your hands up!"

"We're not armed," Stevie called back. "There are handguns on the floor and one in the center of the table where I am sitting. We've got two dead, two wounded… one critically… and three others. It's safe for you to come in."

"Stevie?" another voice called out.

"Yeah!"

"This is Inspector Peterson from IA. We're coming in." A moment later, a middle aged white man peered cautiously around the corner of the doorway. Even Stevie's advance warning wasn't adequate preparation for the carnage he witnessed.

"Christ!" he said, slowly entering the room while conducting his own body count. He was followed by two other detectives in plain clothes. Behind them, the hallway began to fill up with uniformed officers in blue, each struggling to get a look at the devastation inside the apartment.

"Your dad suggested we stop by," Peterson said turning to Stevie. "It looks like we got here a little late."

58

It didn't take long before Stevie and the others were taken in different directions. One team of Emergency Medical Technicians immediately focused all their attention on the seriously wounded Robby Calderone. Within minutes, they had him transferred to a gurney and out the door for an emergency run to the hospital.

Another EMT prepared Stevie to follow in a separate ambulance for his own trip to the emergency room. Once they arrived, he learned from one of the IA detectives that Calderone hadn't made it. He had died in the ambulance.

Lucy, on the other hand, had refused all medical treatment, claiming that she'd been through beatings a lot worse than this one and knew she would be fine. She insisted on staying with Melody and Shaquan when they were taken in for questioning.

After a couple of hours of waiting and various medical treatments, Stevie followed suit and rejected his own doctor's recommendation that he be admitted and spend the night in a hospital bed. The wound, while messy and painful, had apparently done little if any real damage. He promised to take it easy, drink plenty of fluids, and come back for a check-up the following day. The IA detective promised to make sure they got him home safely.

But, first, Stevie had to come to the stationhouse and answer a few questions. After all, he had just killed two New York City police officers and watched a third be murdered.

That was just fine with Stevie. He, too, wanted to share what he knew about Robby Calderone and Jack Schwinn. And, he wanted to learn what, if anything, IA might have on the two crooked cops.

Stevie also wanted to make sure that Shaquan and his mother were being treated appropriately. They were not suspects in this or any other crime. They were witnesses and victims. Given their own histories with the police, that was not a familiar role for either of them. He was worried that everyone concerned – Melody, Shaquan and the cops – might fall back into old and bad habits.

Stevie certainly wanted to ensure that the boy wasn't bundled off to the City's Children's Center where dozens of kids of all ages were forced to stay the night after being freshly removed from their own homes, kicked out of existing foster care placements or picked up on the streets of New York. Shaquan had a home – albeit a BFS group home – where he could go when the police were finished with him.

Back at IA's Brooklyn Borough Headquarters, Stevie was led to a small interview room with a metal table and a half-dozen straight back chairs. The detective who had accompanied him to the hospital left for a few minutes before returning with Inspector Tommy Peterson.

"You've had quite a night," Peterson began.

"Yes," Stevie answered simply. To his own surprise, no witty but cynical quip came to his lips. The dark "gallows" humor that most cops relied on for emotional protection at times like these no longer seemed to work for him. "Where are the others?"

"They're giving statements," Peterson responded. "Don't worry. We're taking care of them. We've got a pretty good idea of who the bad guys were in this one. Why don't you tell me what happened? Start at the very beginning."

"Sure," Stevie said, taking a sip of water from the bottle that Peterson handed him.

Over the next two hours, he recounted the story of his last two weeks, beginning with Shaquan's disappearance and ending with the gunshots earlier that evening. The two detectives had plenty of questions. Once they reached what seemed to be a conclusion, Stevie asked a question of his own.

"So, what can you share with *me*?"

Peterson hesitated for only a moment.

"Well, we've actually been looking at Robby Calderone for quite some time. There were some questions that surfaced about him a few years ago when he was working out of Brooklyn South Narcotics."

Stevie wondered if any of those questions might have come from Artie Schwartz.

"Then, about a year ago, Brian Finnerty, his partner, got himself jammed up for taking some drugs and money from a kid on the street… totally unrelated to Calderone. He kept the money and gave the dope to his CI. Once we had Finnerty, he immediately offered to give us Calderone… not that he actually had anything solid… but he was pretty sure that his partner was into something… something major. Frankly, I think Finnerty was pissed off that Calderone hadn't cut him in on it."

Peterson took a sip of his own water bottle before he continued. "We went back and took a closer look at Calderone's time in Brooklyn South. It started to look like he might have been inserting himself into the local turf wars…picking winners and providing them with protection. Based on what Finnerty was telling us … not that he really understood what he was telling us… it appeared that Calderone had started doing the same thing up in Brooklyn North after he transferred. This time, he seemed to be going even further. There were a couple of drug-related murders, even before the Rue James killing, where Calderone was the lead on the case. He began getting the homicide investigations transferred to Narcotics on the theory that the cases were related. While we haven't been able to prove it … until tonight… it looked like the best of both worlds. Calderone was a hired gun for the dealers he selected… and the lead investigator in the murders they committed."

Stevie nodded. These were the cases that his brother had been so angry about, he thought to himself.

"What about Jack Schwinn?"

"Schwinn was something of a surprise for us," Peterson said, shaking his head with an obvious sadness. "There had never been a hint of trouble throughout his career. You know; you worked with him! But, it turns out that he had known Calderone from way back. The two of them rode together in their early days on the job. And, it looks like Schwinn needed money. He had gotten divorced, for the second time, a few years ago. Between his two ex-wives with alimony, the houses and child support, they had cleaned him out. He was desperate."

Stevie had lost track of Jack's private life. He knew that Schwinn's first marriage had dissolved in the same toxic "cop-life" environment that had killed his own. Unlike Stevie, however, Jack had fancied himself a ladies man. Even after tying the knot a second time, he continued to chase after half the women at The Cumberland and anything else in a skirt he could find.

"We think that Calderone convinced Schwinn that the scheme he'd started in Brooklyn South would work even better… and be safer and more profitable… if he had a Unit Commander running interference for him."

Stevie nodded again. He was still shocked… and really saddened by the fact that Jack Schwin had turned bad. They had worked together for years. And, while he and Jack had never really been close, he had liked the man… and trusted him. But, as Schwinn had said himself, maybe he had always been a little too trusting.

"So, Shaquan and Melody told you that they saw Calderone shoot Rue James?" Stevie asked.

"Yes," Peterson answered. "And, that they saw Schwinn with him."

"Do you think they were working with Back Thompson, the guy who stepped up to take Rue's place?"

"It could be," said Peterson. "It would certainly fit our theory. But, we've got nothing to prove it, at least not yet. Calderone is dead. Maybe we'll find something else that ties the two together – perhaps a money trail. We're really just getting started on this."

"Right," Stevie said with an air of finality. "Do you need anything else from me… or the others… right now?"

"No," said Peterson, pushing his chair back and rising from the table. "You're all free to go. But you know the drill. Stay in touch, we'll probably want to talk to you again at some point soon."

Peterson opened the door and led him down the hall to a large reception area where Lucy, Shaquan and Melody were waiting.

"I'll have an officer here in a few minutes to drive you all home," Peterson said, reaching out to shake Stevie's good hand. "Take care of that shoulder...and say hello to your father for me."

"I will. And thanks... for everything."

Stevie turned to see Lucy rise from the chair where she had been sitting. She was bruised and swollen on both sides of her face, but seemed mainly concerned about his shoulder.

"Are you all right?" she asked.

"Yeah, I'm fine," he answered, leaning forward to kiss her gently on the forehead, the only place he could see where she hadn't been hurt. "How about you? You look like you've gone a few rounds with Mike Tyson."

"I'll be fine...once the swelling goes down and I look normal again... I can take a punch."

Shaquan and Melody were sitting next to each other along the wall; she resting her head on his shoulder; his arm draped protectively around her. This was the way Stevie always thought of them now – the boy absolutely determined to save his mother from the life she'd made for herself, ever ready to defend her against a world filled with danger.

"Hi, Stevie," Shaquan said, rising from the chair to meet him. "Is your shoulder going to be OK?"

"Yeah, I'll be fine. How about you and your mom?"

"We're OK," Shaquan answered; then looked deeply into his eyes. "Thanks for coming to get us. Thanks for everything."

"Sure."

Their conversation was interrupted by the same IA detective who had accompanied Stevie to and from the hospital. "I can give you folks a lift to wherever you want to go," he said. "The car is right outsde."

"Where are we going to go?" Shaquan asked suddenly, a look of panic once again burning in his eyes. "My mom can't go back to that apartment. That's impossible."

Lucy quickly interrupted with a suggestion of her own. "I've made a couple of phone calls and I've found a bed Lucy can use in a domestic violence shelter... at least for couple of nights. If the detective drove us to my place, I can take her there."

"Can I go with her?" Shaquan asked.

"You really need to come back to the group home," Stevie said, trying to sound as gentle and encouraging as possible. "In a day or two, once your mom gets settled somewhere, we can think about arranging for you two to have more time together…a lot more time."

During the exchange, Melody had also risen out of her chair and now approached her son. "You go home, Shaquan," she said softly, reaching out to touch his face. "Steve knows best. I'll go with Lucy now. We'll talk tomorrow."

Then, she turned to her son's caseworker. "Thank you, Steve. Thank you for taking care of me and my son."

"Sure," Stevie said again.

The detective took them to Lucy's apartment first, where she and Melody switched cars for the drive to a DV shelter, the location of which Lucy could not disclose. Stevie and Shaquan watched as they climbed into her car and drove off, each feeling their own very definite sense of loss.

Then, the officer drove them out to the Flatbush Group Home. It was past 11:00 when they arrived.

"I can get home from here," Stevie told the detective. "Thanks for the ride."

Shaquan's return was greeted with screams of excitement and tears of joy. Joseph Otinga had been gone for hours, but Mrs. Ramirez was working an extra shift. She welcomed the boy with a torrent of high speed and high volume Spanish, all punctuated by a repeated series of emotional bear hugs. The other kids who had been watching TV in the living room surrounded Shaquan in the hallway, peppering him with questions and pounding him with affectionate punches, high-fives and fist bumps.

Moments later, Carlos came racing downstairs from the room which he would once again be sharing with his friend.

"Hey, Bro," he said, breaking out into an enormous grin. "I knew you'd be coming back."

"Yeah," Shaquan said almost shyly. "Someone's got to be looking out for your skinny little ass."

"Screw you, man," Carlos shot back. "I knew I should have

rented out your crib."

Stevie interrupted the increasingly testosterone-fueled exchange to say that he was leaving but would be back for a longer meeting with Shaquan the following day.

"Thanks for bringing him back," Carlos said, turning momentarily more serious. "I knew you could find him."

"Yeah,"Shaquan added again. "Thanks."

"Hey, it's nice to have you home again. Now try to get some sleep. That's what I'm going to do."

Stevie gently brushed aside any further questions from Mrs. Ramirez or the other kids, pleading that he was exhausted and needed to get some rest. He promised to provide a full report the next day. Robert Wilkins gave him a quick ride home in the house van. It was almost midnight when he walked in the door.

Stevie dropped his backpack – now minus the handgun, which had been held as evidence – in the hallway and fought a powerful desire to pour a glass of wine on top of the pain medications he'd been given. He slumped down at the dining table and pulled out his cell phone. It had been hours since he'd checked his messages. There were several sets of calls and texts from both his father and his brother Frankie.

Before Stevie could even call back, the cellphone came to life in his hand. He could see from the display that it was Lucy.

"Hi," he answered.

"Hi. I just dropped Melody off and got her settled in for the night." Stevie could hear the fatigue – both physical and emotional – in her voice. "I was hoping you might be in the mood for some company. I know I am."

Her words were like a soothing balm to his bruised and battered nerves. "There's nothing that would make me happier."

"There's one condition. You have to promise not to make fun of the way I look."

"Agreed," Stevie offered. "And, you can't touch my left shoulder."

"That's fair," Lucy said. "I'll see you in about a half hour."

"Great," he said before hanging up.

For the next few moments Stevie stared absently out over his darkened back garden, a soft smile forming on his lips. Then, he picked up the cellphone once again, punched in a different number, and spoke as soon as he got an answer.

"Hi, Dad...."

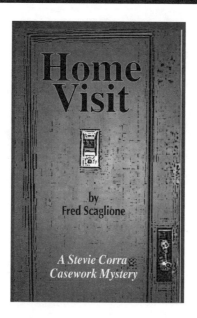

NYNP Books

The "One-Stop Shop" for books on issues relating to nonprofits, charity and human services:

- Fundraising
- Boards & Governance
- Finance & Accounting
- Leadership
- Volunteer Management
- IT, Systems and Telecommunications
- Grant Writing
- Marketing & Communications
- History
- Early Childhood
- Child Welfare
- Behavioral Health
- Senior Services
- Substance and Alcohol Abuse
- Strategic Planning
- Housing & Homelessness
- Youth Development
- Employment Services & Workforce Development
- Program Evaluation, Outcomes & QA
- Biography & Personal Opinion
- Fiction & Mystery

Find Books; Read Reviews; Post Your Own Comments

NYNP Books
New York Nonprofit Press
www.NYNPbooks.com
866-336-6967